BETWEEN THE SKY AND THE SEA

by Lisa Williams Kline

DRAGONBLADE PUBLISHING, INC.

ARE YOU SIGNED UP FOR DRAGONBLADE'S BLOG?

You'll get the latest news and information on exclusive giveaways, exclusive excerpts, coming releases, sales, free books, cover reveals and more.

Check out our complete list of authors, too!

No spam, no junk. That's a promise!

Sign Up Here

www.dragonbladepublishing.com

Dearest Reader;

Thank you for your support of a small press. At Dragonblade Publishing, we strive to bring you the highest quality Historical Romance from some of the best authors in the business. Without your support, there is no 'us', so we sincerely hope you adore these stories and find some new favorite authors along the way.

Happy Reading!

CEO, Dragonblade Publishing

DEDICATION

In honor of my grandparents,
who owned a hat shop

The discovery of the remains of the steamship Pulaski thirty-five miles off the coast of North Carolina in 2018 fascinated me. I devoured the articles describing the ship built for speed, the electrifying explosion, the loss of hundreds of lives and thousands of gold pieces. I happened to stumble upon an article from the *Delaware Gazette* from 1838 that described how a Mr. Ridge from New Orleans and a Miss Onslow from Savannah had survived on two floating settees after the wreck for four days, until they were rescued. When the ship sank, they had seen each other on board, possibly felt drawn to each other, but had not been introduced. When they were rescued four days later, they were engaged.

Was this story true? Some think it might have been the invention of a reporter, especially because the names of Miss Onslow and Mr. Ridge do not appear on the ship's passenger list. Still, it continued to fascinate me. Did they indeed marry? If so, how might their marriage have fared, forged during four such unforgettable days? Catastrophe, attraction, and marriage are intriguing subjects, both in the 1800's and now. The idea took hold and I could not let go.

I spent many hours with the excellent online database JSTOR, researching the wreck itself, but also the millinery business, railroads, ships, the legal status of women, inheritance, married women's property, travel by stagecoach, and slavery.

The main source I used to research the wreck itself was the account called "The Loss of the Steamer Pulaski" by Mrs. Hugh McLeod, which appears in the *Georgia Historical Quarterly*. This is a first-hand account by a survivor.

"Courtship on a Fragment of the Pulaski" came from the

Delaware Gazette, and I found it in *The Museum of Perilous Adventures and Daring Exploits*, pp. 255-270. This is a compilation located in the Library of Congress, published by O.F. Gibbs of Chicago in 1863.

"The Steamship Pulaski's Passengers Survive Her Sinking and Fall in Love" is from a collection called *Magic Masts and Sturdy Ships* by Kathy Warnes, PhD.

I read numerous articles in the *Charlotte Observer* by Mark Price about the exploration of the wreck, and then there was one in particular on January 28, 2018, which described those from Blue Water Ventures, the salvage divers, researching the verity of the story about Miss Onslow and Mr. Ridge.

For background, I used the following books:

Eric J. Brock. *New Orleans*. Arcadia Publishing: Charleston, S.C., 1999.

Susan S. Carson and Jon C. Lewis. *Joshua's Legacy: Dream Makers of Old Southport*. Southport Historical Society: Southport, N.C., 2003.

Susan E. Dick and Mandi D. Johnson. *Savannah 1733 to 2000*. Arcadia Publishing: Charleston, S.C., 2001.

Walter J. Fraser, Jr. *Savannah in the Old South*. University of Georgia Press: Athens, 2003.

Susan B. Johnson. *Savannah's Little Crooked Houses: If These Walls Could Talk*. The History Press: Charleston, S.C., 2007.

Robert C. Jones. *A History of Georgia Railroads*. History Press: Charleston, S.C., 2017.

Spencer Bidwell King, Jr. *Ebb Tide: As Seen Through the Diary of Josephine Clay Habersham 1863*. The University of Georgia Press: Athens, 1958.

Sally G. McMillen. *Motherhood in the Old South: Pregnancy, Childbirth, and Infant Rearing*. Louisiana State University Press, 1990.

Jackson McQuigg, Tammy Galloway, and Scott McIntosh. *Central of Georgia Railway*. Arcadia Publishing: Charleston, S.C., 1998.

Bill Reaves, *Southport (Smithville): A Chronology 1520-1887*. Broadfoot Publishing Company: Wilmington, N.C., 1978.

I also visited the Georgia Historical Society in Savannah. While visiting their beautiful library, along with many other documents, I relied on *The Work of the Federal Courts in Georgia Over Two Centuries* by Erwin C. Surrency to research 19th century treatment of women in Georgia courts. For further background on life in Savannah in 1838, I visited the Telfair Museum's Owen-Thomas House, The Georgia State Railroad Museum, Colonial Cemetery, Savannah's many lovely squares, and The Pink House Restaurant (which was quite enjoyable).

Three excellent novels helped me as I attempted to write about this general time period. They are *The Invention of Wings*, by Sue Monk Kidd, *Dear Miss Cushman* by Paula Martinac, and *Surviving Savannah* by Patti Callahan.

All of the characters in this story, including Lavinia Onslow and Daniel Ridge, are products of my imagination. I imagined all of the events. Though it really occurred, even the shipwreck scene was a product of my imagination, created from the sources I had read. In the end, does it matter if this four-day post-shipwreck courtship was true? I think sometimes fiction can be the truest of all.

ACKNOWLEDGMENTS

My dear longtime writing colleagues Ann Campanella, Liz Hatley, Michelle Moore, Emily Pearce, and Betsy Thorpe were steadfast and inspiring as they read and commented on many drafts of this novel.

I am so grateful to Kathryn Le Veque for giving Lavinia and Daniel's story a home at Dragonblade. Additional thanks go to the team at Dragonblade, especially Courtney Brown, whose commitment to the story improved the authenticity. Thanks also to Shawn Morrison, for keeping everything on track, and to Kim Killion for designing the vivid, evocative cover.

While I was working on this novel, I took writing workshops with Jill McCorkle, John Bemis, and Paula Martinac, and each of them provided insights into the story and its telling. In particular, Paula Martinac's extensive knowledge of historical fiction and her feedback on my pages was of great value. Robin Henry of *Readerly* also gave me feedback on historical details and anachronisms and asked hard questions about the path of my plot, challenging me to strengthen the story.

Thanks to Rachel Minetti of the Georgia Historical Society in Savannah for allowing me to visit their beautiful library, and for assistance in determining a logical place for the Onslows' fictional millinery shop in 1838 Savannah and also with locating the Onslows' fictional home.

Thanks also to Ben Wheeler of the Georgia State Railroad Museum for answering my questions.

Roxanne Lucy was kind enough to read this story as a Beta reader. Kimmery Martin also gave feedback and encouragement, which I deeply appreciated.

Dr. Sally McMillen of Davidson College assisted me with sources about the rights of women at that time. Thanks to Sarah Walls and Landis Wade for their suggestions on legal research.

Last but certainly not least, my gratitude goes out to my husband, Jeff, who enthusiastically read and commented on many drafts and whose love and support sustain me every day.

CHAPTER ONE

June 10, 1838
Savannah

L AVINIA SAT AWKWARDLY with Mr. Grogan in the parlor of her family's home on Oglethorpe Square on a sweltering Sunday afternoon. Outside the window, the Spanish moss hung motionless from the live oak near the street without the slightest whisper of a breeze. Inside, the heavy velvet curtains hung lifeless, and sweat beaded on Mr. Grogan's bald forehead like condensation on a glass of lemonade.

"Tell me your interests," he said. "We never have an opportunity to exchange more than the briefest pleasantries when I see you at church services. I would be most fascinated to hear."

Interests? Lavinia straightened slightly, trying to relieve the corset stays cutting into her ribcage. People seldom asked Lavinia about what occupied her time or her mind. Such a question from a man was a novel experience for her.

She adjusted her skirts. "Perhaps you know, I've been helping my father with Onslow's Millinery for four years now, ever since I turned eighteen. I help direct the styling and displays, and I assist my father with the buying and the bookkeeping. I find it all quite engaging. Of course, as the eldest daughter I also help Father run the household since our mother died many years ago." She hesitated. Should she say more? "Any time not thus occupied I often spend reading. Father is generous in that he allows Sarah and me to read widely." Lavinia had to admit, though, that she had taken much more advantage of the freedom to read than her younger sister Sarah.

"Reading may broaden a person's mind, depending upon the material," Mr. Grogan said diplomatically. He removed a handkerchief from his well-tailored brocade waistcoat and wiped his forehead, then his palms, allowing his eyes to travel over the fashionable dusky rose walls that Lavinia had just had painted. "Perhaps not novels."

Lavinia held her tongue, for she had just begun the novel *The Last of the Mohicans* by James Fenimore Cooper, while a book by Mary Shelley waited enticingly on her nightstand. Perhaps not novels, indeed.

Lavinia had been exchanging books for several years with her closest friend, Harriet, who used to travel to Europe and bring them back. Harriet was blonde and petite and polite, but her appropriate southern appearance hid a rather subversive mind. Harriet had in the past year moved to Augusta with her husband, and Lavinia dearly missed their discussions about books.

Mr. Matthew Grogan was in the brick-making business, Father had told her, and there was lately a great demand for gray bricks in Savannah, and in many other cities, because of their impermeability to fire, which had decimated Savannah several times over past years. The Onslows' own two-story house was built of gray brick. But Mr. Grogan was much older than Lavinia—five and thirty, at least—and with that expanse of bare head and slightly stooped posture, his years showed.

"Your father has told me that you are quite efficient, and that you are in excellent health."

Was he purchasing a horse?

"Of course, our customers demand efficiency and the highest level of service at the millinery shop." She would not offer a rejoinder regarding her own health.

Mr. Grogan cleared his throat. "Your father also says you are to accompany him as his hostess for the summer season in Saratoga Springs in a few days."

"Yes, that's true." She gave him a genuine smile. "I'm very excited about the voyage, as I've never been so far north before."

"You'll travel on the *Pulaski*?"

"Yes. Father is pleased to have obtained tickets." The *Pulaski*, a sumptuous new ship, built in Baltimore, had been partially financed by men in Savannah and was prized for its speed. Father was delighted that many socially prominent families who frequented Onslow's Millinery would be traveling with them.

"Excellent."

That subject exhausted, Mr. Grogan went silent. Lavinia knew that according to Southern decorum she should ask him a question about himself, such as whether he'd ever been to Saratoga Springs, or what types of books he enjoyed reading, though she doubted they'd have any books in common. She might inquire whether he enjoyed hunting, but he did not look in the least like a hunter or sportsman of any kind. She could ask his opinion of Reverend Collins' sermon this morning, but it had been about the respective roles of men and women in the church, and that was a more fraught topic than Lavinia thought would be appropriate.

An awkward silence ensued as Lavinia searched for the right engaging yet noncontroversial question an astute hostess might ask. A bee scrambled laboriously over the pearly petals of a magnolia blossom just outside the window and then relaxed its wings as if the soporific afternoon were too much for even an insect. In spite of her efforts to play the perfect hostess, Lavinia's mind had wandered to the pink ruche lining she'd planned for the new summer bonnets when Mr. Grogan startled her.

"Miss Onslow, I would like to request the high honor of courting you . . . perhaps with the express hope of a deeper commitment when you return from Saratoga Springs." Looking at her with soulful brown eyes with creases around the edges, Mr.

Grogan took Lavinia's hand and brought it to his thin lips for a kiss. His hand felt clammy when it touched hers, and, though barely discernible, Lavinia felt him shaking. "Possibly you need not worry about the millinery shop anymore. I did speak to your father and earned his approval in speaking to you of this, but he said the decision must be yours."

Her heart pounded and dampness spread under her arms at what seemed to have suddenly become a proposal of marriage. Naturally, Father would find him acceptable, since he believed marriage to be primarily a consolidation of property and Mr. Grogan apparently had a great deal of it. Yet, with each new book she read, Lavinia's ideas about marriage had become more modern. Shouldn't she at least feel the stirrings of true attachment toward the man she would marry? And Mr. Grogan seemed to assume that she would be pleased to relinquish the responsibilities of the millinery shop when nothing could be further from the truth.

She wished Clementine, their long-time housekeeper, would come in. She might relieve the awkwardness by asking if they needed more lemonade, but Clementine spent her Sundays at church, so Lavinia was left to fend for herself.

"You're very kind, sir, and I'm honored. Let me think on this. I cannot give you an immediate answer. I will send my answer tomorrow." Lavinia, still surprised, managed her most accommodating smile.

He tipped his elegant top hat and politely bid her good day, nearly tripping as he descended their front steps.

SINCE CLEMENTINE DIDN'T come on Sundays, Lavinia used the warming kitchen just at the back of the house to prepare a cold supper of ham and potato salad for herself, Sarah, and Father. Father liked her to use their best china on Sundays, but it was already packed up to be sent to Saratoga Springs for entertaining, so she used the everyday.

"Did you accept Mr. Grogan's offer?" Father looked pointedly at Lavinia as he reached for the mustard. He rarely wasted time coming to the point. He sat at the head of their dining table, a pine with mahogany veneer which Lavinia had chosen a few years ago when she updated the furnishings in the house to the newer Empire style.

Lavinia had inherited Frederick Onslow's auburn hair and blue eyes, but now gray threaded his hair and his well-trimmed mustache. His face was more florid than Lavinia would have liked, and she worried about his health. Her father wasn't the young man he used to be, and she wondered, not for the first time, what sort of man he'd been when her mother was alive. Lavinia didn't remember her mother, as she had been only three when she died, but she knew her father had tried to give his daughters everything they could wish for in her absence.

She smoothed the linen napkin in her lap and cleared her throat. "I told him I would answer him tomorrow."

"Don't think too long, Lavinia. He is a suitor I approve of."

"What do you mean, Father?" Father seemed to be pressuring her more than she liked. "You have always told me that choosing my husband was my decision."

"Yes, what do you mean?" Sarah's dark eyes, which Father had always declared were just like their mother's, went wide at this possible conflict between Father and Lavinia. She hated disagreement of any sort. Lavinia had often wished she had pale skin and smooth raven hair like her younger sister, but all Lavinia had inherited from her mother was her jewelry, her hairbrush, and a mirror set, which was most often employed in younger days staring at her imperfections and wishing them gone. Lavinia had tried to get rid of her freckles with lemon juice without success and had attempted taming her auburn curls to no avail— ringlets sprang free of her coiled braids with minds of their own.

"I mean that even though you and William are engaged,

Sarah, I feel it's more proper for the elder sister to marry first. I would like you to wait until Lavinia has wed before you do."

"Father!" Sarah blinked back tears. She and William Anderson had danced all night this past March at the only grand ball that had been held this year. Savannah's suffering economy caused the cancellation of many balls and much distress among her sister's social set. It had been Sarah's debutante season, and she and William had become engaged not long after the ball.

Lavinia put down her fork. Why should Father feel that Sarah needed to wait for her? Today's events with Mr. Grogan had caught her off-guard, and now this unexpected pressure from Father made her feel even more anxious. "Father, I beg you, don't make Sarah's union contingent upon mine. I am quite content helping you in the shop. I may never marry."

"You need someone who can take care of you, Lavinia. And ideally, you should marry before Sarah. Mr. Grogan has much to recommend him."

THAT NIGHT, AFTER Sarah went to bed in an unusually quiet mood, Lavinia lay awake in her front bedroom for a long time. Why was Father so old-fashioned about the issue of her marriage? The idea that Sarah not marry on her account was absurd. Sometimes Lavinia had the ability to persuade her father in business matters, and possibly at Saratoga Springs Lavinia could prevail upon Father to change his mind about this. For herself, she had always vividly imagined being drawn to her future husband by mutual intellectual regard and the invisible pull of their hearts' desire. She couldn't imagine his face, but so many of his attributes were crystal clear in her mind—honesty, intelligence, warmth, integrity, passion, possibly even heroism. Many of those attributes came from her reading, but also from her own father, who she considered to be a man of integrity. Yet now

Sarah and William's future depended upon Lavinia's decision about a man her father approved but toward whom she felt no attraction whatsoever.

Men had always been more drawn to Sarah; she'd had her pick of them as a debutante and had chosen William. Lavinia wasn't particularly fond of William, but she hesitated to call it dislike. He was handsome enough and well-mannered, he was studying to become a lawyer, and he came from a very respectable family. In fact, he lived with his family only a few blocks away in a graceful mansion, and the Onslows had known them all for many years. Possibly it was the proprietary attitude he seemed to have acquired lately toward her sister. At any rate, Sarah was smitten with him. Finally, Lavinia lit a candle and tiptoed into Sarah's room, careful not to wake Father, whose bedroom was in the back of the house.

"Sarah, are you awake?" she whispered as she sat down on the bed next to her sister, pulling her knees to her chin.

Sarah turned to her and, in the candlelight, Lavinia saw that Sarah's eyes were worried. "Yes, I cannot sleep."

"Nor can I. Tell me honestly, what did you think of Mr. Grogan?" Sarah had also met Mr. Grogan a few times when their congregation mingled after church.

"He seems very solicitous, Livvy." Sarah hesitated a moment. "What is your complaint?"

"Well, he is quite a bit older. And he doesn't seem much interested in me continuing to manage the shop, which troubles me." She paused, hoping that Sarah would understand her reservations about Mr. Grogan. But possibly her sister, eager to marry William, might overlook them. After all, Mr. Grogan had been the only suitor to actually propose marriage to Lavinia. "I was surprised that he said, 'Tell me your interests.'"

Sarah giggled. "Yes, dear Livvy, I pine to know, what are your interests?"

"I must admit I was somewhat pleased to be asked about them. He is just so much older. And stooped."

"Do you mean like this?" Sarah jumped from the bed and walked across the room imitating Mr. Grogan's stooped posture.

"Oh, Sarah, don't!" Lavinia said, beginning to laugh. Within moments they had both collapsed onto the bed, stifling their amusement. "Stop, Sarah!"

When their laughter had at last subsided, Sarah took her hand. "Don't feel that you have to accept Mr. Grogan because of me."

"I know you feel that way, Sarah, and I love you for it. I only wish he weren't my only suitor."

"Livvy, you're so kind, so intelligent, so caring. I just know you'd have more suitors if you were only less serious."

"But Sarah, I'm a serious person. I like keeping track of figures and working and reading unusual books. I don't want to be expected to change who I am simply for social approval."

"Of course not, but you could on occasion be more vivacious."

"Sarah! I won't act silly for the sake of a man."

"Not silly—vivacious." Sarah squeezed Lavinia's hand. "I love you just as you are. But truly, Livvy, if you could endeavor to form an attachment at Saratoga Springs, I will be the most grateful sister on earth."

LAVINIA SLEPT VERY little the rest of the night. She hated incurring Father's displeasure, and never would she want to cause any pain to Sarah. Her desire to care for and protect them seemed suddenly to be at war with this one desire she had for her own life. Why couldn't Father accept that she wanted more than a merely practical marriage?

Finally, just as the six o'clock church bells began ringing throughout Savannah, she tiptoed downstairs to the dining table with quill, ink, and paper, since she had no writing desk in her room, and, still in her nightgown, drafted a polite letter to Matthew Grogan.

As Lavinia signed her name, Clementine arrived, having walked, as usual, from her home in Oglethorpe Ward, and came into the warming kitchen, noisily preparing coffee. Father descended the stairs, buttoning his waistcoat.

"Is that your answer to Matthew Grogan?"

"I have given him an honest answer. And you did say, Father, that in the end the decision was mine." Lavinia lit a candle and melted the wax to seal the letter before she could change her mind, avoiding her father's gaze.

CHAPTER TWO

June 13, 1838
Savannah

Lavinia looked in the mirror above her dressing table, adjusting the straw bonnet with the white egret feather that she'd designed herself with this voyage in mind.

"Lavinia, you're wearing your gray gloves, aren't you?" Clementine, on her way down the hall with the feather duster, leaned in the doorway.

Gloves! Of course, Clementine was right—she was always right. "Do you know where they are?" Lavinia gave her sunny front bedroom a last look around.

Sarah's laugh came from across the hall. "Honestly, Lavinia, nobody loses gloves oftener than you."

"I put them in the glove box downstairs in the front hall," said Clementine. "Where a pair of gloves ought to be." She headed toward Father's back bedroom with the feather duster. She was one of the few free Black women in Savannah and had cared for the Onslow girls all their lives. Father had long served as guardian for both Clementine and their groom Peter, who was also free.

"Thank you, Clementine." Lavinia rushed down the curving stairs of their stately Savannah home just as her father strode through the back door, his double-breasted tailcoat billowing out behind him, and they nearly collided in the hall.

"Are you ready, Lavinia? Peter has loaded the trunks in the carriage and is bringing it around front. The ship will be boarding in an hour, and we must stop by the shop on the way."

"Just ready, Father!" Lavinia slid her gloves up her arms. "Have you been out?"

"Just a quick visit with Dr. Martin."

"Your physician?" On the morning of their departure? Lavinia immediately began searching his face for signs of disturbance or ill health. "What did he say?"

"We had business, Lavinia. Stop your worrying. Time to go now."

Sarah hurried down the stairs just then looking as fresh and cool as ever in her newest summer frock. "Is it truly time for you to leave? Oh, Livvy, I can't believe the time is already here." Sarah was not accompanying them to Saratoga Springs, and Lavinia was sorry to be leaving her behind. But Sarah had begged Father to be able to stay home to spend more time with William and begin learning the running of a household on her own. She had also been invited to participate with this year's other debutantes in the July Fourth ceremonies and celebrations, and even Father agreed she shouldn't miss that. There would be other trips.

Lavinia embraced her only sister ferociously, taking in the scent of her hair, feeling how fragile she was, and then cupped her face in both hands. "We'll be back in two months." In the front hall mirror, as they embraced, she caught a glimpse of her own serious face framed by her bonnet contrasting with Sarah's sleek dark curls.

Their father embraced Sarah as well. "Take care of yourself, dear, and be sure to have Mrs. Keating accompany you when you go out. I expect William will be of help as well." Mrs. Keating was a close neighbor and had agreed to stay with Sarah at night for the duration of the trip and provide her whatever help she may need. Lavinia had always wondered if the widowed Mrs. Keating secretly hoped Father might have an interest in her. He'd had opportunities to remarry since their mother died when Sarah was born, but he never had.

Lavinia squeezed Sarah's hand as they went out to the front porch. "I will write to you as soon as I possibly can."

"I promise that a letter will be waiting at the hotel when you arrive," Sarah said, then whispered, "And perhaps, indeed, you'll meet someone."

Lavinia laughed. "Oh, of course, that should be easy. I'm sure the first man I see will fall madly in love with me, and I with him." She'd caught Sarah and William in an embrace just yesterday and pretended not to see.

Clementine came out now, her hands folded under her apron. "I've been praying that the Lord will watch over your ship." Clementine had always seemed of an indeterminate age to Lavinia, but in truth was only about fifteen years her senior. Her stern demeanor belied her generous heart. She was also a granny midwife, and much loved throughout the community for the help she provided women giving birth.

"Thank you, Clementine." Father gave her one of his characteristic deferential nods. "I trust that you and Peter will watch over Sarah."

"Yes, sir, we will."

Father headed down the front steps and gave Sarah a pointed look. "Sarah, I've asked Mrs. Keating to also come over in the evenings to join you and William."

"That early?" Sarah glanced at Lavinia, disappointed.

Lavinia drew in her breath. She knew Sarah had been hoping to spend time alone with William—perhaps for more impassioned kissing?—while Father was gone. That would be challenging with Mrs. Keating's hovering presence.

Lavinia felt for her sister and the familiar conflict within over this trip resurfaced. She was certainly excited to go, and she was honored that Father had invited her as his hostess at Saratoga Springs, even if it was an enormous responsibility. Making Father proud had always been a driving force for Lavinia. Yet, she worried over leaving Sarah behind on her own, though she knew Sarah would enjoy her time with William and with the other debutantes. She'd spent so much of her own childhood caring for and mothering Sarah, and she suspected she might always see her as that little girl of long ago, though she was a grown woman now. Almost every night as a child, Sarah had climbed into bed with Lavinia, and Sarah's warm and trusting little body snuggled next to her. Which did Lavinia want more, to help Father, or to care for Sarah and see her happy? This was the first occasion in her life when she couldn't do both.

"I'm sorry about Mrs. Keating, dearest, but she'll probably fall asleep anyway," she whispered, squeezing Sarah's arm.

"I hope you're right. And remember what I said, Livvy, about being light-hearted and flirtatious." Sarah batted her eyelashes theatrically. "Men like vivacious ladies."

Lavinia laughed, though this still seemed to be a broad generalization in her view. But since Sarah had had more success attracting the attention of men, Lavinia could hardly argue the point.

At that moment, Peter urged Daisy, their bay draft horse, to pull up the carriage in front of their house and parked in the shade of their gnarled live oak. Their wagon had gone to the docks earlier, carrying the family silver, china, and crystal for entertaining while at Saratoga Springs, and now the carriage was loaded beyond belief. There were two trunks for Lavinia's clothes, two for Father's, and half a dozen hat boxes. Being in the millinery business naturally required that they maintain a fashionable appearance and that Lavinia show off all their latest wares. There was scarcely room left for people.

Lavinia and Father climbed in behind Peter.

"Bon voyage!" Sarah cried. "I'll miss you!" And she blew them a kiss.

Lavinia did likewise, feeling a pang, resolving to keep her sister's face locked in her memory. "And I as well."

Clementine waved, and Lavinia felt comforted by her presence, hoping Sarah's ardent desires for time alone with William wouldn't test Clementine's patience too much.

"Gee!" Peter said, giving the reins a shake, and Daisy set off for Onslow's Millinery on Ellis Square, a route she knew well. Gray Spanish moss hanging from sprawling trees cast a filigree shadow over the cobbled street and gave an atmospheric sense of mystery to the city. Lavinia had not been to many other cities, but she felt sure Savannah was among the world's most beautiful. The equidistant squares with small parks anchored by graceful live oaks and white-barked sycamores gave the city elegance and style. Wood from these native trees had been used to build many a ship in Savannah.

As they turned down Abercorn Street and headed through Reynolds Square toward East Bay Street, the air felt thick with humidity, heat, and the pungent smells of the Savannah River. June was past the busy season in Savannah, but they still passed several mule-drawn wagons carrying rice and slave women balancing huge loads of laundry and cotton on their heads. As they made their way to the shop, the church bells began ringing to announce the noon hour.

On the way to the commercial district, they passed the elegant Georgian home of Matthew Grogan. Sarah, dear sister that she was, had never said a word about Lavinia refusing Mr. Grogan. It was Father who had been most displeased by Lavinia's decision, bringing it up at every opportunity until Lavinia had finally asked him to please let the subject rest. He had, but she could still feel his displeasure, as though she had somehow betrayed him, and she hated it.

"Here we are, sir," Peter said, pulling up the carriage beside the front windows of Onslow's Millinery. With pride, Lavinia examined the bonnets that she'd arranged in the bay window a few days before. The low platform in the window and the tiered wooden display it held were polished daily and shone in the bright sunlight. On the upper level of the display was a sweet summer straw ladies' bonnet with a bluebird feather and a clutch of blue and yellow flowers, a sweeping woman's bonnet in blue silk with a deep brim and ivory satin sash. Arrayed below was a tasteful spray of matching flowers and feathers and light summer gloves. Just looking at all the hues and textures made Lavinia smile.

"Peter, I will be out in a moment," Father said now, climbing down. "Lavinia, wait with Peter."

Lavinia desperately wanted to go inside and see how the milliners were progressing with the new design they'd copied from the latest ladies' magazine from Milan, yet she knew that she and Father certainly couldn't be delayed, and there was a definite chance of that if she started examining the work. She waited a moment with Peter, alternately fanning herself and drumming her fan on her lap. Finally, she could not contain herself any longer and climbed down, saying, "Peter, I am just going in for a moment."

"Yes, Miss Lavinia, I was expecting that." Peter's voice sounded matter-of-fact, and he gave her a patient smile.

"Truly, just a moment."

"Yes, Miss Lavinia." He pulled out a scrap of wood and began carving one of the wooden animals he habitually made for his grandchildren.

Lavinia hurried into the shop, enjoying the sunshine on the dark floorboards, the colorful displays, the smell of the wax used to dip the flowers, the touch of the fabric, and the bits of feathers that sometimes hung in the air. They sold more than just millinery in the shop. They kept a selection of rich fabrics, such as silks, taffetas, damasks, and satins. Customers could also purchase glazed kid and lamb gloves, powder boxes and puffs, satin petticoats and shoes, silk stockings, hoops, stays, thimbles, and an assortment of paste pins. It was an ongoing family joke that her father stocked gloves at Onslow's Millinery just to defray the expense of replacing all the ones Lavinia lost.

"Good afternoon, Miss Lavinia." Mr. Mason, the young man

who had served as Father's assistant for the past ten years or so, greeted her just inside. He was tall and thin, very careful about his dress, and in his mid-twenties, just a few years older than Lavinia. He seemed, so far at least, to be a confirmed bachelor. Because he didn't have any family, Father had been inviting him to Sunday dinner once a month for several years, which he seemed to greatly enjoy. His business acumen wasn't what Lavinia would have liked—he had a tendency to forget to charge a customer for accessories—but he had an excellent eye for design and display details, and Father was very pleased with his feel for the millinery business and the progress he was making. "Your father is in his office."

"Good afternoon, Mr. Mason. I just wanted to go in the back and see how the new summer bonnet design is coming along."

"It's going well. I believe your father is pleased." Mr. Mason seemed to idolize Father, and Lavinia noticed lately that he had even adopted some of Father's phrases and mannerisms. The slight deferential bow he gave her as he spoke made her smile to herself.

Lavinia nodded and hurried toward the short hall that led to the offices and back room, but she paused to greet Mrs. Smith, a longtime customer, who was perusing the glove selection. "Oh, Mrs. Smith, I think those white kids will look lovely with the straw bonnet you ordered last week."

"They are just the ones I was thinking about." Mrs. Smith smoothed one on and admired it. Lavinia helped her with the buttons. "Yes, thank you, Miss Onslow, I think they will be perfect."

In the back room, the two milliners, Mrs. Thomas and Abby, her daughter, were hard at work on light straw summer bonnets. They were surrounded by all the trimmings from the millinery trade—straw, feathers in every shade from egret white to jet-black plumes, tape, needle and thread, and ribbons of all colors and sizes. The small room had no window, but they often kept the back door open for the light and any breeze they could catch, and the two women made it a congenial place to be.

"How are you getting on, Mrs. Thomas, Abby? I'm eager to see how the pink ruche looks." Lavinia had seen in the magazine from Milan that one of the newest styles was to line bonnet brims in a pinkish ruche material in order to brighten the wearer's complexion, and she had requested the milliners try to reproduce it.

Abby held up the bonnet she was working on. The ruffled pink ruche lining was complete, and Abby was sewing a rose made of red ribbon onto the right side of the brim. "Do you like it, Miss Onslow?"

Lavinia immediately peeled off her gloves and took the proffered bonnet, turning it one way and then another as she scrutinized the look of the ruche inside. "Would you mind putting it on, Abby?" she said. "I would like to see if it does improve the complexion."

Abby obliged, tying the satin ribbon under her chin and smiling for Lavinia. She was a thin, pale girl, but the pink did indeed reflect attractively off her cheeks.

"You have the healthy glow of an afternoon outdoors with a bracing breeze," Lavinia declared. "Do you agree, Mrs. Thomas?"

Mrs. Thomas smiled at her daughter. "You look lovely, dear."

"I think it will be popular—do you?" Lavinia asked.

"I do," said Abby.

"Can you each make five of them over the next week?"

"Yes, miss," Mrs. Thomas said.

Abby, who was a bit slower with her work than her more experienced mother, hesitantly agreed.

"Lavinia?" came Father's voice. "I thought I told you to wait in the carriage with Peter."

"I'm sorry, Father, I was eager to see the new summer bonnets." Lavinia waved good-bye to the milliners and headed for the front of the store.

"Wait, Miss Lavinia, your gloves!" called Mrs. Thomas.

Lavinia raced back to grab them. "Thank you!"

"Safe travels, Mr. Onslow, Miss Lavinia," said Mr. Mason as she passed by the second time. Father gave Mr. Mason a hearty handshake.

"Thank you, Mr. Mason. Write with any questions at all. I trust the shop to your excellent care." Father held the door for Lavinia. "We shall see you in August."

And Lavinia and Father climbed into the carriage and set off for the docks.

THEY PASSED THE waterfront warehouses, the schooners carrying raw cotton, the flatboats loaded with rice, and at last came upon the steamship *Pulaski*, docked by the teeming Savannah wharf. It was the most enormous ship Lavinia had ever seen, three decks high and nearly as long as a city block, with two smokestacks in the center near the wheelhouse, flanked by three massive white furled sails fore and one aft. Nearly brand-new, having completed only four previous voyages, the polished wood gleamed on the *Pulaski's* sides. Sailors scurried across the shining decks, pulling ropes. With a cacophony of shouting and banging, slaves and free longshoremen heaved trunks and crates up the gangplank and onto the deck.

"The *Pulaski* is one of the fastest steamships ever built," said Father. "I heard someone say it sails five miles per hour. Can you believe we'll be in Baltimore by day after tomorrow?" Father asked as he climbed down from the carriage.

"It's very imposing, sir," Peter agreed, craning his neck back to take in the sails.

"Truly a miracle." Lavinia's pulse ran fast, and her mind raced with the trip's possibilities: the excitement of the voyage; the honor and responsibility of hosting soirees for Father; and yes, even the possibility of meeting a man who could appreciate a woman like Lavinia. For the first day after her refusal of Mr.

Grogan, she feared Father had reconsidered bringing her to Saratoga Springs, and she was glad not to have been left behind. Perhaps, as Sarah hoped, there would be a thoughtful man at Saratoga Springs, fascinated by the attractions of a serious-minded woman, and Father would be pleased with her again.

Suddenly the *Pulaski*'s ear-splitting horn sounded, deep and long, making Lavinia jump.

"Time to board." Peter climbed down from the carriage.

Father escorted Lavinia up the walkway to the ship's deck while behind them, Peter and two wharf workers carried their trunks and boxes. Lavinia and Father had a few flurried moments to greet acquaintances on board and admire the luxurious, well-appointed vessel before the steam engine sprang to life and the polished wooden deck beneath them vibrated.

"Bon voyage!" People assembled on the dock waved festively, and Lavinia, trembling with excitement, lifted her gloved hand in response to the well-wishers as the *Pulaski* lurched forward.

CHAPTER THREE

June 14, 1838
At sea

L AVINIA CAREFULLY CLASPED her pink topaz necklace then put on the matching topaz and pearl drop earrings that Father had asked her to wear to dinner. He had given them to her for her eighteenth birthday, and she enjoyed having the opportunity to wear them tonight.

It would be the same in Baltimore when the *Pulaski* arrived—Father was insisting that she adorn herself in her best attire. He liked the world to appreciate his success and used that attention as a way of promoting business for Onslow's Millinery. Some of their more conservative Methodist friends from church disapproved of Father's emphasis on appearance, but he always insisted that their business demanded it.

As the younger son of a rice plantation owner, his older brother had inherited the plantation as well as all its slaves on the death of Lavinia's grandfather. Father had inherited various other investments and the millinery shop, which was, in most people's view, much less prestigious than his brother's plantation. Sometimes Lavinia wondered if the great pride he took in the success of the millinery and their fine appearance had been borne of an early desire to prove himself the equal—or even the better—of his imperious brother.

His first act on moving to Savannah to take over the millinery had been to declare himself a Methodist. He was also an abolitionist, though quietly so, which had created a rift with his older slave-owning brother, and had not made social acceptance easy, but Father had persevered in seeking that as well as business success. In 1825, when Lavinia was only a child of nine, the war hero Marquis de Lafayette had come to Savannah on his tour of the United States and stayed just around the corner from the Onslow's, at Mr. Owens' Regency-style home. The Marquis made a speech that Father attended in which he deplored the ownership of human beings. Lavinia could still remember Father's excitement when he quoted Lafayette to her later as saying that if he had known America would become a slave-owning country, he would never have fought for it. And Father told her that when James Edward Oglethorpe originally founded Savannah, he had outlawed slavery and so it had remained for many years. Lavinia admired her father's position on slavery, agreed with it, and wished it had not become such a large part of life in Savannah. She had always avoided the area in the marketplace where the slave auctions were held and could not imagine ever owning slaves herself.

The bell rang for supper.

Lavinia smoothed her hands over her tight whalebone corset, which cinched her waist but also made it hard to breathe and nigh impossible to enjoy dinner. But the food on the *Pulaski* was sumptuous, and she was growing hungry—unlike many others, she was fortunate not to have suffered from seasickness so far. Thinking twice about it, she quickly reached back and loosened the laces. No one would be the wiser, and now she could eat what she wished.

Through the cabin window, she could see the sun riding low on the horizon as the ship cut through the waves at a fast clip. She'd been on the *Pulaski* since yesterday afternoon, and except for the evening stop in Charleston, the ship had travelled swiftly the entire time. Speed was evidently a badge of honor; Lavinia had heard that all the steamships raced to see who could make it to port faster.

She had spent her time mostly cooped up in this stateroom with her window open, except for the few times Father escorted her above decks for a stroll. Father's cabin was next door, but he was out on deck a good deal. Even in her stateroom, however, there was much to occupy her mind and eyes. Water shifted around her and off into the distance, with no view of land, entrancing her. And she'd been amazed by the ship itself during her strolls with Father—the sailors scurrying around the decks, the steam streaming from the central smokestacks, and the lavishly appointed dining room and staterooms were endlessly fascinating.

A sharp knock sounded at her door. "Lavinia?" Father's voice came through the open window. "Are you ready for dinner?"

"Yes, Father."

She opened the door, her hand still on the pink topaz pendant. The blue floral print, mutton sleeves, fitted bodice and satin sash had all been her own design choices, and this was her favorite of all her new gowns.

Father offered his arm, and he led her toward the dining room. "There is a certain Mr. Whalen that we'll be joining for dinner. He's an architect who's been successful, and we have business to discuss, perhaps about enlarging our home as well as the shop."

"Of course, Father." She sensed from a characteristic twitch of Father's mustache that he felt somewhat apprehensive about the dinner. He had not mentioned any additions to their home or the millinery, though Lavinia could easily think of ways to use extra space in the shop. She was determined to begin her hostess responsibilities now and make every effort to smooth the evening as a good hostess would. She hoped Father would notice and be pleased.

The tables in the first-class dining room bore embroidered

white tablecloths, abundant roses in crystal vases, and richly upholstered red chairs. The dining hall ceiling rose two stories high, with a promenade where people could stroll around the edge and peer down to see who dined with whom. Though Father wished last night that they could have been seated at the Captain's table, tonight he directed their steps toward a smaller table for four without comment. He sat so he could see the door, and when a portly man with gray curls about her father's age entered, Father caught his eye and nodded in greeting.

"Good evening, Mr. Whalen. My daughter Lavinia and I are delighted to dine with you this evening," he said as Mr. Whalen joined them.

Mr. Whalen bowed and kissed the hand Lavinia proffered with thin, dry lips. "Good evening, Miss Onslow. A pleasure to make your acquaintance. You are every bit as lovely as your father described you."

"The pleasure is mine." Mr. Whalen's gallantry was nice, but she sighed inwardly. Was Father indeed thinking of adding onto the shop? She could only hope that Father did not entertain any notions about this man becoming a potential suitor.

Dinner featured turtle soup, beefsteak, and oyster pie, as well as potatoes and boiled cabbage. Father ordered Lavinia oyster pie and a sherry. For himself, he ordered the more expensive claret, turtle soup, and beefsteak. She would have preferred to have made her dinner choices herself—the turtle soup sounded quite good—but was unsurprised that her father preempted her. Indeed, Father did know that she was fond of oysters. She supposed he was concerned about whether it would seem quite proper for Lavinia to have an opinion on the matter herself. She would ask him later if he would permit her to order for herself tomorrow. She'd seen other women do it and felt it could not be seen as improper Yet, make no mistake, tonight she planned to do the oysters justice.

Over his own beefsteak and claret, Mr. Whalen inquired about their travels to Saratoga Springs. As Father detailed their plans for the summer, Lavinia let her gaze travel over the room and observed the headwear, hoping to spy some innovative or inspiring styles she could get Mrs. Thomas and Abby to copy.

At that moment, a young man entered the dining room, carrying a book. Slender and of medium height, he had wavy dark blonde hair, a bit longer than most men were wearing it these days, spectacles over expressive eyes, and a well-trimmed mustache. Almost in spite of herself, Lavinia admired his appearance and was intrigued by the fact that he had brought a book with him to dinner. Instantly, a fashionably dressed young woman sitting at another table with some of her friends pulled out her fan and spread it wide. Lavinia recognized the fan signal—the woman was silently inviting him to come talk to her. Well, that was bold. Would the young man oblige? Apparently not. Instead, he glanced Lavinia's way and, seeing where her attention rested, gave her a look of exaggerated forbearance. Then he sat down and opened his book. Lavinia stifled a smile at their very satisfying moment of accord, shared completely without words.

"Lavinia, Mr. Whalen has asked you a question." Father's face was flushed, and Lavinia feared she had embarrassed him. "Mr. Whalen will think you rude."

"Have you stayed at Saratoga Springs before, Miss Onslow?" Mr. Whalen repeated.

"My apologies. This will be my first visit." Lavinia smiled as graciously as she could but chided herself. It wasn't like her to lose track of a conversation like this. That young man had abstracted her.

"How long will you stay?"

"Until the end of August," Father wiped his mouth with the linen napkin "when we can finally have relief from the heat and the swamp fevers at home."

As Father resumed the conversation, her attention drifted back to the young man. He turned a page in his book. She couldn't tell what he was reading but was intensely curious. He wore a dark coat, light trousers, a double-breasted vest, and a cravat. Almost as if he could sense her noticing him, his eyes flicked to hers and they both quickly looked away again with small, embarrassed smiles. Throughout the rest of dinner, she had the not unpleasant sensation that he glanced her way more than once. Her awareness of his proximity and attention caused her to nearly lose track of the conversation surrounding the possible expansion of the shop several times more.

After dinner Father stood, waiting to pull her chair out. "Mr. Whalen, would you care for a cigar on the promenade deck?"

"Don't mind if I do."

"I'll escort Lavinia back to her cabin, then, and meet you beside the smoking lounge in half an hour."

"Very well," said Mr. Whalen, and he took his leave.

Lavinia wished Father hadn't already said she was going back to her cabin. She was hoping for another chance to see the book-reading young man. Perhaps he was the sort who enjoyed an evening stroll. She must persuade Father to accompany her on a stroll after his cigar, since she couldn't go without him as an escort. Again, as they left the dining room, she apprehended the glance of the young man. As she passed the bold woman who had sent the earlier fan signal, she suddenly saw another significant gesture. The woman held her fan's handle to her lips, which meant "kiss me." Lavinia suppressed a smile at seeing such brazenness. She glanced back to check if the young man had seen, and once more he sent Lavinia what seemed to be a look of understanding, then pointedly turned a page.

Sarah's comments about being flirtatious flashed through her mind. This other woman was certainly determined to attract the man's attention, yet he seemed to share Lavinia's disinterest in such flirtations. Lavinia could not deny having a tantalizing attraction to what seemed to be the young man's more serious nature.

"How did you like Mr. Whalen?" Father and Lavinia navigated the narrow halls on the way to her cabin.

"He seemed nice enough. Are we indeed planning to expand

the shop?"

"I know that he's been recently widowed."

"Widowed! Father, I knew you were scheming. You aren't planning to expand the shop at all, are you?"

"I just worry about you, Lavinia."

A spiral of concern raced through Lavinia, and she remembered how flushed his face was at dinner.

"Father, why did you visit Dr. Martin before our voyage?"

"Never mind that, Lavinia. We need to make an advantageous match for you," Father continued.

Lavinia loved Father so dearly and knew him so well. It was clear there was something he wasn't telling her. She also knew she was much more to him than just a daughter to be married off, but she wished he could understand her feelings about deep love and respect in marriage. "Father, Mr. Whalen is too old for me."

"Age is not the only issue you should be concerned with in a match."

"But Father, you know I want to marry for love. And besides, so far I am happy helping you with the shop. What would happen to my work in the shop should I marry Mr. Whalen?"

"Mr. Mason could take over, I'm sure."

"Mr. Mason!" A flush heated her cheeks. That wasn't an idea that had occurred to Lavinia at all.

"Mr. Whalen is waiting for me, so there isn't time to discuss this."

Lavinia drew a calming breath and remembered her earlier intention. "After you've finished your cigar with Mr. Whalen, will you promenade with me? I would enjoy being out of my cabin for a few minutes this evening. And I understand that being on deck can help prevent seasickness."

Father seemed happy to change the topic as well. "Very well, Lavinia. I'll fetch you at ten thirty for a short stroll."

Lavinia paced the cramped stateroom in frustration after her father left. His comment about Mr. Mason had startled her even more than the idea of Mr. Whalen as a suitor. Mr. Mason was a perfectly nice young man, but Father's assumption that Lavinia would marry, give up her position in the shop, and that Mr. Mason would then take over truly bothered her. Why couldn't a woman marry for love as well as keep an occupation? She had half a mind to go up on deck alone without Father and send a suggestive fan signal to that serious young man.

Finally, she sat down and calmed herself by occupying the rest of the hour reading. At least Frederick Onslow trusted his two daughters to read whatever they liked, though he might have reconsidered had he known all of Lavinia's reading preferences. Recently, in addition to the novels she enjoyed, Lavinia had also read some thought-provoking essays about the evils of slave-holding and also letters published in serial form by a Sarah Grimké from Charleston, South Carolina on the condition and value of women. Miss Grimké and her sister Angelina had caused quite a stir by lecturing in public, even with men present. In her published letters, Miss Grimké had expressed ideas about women's equality that would be shocking to most Savannah ladies, but Lavinia was persuaded by Miss Grimké's argument; she wasn't sure that marriage would make her *more* fortunate, especially if it were with one of these older men Father seemed determined to foist upon her. Father's progressive views on freedom from slavery didn't extend to freedom for women.

Her mind wandered back to portly Mr. Whalen and the young man in the dining hall. Was it too much to ask to find love in a match?

When Father finally knocked on her stateroom door at half past ten, she found a shawl Sarah had crocheted for her and wrapped it around her shoulders. Sarah would love to be here, if not for William and her commitments in Savannah, and Lavinia wished she could talk with her about everything, especially that young man with whom she'd had that provocative wordless conversation.

"Sarah," she'd say, "I didn't attempt to be lively or vivacious and I believe he still found me engaging." She was so lost in this pretend dialogue that Father had to remind her to put on her gloves, which she'd left lying on the end of the bed. She was at all times a walking advertisement for Onslow's Millinery.

The smell of cigar clung to Father's jacket as they headed down the corridor between the cabins. "Did you enjoy your cigar?" Determined to stay on a congenial footing with Father, she took his arm.

"Very much."

"I've been looking forward to strolling out in the breeze. Imagine the ship going so fast that we can be in Baltimore after only two nights aboard."

"The boilers are working at full steam to manage it."

The wind grabbed her shawl and almost wrenched it from her shoulders as they came topside, and her bonnet nearly blew off. Quite a few people leaned against the railings observing the dazzling dance of the half-moon on the shifting water.

As she meandered along with Father, she looked for the young man amongst the others on the upper deck. When they came around the starboard side, there he was! He sat alone on a wooden settee nearly at the back of the boat, facing the water. Her heart beat a bit faster. The book lay beside him on the settee. As she and Father strolled past, she was just able to see the title. *The Last of the Mohicans*! The novel she had recently begun herself. If Father weren't here, she might strike up a conversation and ask the young man his opinion of the book. She herself was finding the concept of friendship between the native Indians and white settlers to be quite intriguing. She realized the young man had once again caused her to lose track of a conversation, and she refocused on Father.

"I hope you are able to find a man to marry, Lavinia. I don't want you to grow to old age taking care of me." Father removed his top hat because of the wind and cradled it under his elbow.

"I would be honored to grow old taking care of you." She affectionately patted his arm. "I would far rather have that than a marriage that is only a business arrangement. I am looking for a love match, a true partner in my life. I always had the feeling that yours was a love match with Mother, and that the two of you had a deep friendship and partnership."

"I certainly felt love for your mother, Lavinia, but you'd be surprised how much of marriage *is* like a business arrangement."

"I disagree, Father." Her frustration rose again. Much as she admired Father, much as she wanted to be able to agree with him, she wouldn't abandon this hope for her own future and couldn't understand why he refused to see her view. "Women and men are partners in love, not business partners."

"Lavinia, you are speaking naively. Believe me, you don't want to make a mistake in the arena of your marriage union."

"Father, please don't call me naïve—"

"But Lavinia, you have no idea of the vicissitudes of life. Think when you're at Saratoga Springs about making an advantageous match. Perhaps you'll meet someone there who pleases you. Or perhaps you'll reconsider Mr. Grogan. He is an honorable man, whatever your objections. Look at me, Lavinia. This is important to me."

Lavinia turned and looked at her father's concerned face. "Father, I didn't mean to upset you—"

But in the space of her breath before her next word, an enormous explosion filled the atmosphere, so loud and close the air shattered around them. The sky lit up with fire, a wave of boiling heat washed over them, and the boat under their feet listed suddenly and sharply down. She screamed and looked to her father in alarm and the look of horror and fear she saw mirrored on his face terrified her. She couldn't remember ever seeing Father afraid. He had hold of the railing and she grabbed for his free arm, but the deck lurched suddenly, and they both lost their footing. One instant he stood beside her and the next he had vanished over the side.

"Father!" She tried to stay standing, but it was impossible. She tumbled across the deck so fast she couldn't grab anything solid, her head spinning. A boiler was on fire, and waves of heat from the inferno blasted her. Everything roared—the fire, the sea, the wind—in a cacophony that filled her head. Through it all came the sound of someone thinly screaming "I am burned! I am burned!" Her transit across the fractured deck took a matter of seconds, though it seemed much longer, then she slid as if in slow motion under the railing, over the side edge of the ship, and into the frigid and choppy water.

She gasped for air, water splashing her face, struggling to keep her head above the surface with her voluminous mutton chop sleeves and full skirt, which had filled with air, billowing around her. Dozens of others in the water with her flailed and screamed. She grabbed a passing couch pillow as she struggled to stay afloat, and was just able to keep her head up. She looked around wildly, attempting to see if any of the struggling figures was Father.

"Father!" She yelled again, then looked up in shock as the ship, with a wrenching, thundering noise, and splintering of wood, broke apart at its center and massive flames and black smoke billowed from the boiler room into the dark sky, eerily silhouetting the massive wheelhouse. The center of the ship began to sink, and the two ends of the ship began to rise toward the sky, with frantic people clinging to the railings. On the front half of the ship, far from Lavinia, men shouted and lowered lifeboats.

"Father!" Roaring and crackling from the massive fires on board continued to overwhelm her senses. None of those struggling around her appeared to be Father. He had disappeared in the blink of an eye. Her head went under as she gasped for breath, and she swallowed a great deal of water. Her dress, instantly waterlogged, threatened to drag her under. She choked and coughed, clutching the couch pillow that was quickly becoming saturated and less buoyant. Holding onto it now barely kept her head above water. Others who knew how to swim were making for the lifeboat being lowered down the looming side of the *Pulaski*. She tried to paddle and kick her way toward the lifeboat that was quickly being lowered down the angled side of the ship, but her skirts hampered her progress.

The lifeboat touched down on the waves but as people nearby clambered in, the boat filled with water and its edges wobbled, then it sank below the surface. Snatches of screams floated through the air as the people inside the lifeboat tumbled into the water. Other crew managed to lower two more lifeboats onto the water, but the remaining boats remained lashed to the ship as the *Pulaski* continued to sink.

"Help!" Could she make it onto a lifeboat? Were they seaworthy? Dozens of people were struggling toward the boats. Some of the men who could swim made progress through the waves, but most, like Lavinia, had never been taught and struggled against the chop and their heavy clothes.

"Miss!" A voice sounded behind her, and she turned to see the handsome young man from dinner, kneeling on a makeshift raft made of two wooden settees. He had lashed them together with the legs upright somehow, the seats facing downward, and they floated.

"Oh, please—"

"Here." He held out his hand but could not reach her. As waves threatened to push her farther away, he grabbed the end of a length of rope that seemed to be part of his lashing, dove into the water, and swam a few strokes toward her. He helped her take hold of his arm and began pulling the two of them back toward his makeshift raft.

"Hold on here." He placed her hand on one of the legs of the settees comprising the homemade craft, then pulled himself up, dripping and gasping. Immediately he firmly grasped her other arm and pulled her halfway aboard. Water streamed from her sleeves and hair and she tried to catch her breath, still dangling partly in the water. He leaned over her, clasped both hands around her waist, and hoisted her the rest of the way onto the settee raft. "Are you all right?"

"I—I don't know. I think so." She gasped with relief and lay there dazed, panting. Screaming rent the air, and surreal flames crackled on the water. The two ends of the ship stood nearly upright. When a woman clinging to the railings with her child fell into the water, Lavinia cried out and covered her mouth with her hand, choking out a sob. This couldn't be happening. It was worse than her worst nightmare.

The young man had found a what seemed to be a side rail from a bed and was using it as an oar to row them away from the flaming wreck, toward one of the lifeboats. It was still afloat and moving quickly in their general direction, away from the ruined *Pulaski*. Lavinia turned herself over, settling more firmly on the joined and semi-submerged settees. Her heart hammered violently in her chest.

"I must find my father." She called for him by name this time, shouting "Frederick Onslow!" at the top of her lungs.

"I will get us as close to a lifeboat as I can." The young man rowed with vigor. "When I do, climb aboard."

As they drew near the closest lifeboat, he called out. "There are two of us here, have you room for two?"

"No, I'm sorry. There's room for only one. Any more and we will be overloaded and sink."

"Please!" She scanned the dark huddled forms to see if one might be Father. "Just two of us."

"No. Only one."

The young man looked at her. "You go. I will be fine here."

He was a stranger—she didn't even know his name—but he had rescued her from almost certain death at risk to himself. This young man was resourceful, and in an inexplicable and visceral way, she felt drawn to him. In truth, she had since the first moment she'd spotted him with his book, striding with self-assurance across the dining room. She thought of Father, who might or might not still live, and of Sarah, who waited for them to return, who had always depended on Lavinia. Whatever the outcome, she knew she would never forgive herself if she left him alone on his settees and took the last spot in the lifeboat. "No, I can't do that."

"Yes, miss, I insist."

He reached for her arm, but she pulled back, staring into his pleading eyes. "No, I won't go. You pulled me from the water, and I won't leave you on this raft alone."

"Last chance, miss." The voice of the man on the lifeboat sounded final.

"No, go on."

"Very well." The boat moved away and within seconds someone else scrambled into it. The young man and Lavinia now floated on either end on the lashed together settee raft, their respective weights balancing the raft's load.

"Why ever would you do that?" The young man gave her a look of despair. "That might have been your chance at life."

"One person alone . . . I simply won't leave you. Not after what you did for me."

It seemed both a matter of minutes and an age since the explosion, and they all floated in silence for a moment, watching as the broken halves of the ship sank rapidly now, and the last people dove or jumped from the decks into the water. The *Pulaski* disappeared beneath the waves as though it had never existed, pulling people who were too close to the ship under as it sank. Lavinia stared helplessly, goosebumps prickling her scalp and tears running down her face, as the water folded over the ship and those desperate people, children included, and they were no more.

Cold waves lapped the edges of their little raft. Exhaustion and shock came over Lavinia and she began to shiver in her wet clothing.

"Please help me search for my father," she begged.

He nodded and paddled toward the second lifeboat, which was still near them.

"Is Frederick Onslow on board?" she called. She heard a murmur go around the boat as they checked.

"No one by that name here!" a man called back.

The young man and Lavinia didn't ask to be taken on board as they knew the answer. The boat was clearly already full and they were likely better off than those in the overloaded lifeboats. So far, the settee raft had managed to keep the two of them afloat quite well.

"What about over there?" She pointed to a patch of floating debris. "Maybe Father is holding onto something."

The young man shook his head. "We should try to stay within sight of the lifeboats. If another ship comes by to save us, it will be best if we are all together."

Knowing he was right, she nevertheless scanned the water for movement as they followed along in the wake of the second lifeboat. They floated, watching as the people in the boat shouted directions and bandaged wounds. A large part of the deck floated by, with several people struggling to climb onto it. Lavinia suddenly noticed a large gash on her arm. It must have happened when she fell. Blood oozed and her arm throbbed, yet she hadn't realized it until now.

"I should introduce myself. Daniel Ridge." Her companion paused in his rowing.

"I suppose since we are marooned on a raft together, we should know each other's names. Lavinia Onslow. A pleasure to meet you, Mr. Ridge."

He gave a little bow of his head. "The pleasure is mine, Miss Onslow."

"How on earth did you manage to tie these settees together in time?"

"When the explosion occurred, and I saw the lifeboats were at the other end of the ship, I knew I needed to create a raft since the boats were beyond my reach. I saw a coil of rope and folded sail nearby and lashed these two settees together with the seats facing each other before they could slide off the deck. I ended up with a sort of protected box that seems to work better in the water when it's upside down."

A cargo crate floated close to them, bumping up against their raft.

"Help me grab that." Mr. Ridge pointed and she caught it before it could drift away again. While Lavinia helped hold the settees together, Mr. Ridge retied the rope to include the crate. "We should look out for anything that will help make us sturdier and float higher." The standing water between the rails of the upside down settees had grown deeper as they grew more waterlogged.

A few minutes later a piece of deck about the size of a table for six floated by and Mr. Ridge made use of that, too, sliding it underneath the settees, shoring up their raft, so it floated higher. Now only a few inches of water covered the settees. It suddenly occurred to them to try to throw a length of rope so that they could tie themselves to the closest lifeboat, but it was already too far away.

For a long while—Lavinia could not tell how long—Mr. Ridge kept the two lifeboats in sight in the moonlight, but as the night wore on, darkness thickened, he tired, and the boats pulled away. But the moaning of the people in the lifeboats, some of whom seemed to be grievously injured, still drifted across the water hauntingly. Some of them had begun to sing hymns.

Then she heard Mr. Ridge sigh quietly, and she realized he was about to collapse.

"Let me try a turn at rowing." She pointed at the makeshift oar. "You must be exhausted."

"I wouldn't hear of it."

"Heavens, I am as able-bodied as you are," she said, keeping her bad arm tucked behind her. "Let me row for a spell."

At last, he handed her the side rail and sank back against one of the settee legs. She clasped the board and rowed steadily but slowly, knowing she needed to conserve strength. Though she shook violently with cold and shock, and the wound on her arm was painful, she focused on following one of the lifeboats until she suddenly realized that in the darkness she could no longer see the other one. The hymn-singing, ominously, had stopped as well.

"I lost one of the lifeboats." Her teeth chattered and her own voice sounded weary.

"Stay with the one you see, if you can."

As the minutes went by, however, the remaining lifeboat drifted farther away over a swell, and the voices of its inhabitants grew fainter. She couldn't keep it in sight for much longer.

"Mr. Ridge, I'm losing the last lifeboat. What will we do if we can't see it?"

Mr. Ridge didn't answer. Had he fallen asleep from exhaustion or of something worse? Her fear was so great that she had no faith she could sleep even if she tried. In her mind's eye she saw, again and again, the moments after the blast when so many people were dragged underwater as the ship sank. She could still hear their piteous cries. She felt horribly alone without the conscious presence of Mr. Ridge, though it was strange to feel so lonely for a person she had known for only a few hours.

She scanned the water, thinking of Father. Had he drowned? Had he managed to get on one of the lifeboats on the other side of the ship, and they had somehow missed seeing it? Her brain ran feverishly over the possible scenarios by which Father might have survived. A part of her mind told her that these hopes were likely foolish, but she clung to them anyway.

An unmeasurable amount of time later, with arms so weak and throbbing she could barely move them, clinging to the settees as they heaved over the waves, water splashing around her legs, exhausted and discouraged that she wasn't able to keep the lifeboats in view, she put their oar over her lap and let herself drift into a shivering stupor. In the morning, the sun would come up and it wouldn't be so cold. They might have land in view. Surely someone would come to save them.

CHAPTER FOUR

June 15, 1838
At sea

L

AVINIA SHOOK HERSELF fully awake. She couldn't say that she had slept; rather, she had lain in a state of stunned exhaustion for what seemed like hours as the raft rocked on the water. They'd both lost their shoes in the wreck, and her right leg had come to rest up against Mr. Ridge's left as they half-sat, half-reclined next to each other. She felt a blush creep up her neck at the sight and considered moving, but she didn't want to wake him, so she simply allowed herself to stay still. Obviously, these weren't ordinary circumstances, and no one could possibly censure them for such contact, and considering her skirts, there were still many layers of fabric between them.

She seemed to have also burned the bottoms of her feet from her short time on the searing deck, which, like the gash on her arm, had gone unnoticed for some time. She had lost one glove in the shipwreck, but strangely, she still had the other. Her bare arm was very stiff, sore, and swollen, though the bleeding had stopped. Her teeth chattered violently and her wet dress made her shiver. She couldn't feel her hands or feet very well.

Faint ribbons of light bled from the east, which meant they needed to row in the opposite direction should they have any hope of going ashore. How far away was the shore? She had no idea.

The lifeboats were long gone. They were completely alone. Steel gray water stretched in every direction and clouds smudged the enormous lightening sky. The events of the previous night played over and over in her head, each time more frightening than before, and it occurred to her that if she had not been strolling on the promenade with Father at the time of the explosion she would likely have died in her stateroom as the ship went down.

She felt so thirsty she cupped water from the ocean in her hands to drink, but one salty taste and she spit it out.

Mr. Ridge lay next to her, still sleeping. She took the chance to study his face. His spectacles were missing, his eyelids looked bruised, and his cravat had come untied. Yet just looking at his resting face, with the flat cheekbones and salt-encrusted mustache, gave her courage. She was not alone. This brave person was here next to her.

As if he knew she watched him, Mr. Ridge stirred and finally sat up, squinting at her wearily in the early morning haze of light. "Are you all right, Miss Onslow?"

"I am doing tolerably well considering the circumstances." She hoped her voice sounded courageous. "I believe I have blisters from rowing, a gash on my arm from when I fell from the boat, and some burns on my feet, but that is all."

"I have blisters, too." He showed her his hands. "And for now, we should save our energy, as it seems useless to try to continue rowing since we have lost the lifeboats. We may be miles from shore. I'd like to see some birds, which might indicate land is near." He looked at her more closely. "That's a bad wound on your arm."

"It's nearly stopped bleeding at least."

"It must be painful." He removed his cravat, and carefully bandaged her arm with it. Her skin tingled at his gentle, careful touch. "Here, take my jacket, though it's wet. You're shivering."

"Oh, no, I couldn't possibly," but her teeth chattered as she said it.

"I insist." He wrapped his jacket over her shoulders. "In fact, we should sit closer for warmth."

She glanced at him gratefully. "That's very thoughtful of you, Mr. Ridge."

He slid closer to her, taking care not to unbalance the raft, and put his arm around her. The feel of his strong arm across her shoulders sent a wave of electricity through her. His body next to hers did indeed create more warmth.

"I apologize for losing the lifeboats."

"No need to apologize, Miss Onslow, I assure you. It was an impossible task."

"What will become of us, Mr. Ridge?"

He sighed, surveying the endless vistas of water in every direction. "Surely there are fairly consistent shipping lanes. And possibly we'll come within view of shore and then we can row in that direction."

"When the time comes for the *Pulaski* to dock in Baltimore and it doesn't arrive, perhaps some passing ship will search for us."

"I would hope so." He arranged his salt-encrusted face into a reassuring expression.

"We were scheduled to dock this afternoon. Since speed was of the utmost concern with the *Pulaski*, I suppose they might wait as much as eight hours before sending out a search party. Or possibly in the morning at first light. So, if we can survive for the next two days, perhaps someone will come and find us."

Mr. Ridge gave her an encouraging nod. "Yes, it's possible. Though I don't know how long people will wait before alerting a vessel to search."

She drew a deep breath. "You are sounding hopeful to prevent me from becoming upset. Is that correct, Mr. Ridge?"

"I am sounding hopeful because one must not lose hope."

She found that statement quite endearing and she ventured a

smile at him. When she smiled it felt as though her tense, salt-covered face cracked into pieces, and then tears leaked from her eyes. Quickly, she wiped them away just as the morning sun eased over the horizon.

"People have said that there is nothing more beautiful than a sunrise on the water." Mr. Ridge gestured at the brilliance surrounding them. "We're surrounded by the most wonderful light. It feels as though we're in a state of glory."

"It does indeed. Ironic to be floating out here in such need but surrounded by glory." She sighed, as the magnificence of the sunrise brought unexpected emotion. She rubbed her gloved hand together with the bare one. "And the sun brings a ray of hope. We will be warmer at least."

She suddenly realized with chagrin that she would need to relieve herself in the presence of Mr. Ridge. Her dress and layers of petticoats were still very wet. The idea was humiliating, but she tried to be practical; surely, he faced the same dilemma.

At that moment, he seemed to read her mind. "Miss Onslow, I must ask you to face away for a few moments if you don't mind. I'd ask you to turn your back, but it will unbalance the raft."

"I completely understand, and may I ask you to do the same for me?"

"Of course. We'll both face away for the sake of propriety."

So as the sun seemed to rise from the very surface of the water, they both did what was necessary the best they could without falling overboard. When she turned back to face him, he had tucked in his shirt and straightened his jacket, and his face looked as red as hers felt.

She quickly changed the subject. "I wonder what's in that crate that we salvaged."

Mr. Ridge released the crate from its lashing and used a pearl-handled folding knife from his vest pocket to pry free a strip of wood. He looked inside and pulled out a bottle of wine with a smile. "Most of the bottles are broken, but three or four remain intact."

Lavinia felt her salt-encrusted face crack as she grinned. "As Methodists, the Onslows do not often partake of wine. But in this instance, I believe an exception should be made."

"Indeed, it could save our lives," Mr. Ridge agreed, as he used his knife to ease out the cork, and then handed the bottle over to Lavinia. The wine, red and sweet, wet her dry mouth and lips and burned her throat as she drank a few measured sips. "Not too much."

"Yes, we must conserve it," Lavinia agreed. Mr. Ridge lifted the bottle to his lips and took several healthy swigs before replacing it carefully in the open crate. With her empty stomach, the wine seemed to go to her head almost immediately, and she speculated whether the same might have happened to Mr. Ridge, as their conversation soon became livelier.

"It seems to me that we will need to keep the sun at our backs as we need to row west to get to shore," Lavinia said.

"Yes, but we have no idea how far away the shore may be. We may be five miles offshore; we may be thirty. If we were within a few miles of land, surely there would be birds, and there are none. We should conserve our strength, as we don't know how long it will be before we're found. I have this pocket knife. Do you have anything in your pockets we might use for fishing or a tool?"

Lavinia touched her earrings and necklace. "I have only items meant for decoration. My jewelry and one glove. Nothing remotely useful."

Mr. Ridge held up a hand in protest. "We may yet find uses for them."

The sun and wine gradually warmed her, and Lavinia's shivering lessened. Just that small thing, that feeling of being warm, gave her some relief, and Mr. Ridge's presence also felt extremely comforting indeed. Recalling his determination not to lose hope, and trying to claim it for her own, she glanced at him shyly as he again tightened some of the ropes holding the raft together. "I suppose since we may have quite a bit of time together, we should get to know each other. I can tell from your accent that you're not from Savannah."

"No, I'm from New Orleans—I'm a purchaser for the Pont-chartrain Railroad. I was traveling to Baltimore to meet a delivery from England of a new steam engine—our first new one in several years." He seemed happy with the tighter knot and began to tighten another.

"You buy your steam engines from England?"

"Yes, from a company called Edward Bury and Company. I traveled to visit my cousin in Charleston before the voyage. I brought his children a book of fairytales as a gift. Their favorite was a story of a fisherman who caught a fish that was in fact an enchanted prince who could grant wishes. The fisherman's wife made many wishes, each one grander than the last."

"I've heard of that story." Lavinia looked around at the rolling waves. "If only we could catch an enchanted fish that could grant wishes!"

"Indeed, we know what we would wish for. The story of the fisherman and his wife became the evening's entertainment when I was with my cousin's family—his children always prepare a play when I visit."

"How industrious! Do the children write all the parts?"

Mr. Ridge laughed. "Yes, well, my cousin's ten-year-old daughter has a flair for drama, and she writes the parts, and she forcefully persuades her younger brother to play the male roles. She played the enchanted fish—in a costume she made herself— as well as the fisherman's wife, and her brother portrayed the fisherman."

"I wish that I could see one of her plays." Childhood memories washed over Lavinia. "My sister and I used to sing for our father when we were still girls." She felt sick that her last conversation with Father had been an argument.

"I'm sure he felt that two little angels were singing to him."

Her face collapsed. "We lost my mother when my younger sister was born. I think my father was so wrapped in grief that he barely noticed our singing most of the time. Though I can't remember my mother, I believe they had a very deep love and respect for each other. Father always spoke about Mother with such tenderness." She paused and took in a shaking breath. "Talking of these things, these ordinary aspects of life, seems so strange under these circumstances." She gestured at the endless expanse of shifting, sparkling water. "Don't you agree?"

"Not at all. On the contrary, it seems soothing to talk of subjects like those. Otherwise, we'd be quaking with fear."

"Perhaps you're right, Mr. Ridge." She rearranged her wet skirts to better let them dry in the sun. Her hands were no longer as cold, and she folded them under her skirts to warm them further. As the swells of the ocean lifted the raft under them and then let it ride down, again and again, they remained silent for a time, exhausted and riding the waves together as the sun continued to fill the sky with the most exquisite colors.

They floated in silence for long moments as the golden light washed over them. The ocean lay fairly quiet today, its surface reflective. Lavinia thought of Father, and Sarah, and Clementine, and tears began to etch their way down her salt-encrusted cheeks. Sarah was at home with Clementine, enjoying time with William, and had no idea of what had happened. At last, she gained control of herself. "I just pray that there is some way Father survived."

Mr. Ridge hesitated before speaking. "It is always possible. Tell me about your father." He gave her a sympathetic look.

"He was—" she drew in a breath and shook herself, determined, "*is* a proud man. Maybe Sarah and I as young girls lived in the shadow of his sadness at losing our mother? But he was—is a doting father. He gave me a pony at age seven. I called him Balderdash. Once I was grown, he was too small for me to ride him, but Father let me keep him and he followed me like a sweet dog."

"How charming! Did you grow up in town or on a plantation?"

"In town. Father wanted to live near the millinery shop he

inherited from my grandfather. I loved going to the shop with him when I was a child—all the colors and textures and beautiful things seemed so magical to me. As soon as he would allow it, I began helping him there. The shop has become quite successful. I have no idea what will become of our shop should Father not survive." That thought shocked her and she abruptly felt huge, raw sobs racking her ribcage. She couldn't seem to get control of herself, and her mind recoiled from the reality of what had happened. "Oh, if I survive this I don't know if Sarah and I can continue on."

"I am sure your father would want you to." He straightened the jacket he had placed on her shoulders.

Mr. Ridge's face became blurred, and she wiped her tears with the edge of her sleeve. "Of course, he would, Mr. Ridge, thank you for reminding me of that." She cleared her throat. They floated over a swell, then slid down. Long moments of silence slipped by, perhaps an hour. Time had no meaning. She tried to stop any desperate or despairing thoughts by continuing conversation with Mr. Ridge. "Please, tell me about yourself."

"Let's see. My father brought our family to New Orleans when I was a boy. I had just finished my schooling when the legislature approved the railroad and so I went to work for them."

"You were lucky to get in with the railroad at the beginning."

"Yes, that first year horses pulled the train. We then went to England to buy an engine, but it still broke down. Sometimes we'd attach a canvas like a sail if the wind was favorable to bring the train into port."

"How innovative." Now her head pounded. Maybe it was the wine, maybe the glare of the morning sun on the water, or maybe simply the constant strain of sorrow and fear pressing on her. She gingerly leaned back against a settee leg and tried to balance herself more firmly on her side of their small, creaking craft. She closed her eyes for a moment. "Tell me about your family."

"My father and mother passed away of yellow fever during the summer three years ago."

"Oh, I'm so sorry." She couldn't help but reach out to put her hand lightly on his arm.

"Thank you, very kind of you." He covered her hand briefly.

"So, we may both be orphans." She felt awkward now, touching his arm, and removed her hand and clasped hers together.

"Now I live with my two older sisters in our family home in one of the newer neighborhoods in New Orleans."

"You are wise to the ways of women, then, Mr. Ridge." Lavinia somewhat surprised herself with this flirtatious comment—flirtatious by her standard, anyway. It seemed ridiculous under the circumstances. Perhaps her brain was becoming addled from the sun and wine. Still, it lightened her heart. She suspected Sarah would approve.

"I was told that my feet didn't touch the ground for my first year, as I had two little mothers. I'm probably lucky I learned to walk."

She actually smiled, thinking about the girls carrying around their little brother. She pictured them taking turns pushing him in a baby carriage.

The sun rose higher in the sky now, and she had at last stopped shivering; in fact, she felt warm in her voluminous clothes. Her bonnet had blown off in the shipwreck, and her hair had come completely down and dried hanging down her back. She touched it self-consciously. Most of her hairpins had come out. She hadn't worn her hair down in company for a few years now. Having it down now felt quite odd. As her auburn ringlets had a mind of their own, she must indeed look a fright.

She ran her hand over her hair. "Funny, at a time like this, you begin to wonder about the worth of things. Gloves, for instance." She held up her hand with the single long glove. "Bonnets, too. Normally I wouldn't dream of being without a bonnet—always proper, always advertising for the shop. But right now, a bonnet of course is of no importance whatsoever. And when I think about the hours of my life that have been consumed by bonnets, I'm of a mind to think that it's all been a waste. Yet I do adore them. Possibly I should think of another purpose for my life."

"Don't say that, Miss Onslow. Bonnets are more than head decorations. They're expressions of who the wearers are. Surely there is worth to that, in letting your customers be themselves. And, as I'm sure you know, they protect from the elements."

She found Mr. Ridge's reassurances comforting. That was exactly the way she felt, and he'd expressed it so succinctly. He certainly seemed to be a sensitive man. She suddenly thought of the pink topaz necklace that father had wanted her to wear. Her hand went to her neckline, and she fingered the now salt-encrusted stone. "This necklace. Father gave it to me for my eighteenth birthday. I treasured it, and he always wanted me to wear it to show that we were prosperous." She hesitated and her voice cracked. "And now Father could be dead, and this pink stone is worth nothing out here. It won't buy us food or water, which we need to survive."

He looked at her soberly. "Please don't give up hope, Miss Onslow. Maybe a boat will come by. Or it'll rain. I'm trying to think of a way to capture water for drinking if we're lucky enough to get some."

It's true, she was growing quite thirsty, and pangs of hunger rumbled in her stomach. She decided not to speak of them, fearing it would only make them worse. They floated in silence again. Mr. Ridge's eyes closed, and she used the moment to study his tired face. He had a wavy shock of dark blonde hair, full lips, and a square jaw. He rubbed the bridge of his nose wearily. He had definitely been wearing spectacles when she spotted him on board last night, and she wondered where they had gone.

"Do you wear spectacles?" she asked when he opened his eyes. "Did you lose them?"

"Unfortunately, yes." He rubbed his eyes and squinted at her. "So, if a ship comes within sight, you will need to spot it."

The weakness of Mr. Ridge's eyes for some reason made her feel closer to him. Perhaps he was the kind of man who believed himself duty bound to protect her in spite of any vulnerabilities he might have.

"I'll keep a sharp lookout. Meanwhile, is there a way to catch a fish? I mean, other than waiting for a flying fish to land on our raft of its own accord."

"I could use a piece of clothing for a line, but we have no bait or lures."

"What about my glove? We will find a use for it after all. And we could use one of my earrings as a lure." She reached up to see if she still wore the pearl drop and topaz earrings from last night. Had it been only a few hours ago? She'd had pierced ears since she was sixteen. She'd started wearing her hair up instead of down over her shoulders then, and she felt at that time she became a mature woman. How foolish she felt now!

She dropped the glove and an earring into Mr. Ridge's hand.

"You're sure, Miss Onslow?"

"I'm sure. And what about something longer to attach to it? The glove will not be enough. A white piece of my petticoat?"

He looked away before answering carefully. "If you don't mind parting with a piece of it."

She laughed for the first time since last night. "Take my entire petticoat if you need it to save us, Mr. Ridge. May I borrow your knife?" She pulled up the edge of her skirt, revealing the multiple layers of petticoat. Mr. Ridge cleared his throat as he pulled the small folding blade from his pocket. Without hesitating, she cut and tugged at the wet fabric until she had ripped a lacy strip from the bottom, and she also tore a thin length of material from the bottom of her skirt and handed both to Mr. Ridge.

"Can you make a fishing line from these?"

Mr. Ridge took the pieces of cloth and knotted them together. Then he tied the glove to one end and the earring to the other. The glove he knotted around one of the legs of a settee and then fed the earring end into the water. "I don't know if there is any use in this, but as you say, we must do something."

"At home I am in the habit of losing gloves. Clementine, our housekeeper, and Sarah, my sister, tease me endlessly about it."

"You must tell them, when we return, that you made good use of this one," Mr. Ridge said, with a smile.

They watched the line of cloth sink into the water, with the shiny earring at the end, trailing behind them.

"In Savannah, we go crabbing by using a string and a chicken neck. The children love it. Do you do the same in New Orleans?"

Mr. Ridge looked at her and smiled. "In fact, we do." Neither of them mentioned that crabbing was a recreational activity, not something they might depend upon for their literal survival. "Once we are rescued, perhaps we should go crabbing together."

"We should." The fact that rescue might never happen hung silently between them. The sun now glared down on them without respite in the cloudless sky.

They needed shade from the sun—that was becoming clear. As far as Lavinia could see, the only possible source of shade was her dress. But what would Mr. Ridge think of her, suggesting that she remove her own dress? As she contemplated this predicament, the sun inched higher and became, if it was possible, even hotter and more glaring. Mr. Ridge removed his shirt collar and made another fishing lure from it. Then a few minutes later he removed his waistcoat.

"Would you like to use my waistcoat to protect your head and neck from blistering?"

"Oh, no, you use it yourself."

"You're sure, Miss Onslow?"

"I'm sure. Your bare neck is in more danger than mine." She gave him a little smile.

He then tied the garment around his head so that the body of the waistcoat protected his head and neck. It did look a little peculiar. And still they floated under the searing sun. Lavinia felt her exposed skin burning. Finally she could take it no longer.

"Possibly we could use my skirt as a tent to shade us from the sun." She picked up some of the voluminous wet yards of blue silk.

Mr. Ridge's face turned red, and he looked away.

"Otherwise, we'll blister. Help me with my buttons, please." She turned her back so he could assist with the long row of tiny buttons. She, too, blushed, as she considered what Father might think about his daughter at this moment. And goodness, she could just hear Clementine. But this was a situation such that it seemed necessary to dispense with propriety for survival.

"I apologize, Miss Onslow, this is quite awkward." He released the first few buttons with shaky hands.

"Think nothing of it." Her voice sounded crisp and decisive.

But she held her breath as the tentative and pleasant pressure of his fingers made their way slowly down her back.

Eventually her bodice came loose. In a business-like way, she pulled the ruined blue mutton chop sleeves down from her shoulders, carefully over her injured arm, and with Mr. Ridge's awkward help, pulled the copious yards of wet skirts over her head. Even though she was still covered by her corset, chemise, and several layers of petticoats, her cheeks burned with embarrassment. She had never been seen in such a state of undress except by Sarah, yet here she sat in her petticoat with a man she had known only for one night. Impulsively, she reached into the crate for the bottle of wine and took another burning swig.

"In fact, let's take off the corset, too. Would you mind unlacing me?" In truth, notions of propriety were quickly fading now, and she was eager to have it off, it felt so uncomfortable. Mr. Ridge unlaced her corset with unsure fingers, then she removed it and tossed the whalebone-lined garment onto the raft behind her, leaving her only in her chemise.

Mr. Ridge assiduously avoided looking at her.

"Mr. Ridge, do you believe me to be a hussy?"

He glanced at her, his face turning red. "Certainly not. I believe you to be the most practical of ladies. A lady who will do what is necessary to survive these circumstances. I admire you, Miss Onslow."

Did he? She wasn't sure, but she nodded. "Thank you for

that."

Lavinia spread the dress out in a wide circle while Mr. Ridge cut free some small lengths of rope from the lashings. He then capably tied one handful of the billowing skirt to the corner leg of the settee on his side of the raft. Lavinia tied another to the settee leg on the adjacent corner. Together they propped the bed rail in the center like a tentpole and stretched the fabric taut to keep the rail standing, always careful not to disturb the balance of the small raft. They wedged the rail in the crack between the two settees and with a few adjustments for stability they soon sat under a wobbly makeshift tent. They folded part of the skirt up over the top so they could see out as they rode the constant swells of the sea.

"Much better."

"Allow me to say that I admire your sacrifice."

His sensitivity to her situation touched her, so she made light of it, laughing as she said, "Father would be horrified to see my most fashionable dress used as a tent."

"I believe he would be proud of your ingenuity."

The idea that Father would be proud of her made tears spring to her eyes, as indeed she'd always wanted that very thing, but she took a deep breath to stop them coming and gave Mr. Ridge a wan smile.

By midday she felt weak with hunger and had a pounding headache, but speaking of it seemed like a useless complaint. What could anyone do about it, after all? If Mr. Ridge were anything like father, he would want to solve any dilemma she might bring up, but there was no solution to this one.

A particularly large swell raised them up and then they slid down into the trough between swells. Over the next swell something appeared, floating toward them in the water.

"What's that?" She peered out over the sea, squinting to see more clearly.

"I can't tell."

She silently watched the thing float closer, wondering at first if it might be a piece of the ship that they could use to fortify their raft. It slid over another swell and floated closer, and a moment later a length of deck flooring the size of a small rug nearly bumped into their raft, one side dipping lower in the water. As it bumped, the tilted edge turned, and Lavinia discerned a jacket, trousers, and a gruesome pale face—a man, lashed to a piece of the Pulaski's fine, polished deck.

She screamed and grabbed Mr. Ridge's arm. "A body! It's a body!"

"Sakes alive!" He grabbed the bed rail and pushed the deck flooring away, then he paddled away from the floating thing like a madman. Lavinia's heart raced and bile licked the back of her throat. The awful vision of that face seared itself into her memory. Yet in all her panic, she did think, *That is not Father's waistcoat. Nor his trousers.*

Mr. Ridge summoned his strength and paddled for a time to make sure they could no longer see the body. "That poor fellow," he said as he gasped for air. "We are lucky beyond measure."

"He was someone's husband, or father, or son." Was it perhaps one of the people Father and Lavinia had passed in the dining room, or out on deck? They might have seen this person alive only days ago. The gravity of the enormous loss of life that they'd survived settled over her. Possibly the Captain, their dining companion Mr. Whalen, entire families from Savannah, and hundreds of other people. But she couldn't accept that Father might have died. Not yet.

"We should say a prayer for him." Mr. Ridge's voice sounded solemn. They both bowed their heads and prayed silently, though the terrible image of that drowned face persisted behind her closed eyelids.

A moment later, Mr. Ridge said, "We might as well make good use of that piece of flooring. He certainly doesn't need it anymore."

With Lavinia's silent consent, Mr. Ridge rowed closer, and cut the rope that had kept the poor dead man on the flooring, and he slid into the water, which quickly claimed him. Mr. Ridge then used the flooring to further shore up their raft.

Lavinia rested for a long while after the shock of seeing that body. Gradually, she began to pass the time by scanning the bright horizon for ships. Sometimes she thought she saw one, then blinked and focused on only a wisp of a cloud near the edge of the water. *Please be a ship.* But then it wasn't.

"Shouldn't a ship be coming for us by now?" She tried to keep the tone of desperation from her voice. "People will know by now that the *Pulaski* didn't arrive in port, and they would have sent ships in search of survivors."

"Our best hope is that they waste no time in sending out search parties."

They floated in silence for a few minutes. She was determined to renew her efforts at conversation to stave off the panic lurking just beyond the next swell of the sea.

"Do you enjoy traveling, generally, Mr. Ridge?"

"Yes, I like meeting people from different backgrounds and seeing different places and learning other customs. Once I took a steamship to England. London is an exhilarating city. I visited Westminster Abbey, which is quite impressive. I read that young Queen Victoria's coronation is to take place there this very month. That should be quite the spectacle! Imagine becoming queen of such an empire at the age of eighteen."

"That is a young age to take on such responsibility and power." The new queen was even younger than Sarah. She tried to imagine her sister as the ruler of an empire but couldn't quite manage it. "I'm envious of your travels, Mr. Ridge. This voyage is the first time I have ever been outside the south."

"Let us make a pact that you will go on to exciting travels in future days."

"Yes, I would enjoy that."

The sun beat down upon them mercilessly as their little raft shifted and slid over the hills of water. They were silent for a long while before he spoke again, possibly mid-afternoon. "You have not mentioned a word about being hungry, though I know you must be because I am."

"No good can come of talking about it, since we have nothing to eat. At least I don't believe we've caught any fish, have we?"

He pulled the strip of her petticoat with the earring dangling from the raft out of the water, then checked for his collar, which had become their second lure, but it had washed away. "No, we have not caught any fish."

For the latter part of the afternoon Lavinia tried to sleep while Mr. Ridge kept watch for a ship as best he could. Her hollow, empty stomach made sleep difficult. The pangs kept waking her and whenever she raised her head, she felt lightheaded. When she'd had as much rest as she could, she insisted that he sleep while she kept watch, but he didn't sleep much more than she had. The horizon remained unchanging with no glimpse of land anywhere.

As evening began to fall, they were both tempted to drink more of the wine but decided only to allow themselves four swigs a day. The wine on their empty stomachs was liable to make them too giddy otherwise. Lavinia's tongue and lips were swollen with thirst, and she knew Mr. Ridge's must be also, but neither spoke of it.

At last, the sun slid down the sky toward the water in the west and the air grew a bit cooler. Still, they spotted no ships.

"What if a ship should come at night? We may not even see it."

"One of us should keep watch all the time. Take turns sleeping."

She agreed, though she had no idea how they would manage that. Had it been only just one day that they'd been here floating together? Yes, she and Mr. Ridge had now seen both a sunrise and a sunset from their rickety little raft. In some ways, it seemed like a whole lifetime rather than just one day, and she and Mr. Ridge had known each other for the entirety of that life.

There wasn't the slightest sign of land anywhere. Nothing but water as far as she could see in every direction.

CHAPTER FIVE

June 15, 1838
At sea

THE STARS THAT night were brilliant. The moon had waned from the night before, and the stars covered the expanse like a sparkling blanket, dominating the skyscape.

"Just look." It was a relief to think about something other than hunger and tiredness and fear. Her mouth was so dry her swollen tongue stuck to the roof of her mouth. Talking was difficult, but she persevered.

In awe, they stared at the constellations spread across the dark sky. The stars were so bright the night sky pulsed and glowed.

"I can't see the stars quite clearly since I lost my spectacles, but still they're breathtaking. They seem alive, don't they?"

"Do you know anything about the constellations, Mr. Ridge?"

"I know some of them. Ursa Major and Ursa Minor. The end of the tail of the little bear is the north star, which sailors use for navigation."

"Oh, let there be a ship nearby. Oh, Lord, please."

"Can you find Orion's belt? Three stars in a line."

"Father taught us where that was. Yes, I see it."

"See if you can find Leo. There's a large orange star just underneath it."

He waited as she studied the sky for a moment. "Do you see?" She continued scanning the sky. "There should be a backward question mark that makes the lion's head and chest. And a bright star that is the lion's front leg. See it?"

"Oh, yes. I do see it, Mr. Ridge. Did you ever learn any of the myths associated with the constellations? Father had a book on Greek mythology in our home library and I used to read it all the time. For example, Orion was the great hunter and he claimed he could kill all of the animals. He fought the scorpion, however, and could not defeat him, so Zeus raised the scorpion up into the night sky for all time. I wonder if I can spot the Scorpion."

She looked but was unable to find it. Finally, near the edge of the water, she found the curl of the scorpion's tail and traced upwards to see its pincers and head.

As it grew colder that night, the two of them took down her dress and made a blanket of it. It grew damp quickly as the water in their raft soaked into the fading material, but it was better than nothing. They warmed their throats and stomachs with one final swig of the wine and Mr. Ridge agreed to keep the first watch. Sleep was an escape from hunger and so Lavinia curled next to Mr. Ridge, and, as the dark waves lapped her legs and the bottom of the settee and the stars spread over them, she let herself float into a troubled, anxious, exhausted sleep.

"MISS ONSLOW."

Mr. Ridge's hand gently touched Lavinia's shoulder. The stars were gone. Clouds had moved in, and rain splattered on her hair and face.

"Try to drink as much as you can."

They tilted their heads back to catch water in their mouths. The rain came down more swiftly, cold on their skin, and they let it stream over their faces and between their parched lips. They caught it in their cupped hands and drained it into their yearning mouths. The rain smelled fresh, and the water tasted delicious.

They made a pool of the skirt of her dress to catch the rain, and it did hold it for a few seconds. They quickly took turns drinking before it leeched through and even wrung some from the material, allowing the precious water to fill their mouths.

The wind began to howl as the storm picked up, frigid air battered them, and choppy waves splashed over them. In the increasingly rough seas, Lavinia had to grasp Mr. Ridge's arm as they scaled the sides of the waves and then slid down the other sides, terrified she might fall over the edge. They couldn't drink as much now but let themselves get completely drenched, rain and saltwater mingling to plaster their hair to their skulls and soak deliciously into their skin.

The storm passed quickly, and the seas quieted. The two of them had drunk their fill, and Lavinia's empty stomach felt bloated.

Then Mr. Ridge gasped. "Blast!"

"What's wrong?"

"The storm washed the wine crate away."

They looked across the dark undulating waves in despairing silence, hoping to see it bobbing nearby, but saw nothing. That wine could have sustained them for several more days if they were careful.

"I should have lashed it more firmly to the raft. What a fool I am!"

"You are far from a fool, Mr. Ridge."

"I fear I am, yet there is nothing to be done. And I wish we had drunk more of it!" Mr. Ridge's voice held a sigh. Afterward Lavinia insisted that Mr. Ridge sleep, promising she'd stay awake and keep watch. The soporific monotony of watching the dark waves rise and fall several times caused her to nod off, from exhaustion as much as anything else. Although the water and wine had helped, hunger made her lightheaded, with murky and formless thoughts.

THAT MORNING, AS the sky lightened ever so slightly, she renewed her search for vessels. Something—a smudge—lay at the horizon. Was it moving or stationary? She couldn't tell. She rubbed her eyes, waiting for more light. Her mind reeled. It could be land. Or maybe a ship. What if her exhaustion was such that she imagined things?

As they continued to float, and the sky lightened a bit more, she deciphered a thin line of green in the distance to the west. Her heart began to beat faster as she squinted at it, hardly daring to hope. But, yes, it had to be! Oh, hallelujah, it was land!

"Mr. Ridge," she shook his shoulder.

Mr. Ridge's eyes fluttered open. "Yes?" He sat up.

"Land!" She pointed.

He was alert at once. "Row!" Mr. Ridge grabbed the bed rail and Lavinia grabbed a board he had pried loose from the crate that hadn't been washed away with the rest. They both rowed as though they were mad, using every bit of energy they could muster and then more, but the thin line of green did not get any larger. They rowed constantly through the sunrise and a long time after, still the land did not move any closer. Lavinia's arms burned with such exertion she knew she was near collapsing.

"It is no closer."

They stopped to rest, breathless, arms seizing and heavy after their efforts.

"No matter how much we paddle, the currents will take us where they will."

"I can't accept that!" Lavinia grabbed the oar and paddled with all her might for as long as she was able in her weakened state. The line of green remained unchanging.

She finally sat back in such weariness her head swam, and for a moment she simply fainted with the paddle across her lap. When she came to, Mr. Ridge was rowing hard. He tried for long minutes, panting and drenched in sweat.

"I am in complete despair," he moaned. "If anything, the line of green seems even farther away."

They lay resting on the little raft in silence. Long minutes dragged by, the only sounds the waves lapping against the raft and their exhausted breath. After resting for a few minutes, Lavinia recalled Mr. Ridge's story of using a sail to move the train, and they tried using the billowing skirt of Lavinia's dress as a sail, but they had no long implement sturdy enough to use as a mast. Mr. Ridge tried to act as a mast, standing and holding the skirt up, but the raft became so wobbly he nearly fell off. He sat back down and Lavinia helped him put up the makeshift tent again.

Then Lavinia looked at the horizon and the strip of green was gone. Had she ever really seen it? Tears ran down her cheeks.

Very gently, Mr. Ridge took her blistered hand in both of his and kissed it with his dry, cracked lips. "I am so sorry, Miss Onslow."

She lay on the raft, letting herself feel the comfort of Mr. Ridge holding her blistered hand. Somehow his touch made her feel less hopeless.

As a little girl, Lavinia often dreamed that her mother came to her, sat beside her on the bed, and laid her cool palm gently on her cheek.

"Father," she'd asked as a girl of ten, when leaving church services in their carriage, "do you believe that Mama ever comes to visit us? Comes to see how we're getting along without her?"

Father had given her a kind look. "No, Lavinia. She has gone to be with God. Perhaps sometimes you feel her spirit simply because you long to see her, but she can't come visit you."

Sarah, sitting next to her in the carriage, squeezed her hand. The two of them had whispered together at night about whether their mother's spirit could come to them, and Sarah had confided to Lavinia that she wished for it as well.

When Father took them to the Methodist church growing up, she had often repeated the Apostles' Creed, declaring that she believed in "the resurrection of the body and the life everlasting," but as a child she had trouble grasping it, and there was no one who could explain it to her. What was everlasting life like? If her mother had everlasting life, where was she and who was she with? Should Mr. Ridge and Lavinia die out here now, where would they go?

"Do you believe in life after death, Mr. Ridge?" They'd been silent and lost in their thoughts, possibly barely conscious, for some time. Conversation took her mind off her hunger, the discomfort, and the black spots that floated in front of her eyes, in spite of the fact that it was growing more and more difficult to talk with her dry, swollen lips.

Mr. Ridge hesitated. "I grew up Catholic. I was taught to believe in Heaven and Hell and Purgatory, that the kind of life you live determines where you go."

"But what do you believe now? If we die out here, do you believe everlasting life awaits us?"

Mr. Ridge hesitated for a long moment. "I must hope for it. Don't you think so?" He responded as kindly as Father had when she'd asked the questions about her mother. "I don't know that anyone alive knows the definitive answer, but our Lord Jesus is proof that there is life after death with God. I've tried to live a good life. I hope to see God face to face."

"But what do you suppose life after death is like? We don't have our physical bodies, at least I don't imagine that we would. What do our souls look like? Do we become like beams of light? Do we become stars in the sky? Do we become part of God?"

Mr. Ridge smiled at her wearily. "You ask some thought-provoking questions. I wish I knew the answers, but I don't"

"Of course. No one living knows."

"The sun is rising higher. We should put up our tent."

She helped Mr. Ridge put up their tent and noted that the water seemed to be about an inch deeper on the settees. She helped him tighten and double knot the fraying ropes.

"I'VE BEEN THINKING about the idea of time." She whispered this to Mr. Ridge after they floated for a long while. The sun beat down upon the faded blue dress stretched over their heads. A haze of confusion had enveloped her.

"I believe this is the second day. We floated for the first night after the accident, then the first day passed, and last night we looked at the stars and then it rained. And today is the second day."

"No, I mean the idea that time can inch by or race by. Or that each day that passes can seem like time folding over itself."

"Miss Onslow, are you all right?" Mr. Ridge turned toward her and peered at her with some concern. "It's true that the days can seem to run together as we float out here. Why don't I use my pocketknife to make a score on the settee leg for each day?" He took out the pearl-handled knife and did just that, creating two slashes in the mahogany. "There. Two days." He rubbed his finger over the cuts and searched her face. "Better?"

She could not help but smile and nod. "Yes. And indeed, I admire your practicality." She stared in silence for a moment at the two little parallel lines. "Do you believe in fate, Mr. Ridge? Do you believe we were fated to be together on this raft?"

"Fated?" Mr. Ridge slid the pocketknife back into his vest. "It's true, never would I have thought that I would be spending the better part of two days alone with a young lady as lovely as you." He gave her a sideways glance, smiling.

She might have blushed at such a compliment a few days ago, but now her capacity for embarrassment seemed to have disappeared, and she broadened her smile of appreciation. "Thank you, Mr. Ridge." She took a breath. "I'll never forget the moment I first saw you in the dining room."

"Yes. Our eyes met."

"Yes. Do you remember the woman with the fan?"

Mr. Ridge looked a little abashed. "Ah, yes, her. The signals with the fan. She was quite forward. Yet it was you I noticed. I could not take my eyes off you. When I saw you in the water, even though we'd endured a horrible accident, I remembered the way we'd exchanged glances, and yes, I suppose the thought flashed through my mind that perhaps it had been fate that put us together in the water at that moment."

She ducked her head. All her years in Savannah no young man had ever said such a thing to her. Sarah's voice came back to her, asking Lavinia to behave in a more lighthearted way. She wondered what Sarah would make of this conversation. "I noticed you, too," she finally said. "Reading *The Last of the Mohicans*. I was with Father but wished I could speak with you about your thoughts on the book."

"Oh?"

"I could have asked your opinion about friendships between the different races. Indians and settlers, for example."

He smiled. "I would have responded that, in my view, we are all people, all equally valuable, and I believe that is one of the lessons of that book. Though there of course are dangers and difficulties in having such friendships, I believe it would be worthwhile to make that effort."

"My thoughts as well! I was reading the book in preparation for our trip, since it took place near Lake George and Saratoga Springs. What were your thoughts on the characters? I liked Cora, who was serious and level-headed. I've always been a serious person, and I enjoyed seeing a serious woman portrayed in a novel. Her younger sister was more light-hearted, like my sister

Sarah, in fact. What character appealed most to you?"

"Hawkeye, I must say. I found him heroic and quick-thinking. Yet I admired Uncas and his father as well."

Lavinia hesitated. A wave of nausea twisted her stomach. She tried to push on with the conversation. "What, then, are your thoughts about the Indians now being driven from their lands? I read in our paper that many from Georgia are being made to leave and move out west. Some of Father's friends say that we need the land to grow cotton."

Mr. Ridge looked uncomfortable. "I am not sure what my feelings are about that. As an employee of the railroad, I know a great deal of land will be needed for the tracks as it expands. And that some solution must be reached."

They were silent for a moment, as the raft slid over a swell and the sun beat down on their little tent. Lavinia wished she knew more about the situation; possibly she and Mr. Ridge did not agree on this topic. She was also beginning to feel even worse. She decided to return to the topic of the book. "I hope one day to know how the book ends."

"Oh, I hope so, too. Both our copies are now at the bottom of the sea."

"I wonder if Cora and Uncas will be drawn to each other in affection, even though such a friendship between them seems impossible."

"Miss Onslow, I submit that that there is a difference between love and friendship."

She had to agree, but responding aloud to this last comment felt dangerous, a foray into romantic territory she and Mr. Ridge had not heretofore greatly explored. She looked back at the two lines on the settee leg, two little specks floating on a sea of mahogany. Her head swam and her breath was shallow. The lines grew blurred as she stared. "Do you believe we're fated to die together, Mr. Ridge?"

"I'm sorry, Miss Onslow, please, I'd rather not speak about death."

"I am beginning to understand that you're a practical and optimistic man. Perhaps conceptual conversations don't interest you much."

"It's true, I don't think such conversations bring us closer to solutions for problems."

"Conversations like that occupied my sister and me quite a lot during our childhood, possibly because of the death of our mother. Sarah and I used to spend hours discussing whether ghosts existed and whether you could communicate with a person—such as our mother—who had gone to the other side."

"I'm sorry for the loss of your mother, Miss Onslow. I feel deeply for you two motherless girls. But I beg you, let's not talk about death."

Mr. Ridge was doubtless right that speaking of death was not a good idea in their situation. She laid her head back and went silent. She was feeling very sick now.

As the raft drifted over a swell, and the sun bore down upon them, Lavinia felt weaker and more nauseated. All of a sudden, nausea overcame her, and hot, sour bile raced up her throat. She leaned to the side and dry-heaved over the water.

"Miss Onslow, are you all right?"

She leaned listlessly against the settee leg. "I am not fine, but conversation takes my mind off the fact that I'm starving and terrified and would trade this topaz necklace for a cool glass of water."

"I wish I had one to offer you. But perhaps we should cease our conversation for a bit and you can rest."

"No, please keep talking." Lavinia laid her head back down. "It helps me."

"What should I talk about, then? Our favorite foods?" Mr. Ridge gave her a concerned glance. "That's a pleasant enough topic. New Orleans is such a mecca for fine food I couldn't begin to name my favorite meal, though if I had to choose, I believe it's roast mutton with potatoes smothered in gravy. Or shrimp étouffée. What about yours?"

A sharp pang shot through her stomach as she remembered the mashed potatoes Clementine often made for Saturday dinner. She wasn't fond of Clementine's regular Saturday mutton, but she dearly loved the mashed potatoes that accompanied it. She broke out in a cold, clammy sweat and black dots again floated in front of her eyes.

"Perhaps we shouldn't talk about food. It will only make us weaker with hunger. Besides, you know that a real lady is not supposed to have an appetite, so ideally my favorite food should be air. Of which there is plenty around here." She drew in a couple of shaky breaths. "Why hasn't a ship come for us?"

"Stay still." Mr. Ridge suddenly sat up straighter.

"What?" The tent made from her dress fluttered energetically in a gust of wind that blew the raft across the swells. The glaring sun cast reflections on the choppy waves, and Mr. Ridge silently pointed. A fin.

Lavinia drew in her breath, her blood ran cold, and her heart thundered in her chest. Mr. Ridge gestured for her to slowly pull her legs up under her and slide closer to him. Very slowly, so as not to tip the raft, she did, and the gray triangular fin cut through the water in a meandering, exploratory way, coming closer. Silence stretched out.

Mr. Ridge's breath was next to her ear. "Don't move."

They held completely still as the shark came close and circled. The gray body slid beneath the water. The gills rippled. The spiked tail propelled it smoothly forward.

Then, a bump.

She gasped.

Mr. Ridge held her closer to him.

Another bump. All of a sudden, Mr. Ridge lunged for the oar to strike the beast. As the raft shifted under him, Lavinia, already unsteady, tumbled off. In an instant, the water closed over her head, and she gulped salty mouthfuls. She struggled to get her head above the surface, kicking and flailing her arms, terror giving her energy.

The burning salt water went down her throat and she coughed and choked. On his knees on the raft, Mr. Ridge struck repeatedly at the shark's nose with the oar, shoving it away from Lavinia again and again. For her part, Lavinia grabbed onto two settee legs and kicked at the powerful beast with all her strength, her feet thudding against the sandpapery, muscled body. As it circled around the raft again, she managed to pull herself halfway back onto the raft.

"Kick!"

She kicked, in spite of her weakness and exhaustion, not knowing where to aim, barely escaping the snap of the shark's teeth, just as Mr. Ridge smashed the bed rail into the shark's eye. He dropped it beside him and all at once heaved her back onto the raft. She landed on top of him, breathless and panting with exertion. Instead of moving away she clasped her arms around his chest, and they lay half-prone together.

He held her tightly in his arms as the water quieted.

"The shark has left." His voice was raw with emotion.

Her relief was so complete that all strength drained away. They floated in exhausted silence, peering at the water for the fin, marveling at their survival, until Lavinia finally succumbed to sleep.

When Lavinia finally awoke, the sun was beginning to set. Mr. Ridge caressed her hair. As she stirred, he spoke softly. "Miss Onslow, I wish I could be the hero you want me to be. I wish I could summon a ship for us. I believe you're right; we were fated to be together on this raft."

Lavinia could not speak.

"It's all right, dear Miss Onslow. I shall tell you more about the fisherman who caught the enchanted fish, and other fairytales from the book I gave my niece and nephew, to pass the time."

"All right," she whispered. "How did that story end?"

"The fisherman's wife made grander and grander wishes, which the fish granted, until at last she wished to control the sun and the moon, and at that, the fish refused and sent the fisherman and his wife back to their ditch."

"We are powerless to control nature."

"Yes."

She lay in his arms for a long time, floating in and out of awareness, feeling the comfort of his heart beating beneath her cheek.

CHAPTER SIX

June 16, 1838
At sea

THE THIRD MORNING on the settee raft Lavinia felt far weaker, and the inside of her mouth was so dry she wasn't sure she could talk. Swallowing felt painful, and her lips were swollen and cracked. Her head pounded, and every time she tried to move the black spots floated in front of her eyes. She shivered under the fading blue dress they'd used again as a damp blanket. Angry vermillion flesh surrounded the gash on her arm, hot and sore. Yet Mr. Ridge held her hand, even in sleep, and just his touch made her feel safer.

Mr. Ridge's eyes were closed, and she didn't want to wake him. She gently ran her fingertip down the back of each of his fingers as he slept. He had very fine hands, though they were now inflamed with blisters from rowing. His lips were chapped, and a white salt spray had dried on his burned cheeks.

His eyes flew open, and he started when he saw her looking at him.

"I'm sorry, Miss Onslow, I must've been dreaming. I didn't mean to start like that." His voice was a whisper.

She felt embarrassed that he'd caught her staring, but poor man, he looked exhausted. More than a day had passed since the rainstorm. How long could a person survive without water? Water lapped the edge of the settees and the rising sun grew on the horizon, mocking their extreme and all-consuming thirst.

"How are you feeling today?"

He tried to smile, and his lips cracked and began to bleed a little. "Oh, tolerably well. What about you?"

"I am as well."

They set up their tent and lay beneath it quietly. Mr. Ridge carefully carved a third notch onto the leg of the settee, signifying the passing of another day. The ocean swells flowed smooth and glassy today and the sun burned with a penetrating glare. Lavinia hadn't had to relieve herself since that first day simply because she hadn't ingested any food or drink other than the few swigs of wine and the rainwater.

She looked down into the water surrounding the raft. Would the shark return? Lavinia shivered. Yet she didn't see any fish at all. Just the deep blue of the water going down, darker and darker, as if to infinity. She and Daniel Ridge were tiny beings floating on an endless sea.

They floated in silence for a long while. The water lapped the edges of their raft with a soporific rhythm, Lavinia's arm throbbed. Conversation seemed the only way to fight the despondency she felt.

"I believe my favorite food is deviled crab." Lavinia told Mr. Ridge, giving up her moratorium on the subject with a sideways glance. "With lemonade. Could you imagine how delicious a glass of lemonade might be right now?" Her voice was so cracked and hoarse now that she hardly sounded like herself, even to her own ears.

"Yes. You must know that New Orleans has the best deviled crab in all of America." His voice was now barely a whisper.

"Well, I have never been to New Orleans so I could not say how good the deviled crab is there, but I cannot imagine it would be better than in Savannah."

"I thought you weren't going to speak of food."

"I have decided to humor you, Mr. Ridge." She gave him what she hoped was a light-hearted smile. In return, he gave her a slow, cracked grin and closed his eyes again. A feeling of worry seized her. Was Mr. Ridge even weaker than she was?

"And Clementine's cheese grits. When I think of food that would comfort me, I think of Clementine's cheese grits."

Mr. Ridge didn't open his eyes. She tried to keep from panicking. Someone simply had to come rescue them. She scanned the horizon in desperation. Something white inched along. Her breath hitched.

"Mr. Ridge, look over there. Is that a ship?"

Mr. Ridge stirred, opened his eyes, and squinted. "I'm afraid I can't see. Do you indeed see a ship? That would be a miracle."

"Something is moving. Quite a distance away."

She watched the tiny patch of white slide along the surface of the water for a few minutes, trying to determine if it was real or a mirage. At last, she scrambled to her knees and waved her arms. "Help! Help!" She'd once learned to whistle to get the attention of her pony, and she put her fingers in her mouth now and whistled as loudly as she was able.

Mr. Ridge got up on his knees as well, and they knocked down their tent and both nearly fell into the water from waving their arms and shouting. She didn't know how long they yelled and waved, but it felt like eternity. Her throat felt hoarse, and her arms and knees ached, and still she waved one arm, holding onto Mr. Ridge's elbow with the other. The seconds dragged by as exhaustion overtook her, but the ship never wavered in its progress, and they watched helplessly as the tiny white sails slid across the horizon and then out of sight.

She sank onto the skirt of her now sodden petticoat, and wept, although she had no tears, only dry sobs. Mr. Ridge lay down beside her and took her into his arms. She let him hold her as she cried uncontrollably, their sunburned faces touching.

"They couldn't see us." She felt such hopelessness.

"They were too far away."

"That was quite an impressive whistle," he said at last.

"Thank you. I learned it as a girl to call my pony, Balder-dash."

They lay together for a long time after that, feeling complete-ly emptied of any remaining energy or hope, then they set up their tent again and lay back down in each other's arms.

Long stretches of time drifted by. The sun rose higher in the sky and seemed determined to burn them to ash. The horizon was empty in all directions. Lavinia's spirits plunged, and she concluded with unassailable certainty that they would indeed die out here.

"Is there anything that you wish you'd done in your life that you haven't, Mr. Ridge? Do you wish you had traveled more? Seen the Taj Mahal?"

He lay still for a few seconds, his eyes closed. "I would have liked to have had a wife and children. What about you?"

She regarded him. "I've come to the ripe age of twenty-two without being kissed. I always wished for a love match but never found one. I wish just once that I might have been kissed."

Mr. Ridge opened his eyes and sat up. He looked into hers and reached up and gently pushed a strand of hair from her face. "I will kiss you, Miss Onslow. It would be my great honor and pleasure to do so." He leaned toward her and very gently touched his dry, cracked lips to hers. She caught her breath. Despite the pain of their sore lips, a pleasant heady feeling swirled and she felt a faint shiver, a tingling lightness through her whole body. Then he held her close and they floated in a golden silence for a long time. Or perhaps it was only for a few moments. Time seemed to have stopped.

"So that's how a kiss feels."

"If we weren't in such a disastrous situation, I would find this to be perfect. Lying here with you in my arms."

She snuggled closer. "Do you believe in love, Mr. Ridge?"

"Of course. Don't you?"

"And do you believe that every person has a person that fate intends for them, that they may need to go to the ends of the earth to find?"

"I'm not sure one would need to go to the ends of the earth for that," he said. "Love can be found even close to home."

"Ever practical, I see. My dearest hope is to feel love before I die."

"I feel it right now, Miss Onslow. And no need to associate death with it."

"You do? You feel love?" His words caressed her skin like a light dusting of snow. She didn't want to think about anything any longer. She wanted to float here with Mr. Ridge until she fell asleep. And then possibly she would not wake up. That would not be so bad a death.

LATE IN THE afternoon, the surface of the water became rippled, and Mr. Ridge sat up abruptly.

"Fish." He pulled up the lace strip that was anchored to the settee leg with the glove and checked to make sure the earring was still attached. "Perhaps we'll catch one."

The two of them sat up to look at the disturbed surface of the water. Flashes of hundreds of lean silvery bodies raced by beside them.

Mr. Ridge reached for his pocketknife then glanced at her corset, which was lying on the raft next to them, as if inspired. "Aren't there are whalebone stays in your corset? We could use one to try to stab a fish."

"Yes—quickly!"

He slid free one of the long stays, which looked remarkably like a thin ivory knife and wrapped one end in a stocking that had been discarded not long after the corset. Thus able to hold the stay more firmly, he leaned over the edge of the raft, stabbing at the water. His movements were so forceful that Lavinia had to grab one of the settee legs to prevent herself from falling in.

"Ah! Ah!" He stabbed again and again, splashing water all over them, exclaiming with frustration every time he missed. He leaned so far over the edge that Lavinia grasped his foot to keep him from falling overboard.

Seconds went by and the water quieted. The school of fish had nearly passed by without Mr. Ridge stabbing a single one. With a last furious effort, he leaned over the edge and struck once more.

"Aha!" He reached into the water and grasped a small writhing fish on the end of the whalebone stay. "I got one!" The desperate fish wiggled and flopped about as Mr. Ridge struggled to keep a grip on it.

"No, no, get it, it can't get away!" She grabbed for it herself and felt the slick scales as the raft shifted beneath her weight. The fish's sharp tail cut her palm and a fine line of blood appeared.

Mr. Ridge grabbed the fish up and slammed its head on one of the wooden settee legs and it went still. "We caught one! By George, we caught one!"

The dead fish lay on their raft, its eye clouding and silvery rainbow scales going dull, its gills now still.

"Oh, my lord. What kind do you think it is?"

"I'm not much of a fisherman. Sea mullet, perhaps? Or—" He grinned at her. "Perhaps it's enchanted. Using the pocket knife he cut off the fish's head and tail, gutted it, and began sawing the fish in half with hands that Lavinia could see were shaking with excitement. "Half for you, half for me. I've cleaned fish in my day, but fileting is not easily done while raw."

She took the section of fish he handed her. As hungry as she was, could she stomach raw fish with the bones in it? Watching Mr. Ridge bite into the fish, she did the same. The sound as her teeth pierced the fish's skin made her skin crawl. The meat tasted slimy, still warm, and prickly with bones. Saliva flowed into her mouth and her stomach churned. Yet she must choke it down, and so she did.

With an air of victory, Mr. Ridge threw the tail and bones into the sea, then kept the head to use for bait.

Eating the fish created painful stomach cramps and Lavinia nearly vomited. With great effort she managed to keep the raw meal down. Catching and eating the fish had given both of them renewed strength. Mr. Ridge in particular seemed more hopeful. They rested in each other's arms, occasionally sleeping, and floated on the now nearly glassy sea for most of what remained of the day. They were hot and sweaty lying under the fading silk dress but dared not let themselves be open to the elements.

Eventually, Mr. Ridge had to again tighten the ropes holding the settees together, as they had begun working themselves loose. Was the water surrounding them on the settee slightly deeper? Was their raft sinking? Lavinia felt a stab of fear at the thought. She was beginning to accept her inevitable death, but she feared drowning. The disappointment from the passing ship still lay over her like a heavy blanket, but she tried not to show it for Mr. Ridge's sake.

As he attended to the last rope, he spoke. "How are you feeling, Miss Onslow?"

"Not as weak as before. And you?"

"The same. And I won't give in to despair because I have you. I've been giving this a great deal of thought over the past hours as we have been floating here and I would like to make a serious proposal to you."

She raised herself up on her elbow to examine his salt-crusted face. "What kind of proposal?"

Carefully rising to his knees, he took one of her hands in his and kissed it. "Once we're rescued, will you become my wife? In these days together you've shown yourself to be so quick-witted and perseverant, strong of spirit and kindhearted, a woman I would be proud and humbled to call my life's partner. You are a treasure, and I want to spend the rest of my life with you."

She stared at him. Her mouth fell open. Was this a delusion? She put her hand to his face, then touched his lips to see if he was indeed speaking. Everything seemed so strange now.

"What are you saying to me?"

"We've surely endured more in these three days together than many betrothed couples ever experience." He took her hand in his. "The hopes and disappointments. The greatest desires and the greatest sorrows. Please tell me that you will consent to be my wife."

Wife? Her mind reeled. A home of her own with a partner who loved her, a partner she loved—that was the desire of her heart. She'd always believed that she would rather remain alone and never marry than to give up that ideal. Was this the passion that she'd been dreaming of? It was certainly true that after these few days she could not imagine her life without Mr. Ridge.

Tears came into her eyes. "Of course. I also admire your bravery and resourcefulness. I'd be honored to become your wife, Mr. Ridge." It was a bittersweet moment. She had given up the hope that any ship would come for them. Only the two of them would ever know of their intentions for each other. But the idea of becoming engaged to Mr. Ridge before they died held a precious sort of romance, and indeed, they would spend the rest of their lives together.

With that, Mr. Ridge kissed her again, deeper this time. Her heart beat next to his and a low twinge of desire quickened with each second of their kiss.

"I should give you a ring. What about a ring made from the lace of your petticoat?"

"I think that would be perfect."

So, he tore a piece of lace from her petticoat and with great care tied it around her finger. Then he kissed her hand, her arm, and her neck. They floated the rest of the afternoon in each other's arms.

That evening the magnificence of the sunset took Lavinia's breath away. Orange and pink spread across the sky in brilliant swaths as the azure of the sky above deepened into indigo. "The beauty of it makes me want to cry. How many more sunsets do you believe we will see?"

"Now, now, we agreed not to talk about things like that. Let's think of happy memories." Mr. Ridge now appeared, as her fiancé, to have assigned himself the role of chief optimist for their small raft. "What is your happiest memory?"

She stared at the colors in the water below the sinking sun, and took Mr. Ridge's hand, thinking. What was her happiest memory?

"Hmm. I think the happiest memory of my childhood is when Father and Sarah and I went flower-picking in Oglethorpe Square one afternoon when we were little. Father almost never did things like this with us so both of us were filled with delight. He was in an uncharacteristically good humor and sang 'Home, Sweet Home' to us. We girls joined in on the chorus, giggling as Father sang deep and low."

"You mean like this?" And Mr. Ridge sang a few words of the chorus of "Home, Sweet Home" in his deepest voice, but then it cracked with exhaustion.

She laughed softly, and at the same moment her eyes teared, but tears never fell. Her body didn't have that much moisture left to give. "And what's yours? Your happiest memory?"

"I believe it might be this moment, right now. On this raft watching a breathtaking sunset with you, my treasured wife to be."

"Oh, Mr. Ridge, you don't mean that!"

"I do. I certainly do." He kissed her hand and then her mouth, then they floated together in silence and watched as the sun dropped below the horizon and darkness set in.

CHAPTER SEVEN

June 18, 1838
At sea

S HE ALREADY LAY awake writhing with hunger pains by the time the sun rose on the fourth day. Just after sunrise, after Mr. Ridge carved the fourth notch in the mahogany leg of the settee and futilely checked to see if the fish head bait had attracted anything, they spotted a second boat, this one on the western horizon, heading south. Its sails seemed bigger, closer.

"Mr. Ridge!" She shook his shoulder. "Another boat!" They scrambled to their knees, holding onto each other, and waved their arms, screaming and yelling. She employed her whistle again and again, sending the sound shrieking through the morning air.

"Help!" Mr. Ridge yelled. "Help!"

They watched in horror as the boat sailed across the horizon and out of their sight without slowing down. Within a few minutes it was gone.

"No!" She screamed. "No, no, no!" Her throat felt raw from screaming. Slowly, she collapsed onto the half-submerged settees. "Another ship can't have sailed right by without seeing us." She wished she could cry.

Mr. Ridge sat down wearily. "That ship sailed closer than the first one. But I suppose it's so early in the morning that not many of the crew were up and about. Ah, my heart is breaking."

Another ship went by later in the morning with the same result. They lay down, after waving and shouting and whistling, spent and exhausted. Lavinia had thought she was prepared to die, but realized, when she saw the ships and the chance for rescue, that she was not. Perhaps Mr. Ridge's optimism had worked its way into her after all. She wasn't sure which was harder to live with now—the hope or the lack of it.

Mr. Ridge now spoke in a whisper after all their hoarse shouting. "We must be in a shipping lane since we've seen three ships go by. More will come. Someone will come close enough to see us."

And so they continued to float under their makeshift tent. The minutes turned to hours, the morning to afternoon, and Lavinia's hope ebbed away again. They floated, barely conscious.

"Mr. Ridge," Lavinia whispered at last, "since we're to be married, should I call you by your first name?"

"You have always called me Mr. Ridge, haven't you?" He laughed weakly. "Yes, please call me Daniel."

"Daniel. Daniel in the lion's den, like in the Bible. We've had our own sort of lion's den, haven't we? And you've been so brave."

"You've been brave too, Miss Onslow."

"Lavinia."

"You've been brave too, Lavinia." He kissed her shoulder. They drifted again in nearly unconscious silence for long minutes.

"Well, Daniel." After a time, she took his hand. "I don't want a large wedding, do you? Just a few friends and family." As she whispered these words, they sounded ridiculous to her. Making wedding plans in their present circumstances felt like a delusion, like spinning gossamer from the air. But reality lay a bit beyond her grasp at the moment, and she continued on. "Perhaps a service at the Wesley Chapel and a small reception at the house. Sarah will be my only attendant. Mrs. Thomas will help make my dress."

"Any plans you want to make are fine. But I suppose I should remind you that I'm Catholic. Many of us in New Orleans are."

Silence fell over them as they contemplated this. She never thought much about Catholicism. She had, in fact, met only a few Catholics in her short life and felt hazy about what they believed and how it was different from Protestants. Father had considered their beliefs to be different. Yet, Mr. Ridge was indeed one of the kindest and bravest men she'd ever met. Had Mr. Ridge—Daniel—ever contemplated marrying a woman outside of his Catholic faith? She had heard that Catholics, unlike Protestants, were often insistent upon conversion.

"Would you want me to convert?"

He remained silent for a long moment. "I've never been very religious. My sisters might make that request."

"But what are *your* feelings?"

He spent some moments in thought, so long that she believed he might have fallen asleep or unconscious. She squeezed his hand to wake him. Finally, he spoke. "I think that while we have been out here floating and fighting for our lives with miles of empty sea around us, religious differences have come to seem unimportant."

She nodded in agreement. How would Father feel, if perchance he were still alive? The thought brought a pang of loss. Father's estranged brother, Uncle Timothy, and his wife Eunice would probably disapprove if she married a Catholic man. They might refuse to attend such a wedding. But since their families hadn't seen each other for years, they would likely refuse anyway. And what did her aunt and uncle know of what she and Mr. Ridge—Daniel—had endured out here? What did anyone know? She could hardly hold it all in her own mind.

"Do you agree?"

"Yes." She hesitated. "They seem unimportant now. But if we're rescued, they could become important once again."

"If we're rescued our lives will be changed so much, I wager our former lives will seem to be a dream."

Their conversation had involved them so that only now did Lavinia see another ship under sail, much closer than any had been before, approaching from the north. She ran her hand over her eyes to make sure she wasn't seeing things, but it continued to move closer still. Her heart rose to her throat; she didn't believe she could survive another ship sailing past them.

She touched Daniel's arm. "Daniel . . ."

Gripping each other's hands to support each other, they raised themselves to their knees and waved and shouted again, and she stuck her fingers between her dry and bleeding lips to make the whistle once more. The raft shifted and creaked under their weight. Once a swell rose and blocked their view of the ship and Lavinia felt a corresponding swell of panic.

But soon the swell passed, and the ship was still there. A few minutes more and she had sailed near enough for them to see tiny figures moving about on the deck, shouting and pointing. Pointing at them!

The realization that they'd been seen raised prickles on Lavinia's scalp "They've seen us!"

They watched in thrall as the angle of the sails on the sleek ship changed slightly and it headed their way. Thirty yards away the ship stopped and dropped anchor.

Lavinia and Daniel grabbed each other in a fierce hug, both breathless and sobbing with joy.

"Oh, Lavinia, we're saved!" Daniel hugged her so tightly to him that black spots whirled before her, and she thought she might faint.

Someone shouted to them, "We'll drop a lifeboat!"

They watched, holding onto each other as the sailors lowered a lifeboat carrying two men down the side. An age went by as the lifeboat splashed onto the water's surface and the sailors rowed vigorously in their direction. She had a flash of desperate fear that the boat would never reach them.

As the boat drew near, the sailors' faces showed surprise at her appearance. She had quite forgotten that she wore only her chemise, and her corset lay discarded on the raft. She tried to cover herself with the skirt of her dress, then her weakness overtook her. Such worries were foolish at a time like this, anyway.

At last, the sailors were close enough to speak.

"Thank the lord we saw you!" said one sailor, wiry with a wizened face.

"Oh, thank you! You're the fourth ship we've seen, and the only one who's seen us!" Daniel called back.

"Yes, thank God!" Lavinia whispered, her voice almost completely gone.

"How long you been floating here?" asked the other sailor, more muscular and with a full red beard.

"Four days now. We were on the *Pulaski,* but it exploded in a horrible accident—the boiler."

"Yes, we heard of the *Pulaski.*"

Daniel wrapped his arm around her back to help her onto the lifeboat. "Ladies first."

"Here, take my hand." The muscular sailor and Daniel helped Lavinia crawl into the lifeboat. She nearly fell into the floor of the boat, feeling, as Father sometimes used to say, as weak as a kitten.

Then Daniel clambered into the lifeboat with her, and the sailors made to turn the boat back toward the ship.

"Wait! I'll need my dress." What else would she wear on a ship full of sailors? Then she also remembered the earring. "And there's an earring of mine hanging in the water." They might be able to sell the earring for passage back to Savannah.

The sailors hesitated for a moment, then rowed back to the two settees. She looked at those two settees, so small and disheveled, nothing more than a half-sunken bit of flotsam. So unbelievable that this flimsy pile of furniture had saved their lives and had been their whole world for four terrifying and extraordinary days.

One of the sailors grasped her faded blue dress and pulled it onto the boat.

"I'll get your earring." As Daniel leaned over to try to find the earring hanging in the water, however, he collapsed.

One of the sailors reached over and pulled at the glove and strip of lace and with wiry fingers pulled it to the surface. Nothing. The earring was gone.

Lavinia's hands went to her neck and earlobe. At least she still had her necklace and the other earring.

"Sorry. Do you also want the corset, miss?"

"No!" The sailor laughed and tossed the corset back at the raft. It fell into the water, and as she watched it sink she swore to herself that it would be her last corset.

As the sailors rowed toward the ship, Daniel asked, "How far off the coast are we?"

"About fifty miles, give or take."

Lavinia gasped, glancing at Daniel. "We never could have rowed to shore."

"No, never."

CHAPTER EIGHT

June 1838
At sea

THEY WERE TO be a full day on the cargo ship, which was enroute to Smithville, North Carolina with a load of tea and spices and expected to arrive the following afternoon. After the sailors pulled them up the side, they took them to the ship's mess and gave them coffee, fish stew, and hardtack to eat.

"Mind you, don't eat too much." The cook, a small, bearded man with dark eyes and a dirty apron, spooned the fish stew into metal bowls. "When you haven't eaten in a few days it's best to eat sparingly."

"Yes, of course. Thank you." Daniel and Lavinia sat close to each other as they ate, not wanting to be separated after their experience. The hardtack tasted stale and dry, but Lavinia felt so hungry she persevered slowly, dipping it into the watery fish stew to soften it. Someone had kindly given her a rough blanket to drape over herself, and another applied a poultice and rebandaged the gash on her arm.

"Did you hear of other survivors of the *Pulaski?*" Daniel asked the cook.

"We heard two lifeboats came ashore, but some died while attempting to swim over the breakers. A terrible loss. Yet some lived."

Lavinia had a flash memory of the lifeboats being lowered and sinking within minutes, leaving people floundering in the sea. Had Father been one of those who lived?

Daniel put his arm around her, as if he knew what was in her mind and wished to protect her from it.

"The two of you ought to rest."

One of the officers gave up his stateroom for Lavinia, so that there would be a place for her to wash up nearby, and another gave Daniel a room as well. She felt so exhausted that she could not sit in the ship's mess for long before wanting to crawl into the bed in the cabin. She didn't want to be separated from Daniel, but once she got into bed she fell into a deep and heavy sleep. She slept for hours, her body desperate for rest, but she woke up with renewed sorrow for her father and spent the morning floating in and out of consciousness, like a raft adrift on the open sea.

Once she was fully awake, she washed up in the basin in her room and pulled on her faded, salt-stiffened blue dress. It was a sight, but it had finally dried overnight, and she had nothing else to wear. She noticed it hung more loosely after the days without food. She still wore the pink topaz necklace, and the single earring, and used the basin to wash the crusted salt away from the gems.

When she next saw Daniel in the mess hall, joining the other sailors for the midday meal as before, they both had better appetites and were able to slowly drink the ale and eat the salted pork the ship's cook had prepared.

"I need to speak with you privately." Daniel said when they had finished. He seemed nervous, with a look of deep concern on his face.

She looked around at the sailors at the table with them. What was on Daniel's mind?

"Do you feel able to take a turn around the deck?"

"I believe I could manage it." What could be worrying him?

She wrapped her blanket around her shoulders and together

they headed up above decks and into the breeze. Since they were engaged, no one could object to them spending time alone together, though the sailors generally did not seem to care about such social niceties. After what they had been through, neither did Lavinia. Someone had given Daniel a pair of shoes, but she was still barefoot, so she padded carefully and slowly around the deck. They made their way to a railing and watched the whitecaps.

"Four days on that water. It's a miracle we have been saved, that we are alive, Daniel. So many must have died." She waited for Daniel to speak.

"I have a confession to make." They watched the evershifting water, and Daniel took her hand.

She looked at him in surprise. "A confession?" Her mind whirled through the possibilities of what he could be referring to. Had he lied to her about his intentions or hidden something from his past?

"I feel that I must tell you this." His eyes widened with intensity as he looked at her. He gripped her hand so tightly it hurt. "And if you wish to break our engagement after you learn this, you are completely free to do so, Lavinia."

"What in the world do you mean?" She stared at him without understanding, her heart beating ferociously.

He took a deep breath, as if steeling himself, then it all tumbled out at once. "I boarded the *Pulaski* as a man with means. I had family money that kept me and my sisters comfortable and more that I had accrued through my work on the railroad. I was doing quite well. In fact, I planned to use my growing funds to invest in the Philadelphia, Wilmington, and Baltimore Railroad. I left sufficient funds at home for my sisters' comfort and the upkeep of our home for a time, but I carried most of my wealth with me on the *Pulaski*. I was meant to meet with PW&B people a few days before taking possession of the Pontchartrain engine. It's why I was on the *Pulaski*." He looked rueful, apologetic. "It was so fast, you see. I'd have time to complete my deal and satisfy my employers all in one trip. I had twenty-five thousand dollars with me in gold coins. All of those gold coins went down with the ship. I am now penniless. I have nothing left." He paused.

She stared at him. Father had brought a substantial amount of money, too, but since Sarah and William were still at home, he hadn't seen the need to bring it all or even most of it. But she knew others traveled more lavishly and preferred to bring their wealth with them. She hadn't considered it before, but now she supposed there must be many family fortunes lying at the bottom of the ocean with the remains of the *Pulaski*.

"I realize how shocking this must be to you," Daniel continued when she didn't speak. "It's a shock to me, too, as I worked so hard for it. But now that we're saved, I feel obligated to release you from our engagement if you wish."

She could feel nothing other than relief.

"Daniel, I don't care how much or how little you have. You have shown yourself to be the most courageous and steadfast of men, and I'll still be honored to become your wife. I realize, however, that we've only known each other for four days. We have much to learn about each other."

"True. We could be rushing headlong into this." He brushed a strand of hair from her cheek.

"We may be making an impulsive decision." She leaned closer to him.

"And I will need to rebuild my life."

"As will I." The idea of kissing became irresistible and they drew together, their lips touching gently. Lavinia closed her eyes.

Eventually, they pulled apart with reluctance, and Daniel picked up her hand, kissing it. "You're sure you still want to become my wife?" He searched her face with his eyes.

"Quite sure." She touched the pink topaz stone. "I can sell my necklace. We'll start again." She kissed him again lightly.

"I can hardly believe my ears. I have held my tongue for days now, but it's always been in the back of my mind." He held her at arms' length, seeming to drink in the sight of her, then pulled her close, her body nestled next to his stronger one.

"It's not only a miracle that we've been saved. It's a miracle that you, who I only glimpsed at dinner on the *Pulaski*, are now to be my wife. But I fear you think me a hero when I'm not, and I will not live up to your expectations."

"You are a hero, Daniel."

"No. I am simply a man who sees what needs to be done and tries to do it as quickly as he can. My sisters sometimes criticize me for being too single-minded, Lavinia, but I thank God for it if I have managed to capture your admiration."

"You have.

As they leaned together against the railing, he ran his fingers over the dirty lace ring he had tied there and took a quick breath. "I'll give you a real ring. Once I get back with the railroad. One that does justice to all the fine qualities that I admire in you."

"I like this one, Daniel. Just as it is."

"Should your father still be alive, I suspect he would not be satisfied with the lace ring whatsoever. And possibly you yourself might change your mind. We built up such trust over those four days. We have told each other much about ourselves. Yet, now, back in the world, will you still admire me?"

"Of course! You seem to think that I only wanted to marry a man of means." In truth, what *would* Father think about the lace ring? Appearances and having means were very important to Father. Yet the wreck had changed so much about the way Lavinia saw the world.

"Then let's marry as soon as we set food on land. What do you say?

She looked deeply into his eyes and clasped his hands. "That would be wonderful. Though I do wish Sarah could meet you," she added with a touch of sorrow.

"There will be plenty of time for us to meet after we're married."

After that, she strolled with Daniel along the deck, holding his hand, feeling happy and expectant. She looked out over the water, recalling floating there for those hundred hours or so. A sailor shouldering a coil of rope passed, smiling at them, and Lavinia recognized him as the wizened man who had rowed out to rescue them. She and Daniel retuned his smile and wished him good afternoon. Several of the sailors had been friendly toward them, and she felt a little guilty to be strolling along the deck in a leisurely way with Daniel while they were hauling sails and swabbing decks.

"The minute we land we should send word to Sarah and to your sisters that we're still alive. By now they've probably heard news of the sinking of the *Pulaski* and think we're dead."

"I agree. It will be like coming back to life." He smiled down at her as they headed back into the cabins to rest.

LATE THAT AFTERNOON Daniel and Lavinia, still very weak, joined the crew on the deck as land came into view.

"I wrote my sisters Sally and Imogene this afternoon. But I wanted to tell them about the loss of the money in person. It would be too shocking in a letter, and I don't want them to be afraid. In truth, just thinking about all those gold pieces at the bottom of the ocean makes my own stomach clench with fear for the future. But I'm still a young man, and I can begin again, as you said, and build up another fortune."

"We escaped with our lives. The gold doesn't matter." An image of the dead man who had floated up to their raft rose up in her mind and she shuddered. That poor man. How many bodies must there be floating now, their sightless eyes turned to face the sun? She shook herself, as though it might help her shake free of the memory and tried to focus on Daniel's words.

"In my letter, I told my sisters about you. Sally is friendly and kind. I think you will like her immensely and she will be excited to meet you as well. Imogene is the oldest, and she has always been more protective, though—harder to get to know. Imogene found fault with another young lady I spent time with several years ago now. We will have to find a way to be sure she has a good impression of you so she can see you as I do."

"I hope I can win her over." She looked forward to one day meeting Daniel's sisters and adding them to her family.

She tried not to think about the other young lady Daniel had mentioned.

CHAPTER NINE

June 1838
Smithville

W ITHIN AN HOUR, the cargo ship landed at the bustling port of Smithville, North Carolina, located at the mouth of the Cape Fear River. Daniel took her hand to help her down the walkway and onto the dock. They both felt unsteady on their feet after floating for four days and then traveling on the ship for another.

"Think how close we came to never setting foot on firm ground again."

"Yes, so close it makes me shiver." She squeezed his hand more tightly. She still used the blanket the sailors had given her as a shawl over her faded blue dress and tiptoed over the wooden dock in her still-bare feet. Daniel also wore his own clothes, faded and threadbare from their days in the salt and sun.

As Lavinia and Daniel disembarked, a smartly-dressed newspaper reporter with a carefully waxed mustache elbowed forward through the small knot of people clustered by the docks and introduced himself. "Hello, sir and madam, could I have a moment of your time?" The reporter wore a straw top hat and brandished a pencil and notebook. "I represent the *Delaware Gazette,* the oldest newspaper in Delaware. I understand you were rescued from the *Pulaski*. Would you be willing to share the story of your adventures with our readers? The sinking of the *Pulaski* has been a front-page story all week, as many bodies from that ship have washed ashore in these parts, and your story seems to be a rare happy one among the tragic."

"Bodies have washed up here?" She felt faint, again seeing the ravaged balloon-like face of the one that floated up to their raft. And Father?

Daniel put his arm around her and pulled her closer. "It was a harrowing experience, and I am sure my fiancée has not the strength."

"Your fiancée?" The reporter raised his eyebrows. "How charming. And how long have you been engaged?"

"We became engaged while floating on our raft." Daniel tried to push by. "But please, as you can see, my fiancée is not feeling well."

Maybe Daniel assumed Lavinia held to the notion that good southern women wouldn't want their names in the paper except on the days of their birth, marriage, and death. Whatever his motivation, it was clear he was determined to be protective of her.

"It's all right, Daniel." She recovered herself. "Maybe if the story appears in the newspaper our families will see it and learn that we are alive sooner than we could write them ourselves. And if Father survived, he might read about me and know that I survived, too."

Before they could speak further to the reporter, the captain approached and the reporter withdrew, a vexed expression on his face.

"Miss Onslow and Mr. Ridge." The captain gave a slight bow. "I've informed an elder at the Smithville Methodist Church of your situation and he has left to canvass members of the congregation to help with food, lodging, and clothing for you. He should be returning to the docks any minute."

"Thank you, Captain." Daniel shook his hand energetically.

"We owe you our lives."

"We are so very thankful for all that you have done." Lavinia picked up her skirts as they stepped off the dock onto the muddy ground.

Since Daniel and Lavinia weren't yet married, two different parishioners several blocks apart generously volunteered to take them in. Daniel stayed with Mr. Nast, the owner of the general store, and Lavinia stayed with Dr. Gosher, the local physician, and his wife, who both turned out to be very kind.

That night, as she drifted to sleep in the Goshers' guest bedroom, listening to the water lapping at the shore and the seabirds calling outside her window, her mind returned to the scene of the wreck. She imagined Daniel frantically lashing the two settees together and relived him pulling her from the water. In her mind's eye she saw Daniel catch the fish, felt its scales between her fingers, felt the slithery crunch in her mouth as she ate it. With each remembered sensation she felt her heart begin to beat more rapidly.

She also had visions of Daniel's gold pieces drifting down, down, down to the bottom of the ocean and scattering on the sand where fishes would peck at the shiny coins as if they were food. She wondered about the letter Daniel had written to his sisters, failing to mention the loss. They would be so happy that their brother had survived, but they might suspect the rest. Their entire life savings.

She felt a bit panicked herself, despite the assurances she had given him of starting again. At least she knew if the worst happened and Father were gone, she had part ownership of the Onslow house on Oglethorpe Square, the millinery shop, and the rest of Father's considerable estate. She wished Daniel had told her about the loss sooner. It was almost as though he didn't trust her.

After being with Daniel night and day for nearly a week, the separation grieved her keenly and she worried about how he fared. Only he and Lavinia knew what they'd survived. In spite of the tasty food, the comfortable bed, and the clothes that were kindly given by her hosts, she felt lonely for his company. Only his company would do, and she asked Mrs. Gosher that evening before bed if she would mind having a note sent to Daniel.

He visited her as soon as decently possible the following morning at the Goshers' waterfront home, and she descended the stairs as quickly as she could in her weakened state to meet him, wearing clothes and shoes loaned by her generous hostess. But he arrived barely early enough to beat the nattily-dressed reporter who had missed his opportunity for a story the day before when the captain interrupted. He turned up to on the Goshers' doorstep on Daniel's heels.

When Mrs. Gosher opened the door for Daniel, Lavinia saw, from her position halfway down the stairs, that Daniel placed himself between the reporter and the door.

"You again! I told you yesterday my fiancée was not well enough to speak with you!"

"Let the lady speak for herself," said the reporter, trying to push past Daniel.

Then, to her immense shock, Daniel shoved the man, sending him sprawling noisily down the front porch steps onto the muddy street.

"Oof, ow!" The reporter tried to regain his footing, fumbling for his pencil and paper.

"Oh, my goodness!" Mrs. Gosher exclaimed.

"Daniel!" Lavinia, rushed down the remaining stairs, her hands flying to her cheeks. "What has come over you? You know I said I was amenable to an interview!"

Daniel stared at the man on the muddy stones. After a moment, which he apparently needed to gather himself, he leaned down to help the man up, grasping his hand. "My apologies, I don't know what came over me."

Perhaps Daniel had developed an excessive desire to protect Lavinia from anything he perceived might threaten her. But goodness, he had more of a temper than she'd realized.

The reporter scrambled to his feet, pulling his arm away from Daniel. "What's the matter with you?" he demanded, ruefully dusting off his muddied jacket. "I'm simply trying to do my job and ask a few questions."

"Which we would be pleased to answer!" Lavinia gave Daniel a hard look then glanced at Mrs. Gosher. "Mrs. Gosher, is it all right if we invite Mr. Morgan in?

Mrs. Gosher nodded. "Certainly. Please, sir, come into the parlor."

Daniel, somewhat abashed, followed them into the parlor.

"May I offer you some tea?" asked Mrs. Gosher, clearly trying to smooth the awkward situation. They all declined. "Then, please have a seat."

Lavinia sat on the loveseat and Daniel quickly sat beside her and took her hand. The reporter sat in one rocker by the fireplace while Mrs. Gosher sat in another.

"Thank you for your cooperation." The reporter cleared his throat and pointedly addressed Lavinia. He took out a handkerchief and held it to his wrist, now bleeding from his fall. "Let me properly introduce myself. My name is Andrew Morgan, and, as I mentioned yesterday, I work for the *Delaware Gazette*. Our readers are fascinated by the wreck of the *Pulaski* and are anxious to hear of any stories of survival. As I also mentioned yesterday, bodies have been floating up on beaches here in Smithville from the wreck and there is much to mourn. Your story offers such hope in the face of such tragedy. We would like to print a story of your account of the incredible experience you have had."

"It was quite traumatic." Lavinia nodded, smoothing the skirt that Mrs. Gosher had so kindly given her. "But I, for one, would be glad to talk about it."

Daniel grabbed up the lace protector on the loveseat's armrest and then made a mess of trying to put it back in place. "Are you sure you want our story displayed on the front page of the paper for everyone to see? I am not at all sure of this. What if, as your fiancé, I forbade you to speak to him?

"You cannot forbid me to speak. I am not yet your wife, and even then, I would hope that you would be the sort of husband who knows his wife holds her own opinions." Lavinia felt a bit brash but also confident. "And I feel that speaking to the reporter might be helpful. I think we should talk to the papers so possibly our families can learn we are alive more quickly than a letter might carry the news." She then turned back to the reporter. "Mr. Morgan, do you by chance have any lists of survivors? My father travelled on the ship with me. He was strolling next to me on the deck and then there occurred a horrific explosion and suddenly my father was gone. I am desperate to know if he is by any chance among the survivors."

"We did publish a list of the few survivors we know about so far. It was in yesterday's paper."

"Oh, that is wonderful news!" She clasped her hands to her heart. "Was the name Frederick Onslow on that list?"

Mr. Morgan wrinkled his brow in thought, then carefully measured his words. "Perhaps the mistress of the house can get you a copy and you can look for yourself. I don't rightly trust my memory."

Lavinia's chest tightened. He didn't want to tell her that Frederick Onslow's name was not listed among the survivors. But she had to see it for herself.

"Mrs. Gosher, do you have yesterday's paper?"

"I believe I may." She stood and left the room quickly. They heard a rustling of papers in the next room, and a moment later she returned with the paper and handed it to Lavinia.

She cast her eyes quickly over the pages, looking for the list of survivors. It was a sorrowful issue indeed. Past the typical community notices and advertisements for shops and sales, there was also a lengthy article about hundreds of Cherokee Indians in western North Carolina, South Carolina, and Georgia who were being relocated to the Western territories by troops of soldiers on President Jackson's orders. The Cherokee were to travel on foot. Lavinia felt a sudden kinship with them over what was sure to be a long and brutal journey, but she didn't have much heart to spare as she looked for the survivor list. Finally she spotted an article with the headline "Survivors of the *Pulaski*," with a list of about thirty names. Frederick Onslow did not appear among them. She ran her finger down the list twice to make sure. Not there. Tears glazed her eyes, but she laid the paper on her lap and carefully ran her finger down the list of names a third time.

Daniel drew a deep breath, and she glimpsed him catching the eye of the reporter. "I'm so sorry, Lavinia."

"My deepest condolences, miss. Though I must say, it's early yet. More survivors may be discovered. As you were."

She sat, her mouth slightly open, with the tears now running down her cheeks. "All along, even though we didn't see him on the lifeboats, I still had a sliver of hope." Lavinia let the newspaper drop to the floor and put her face in her hands.

Daniel sat next to her and put his hand on her shoulder. Her sobs were raw and unfettered.

Mr. Morgan stood. "I should come back tomorrow perhaps?"

Daniel nodded. "Please."

As soon as Mr. Morgan left Daniel took her hand and tried to comfort her. "I remember my misery when my own parents died—no one could have ever consoled me. The only help was that my sisters were just as devastated. I took a great deal of comfort in being with them."

"I'd like to lie down."

"Let me be a comfort to you, Lavinia. I know what it's like to lose a father."

"I want to be alone. I don't want anyone to see me this way."

He hesitated. "Of course." He rose and helped her into the front hallway and up the stairs into the bedroom. He lay a blanket over her and kissed her hand. "I'll come back later."

She only nodded. His footsteps sounded on the stairs.

"Thank you, Mrs. Gosher, I think Miss Onslow needs to rest."

"Will you join us for dinner then?"

"Thank you, I will. I'll see you this evening," After that the door closed.

A FEW HOURS later, Lavinia stood on the wooden walkway next to the water. She had needed some air, and Mrs. Gosher had kindly insisted on accompanying her. Just across the street were the living quarters built on stilts for the ship pilots, and Lavinia gazed at the building curiously.

"What is that structure?"

"It's for the pilots who board the ships and guide them into the Smithville port through the dangerous Frying Pan shoals." Mrs. Gosher said by way of explanation, taking her arm.

They strolled slowly along the river, Mrs. Gosher helping Lavinia as she still felt so weak. If she were in a different frame of mind, Smithville would seem a charming little port town, with well-maintained homes along the waterfront. Mrs. Gosher told her that many of the homes in Smithville had been built forty or fifty years before, in the 1790's, similar to when many homes in Savannah had been built, as well, and that many of the town's residents made their livings from the sea. They passed an inn, a tavern, and even a jail, then stopped and spoke with a soldier at Fort Johnston, right on the waterfront, who greeted Mrs. Gosher and chatted about the town's upcoming Fourth of July celebrations.

As they talked, Lavinia gazed across the inlet at the relatively new stucco and whitewash lighthouse on Smith Island. The soldier followed her gaze. "It was built about twenty years ago. It can be reached only by boat." Apparently, the shoals around the mouth of the Cape Fear were some of the most dangerous on the coast, and the lighthouse helped guide ships through these waters. "There's been many a shipwreck, though," the soldier added, "so I'm not so sure Old Baldy is doing its job. And just here, you can see the billet head of the *Pulaski* that washed up just last week."

"Oh." Lavinia caught her breath. She looked at the familiar

but now battered and cracked billet head displayed in the sand near the pilot's house. It had looked so imposing and shiny only days before. Four or five people were digging in the dunes in the near distance.

"What are those people doing?"

"Don't look at that, dear." Mrs. Gosher tried to steer her away.

"They're burying bodies." The soldier spoke before Mrs. Gosher could stop him.

She glimpsed a worker quickly repositioning a wind-ruffled sheet that covered an oblong shape on the beach and weakness washed over her. The ravished face on the body that had floated up beside their raft remained in her mind's eye. And now they buried more bodies here, bodies that might have been people she had seen in the dining hall or on the deck of the *Pulaski*, or even on the streets of Savannah. And maybe even Father! As the awful scene unfolded, she fought powerful desires both to look away and to rush over and examine the grisly face of each one.

"You have upset my guest, sir." Mrs. Gosher, wrapped a caring arm around her waist, pulling her back from walking closer.

"Oh, my Lord, I heard from my neighbor about the young woman saved by the brave man who lashed together two settees. Are you that young lady?"

Her face heated up. "I see our story has preceded us."

"People hereabouts are amazed that you survived when so many others died."

"Come on, Miss Onslow, we should be getting back." Mrs. Gosher now took her arm with firmness. She turned Lavinia away from the people digging.

"Dear, I'm sorry that happened."

"Yes. I apologize for my emotions—"

"No apology needed, dear, certainly." A moment later, she spoke again. "I must say, Mr. Ridge seems to be quite a resourceful young man."

"Yes, of course. He saved our lives." Lavinia studied her feet, in Mrs. Gosher's second-best shoes, advancing on the wooden walkway. Mrs. Gosher cleared her throat. She seemed to be working up to saying something. What was Mrs. Gosher aiming at?

"I just wondered if you might be concerned about him pushing that reporter."

She glanced at Mrs. Gosher's observant eyes and well-meaning face. She had been trying not to dwell on it, but the older woman's words had given voice to a doubt that had been slowly growing in her mind. "It has given me something to think about," she said at last.

And there were other things, too, such as his near threat to forbid her to speak. And the fact that he had initially withheld the information about the lost gold pieces from her and now still from his sisters. She didn't mention that one to Mrs. Gosher.

"Forgive me for saying this, but I think he has strong feelings about you, dear, and is driven to protect you."

"I have never seen my father push a man like that. Shouldn't men control their tempers?"

"Sometimes life requires passion. Try not to hold it against him too much."

She looked again at the sweet, forbearing face of her Smithville host. What kinds of experiences had Mrs. Gosher had with her own marriage that might have influenced her to tell Lavinia this? And with her mention of passion, it felt like she was reading Lavinia's mind. "I've always hoped for a love match, one of true affection and great feeling," Lavinia replied. "But now that I've made one, it gives me pause. I see there is a darker side to passion."

"You may just need a bit more rest, dear."

"I'm sure you're right." Her feelings about Daniel were so jumbled and confused. She could hardly wait for him to take her in his arms and kiss her again. Yet doubts remained. Was Daniel indeed a good man?

TWO DAYS LATER, Lavinia looked at herself in the full-length mirror in Mrs. Gosher's bedroom and touched her pink topaz necklace. Since failing to find Father's name on the list of survivors, she'd been forced to face the certainty that he had perished that night. As the reality of his death had descended upon her, she'd fallen into a dark dream-like state, as though she were living in a cave that had no entrance or exit. Even Daniel's nearness couldn't bring her up out of it. Though nothing else occurred to cause her worry, the misgivings in the back of her clouded mind refused to dispel. When she agreed to marry him, she'd believed they were going to die. Would their reasons for marrying be enough now that they were going to live?

Dr. Gosher tended to her arm each morning and seemed pleased with how it was healing, and Mrs. Gosher and Daniel continued making what plans were necessary for the wedding. Lavinia herself had difficulty taking part in the activity, though she tried.

Mrs. Gosher had offered to lend Lavinia the dress she wore for her wedding, and Lavinia objected at first, saying that she should wear the same faded blue one she wore when Daniel saved her life. But it was in tatters and could barely be considered a dress anymore. Mrs. Gosher had insisted she have a real gown to wear for her wedding, and now here Lavinia stood in this lovely, if a bit dated, antique yellow lace gown with mutton sleeves and a satin sash, waiting for Mrs. Gosher to pin it for fitting. She hadn't had an appetite and had not regained the weight she'd lost while shipwrecked, and Mrs. Gosher was a bit taller than Lavinia, so the dress hung loosely.

Daniel had engaged a certain Judge Johnson, who had offered to marry them this Saturday, two days from now, in the Gosher's parlor.

"Here, look what I've made for you." Mrs. Gosher came back

into the room with her pincushion. She showed Lavinia a small blue handkerchief she'd made from the hem of Lavinia's blue dress. "So that you can carry something blue—and a piece of that dress as a keepsake."

"Thank you, Mrs. Gosher. How kind of you." Lavinia took the blue handkerchief and smoothed her fingers over it, touched by the gesture. She wished she and Daniel could be married in Savannah with Sarah there. She wasn't sure she wanted to get married in Smithville surrounded by strangers, as kind as they had been.

She wanted to get to Savannah and have Sarah meet Daniel. She wanted and needed Sarah's approval. And Clementine's. If she were being truthful with herself, she most of all wished she could have Father's approval, in spite of the disagreements she and Father had had on the subject. And it was Father's approval that she could never receive. Father was gone and would never be present to give her advice or care for her again. She just wanted more time to make her decision, and then she would feel more at peace.

"Hold still, now." Mrs. Gosher pulled the bodice tighter and brandished her pins.

The room seemed to contract around her with the bodice, and Lavinia felt she could barely draw breath. "Stop, stop. I'm not sure I want to do this."

Mrs. Gosher sat back on her heels. "What do you mean, dear? You don't want to wear the dress?"

"No." Lavinia began unbuttoning the back buttons, tearing at them, nearly ripping the lacy fabric. "I should go back to Savannah to get married. I want my sister and Clementine to meet Daniel before I marry him." Lavinia felt light-headed, almost dizzy, on the verge of panicking and running from the room.

"Take a breath, dear. Slowly in, slowly out." Mrs. Gosher put her hand on her arm, and stroked it gently, almost like comforting a child. "I understand that things have moved quickly, and there is much that might cause upset. And of course, you'd like your sister and Clementine to approve. But you do want to marry Mr. Ridge, do you not, Lavinia?"

Lavinia drew a deep, slow breath and stared into Mrs. Gosher's well-meaning eyes. "Yes. Yes, I do." Her heart was beating all out of time.

"Then it's simply a matter of timing, isn't it? You can go ahead and get married here and then travel to Savannah as a married couple. It will be much more proper since you won't have a chaperone to go with you."

To get married, until death would they part, in a rush simply to be more proper? So many people thought that way. And perhaps she had, too, before. Having accepted her own end and been drawn back again from the precipice, now such concern seemed absurd.

In truth, she was still in a state of disbelief that she even remained alive—and on dry land! Against every expectation and all odds, she hadn't died in the shipwreck or sunk to the bottom of the sea. When she thought of her father and all of the other people who had perished, she couldn't understand why she remained while they had gone. She was gripped by the sudden certainty that she had to find a true purpose for her life, something meaningful to herself and others, something that would make it worth her surviving when so many hadn't. What would that be?

She didn't know. Perhaps indeed it was to marry Daniel. Maybe they could do something useful together, as survivors. They did share those unforgettable days together. Or was she simply trying to justify the decision for their marriage that was happening around her? There were as many reasons to go through with it as there were to delay. And she couldn't deny that she desired Daniel—ever since the kiss on the raft—and wanted to know what it would be like to be intimate with him, for her skin to touch his. If the panic of the moment hadn't already made her flushed, her face would have flamed now.

She did want to marry Daniel, whatever the consequences. She wanted her love match and passionate encounters, and Daniel was the one who had been fated to her on that raft. So Mrs. Gosher was right—it was a matter of timing. Perhaps wedding location wasn't the obstacle it had seemed a few moments ago.

She breathed deeply, regained a measure of her composure, and smiled at Mrs. Gosher, allowing her to rebutton the dress. "You've been so kind, lending me clothes and giving me food and shelter. And offering to host our wedding in your parlor. I can never repay you."

"No need to worry." Mrs. Gosher's concerned face relaxed. "It's our great pleasure. And it's a joy to celebrate your survival and romance in the face of such tragedy." She pulled a hatbox from the closet. "Would you like to wear my wedding bonnet as well?"

She opened the hatbox and pulled out a small cottage bonnet made of ivory-colored lace and trimmed with roses with a sweet satin tie. The bonnet was out of style by Savannah standards, Lavinia knew, but it was very pretty. She put it on and looked at herself in the mirror. Then she studied Mrs. Gosher behind her, as she wound up thread and put pins back into the pincushion.

Again Lavinia wondered about Mrs. Gosher's experiences and what had given her the views she held. Did Mrs. Gosher have a lack of romance in her life? Yet, how kind she had been. And Dr. Gosher was so busy helping both townspeople and those in the country as the only doctor for miles around. He was away from home on his horse with his medical bag a great deal.

Perhaps Lavinia's doubts were only her own worn nerves causing her worry for no reason.

THE SATURDAY AFTERNOON sun filtering through the Goshers'

parlor curtains highlighted Judge Johnson's threadbare black coat. His eyes were rheumy and bloodshot. Did Lavinia smell a whiff of whiskey as he spoke? She pushed those thoughts from her head as he made some introductory comments about the sanctity of marriage, and then added, "Please join hands."

Daniel took both of her hands in his, which were warm.

"By joining hands," said Judge Johnson, "you are consenting to be bound together as husband and wife. You are promising to honor, love, and support each other for the rest of your lives."

Lavinia studied Daniel's shining, eager face, the new spectacles he'd gotten free of charge from the general store courtesy of his host, Mr. Nast, and the crisp haircut he'd received yesterday from the town barber, who had also refused to accept payment.

Bound together. The rest of their lives.

Judge Johnson looked at Daniel. "Do you, Daniel, take Lavinia to be your wedded wife, to have and to hold from this day forward, for better, for worse, for richer, for poorer, in sickness and in health, to love and to cherish, till death do you part, according to God's holy ordinance?"

"I do." Daniel, without hesitation, turned to her. His face and lips were peeling from the sun exposure during their ordeal, but he still looked radiant with happiness and desire.

Judge Johnson fixed his watery eyes on her. "And do you, Lavinia, take Daniel to be your wedded husband, to have and to hold from this day forward, for better, for worse, for richer, for poorer, in sickness and in health, to love and to cherish, till death do you part, according to God's holy ordinance?"

She tried to focus on Daniel's loving face, so close to her own. The moment spun out slowly. In the past week and a half she had been shipwrecked, lost her father, nearly lost her life, and been saved while hundreds of others had died. And now here she stood in the sunlit parlor of people she'd known less than five days, marrying a man she'd known for less than two weeks. The moment hung in the air and everyone else waited expectantly.

"I do." Her heart palpitated. Sweat coated her temples.

Goodness, it was hot and stifling in this parlor.

"By the authority vested in me by the laws of the state of North Carolina, I now pronounce you man and wife." Judge Johnson turned to Daniel. "You may kiss the bride."

Daniel smiled, took her face in his hands, and very gently kissed her healing and tender lips with his own. The closeness of him was heady. Unbidden in this moment that was meant to be full of joy, she had a flash memory of the sinking ship and overfull lifeboats. Once one broke through, other images tumbled across her consciousness—the floating dead body, the shark, the passing ships. Her pulse quickened and she couldn't tell if it was from the kiss or the memories running riot in her mind. As Daniel pulled back, smiling down at her, she forced the terrible visions from her mind with all the willpower she had and prayed she would not see them again the next time they kissed. She focused on his yearning hazel eyes behind the new spectacles and summoned the feelings of love and trust that those days on the raft had forged.

Dr. and Mrs. Gosher, the only witnesses, clapped quietly.

As Daniel embraced her in his strong arms, outside the window, the reporter, Mr. Morgan, peeked in, sketching them. Lavinia took a quick breath but decided not to say anything to Daniel about it. He might become irate and rush out to fight with Mr. Morgan again. She breathed deeply, and pulled Daniel closer, inhaling the clean scent of his shaving soap.

Her knees buckled without warning. Daniel grasped her waist and whisked her to one of the dining room chairs, and she sank into it.

THE GOSHERS OWNED a small rental house a few blocks from the shoreline, and they offered it to Daniel and Lavinia for their wedding night, or as long as they wished to stay, as their last tenants had just moved to New Bern. The sun set and the sky filled with vivid colors as they at last trudged up the gentle hill to the little white clapboard house. She lifted her skirts to avoid the ever-present mud on the roads of Smithville.

"We're married! Truly married!" With a rush of affection, Daniel threaded his arm under hers and drew her to him. "You're my wife."

"I'm your wife. Yet ten days ago we didn't even know each other." She leaned on him as they climbed the front steps to the little house. "Do you have any fears about us marrying so quickly?"

Daniel took her into his arms with an energy that squeezed the breath from her lungs. "None. The moment I saw you, Lavinia, I wanted you for my wife. From that moment in the dining hall on the *Pulaski*."

"But I don't even know when your birthday is! Or your favorite color. What's your favorite place? I know practically nothing about you or your family and yet now you're my husband for life! Why, my sister Sarah is engaged to a man we've known practically all our lives. We know his family, we know where he lives, where he attends church, and what his father's business is." She could feel her own heart beating thunderously as she rattled on nonsensically about William. Why should she be thinking of William at a moment like this?

Daniel turned the doorknob and the swollen door opened, startling her with its loud squeak.

"You know that I love the stars at night. You know how I behave in a dangerous situation. You know that I'm not overly religious. You know that I am not much of a fisherman."

They both had to laugh at that.

"That could be a liability in these parts. Most everyone in Smithville seems to have something to do with the fishing life."

"Tell me, what more do you need to know about me?"

"Daniel, you know full well that we barely know each other. And what if your family doesn't like me?" She chattered nervously in anticipation of what was to come, the physical aspect of her union with Daniel, about his body, her own body, and what it would be like. Her book-loving friend Harriet, who had married young, had warned Sarah and Lavinia, one afternoon when they were sitting on the veranda sharing secrets, that relations between a husband and wife were painful at first. A heightened awareness and expectation filled her, Daniel's arms around her seeming to create a sensation of electricity there. As Daniel relinquished her and moved inside to explore the small house, Lavinia stood in the doorway, poised between anticipation and fear.

The setting sun spread rosy stripes across the rough wood floor of the one-room cottage. A narrow bed, a nightstand, and a wardrobe stood on one side of the room. Someone, possibly from the church, had left a Bible on the nightstand for their edification. A fireplace occupied the center wall. On the other side of the room stood a small cast iron stove, a small pine table and two chairs, and a dish cabinet with two plates, two mugs, and two forks and knives.

She came slowly and deliberately inside and closed the door behind her. Looking around this plain little home, she couldn't help but think about her own room back in Savannah, with the high coffered ceiling, tall window, elevated four-poster rosewood bed with the fluffy goose down mattress, and fine Aubusson rug that Father had ordered from France. She'd never fully appreciated the beauty of the heart of pine floors of her home. She touched the pink topaz around her neck. Such luxuries she was used to.

"May thirty-first." Daniel closed the curtains on the cottage's single window, then returned to her and slid his arms around her waist.

She looked up at him questioningly. "What?"

"My birthday." He guided her chin toward his lips with two fingers. "And my favorite color is blue. Like the color of the dress you wore when we met."

The touch of his lips on hers brought back the sharp memory

of that first kiss while they were floating on the settees just a week ago. The desperate, breathless yet hopeful feel of it. Their dry lips had cracked further with the pressure. Now their lips were healing, and they were both clean and smelling of soap, both in wedding attire. A member of the congregation at the Methodist Church had loaned Daniel a fine jacket and breeches, and Mrs. Gosher's alterations to her yellow lace wedding dress had been expertly done.

Yet in spite of her fears, she knew his touch like a familiar coat, and they embraced, their lips fitting together like pieces of a puzzle. When they broke apart again, he slowly untied the satin sash under her chin and removed her bonnet, letting it drop onto the small bedside table. He took the pins from her hair and it sprung free and tumbled down her back with a sound like a breeze through tall grass. Holding her breath, she slid her hands under the lapels of his jacket and pushed it off his shoulders, revealing a worn but clean cotton shirt and borrowed suspenders. Pulling free of his jacket in a hurried motion, he then stroked her hair, awkwardly and reverently. She ran her finger over his jaw, feeling the softness of newly shaved skin.

"I love your hair. I have dreamed of touching it like this." He seemed barely able to control his breath.

With shaking hands, she removed his new spectacles, placed them on the nightstand, and teased back the freshly pomaded dark blonde curls at his temples, which had been so tousled while they had been at sea.

He ran his hand down her back. "What should we do with this tedious row of buttons?"

"Remember the way you removed my blue dress that first day so we could use it as a tent?" She turned her back to him, vividly remembering the feel of his hands on her back as they floated under the hot sun, his fingers patiently unbuttoning. And now, again, she felt them moving slowly down, this time for a much different reason.

And then, at last, the dress slid down, and Lavinia, in her

chemise, and Daniel in his shirtsleeves moved to the bed. They scrambled a little self-consciously under the thin quilt with its wedding ring pattern, and mouth touched mouth and skin touched skin, Daniel's hot breath on her neck. His hands began exploring every inch of her, and she forgot about feeling afraid, lost in the throbbing, the sheer tactile pleasure of it. They tumbled headlong toward their physical union in a matter of minutes and lay together afterward, holding each other tightly, breathing hard.

"Was it all right? Are you all right?"

She nodded, still feeling a burning, throbbing sensation below. Just as Harriet had told her and Sarah on the veranda that distant afternoon, there was pain, and strangely she thought with longing of Sarah, wishing she could have met Daniel and that she could have been present at their wedding. The pain also reminded her of the finality of this act, all the actions of this day. They were cleaved together now, Daniel and Lavinia.

"We are clinging together as if shipwrecked," Daniel whispered.

"Yes."

CHAPTER TEN

June 1838
Smithville

T HE DAY AFTER Lavinia and Daniel's wedding, a thoughtful member of the Smithville Methodist Church left a pot of crab soup, a flat pan of corn bread, and a copy of the *Delaware Gazette* on the front porch. Daniel leaned out the door shirtless and brought them both inside.

"I'm ravenous. This soup smells divine." Daniel brought the soup, the paper and two spoons to the bed. They ate the thick soup while staring at the front page, where there appeared a long and embellished description of their marriage ceremony as glimpsed through the Goshers' parlor window. Mr. Morgan, eavesdropping all the while, had written down their vows word for word in his article.

They lay entwined together on the small bed, sharing the soup, still reveling in the married freedom to touch each other, and reading Mr. Morgan's flowery description of their nuptials.

"'Miss Onslow, looking radiant in a delicate, yellow lace wedding dress and cottage bonnet, said "I do" to an adoring Mr. Ridge as they exchanged marriage vows at two o'clock this afternoon,'" Lavinia read.

"You were indeed radiant," Daniel brushed a strand of hair

back from her face. "And I am indeed adoring."

They finished the soup and used the cornbread to soak up the remnants from the bottom of the pot. Daniel stood, taking the empty pot to the table. "I suppose I was hasty in my judgment of Mr. Morgan. This article captures our wedding in a moving way. Still, I worry about people knowing about us." He pointed to Morgan's byline, as if to emphasize his point.

"People are happy for us, Daniel. Ours is a story of survival and love. It appeals to people, especially after such a disaster as the *Pulaski* and those tough times last year."

"I know the depression has affected many people, and the wreck was a horrible event that will live with us forever, but our lives are none of their business. Half the time those journalists just want to increase newspaper readership and care little for truth-telling. You know I'm right." Daniel paced the small room, suddenly restless.

"I know, Daniel, but look how kind people have been, giving us clothing and food. And without Mr. Morgan's previous article about our story, some of them might not even know of our plight. What would we have done without the good people of Smithville?" She dressed in an everyday frock in a green and yellow floral print that Mrs. Gosher had altered for her and left in the wardrobe yesterday morning with a few essentials. Even after last night, she felt self-conscious to be stepping into the dress with Daniel watching, but with only one room in the house it could hardly be avoided.

"I know the people have been good to us, Lavinia, but I am weary of relying on charity. I need to find a way to be self-sufficient again."

"I know we will, Daniel. Can you try to contact the railroad to make sure they know you are still alive, that you still want your job there?"

"Yes, I've done that. But it may not be that straightforward. I didn't mention this to you before, but not only did I lose my own money when the boat sank, I also lost the ten thousand dollars that the railroad had sent to purchase the new engine from England." Daniel put on the worn white everyday shirt he'd been given, tucked it in, and put on his suspenders. He ran his hand through his hair.

Another revelation. "But surely they can't hold you responsible for that! Our ship sank!" Why hadn't he mentioned it when he'd told her the rest?

"I should still have my position when I get back. I simply need to get there and speak to them face to face. But what would we use for steamboat fare? We can't ask the good people of Smithville for that much."

"A steamboat." Her stomach contracted and she began to shake. She suddenly realized that the very thought of sea travel was terrifying. "I cannot get back on a boat." Her voice shook, and Daniel stopped and looked at her.

"You were on the cargo ship."

"But that was only for a day and a night, with land in sight, and not far out to sea. And what choice did we have?

"We'll take a stagecoach, then," he said swiftly. "It will take much longer, but we could make the trip over land."

She tried to calm her breathing and touched the pink topaz around her neck. "What about this?"

"I would never dream of asking you to part with that necklace. Your father gave it to you."

"Yes, he did. But this necklace and the one earring that I didn't lose at sea are all we have of any value. We could trade my jewelry for stage passage to Savannah." As soon as she said it out loud, she knew this was what she wanted. She and Daniel had talked about New Orleans, his job at the railroad, meeting his sisters, but Lavinia wanted to go home. If she could persuade him to go to Savannah, perhaps there would be a way to entice him to stay. "Sarah is there, my family's home and business are there. And now that we're married, what's mine is yours." All that Lavinia owned now equally belonged to Daniel based on the ceremony they'd had yesterday. In fact, she suddenly realized, since married women could not inherit land in Georgia, any property Lavinia would inherit from her father would belong to him as well.

He saved my life, she reminded herself. *I love and trust him.*

Daniel crossed the room and took her in his arms, brushing his lips across her temple. "Dearest Lavinia, let's go to Savannah then, and I'll meet Sarah and her fiancé. I promise you on my honor that once we're established back in New Orleans, I will buy you a necklace that is more beautiful than this one two times over."

She reached back and tried to undo the clasp, but because her fingers were trembling, she could not.

"Take it off."

Bending to kiss her neck in a dozen places, he did.

As it turned out, two stagecoach seats from Smithville to Savannah cost them nothing. The manager of the stagecoach company, like Daniel's barber and Mr. Nast at the general store, refused to take any payment from *Pulaski* survivors, so Lavinia was able to keep her jewelry. And they didn't have much luggage to take with them—only what the Goshers and the other Methodists had donated to them. Lavinia was relieved, not only because she felt sentimental about the necklace, but for practical purposes it would be good to save it in case they met future catastrophe between here and Savannah. And so, two days later in the wee hours of the morning—the middle of the night, really—Daniel and Lavinia said heartfelt goodbyes to Dr. and Mrs. Gosher at the inn that stood as a waystation for those going into Wilmington to catch the stage.

"Be sure and write to let us know how you get along," Mrs. Gosher clasped her hand with affection.

"There is no way we can adequately thank you for all you

have done, Mrs. Gosher." Much as she wanted to go home to Savannah, she was nervous about leaving Smithville and this kind woman who had cared for her so well and selflessly. Mrs. Gosher had anticipated Lavinia's every need and had even thought to give her writing paper and an envelope to send a letter to Sarah. She'd written to Sarah as soon as she had strength to hold a dip pen, describing their rescue and her inability to find evidence of Father's survival, and Dr. Gosher had posted it for her a few days ago. And now Lavinia was about to follow that letter home.

Dr. Gosher shook Daniel's hand in farewell, surreptitiously pressing some coins into it. "You'll need to pay at the inns along the way."

The first stage of the journey would be a two-day trip to Charleston, where they would change coaches for a further two-day drive through Beaufort to Savannah. Their first coach was full, with two gentlemen traveling on business and a family of five on their way to visit relatives.

"So, you are newly wed?" The mother held two of her three children on her lap, while the other sat on her husband's.

"Yes." Lavinia suddenly thought of the intimate relations she had enjoyed with Daniel the night before, blushing when the woman said "newly wed." The wide eyes of the children regarded the two of them soberly.

As the stage jounced and creaked along, she sat next to Daniel and looked out the window at the changing view. After traveling inland for a time on the first day, the road had veered again toward the coast, and a beautiful yet scrubby coastal landscape unraveled before them with gnarled yaupon trees, the ever-changing marshes with their teeming bird life, and the maritime forests.

The ride itself was miserable. Every day they were to be awake and ready to board by three in the morning. The wheels churned up billowing clouds of dust in the July heat, which covered their skin and clothing. The children became tired and cried. Every fifteen miles or so they stopped for fresh horses.

Sometimes the horses walked so slowly that Daniel and Lavinia clambered out and walked alongside, holding hands, which at least gave them a chance to escape from the crowded coach interior. Traveling so close to the coast, the stage had to cross numerous streams, which obliged everyone to disembark and wait for the driver to make sure the flimsy and loose log bridges were aligned properly, and then drive the empty coach over. Then Daniel and Lavinia and the seven other passengers would carefully walk across and climb back on board.

At one point, after bouncing over a particularly deep rut, one of the leather straps supporting the coach broke, with a resounding noise and a grinding lurch, throwing them into each other's laps. They disembarked while the driver went into the woods and cut down a small pine tree to replace the strap and wedged it cleverly under the coach, after which they resumed their journey.

Daniel's affinity for the children charmed Lavinia. He played games and told them stories to help pass the time, and occasionally took one to sit or sleep on his lap for a while. Lavinia herself felt awkward and tongue-tied around the children. She began to wonder how she would manage if she ever had one of her own.

The inns separated men and women so Daniel and Lavinia couldn't share a room on the journey. She might still feel embarrassed thinking about the things they had done together in the Smithville cottage, but she missed being able to fall asleep in his arms. It seemed so strange that having relations was now permitted when for her entire life she had been taught that such things were forbidden. Perhaps it would have felt more real if they'd had a church wedding and Sarah's blessing. She still shuddered when she thought about the shabby and disheveled appearance of Mr. Johnson, the justice of the peace.

When the stage arrived in Charleston, she remembered the trip that she and Sarah had taken with Father a few years before. They had stayed at the Mills House, within walking distance of the market square, with second floor porches and a charming courtyard filled with roses and azaleas. Lavinia felt disappointed not to be able to walk into town and see the sights as she had with Father and Sarah. Before, they had walked the lovely streets of Charleston and bought a delicate handwoven basket from one of the ladies there. In fact, this was where Lavinia had become familiar with the writings of Sarah Grimké, whose family came from Charleston. She and Daniel could never stay in such a place on this journey. The inn where the stage stopped was humble and cramped, and the bed looked filthy and flea-ridden.

"Do you think Sarah has received my letter by now? She must have, don't you think?" Daniel and Lavinia had just finished the salted pork and cornbread they'd been served for a late dinner. "She had to have been overjoyed to find out I'm alive. She's probably waiting for me on pins and needles."

"You've asked me that about a dozen times, my love," Daniel teased her. "I wish we could have sent the letter by carrier pigeon, and that way we'd be sure it had arrived, rather than depending on the mail service. But yes, I would be willing to bet that your sister has your letter." He gave her a mischievous smile.

"Daniel!" She gave him a light smack on his arm. "You're making light of my worries. Sarah might have sent a reply or even some money for our journey." She took a sip of the bitter coffee they'd been served. "And she'll be heartbroken about Father."

"Everything will be fine once we arrive in Savannah and you see your sister with your own eyes." Daniel then took her face in his hands and gave her a kiss. Not being able to sleep next to each other while traveling increased their desire, and they lingered with their kiss.

And so, her worries were forgotten for another night. After two days of traveling she fell into bed and was asleep immediately.

They embarked on the second stage of the journey to Savannah the next day long before sunrise. All their companions this time were men traveling for business purposes. Lavinia was the only woman in the party. The men were deferential and called her Mrs. Ridge, which she found a bit jarring at first. It was difficult growing used to her new name and status.

This coach, one of the newer styles called the Concord and painted an elegant crimson, offered a more comfortable ride, more like the rocking of a cradle than the jouncing of a wagon. They conversed with more ease than in the more open wagon they'd ridden to Charleston, though the roads, if possible, were even worse, and the coachman ordered the group to get out and walk almost once an hour. As the flat coastal countryside rolled slowly by, graced with live oaks and scrub pines, the men discussed business, inventions, and the recession, and Lavinia listened with interest.

"Have any of you seen or heard of the electric telegraph?" One gentleman, who introduced himself as Maurice Levy and was handsomely dressed in a waistcoat and cravat—the way Daniel had been when she first saw him—seemed eager for a discussion. She thought of how Daniel looked now, in his faded and donated clothing, and how she must look. She wanted these gentlemen to know that she and Daniel were not as poor as they looked but then felt ashamed. Father had always taught them to care about appearances as a way to bolster the business, but she had been reminded of late that the impression of wealth was not the same as integrity or depth of character. Some of the kind people of Smithville had very little to call their own but they had seen their way clear to helping Daniel and Lavinia time and time again, and she would surely never forget it.

"I read that a man named Mr. Samuel Morse has conducted an experiment in New Jersey with sending a message over a wire for a distance of two miles," Mr. Levy continued, speaking with authority. "And he gave a demonstration to President Van Buren."

"I never heard of such a thing," said Mr. Marron, a cynical-looking man. "It's too far-fetched. Something like that will never get funding."

"Funding for the railroad was voted down at first as well,"

Daniel said. "But now there's more support, and the railroads are beginning to flourish. I can envision a time when this land is connected by railroads from Chicago to Charleston to New Orleans and all the way out west."

"Think of the massive amount of work. Who will lay all that track?" Mr. Bishop, a young man in a fine top hat, gave Daniel a skeptical look.

"It is backbreaking work, but there are plenty of men eager to have it."

"Yes, slaves, who haven't a choice. I'm sure they're quite eager." Mr. Marron glanced at Daniel. "Do you work for the railroad?"

"I do." Daniel sat straighter. "I'm employed by the Pontchartrain Railroad between the Mississippi River and Lake Pontchartrain. It's been successfully operating since 1831. We built six miles of track, some of it directly through swampland where the roadbeds had to be built up."

"You speak of only six miles of successful track. To cross our country would require thousands of miles of track. Over mountains and rivers no less. I can't see how it can be done," said Mr. Marron.

"Look at the aqueducts built by the Romans." Lavinia couldn't help herself, she had to speak. "I think that mankind can do whatever we set out to do. Besides, aren't they already building a railroad from Savannah to Macon?"

All of the men stopped and stared at her as if they had forgotten she was there, but Daniel squeezed her hand to show his support, endearing himself to her.

"Railroads are the future of this country." Daniel added. "We make seven round trips per day on the Pontchartrain. In fact, I recently sailed on the *Pulaski* for Baltimore to take delivery on a new steam engine."

"The *Pulaski*?" Mr. Levy sat forward. "The shipwrecked *Pulaski*?"

"The same." Daniel kept gentle hold of her hand. "My wife

and I were fortunate to be among very few survivors, though we still feel the effects of our time floating on the water."

"But we also fell in love on the water and were just married," Lavinia interjected.

"Best wishes to you both." Mr. Bishop tipped his hat. "I believe I read a newspaper account of you. What an astonishing story of survival!"

Lavinia thought about Mr. Morgan, who had stood outside the window during their wedding ceremony. That story must have carried to other papers. She hoped it had made it to Sarah and William in Savannah. And even to Daniel's sisters in New Orleans.

"We were greatly blessed to have survived. Thank God the cargo ship that picked us up saw us when they did. Three previous ships had sailed by without seeing us."

"A miracle!" Mr. Marron no longer looked so cynical.

At that moment, they heard shouting out in front of the horses, and the coach came to a screeching stop so violent that Lavinia, most embarrassingly, landed in the lap of the man on the bench across from her. As she scrambled away, the shouts became more recognizable.

"Stop there!" The sharp ear-ringing report of a rifle shot rang out.

What in the world was happening? She squeezed next to Daniel, and grabbed his arm, her heart pounding.

"Everyone out!" came a shouted command.

"Stagecoach robbers!" whispered Mr. Bishop.

Daniel pressed her to her seat behind him, placing himself between her and the sounds of the commotion outside. "Don't get out."

"I said get out of the coach! Everybody!"

"Does anyone have a pistol?" Mr. Marron's hoarse whisper sounded just behind Lavinia.

The other men began climbing out of the carriage.

"Give me your hatpin," Daniel whispered. "And stand behind

me."

She glanced at his intense face, then quickly reached up and pulled the hatpin from the wedding bonnet Mrs. Gosher had given her. She slipped it to him, and he slid it up his sleeve as they clambered out, legs wobbly, onto the muddy road.

Two skinny and ill-clad young men stood with long rifles, one with a dirty beard, the other clean-shaven, looking little more than a boy. Both wore patched and threadbare clothing and looks of desperation.

"Empty your pockets on the ground!" The bearded one's voice cracked with stress, while the younger one, who had one black and bloodshot eye, gestured with his rifle.

The three businessmen tossed clinking bags of coins on the ground. With regret, Daniel threw down the three gold pieces that Dr. Gosher had given him for their travels. They clattered forlornly in contrast to the fat bags the others had tossed. He took Lavinia's trembling hand and pulled her further behind him.

The bearded man told the younger one to kick the bags over toward him and he kept the rifle pointed at the driver while he gathered them into his saddlebag.

"Now the mailbag." The bearded one gestured threateningly toward the driver with his rifle. The driver quickly retrieved it and handed it to him.

"Keep them covered." The bearded one addressed the younger one and ran to his horse with the mailbag and tied it quickly to his saddlebag. In an instant, he had mounted his horse, jabbed his spurs into its sides and galloped away, leaving his partner alone and just as penniless as he had been when they rode up.

The younger man's mouth fell open; he staggered with disbelief at his partner's treachery, and then he retrained his rifle on the group of them and cleared his throat. "Nobody moves! I know you have more!" The young gunman shook, and the barrel of the rifle wavered.

Mr. Marron and Mr. Bishop spread their arms to indicate they had nothing more. Mr. Levy shook his head as well. Everyone had turned breathless and pale.

The gunman hesitated, uncertain and dangerous, then saw Lavinia's topaz necklace.

"Give it to me." He moved closer and reached out his hand for her to toss it to him. He was near enough that she could smell the woods and the days on him, the sourness of his fear.

Just as she reached for the clasp behind her neck, Daniel darted forward and stabbed the bandit's trigger hand with the hat pin. With a shout, the young man dropped the rifle.

They both scrambled for the gun, but Daniel got hold of it first and turned it on the robber. "If you leave now, I won't shoot." With a look of horror and fear, the young man began to back away.

As a warning, Daniel shot the rifle into the air, with an exploding report and sprinkling of leaves raining down. Both of the carriage horses neighed and reared, and the young gunman's horse wheeled and galloped away through the woods.

The boy turned and sprinted away into the woods after his horse, the underbrush crashing around them.

Mr. Bishop removed his top hat and wiped his brow while Mr. Marron and Mr. Levy collapsed against the side of the carriage. The driver moved to calm the horses.

No one spoke for several moments.

Lavinia drew a deep shaking breath.

"Are you all right?" Daniel took both of her hands in his.

She nodded, feeling weak.

"Everyone else all right?" Daniel looked around at the men, who nodded their assent. "Shall we get on with our journey?"

THE ATMOSPHERE INSIDE the carriage altered after that. The travelers expressed amazement about Daniel's boldness, and

Lavinia could see the way he had risen in esteem in their eyes. She squeezed into the back corner of the carriage, exhausted but inordinately proud of Daniel. He had protected them all, and he'd saved her necklace, her last remaining gift from her father. Mr. Bishop even asked for Daniel's card, and when Daniel replied he had none that had survived the shipwreck, Mr. Bishop gave his to Daniel, expressing interest in the Pontchartrain Railroad. Mr. Levy followed suit.

The landscape, as they neared Savannah, became more familiar to her, with the Spanish moss hanging from the trees, the sweeping rice and cotton plantations, the red clay roads, the shaded squares, and the graceful Georgian houses with their large columned porches. Anticipation built up inside her, with a more rapid beating of her heart and a growing breathlessness. They were alive and she was finally back in Savannah.

Home!

CHAPTER ELEVEN

June 1838
Savannah

IT WAS LATE in the day when the carriage at last stopped at the end of the line—the Pulaski Hotel on Old Bay Street in Savannah. Lavinia would never have walked the distance to her house on Oglethorpe Square in the past—not at this time of the evening and with all the mud and horse manure in the streets—but she thought differently now and was too excited to be home to pause another moment. Daniel and Lavinia bid their traveling companions goodbye and grasped their small bags of belongings.

"This way." She led Daniel south down East Bay Street toward Abercorn Street, and down to Oglethorpe Square, where the Onslows' Georgia gray brick residence stood. Her knees were weak and weary from traveling, yet the thought of being so close to home energized her. "When I think of the amount of luggage that Father and I brought on the *Pulaski*—we each had two full trunks of clothing, shoes, bonnets, and hats—Lord, it was so important for us to be wearing the proper headwear." She walked with Daniel along the river. "The entire back of our carriage was full of our luggage."

"I like you better without a hat anyway." He smiled at her. "You survived—we both did—that's what's important."

Thinking of arriving home again, of seeing Sarah, and Clementine, and Peter, and of all the changes that had taken place, tears streamed down her face as she shuffled down the road.

Daniel stopped and took her in his arms. "Oh, my dear, I am here with you. And Sarah will be overcome with joy to see you."

"I look such a mess after all this traveling. She may not even recognize me! And I'm coming home without Father!"

"You've . . . we've . . . been through a great tragedy. Now you will be able to mourn your father together. Do you think she will like me?" he added with a smile.

She laughed through her tears. "Sarah wants to marry William, and Father told her she ought to wait for me to marry. She will adore you!"

She felt ready to drop by the time they approached their block on Oglethorpe Square. With a pounding heart and aching feet, she looked up at the white columns, the elegant gray door, and the second story porch with the white trim and the potted roses. Black mourning bunting spread over the front windows and hung from the upstairs porch. Clearly they'd already begun mourning Father's death. She hoped they had indeed received her letter and that the bunting was not also for her. It was an unsettling thought.

She climbed the front steps and turned the brass doorknob.

Then the door squeaked open, and she stepped inside.

"Sarah? Clementine?" Sarah walked into the hall, a question in her lovely dark eyes. Her pale face was drawn, her dark brown hair pulled back and braided.

"May I . . ." Sarah started, then stared. Her mouth fell open as she took in Lavinia's appearance. Lavinia could only imagine—her frame still a bit thin, her hair unkempt from days of travel, her faded clothes, the flea bites, dust and dirt from the road.

"It's me."

"Lavinia?" Sarah put her hand over her mouth, bursting into tears. "Oh my God—you're alive!" She took Lavinia into her arms and Lavinia cried again, too. They hugged each other, rocking each other back and forth, for a long time. Finally, Sarah held her at arm's length.

"I thought you were dead."

"I saw the black bunting and wondered if you'd received my letter."

"No. No letter ever came."

Her heart squeezed in pain, for now she would need to confirm for Sarah that Father was gone. And tell her about Daniel. "It should have arrived days ago—long before me. I'm sorry it took me so long to come home, dearest. We've been traveling by stagecoach because I couldn't bear the idea of getting back on a ship. And I know I must look a fright, too. Oh, and I should introduce Daniel Ridge." She hesitated a moment, then plunged in. "My husband."

"Your *husband?*" Sarah, wide-eyed, examined Daniel in his threadbare borrowed clothes. At least Daniel had managed to shave before they left last night's inn.

Daniel stepped forward to kiss Sarah's hand. "It's an honor and a pleasure to meet the dear sister of my treasured wife. Lavinia speaks of you with such fondness."

"A pleasure, yes, Mr. Ridge." Sarah put her hand over her chest and shook her head in disbelief. "You're alive and you're married!"

Lavinia nodded. "Yes."

"And Father—?"

Lavinia tried to answer but couldn't. Her lips tried to form the words but only tears came. Sarah wilted, seeing the answer in Lavinia's eyes. And then they fell into each other's arms again and cried together, Lavinia holding her sister's slim shoulders as she sobbed.

At that moment Clementine came downstairs, her dark skin and hair gleaming. "Miss Lavinia!" She immediately began to cry, drawing a handkerchief from her apron pocket to her face. "I don't believe my eyes."

ONCE INSIDE HER childhood room with the blue wallpaper, Lavinia skimmed out of her filthy clothes, put on one of her old soft cotton nightgowns, and climbed into bed. Daniel borrowed some of her father's nightclothes and climbed in next to her, equally exhausted. Now that they were safely home, the full effects of the last two weeks overwhelmed them both. Lavinia began having nightmares of floating back on the water and Daniel experienced bouts of shouting in his sleep. Dr. Mallard came and examined them both and prescribed bedrest. He treated the nearly healed gash on Lavinia's arm and pronounced that she was lucky it had not become infected. Clementine and Sarah nursed them back to health gently with tea and toast with jam.

Lavinia awoke one morning after several days of agitated sleeping and dreamlike waking, to find Sarah sitting beside her bed. She took her hand.

"How are you feeling, Livvy?"

She put her other hand over Sarah's and took a deep breath. Her sister's dark hair curled smoothly and beautifully as always, but her face was pale and tired.

"I believe I'm a bit better." She pushed herself up on her elbows. "Where's Daniel?"

"He's up and about today for the first time." Sarah held her hand tighter and took a shaky breath. "I thank God that you survived, Livvy! It was a miracle! You wouldn't believe the loss of so many people from Savannah. The mayor has declared a time of mourning and has canceled all the Fourth of July celebrations. More than half the passengers on the *Pulaski* died."

"Oh, how heartbreaking. I can't imagine how many people must be grieving." Lavinia remembered Sarah's previous plans which had kept her at home. "If not for those celebrations, Sarah, you might have been on the *Pulaski*."

"I did think about that, Livvy. I can't tell you how afraid we all were, waiting for news. And then you and Father weren't on the lists of survivors in the paper. I couldn't eat or sleep for days. Clementine had a terrible time with me." Sarah then held up a tattered and stained letter. "And look what finally arrived by stage."

Lavinia's own handwriting looped across the battered letter. She sighed. "Oh, it finally arrived. I wonder where it's been."

That afternoon, Lavinia put on a cool lilac muslin frock that hadn't been new enough to take to Saratoga Springs. Though most of her elegant dresses had gone down with the ship, what had remained in her wardrobe was comfortable and familiar and hers. Having access once again to her closet of clothing was a luxury that Lavinia vowed never to take for granted again. She and Sarah sat in rockers on the upstairs porch, enjoying each other's company and fanning away the heat of the day. Daniel joined them after a while in some old summer trousers, a shirt, and suspenders that had belonged to Father. He was slightly shorter than Father, and it looked as though Clementine had hemmed the pants legs for him. Daniel's blonde curls were struggling to free themselves from the pomade he'd used, presumably also Father's. It was slightly startling at first to see him in Father's clothes, and Lavinia could tell that Sarah noticed, too, but neither woman mentioned it.

After he settled into his own rocker, Sarah asked Daniel how he was feeling. Like Lavinia, he was finally starting to feel himself again.

"Thank you from the bottom of my heart, Mr. Ridge," Sarah went on, "for bringing my sister back alive."

Daniel nodded. "I am grateful that both of us have lived to return and that I can meet you and see Lavinia's home."

"You are very welcome here."

Lavinia was touched by Sarah's overture to this stranger in her home and the three of them sat in pleasant conversation for some time. Eventually, Daniel and Lavinia took turns telling parts of the story of their shipwreck, deliverance to Smithville, marriage, journey to Savannah, and stagecoach robbery.

"Lavinia told me while we floated on the sea that she felt bonnets now seemed somewhat useless, but look how useful even your hatpin was!" Daniel observed.

"That is a way of looking at it," Lavinia agreed with a laugh. They had just settled into a companionable silence when Clementine appeared with glasses of lemonade on a tray.

"Thank you, Clementine, for altering these trousers for me." Daniel smiled his gratitude.

"You're welcome, Mr. Ridge." Clementine gave him a nod. "Somebody ought to get some use out of his clothes."

Tears started to fill Lavinia's eyes, and she saw the same happening to Sarah.

"I think we should have a funeral, Sarah. If he had survived, we would have had word by now. It will be good to say farewell properly."

Sarah's voice broke. "I suppose you're right."

"Yes, it's time," Clementine agreed before she withdrew into the house.

As the younger sister, Sarah would be looking to Lavinia to know what to do. Yet neither of them had ever been involved in planning a funeral before; Lavinia had been only three and Sarah had been an infant when their mother had died. Possibly Daniel could help, since his parents had died only a few years ago.

Lavinia struggled to get her thoughts in order. "We should go to the church tomorrow and speak to the Reverend, should we not? Is that how you did it, Daniel?"

"Yes, I contacted our priest. The church leaders handle these situations all the time."

"I'll write Reverend Collins this afternoon, requesting a meeting."

Sarah agreed, wiping her cheeks. At that moment, a gig pulled up just below them on the cobblestone street and William stepped out, tying his hackney to the narrow stone hitching post out front. A few moments later, Clementine showed him onto the porch, and Sarah introduced him to Daniel.

"Lavinia, what a blessing you've survived! And Mr. Ridge, a pleasure to make your acquaintance." William kissed Lavinia's hand, and then shook Daniel's. He was a thin, scholarly young man who studied law with a local firm and was completing his final clerkship before being admitted to the bar. "I spent the better part of two weeks shoring up your sister. She was beside herself with worry and sorrow when we received news of the *Pulaski*. She prayed every day to see your names on any of the survivors' lists in the papers."

"Oh, I can only imagine how it must have been, poor Sarah." She took her younger sister's hand. "She and Clementine have been wonderful nurses for us since we arrived home in such sad shape."

"Truly, you are quite the hero, Mr. Ridge." William sat down next to Daniel. "You shepherded Miss Onslow through this ordeal. And now married! Sarah and I just learned before the trip that Mr. Onslow wanted us to delay our nuptials until such time as Lavinia might wed, and suddenly it has happened in one fell swoop!"

Did William need to bring up how inconvenienced he'd been so directly, and with Daniel sitting right there? Lavinia felt a muscle tighten in her jaw, and she changed the subject.

"How is the shop?" she asked Sarah. "Has Mr. Mason been in charge these past few weeks? Have you been in to visit or to look at the books?"

Sarah shook her head. "Clementine advised me that I should go in, but I was too worried and grieved about you and father. I must admit I allowed Mr. Mason to take care of everything."

"We should go by the store tomorrow as well." Perhaps it was just that she'd been too long abed, but Lavinia suddenly felt an urgency to take an overseer's role in her father's business. Mr. Mason was certainly trustworthy, but Lavinia wanted to review the books for herself.

"You should be careful not to overdo, my dear." Daniel patted her hand. "We're both recovering, and I wouldn't want you to relapse."

"But Father would want us to keep a close eye on our business." Lavinia folded her fan and placed it on her lap, certain in her decision to turn her attention to the shop.

"Well," said William drily, "due to coverture, control of the business in all likelihood now belongs to Mr. Ridge, depending, of course, on the terms of your father's will."

Sarah nodded but turned pale. "We know about coverture. But no one expected Father to die and Lavinia to marry all in a few weeks. What are you planning for the shop, Livvy?"

Lavinia glanced at Daniel, and then Sarah. "Well, I hadn't yet worked things out in my head. Of course, I've been helping Father with the store for several years now, and I've long anticipated that I would always be involved with the store on some level. But Daniel has a position with the railroad down in New Orleans that he is eager to return to. So, clearly, there are quite a few issues that Daniel and I still need to work out."

Sarah fanned herself weakly. "Lavinia, Father spent his entire life building Onslow's Millinery from the bottom up. It's our family business."

"Sarah, Daniel *is* family now. He is my husband." Even as Lavinia said this, though, she understood Sarah's meaning. Why, she'd known Daniel for less than three weeks! And now he had a right to control her father's business, possibly jointly with Sarah, as an unmarried woman. That was the law, and it had occurred to her, certainly, but it was still strange to contemplate. "Besides, we haven't even seen Father's will. Let's get through the funeral first, before we begin concerning ourselves with these matters."

She glanced at Daniel. He had been looking uncomfortable but seemed to relax at that.

"Let me point out that once Sarah and I are married, I will be family, too," William leaned forward for emphasis. "And I will be a joint owner."

"Mr. Ridge." Sarah crossed her arms. "Please, tell me what

you know about the millinery business." Lavinia wasn't surprised that William would bring up his own interests this way, but Sarah's reaction took her aback. She had expected that Sarah would agree with her and leave this unpleasant conversation to a more appropriate time.

"I'm not familiar with the millinery business." Daniel cleared his throat, then used a conciliatory tone. "I've never once in my life thought of myself as a milliner. The business I know is the railroad business. That said, I am a quick study. And that I trust Lavinia implicitly goes without saying. I agree with Lavinia—now is the time to plan the funeral, not concern ourselves with the disposition of property." Daniel took her hand as he spoke.

Lavinia studied Daniel, then watched Sarah's face.

Sarah seemed to be about to protest but then thought better of it. She closed her mouth and fanned herself with renewed energy. "Lavinia," she finally said. "I would like to speak with you in private."

Sarah and Lavinia excused themselves. As they withdrew Daniel gave Lavinia a concerned look, and then she overheard Daniel asking William how many employees worked for Onslow's Millinery.

Sarah and Lavinia went into her bedroom, where Sarah shut the door and then exclaimed, "Livvy, what are we to do? And what will become of *me* now that Onslow's Millinery will be co-owned by your husband?" Red spots of anger shone on Sarah's pale cheeks. "And what about this house? Does your husband now co-own this house as well?"

"Sarah, we have no idea what Father has put in his will. There are many decisions that must be made. Let's plan a funeral we know will properly honor Father, and deal with the other issues later." Up until now, the two sisters had never questioned what they had. They had both used their father's accounts at shops in town and bought whatever they wanted. Lavinia truly did not know how that might change. "Why don't you and William set a date?"

"William hasn't even been admitted to the bar yet."

"But of course, he will be, Sarah. He's very knowledgeable and well-connected." William's family home was only a few blocks away, in one of the fashionable Savannah neighborhoods, an historic Federal-style mansion with a graceful side porch. His family's consequence in the community all but ensured him a bright career.

But Sarah would not be placated. "Everything that's happened has been horrible, Livvy! As much as I'd wished you would marry, I never thought things would end up like this. Why, you don't even know what kind of family Daniel comes from. At least we know William's family."

"Sarah! That's not fair!"

"Why not? All you know about him is that he's handsome and he saved your life."

"I—I know more than that. He's told me stories about his family." Lavinia hesitated, though. She did know very little about Daniel. Had they indeed been too hasty in their decision to marry, basing it on desire rather than higher qualities of character? As she often did in her arguments with Sarah, she changed the subject. "Sarah, I meant what I said before. You and William could marry right away. Why don't you set a date? You're already engaged."

Sarah's eyes filled with tears as the fight left her. "Why did Father need to die?" she whispered. Lavinia, her heart breaking for her sister, for her father, for herself, wrapped her arms around Sarah and the two of them stood in that childhood bedroom and held each other for a long moment.

A knock sounded at the door, and Clementine, carrying the tray of empty lemonade glasses, poked her head into the room. "Everything all right in here, Miss Lavinia? Miss Sarah?"

"Yes, Clementine." Lavinia stroked Sarah's hair and then they pulled apart.

"Clementine, could you ask Peter to have the horses ready to take the carriage out tomorrow morning? Sarah and I need to go see Reverend Collins."

"That sounds real good." Clementine nodded and headed down the hall.

THAT NIGHT, DANIEL reached for Lavinia in bed. It felt somehow sinful for them to be together in her childhood bed. Everything about life and the world was so strange now that they were back here. Did her girlhood room seem smaller, more constricting?

"Quiet, Sarah may still be up reading." She smelled soap as he nestled her closer to him.

"She knows we are husband and wife. I want to sleep with my arms around you." He took her face in his hands and kissed her. When his lips touched hers, a tingle awoke senses over her entire body, but she pulled away.

"Still, she's right next door, and she might hear us. I don't want to offend her. She is already upset enough."

"I will be quiet as a little mouse." Daniel's hands touched her in places that made her skin feel on fire. "Let's enjoy being married tonight. We're finally well enough again. If you think Sarah will hear us, let's move to the guest room across the hall."

The guest room seemed infinitely better than this room, with all her childhood memories and even one or two of her old dolls watching from atop her bookshelf, so they took the candle and tiptoed across the hall to the guest room, and nestled in together, giggling with every telltale rustle of the bedsheets.

Later, when they were lying entwined in each other's arms, slightly sweaty and out of breath, as the night was hot, Daniel said, "I bet she didn't hear a thing."

"Oh, she most likely did. She's a light sleeper."

"I'm afraid your sister isn't fond of me."

"It's not that, Daniel. She's vexed by the situation. Imagine how she must feel. This stranger appears who suddenly has become the joint owner of *everything* in her life, possibly including the house she lives in. She's been cared for by our father all her life and now he's gone."

"Surely she understands that I would never pretend to be a milliner."

"She only just met you, Daniel. We need to protect her until she and William get married. William comes from a good family here in Savannah, a family we know well."

"We should promote their marriage," Daniel said. "I think, yes, as soon as possible."

Why was Lavinia so annoyed by this statement? Hadn't she suggested the same thing to Sarah just hours ago? And she hadn't told Daniel about her vague misgivings about William's possessive treatment of Sarah or about his rudeness to Peter and Clementine. Maybe he actually believed them a good match. Or was he in a hurry to marry off her sister so that he could get her out of the house?

"He seems like a fine fellow, if a bit on the pompous side."

Lavinia had to admit she agreed with Daniel's assessment of William.

As she lay with Daniel, her mind drifted back to her disagreement with Sarah. She and Sarah almost never disagreed; this deeply troubled Lavinia. Sarah was right that she didn't know whether Daniel came from a good family or not. She'd heard his stories, while they were floating, about his parents' death, life with his sisters, of the plays his young cousins performed. She had seen his kindness to children. But what in fact did she know about him? Nothing except that he was brave and resourceful and loving and that he had saved her life more than once. She felt passion for him, which was what she had always wanted. But was that enough? All of a sudden she wondered—were there advantages to Father's business-like and analytical approach to marriage?

What would Father have thought of her choice?

"I'd better go back to my own room."

"Why? We're man and wife. We should sleep together."

But now the bed with the two of them in it felt insufferably hot and small.

"I'm stifling. I'm going back to my own room." So she went back to her room, washed up in the basin, crawled under the quilt, then lay awake for a long time, thinking.

CHAPTER TWELVE

July 1838
Savannah

L AVINIA AWOKE THE next morning, her senses still alive with
Daniel's touches from the night before and feeling regretful
for having left his side. Still in her nightclothes, she tiptoed across
the hall to the guest room, but the bed was empty, neatly made.
She ran down the hall, glanced downstairs, then back in her
bedroom to peer out the window at the live oak shading their
empty street on Oglethorpe Square below. Where had Daniel
gone? Were they in good standing with each other? She'd never
left his bed before. In fact, they'd almost never had a disagreement, except the one on the raft about food and death when they
were half-delirious. She wasn't even sure if what had happened
the night before qualified as a quarrel. But it fueled her doubts.

In a state of agitation, she went out again into the upstairs
hall, where Sarah stopped her.

"Livvy, Reverend Collins sent an answer to our note and can
meet with us at ten this morning." She smiled. "Don't forget your
gloves.

Reverend Collins! Lavinia's hand went to her bare head, flus-
tered, as she thought of her time in Smithville when she'd
considered herself simply lucky to be alive, and gone about bare-

headed and without gloves. In her bedroom, she dressed as quickly as she could, sliding her chemise over her head, pulling on her crinolines and hoop skirt, finding a suitable day dress and searching until she found dark gray gloves and a restrained bonnet that reflected the proper mood.

Back out in the hall, she pulled on the gloves. "We'll need to make ourselves each a black dress. I'll ask Mrs. Thomas to help." She felt a little lightheaded; so many societal requirements, such a part of her life before, seemed to have escaped her since the shipwreck.

Sarah nodded and squeezed her hand. "Of course, Mrs. Thomas will help."

Lavinia hesitated. She hated needing to ask Sarah the whereabouts of her own husband, but she could avoid the question no longer. "Sarah, have you seen Daniel?"

Sarah looked surprised. "Why, no. He's not in your room?"

"I'll ask Clementine." If anything happened in the Onslow household, Clementine knew about it. Lavinia drew a deep breath, trying to calm herself, and skimmed down the stairs. She found Clementine, white-aproned, spooning biscuits into a basket in the warming kitchen.

"Miss Lavinia, you best eat something before meeting with the Reverend."

"Yes, I will, but have you seen—"

"Peter said he took the draft horse but didn't say where he was going."

Lavinia caught her breath. Possibly he had simply gone for a ride, or to the site far out Oglethorpe Avenue, to Louisville Road, where they were working on the railroad depot, machine shops, and track to Macon. He had mentioned wanting to see it.

As soon as Lavinia and Sarah finished breakfast, Peter had the carriage ready. On the way to the chapel they passed stately Savannah homes, the sandy streets shaded by the magnolia, palmetto, and live oak trees, with black bunting hanging over the windows and from the porches of many. A gloomy pall hung over the city, after the tragedy, and the departure of so many to cooler northern climes. The July air in Savannah was so sultry and thick that sweat trickled down Lavinia's ribcage, between her breasts, and into the tops of her long gloves. Just blocks away, the sails shimmered on dozens of ships moored at the docks on the Savannah River.

Sarah broke the silence. "I feel terrible about yesterday, Livvy. I'm so grateful you're back, and I see that Daniel is a good man. I'm sorry for the things I said about him."

Lavinia squeezed Sarah's hand, relieved to have the air cleared but still wishing she knew where her husband had gone.

At last, they arrived at Wesley Chapel.

"May the Lord watch over you in your grief," Reverend Collins, dressed in his somber black suit clasped Lavinia's hands and then Sarah's. "Your father was an outstanding citizen of this city, always generous, respected and admired by many. He will be greatly missed. It's a blessing, Miss Onslow, that God was with you and you survived."

"Actually, it's Mrs. Ridge," Sarah said quietly. "My sister is newly married."

Reverend Collins' abundant eyebrows shot up. "Married! Now that is a surprise. I always thought I would have the pleasure of performing your marriage ceremony."

Lavinia should have expected this. "Oh, and I wished for that as well, but my husband was very eager for us to join in matrimony after we were rescued."

"Of course. Well, I offer you my best wishes for a productive and obedient life together in the Lord." The Reverend invited them to sit in the straight-backed chairs around a small octagonal leather-covered table in his office. Lavinia and Sarah removed their gloves, arranged their skirts, and sat down.

"As you know, many residents of Savannah died in the wreck of the *Pulaski*, and I've been holding numerous memorial services. In cases such as this . . ." Reverend Collins hesitated, delicately avoiding mentioning that their father's body had not been recovered. A lump rose in Lavinia's throat. The last conversation she'd had with Father had been a disagreement. Tears sprang to her eyes. Her last words to him had been in a raised voice. She could blame the wind, but in her heart she still felt regrets. She pulled a handkerchief from her velvet drawstring reticule, but before she could mop her wet cheeks, she noticed Sarah crying, too, so she handed the handkerchief to Sarah and fished out a spare one for herself. Sarah dabbed her eyes.

"We've been conducting memorial services in the sanctuary. And his name can be added to the family headstone at Colonial Park Cemetery. If you like, the family can be present, and I can say a few words."

Lavinia only nodded as she didn't trust herself to speak just yet.

"What were your father's favorite Bible verses? And favorite hymns?" Reverend Collins, allowing them a moment to recover, then produced a well-used leather notebook and quill pen.

"We should know Father's favorites." Sarah's voice broke. "But I must admit I don't."

Lavinia swallowed hard, clearing her throat. "Father was fond of quoting John 3:15—'That whosoever believeth in him should not perish, but have eternal life.' And I believe he liked the hymn 'Rock of Ages.'" A wistful memory of Father's trembly and earnest tenor as he stood singing beside her in church enveloped her. And it dawned on her that her new husband—whose whereabouts she hoped to know soon—would not have learned those hymns.

"I think he also liked 'Christ the Lord is Risen Today,'" Sarah added. "Remember?" She smiled at Lavinia, putting her hand on her arm. "He always strained to reach that high note?"

This memory brought a smile, but Lavinia felt her face collapse again, and she searched her reticule for another handkerchief.

Reverend Collins was not a man of few words. Sarah and Lavinia sat, weeping on and off, sharing their grief as they had shared so many things before in their lives, their eyes downcast as he described the verses he would read and gave them a sampling of the topics he would cover in his sermon for their father's service. They set a date for the following week, giving enough time for Father's obituary and announcement, which she and Sarah planned to write that afternoon, to appear in the *Savannah Georgian.*

After bidding Reverend Collins good-bye, Lavinia made a mental note to make a contribution to Wesley Chapel in Father's memory and then directed Peter to drive the carriage to Onslow's Millinery. En route, they passed carts and carriages, well-dressed men and women on horseback, slave women carrying baskets of laundry, rice, and cotton on their heads, and a few cows. Artfully arranged dry goods from rugs to foodstuffs beckoned from the glassed storefronts. Lavinia gazed with yearning at the window of the bookseller, which she had frequented so often to buy books. She remembered the conversation at sea with Daniel about *The Last of the Mohicans,* the memory a spark of pleasure on this sad day.

As the carriage rocked along, Sarah returned Lavinia's handkerchief. "Did Clementine know where Daniel went?"

Lavinia ran worried fingers over her recalcitrant coiled braids, shaking her head. "Only that he took the draft horse." She thought it was strange that he had left the house without telling her where he was going. Perhaps he had simply wanted to let her rest. If she hadn't left his bed she would know.

"I'm sure we'll find out soon enough. Don't worry, Livvy." Sarah touched her arm reassuringly.

At Onslow's Millinery, black bunting hung from the storefront windows. The same bonnets were displayed on the mannequins in the windows as the day Father and Lavinia had left on the *Pulaski,* which gave her a pang of sadness. Yet a new one with a bird of paradise feather—one of Father's favorite embellishments—and a beautiful black satin ribbon, adorned the mannequin next to the door. Lavinia wondered if it was Mrs.

Thomas' work or Abby's. And had Mr. Mason designed it? It must have been made in response to Savannah's current state of sorrow. It occurred to Lavinia that she might be able to wear it to Father's funeral. A hat from his shop with touches of his favorites seemed like just the right way to honor him.

Mr. Mason, dressed impeccably as ever, greeted her warmly. "Miss Lavinia, thank God you are alive! We were overjoyed when we heard the news." He kissed both her hand and Sarah's. "Of course we are all still devastated about your father." His eyes brimmed and reddened as he addressed both sisters.

"Thank you, Mr. Mason, that means a great deal," Lavinia said.

"I admired your father more than I can say."

Lavinia realized that Mr. Mason was close to losing his equanimity, and she tried to angle the conversation away from such personal sorrow. "The entire city seems to be in mourning—so many people were lost."

Mr. Mason went on. "Indeed, it is almost impossible to fathom this disaster."

"I'm sorry I haven't come before, Mr. Mason." Sarah gave Mr. Mason an apologetic look. "I have been overcome."

"I understand, Miss Sarah. And I have tried to do everything as I thought your father might want me to do it. I hope the two of you approve." Mr. Mason turned away, possibly trying to hide the fact that he wiped away a tear.

"You're very kind, Mr. Mason, and I know that you were very fond of Father." Lavinia lightly touched his sleeve in sympathy.

"Yes, indeed I was." Mr. Mason straightened his shoulders and cleared his throat. "Would you like to look at the books, Miss Lavinia? I must tell you, with this disaster, business has been slow, and the only bonnets we've been selling have been black. I had to order more black satin and silk. And bombazine."

Lavinia strolled with Sarah through the store toward the offices. Mr. Mason had kept everything immaculately dusted and displayed. All the black made the store look sedately fashionable.

As Mr. Mason was already upset, it did not seem appropriate to introduce the more festive subject of her marriage. She decided to save the news for another time.

She went for a moment into Father's office in the back, just off the hall to the work room. His pedestal desk stood solid and ordered. The leather-trimmed desk mat was aligned just so, the account books were neatly stacked, his favorite fountain pen lay in its case on the right-hand side, and the shelves were full of samples of fabrics, feathers, silk wildflowers, and ribbons.

Near his fountain pen stood three miniatures that he'd had painted—of their mother, Lavinia, and Sarah. Lavinia picked up each of the miniatures and studied them. The miniature of her mother showed her sweet smile, her lively dark eyes, and her dark hair, pulled into a sleek chignon under an elegant blue silk bonnet. How Lavinia wished she could remember her! The same artist painted the miniatures of Sarah and Lavinia several years later. Sarah was a girl of five, looking very much like her mother, dressed in pink, with the same smooth dark hair and sweet expression. Lavinia was a bare-headed girl of eight, somewhat gangly, auburn-haired and freckly. Her ringlets, as usual, strained free of her braids. The expression on her face could not have been called sweet. Determined, perhaps.

The faint smell of cigars permeated the office, making Lavinia feel almost as though Father were in the room. One of his top hats hung on the hat rack waiting for his return, and Lavinia ran her finger along the brim, remembering those last few moments with him on the *Pulaski*. With an ache in her chest, she shut the door and went back out to the floor.

"Everything looks excellent, Mr. Mason. We won't change any of the displays until after the last memorial service here in Savannah." She made the decision on a whim. "Father's service will be on Thursday of next week. And do you agree that the store should be closed?"

"I do, Miss Lavinia." Mr. Mason's chin trembled.

"We can look at the books sometime after the service. I'm

afraid I wouldn't be able to concentrate on it right now."

"Of course, Miss Lavinia."

Lavinia and Sarah then went into the back room, where Mrs. Thomas and Abby were at work. After the mother and daughter had offered their condolences, Lavinia asked if Mrs. Thomas might have some time to help them with mourning dresses.

"Yes, of course I can. I can come over in the evenings this week after I leave the shop," Mrs. Thomas assured them. "These are sad times in Savannah."

"Thank you, Mrs. Thomas," Sarah said. "I realize that will be a lot of time and effort for you, and we appreciate it."

As they prepared to depart the store, Sarah stopped beside the black bonnet in the window—the one with the bird of paradise feather. "Lavinia, I feel sure Father would want us to look our best for his memorial service. What would you think if I wore this bonnet?"

Lavinia hesitated for only a moment. "I think it would look wonderful on you. And I'm sure Father would like it." She quickly chose another, one more understated, for herself. Mr. Mason put both bonnets in boxes for them.

"Gee!" said Peter, slapping the reins, and Daisy headed down the street. Lavinia and Sarah discussed ideas for what to include in Father's obituary. But Lavinia was quieter than usual, preoccupied by questions about her husband's absence this morning, and she had to restrain herself from telling Peter to urge Daisy to a gallop so they could get home.

CHAPTER THIRTEEN

July 1838
Savannah

MIDAFTERNOON, THE SISTERS arrived home from the visits with Reverend Collins and the shop. After a light midday meal, Sarah felt tired and told Lavinia she was going to her room to rest before continuing with Father's obituary, while Clementine brought Lavinia some lemon water on the upstairs porch.

Worries about where Daniel might have gone kept insinuating themselves into Lavinia's thoughts. Lavinia was sorry now that she'd left his bed and couldn't think why she had done it. She'd carried her worries about last night throughout the day.

"Clementine, did Daniel return yet?" She attempted to make her tone casual.

"No, Miss Lavinia. Not yet." Clementine was usually so plainspoken, but she seemed disinclined to say more, and Lavinia could not read her face on the subject of Daniel today. She reached in her apron pocket and handed Lavinia a handful of calling cards she had gathered from the tray on the front hall table. "Some people came by to express their condolences since they heard you were feeling more yourself again."

"Thank you, Clementine."

"One of them was Mr. Trask," Clementine added, pointing to

one in particular. "He would like to meet with you after the funeral."

"Who is Mr. Trask?" Daniel's voice came from the porch door—he had returned.

Lavinia started and put a hand over her thudding heart. He must have come in at the back of the house from the stable.

"Father's lawyer." She turned to look at him. His dark blonde curls and cheeks were coated with dust and dirt, as were the frockcoat and breeches that he'd borrowed from Father's wardrobe. Where had he been? "Sarah and I need to meet with him anyway, but I suppose it will keep until after the funeral. I expect he'll want to be reading Father's will."

"Yes, of course." Daniel indicated his dirty clothes. "I'll go in and wash up in just a moment." He sat down beside her to rest for a moment, apparently at ease. Lavinia thought he might ask about the meeting this morning with Reverend Collins, but Daniel seemed satisfied to sit in silence, and Lavinia was having trouble interpreting his demeanor.

"How did you spend the day, Daniel?" She searched his face for clues that he harbored anger toward her, scrutinizing his hazel eyes behind his spectacles, but saw only goodwill and affection. He took her hand and caressed her palm with his thumb.

"I went out Oglethorpe Avenue to Louisville Road see some of the rail line on the Central of Georgia Railway that's been laid toward Macon and talked with some of the men there. It's very interesting—they plan to run trains in each direction on alternate days. It'll require several more years' work to complete the line, but I predict it'll become an efficient way to transport cotton from Macon."

"If you're right, it'll be good for Savannah and also save the life of many a poor horse." She ventured a smile at him. He did not seem angry after all. Her fears began to recede and, in their place, his touch on her palm inflamed her senses.

Daniel nodded. "Before I left this morning, I also wrote a letter to my sisters in New Orleans to let them know how to reach me here. And I've been thinking that once your father's memorial service is over, we should prepare to go back to New Orleans. I should write to my employers that I am on my way. The loss of their money for the engine is weighing on my mind. Also I'd like you to meet my sisters, Lavinia."

"I want to meet your sisters, too. And I know you are eager to see about your job." Lavinia's jaw and chest tightened. "But what about the shop? And this house? Decisions need to be made here. There's so much to think about with Father gone. The meeting with Mr. Trask should help. He'll be able to tell us what's in Father's will, and that will let us know how much needs to be done with the business and property. And since you are now my husband, you should be there, too." She gave Daniel a look of appeal and squeezed his hand. "Is there a chance that you could get on with the railroad here?"

He sighed and shook his head, letting go of her hand. "The men were welcoming, but because of the recession, the Georgia railroad hasn't the means to pay people in cash right now. They are paying mostly in stock, and I just don't have the wherewithal to be paid in stock right now. We should certainly attend the meeting with Trask, but at the nearest opportunity I'm eager to get back to New Orleans."

SARAH AND LAVINIA stood together in the chapel in the black dresses that Mrs. Thomas had spent several evenings helping them assemble over the last few days, as one visitor after another came to clasp their hands and offer their condolences. Reverend Collins' eulogy was what Lavinia expected—respectful and appreciative for all Father had done for the community, and also very long. The words played back in her mind, and she thought again about that terrible moment when Father had been there beside her on the deck of the *Pulaski*, his hand at her elbow, and then suddenly, with a blast and a horrible tremor, he was gone. She felt a chill even now as she remembered it. Father had left too soon, with too much more to do. Sarah and Lavinia had decided that there would be no trip to the cemetery. They planned to have his name added to the family headstone, as many other grieving families were doing, but it would be some time before that was ready. In the meantime, with no body to bury, there was no reason to go.

After the service, it was only fitting that mourners and friends be welcomed at the house, though Sarah and Lavinia agreed that they'd like nothing more than to close the curtains and go to bed for a week instead. Clementine had fixed ham biscuits, watercress sandwiches, a beef roast, and potato salad.

"Oh, Clementine, I cannot tell you how grateful we are for this." Lavinia helped her arrange the platters and pitchers of lemon water and coffee on the dining room table.

"We might have a crowd here today, Miss Lavinia." Clementine smoothed her apron. "You got to give people something to eat."

And the house filled within the hour. So many good people who had remembered her father. One sweet-looking woman sought her out.

"We used to be customers of Onslow's Millinery, you know, before my father lost his business. He died soon after, and we had no money for a burial or for clothing to wear. Your father was so kind to our family, Miss Lavinia. Not only did he help us with the expenses, but he sent bonnets and gloves for all the women in our family. It was a gesture we've never forgotten."

In the midst of her loss, it soothed Lavinia to learn how generous their father was to the people of Savannah when he was able.

After an hour in the front hall receiving visitors, she accepted a plate from Clementine.

"You'd best eat something." Lavinia found Clementine's brusque way of caretaking comforting. She had never said so, but

Lavinia wondered if Clementine didn't think that Lavinia's and Sarah's lives were mighty easy. Except, perhaps having lost their mother so young.

And now they were orphans.

A few moments later Daniel brought her a glass of Madeira. "It's been opened for the guests, and you'll be on your feet for a good long time this evening."

It made her remember the bottle of wine on the raft with Daniel. After drinking the Madeira, the conversations began to run together and she had little idea what she said to the rest of the many people she spoke to. Some of the visitors stayed until nightfall and found the single bottle of medicinal whiskey that Father kept in the house.

She felt grateful when Daniel and William showed the rest of the guests to the door, one by one. Then she fell into bed like a stone.

CHAPTER FOURTEEN

July 1838
Savannah

M R. TRASK KEPT an office on Oglethorpe Avenue, not far
from the courthouse, on a cobblestone street lined with
tall, white-barked sycamore trees in the heart of Savannah's
business district. Daniel and William both accompanied the sisters
to the meeting. While it made sense for Daniel to accompany her,
as they were married, William insisted on escorting Sarah even
though they were only betrothed. True, he was studying the law
and he and Sarah would be married soon, but it vexed Lavinia.

They didn't wait long before the clerk, Mr. Wilson, directed
them into Mr. Trask's office. The mahogany of Mr. Trask's
rolltop desk shone dark and sleek, and a stack of bound files
teetered on one edge.

To Lavinia's great surprise, young Mr. Mason was in the
room, seated somewhat awkwardly with his top hat on his knee.
He stood when they entered, looking somewhat abashed.

"Well, hello, Mr. Mason," said Lavinia, a little puzzled as to
why he should be present at the reading of her father's will. "I'm
surprised to see you here."

"I am sure I'm equally surprised to be here," Mr. Mason replied.

Possibly Father had left Mr. Mason some token of his esteem. That would be very like him to remember his faithful assistant.

"I'm glad to see you all," said Mr. Trask, heaving his bulky frame to his feet to shake William and Daniel's hands while Lavinia and Sarah removed their gloves. William and Daniel then helped them arrange their skirts and get seated on the settee across from Mr. Trask's desk. "And may I offer my condolences on the loss of your father, Miss Lavinia and Miss Sarah. His memorial service was very fitting for a man of stature in our Savannah community."

"We appreciated your attendance last evening, Mr. Trask."

Mr. Trask reached for a slim bound collection of papers on top of the stack on his desk. He produced a yellowed hand-written document on vellum paper. Lavinia recognized her father's signature at the bottom.

"You are a student of law, are you not, Mr. Anderson?"

"I am." William nodded.

"This will was executed ten years ago, when Lavinia and Sarah were both young girls." He seemed to be addressing his remarks primarily to William. Lavinia wished he would look at her. "It provides for the girls to have house privileges until such time as they might marry. He offers a cash fitting out gift for marriage for each of them of two hundred and fifty dollars, quite generous, and I have that here to give each of you. The two of them are to divide any cash resources from the business once all debts are paid. And the two of them are to divide their deceased mother's jewelry evenly between them."

"We've already done that." Sarah and Lavinia both remained silent after Lavinia's quick response. These small bequests were nothing they hadn't anticipated, and Lavinia was growing more anxious waiting for Mr. Trask to move on to how the bulk of the estate was meant to be handled. Had he given them different assets as his own father had done? Were she and Sarah to share everything equally?

"The millinery business and his two hundred thousand dollars in assets he has left are left to Mr. Mason, for his long-time service."

Mr. Mason's hat made a sharp thud as it fell from his lap to the floor. "I don't understand."

"Mr. Mason?" William raised his eyebrows, looking at Mr. Trask for confirmation.

"Excuse me?" Had she not heard correctly? Sarah and Lavinia sat in shocked silence, and Lavinia felt barely able to breathe. She glanced at Daniel, who seemed to be simply listening and taking things in. How could Father have left their only means of support to Mr. Mason? A person outside the family? And after all the years Lavinia helped Father with the bonnet designs and the bookkeeping? After a long moment, she drew in a breath and grasped Sarah's hand.

"How can that be?" Sarah threw her fan on the settee beside her.

I am the one who helped Father with the millinery shop! Lavinia's thoughts exploded, but due to Mr. Mason's presence she held her tongue.

"As I said, Mr. Onslow executed this will ten years ago. He wanted to provide for his unmarried daughters, but naturally assumed, I am sure, that once you were married your husbands would provide for you."

Lavinia felt faint. She couldn't blame it on a corset because she'd kept her word to herself after the shipwreck and had stopped wearing them. She pulled her fan from her sleeve and flapped it, trying to catch her breath.

"I—I didn't know, Miss Onslow," Mr. Mason stammered. "Please believe I had no idea. I thought possibly he'd left me his desk or something similar. May I assure you I'm just as stunned as you are."

"I don't think either you or Sarah want to be bothered with any of that, do you?" Mr. Trask's voice sounded smooth. "Mr. Mason, it is possible you could speak with Mrs. Ridge about hiring her to help with some of the duties she has been taking care of."

He's suggesting that I work for Mr. Mason? Lavinia's jumbled thoughts raced.

Mr. Trask nodded at Daniel. "Perhaps Mr. Mason and your husband could discuss such an arrangement, that is, if Mr. Ridge would agree to you being involved."

Lavinia fought a desire to slam her fan down on Mr. Trask's fat ringed fingers.

"Of course I would be agreeable," Daniel offered, in a reasonable tone.

William leaned forward. "Who owns the house?" His tone was sharp. He at least could see the injustice of this, though Lavinia suspected he was mostly concerned with his own expectation of a portion of the estate.

"Sarah and Lavinia each own half of it until marriage. After that, naturally their half becomes part of their husbands' estates."

"So, Lavinia and I own half of the house?" Daniel asked.

"Yes, you share the house with Miss Sarah and either party is able to buy the other out if you would like." Mr. Trask smiled indulgently at the sisters. "Your father loved both his daughters very much," he turned his attention back to William and Daniel, "and provided for them well until their husbands could do so. And don't forget, he's left his daughters cash as well as the house. Not all fathers are so generous."

William spoke again, his voice measured. "But the bulk of Mr. Onslow's fortune and his very profitable business have been settled irrevocably away from his own children?"

"As you must know, Mr. Anderson, it was Mr. Onslow's to bestow as he would. The girls are taken care of, and I can't imagine what they would want with the shop anyway—far too taxing for such gentle women." He favored them with another condescending smile. "In any case, you know it's not even legal for a married woman to own or control a business."

"But many women watch over businesses and farms when their husbands travel, or are otherwise occupied, as Sarah and I certainly could," Lavinia said, sitting up as straight as she could, fanning herself with furious energy.

"And I trust Lavinia implicitly," Daniel added. "I'm not a milliner. I'm a railroad man."

Mr. Trask ignored her and spoke to Daniel. "And you have an income from the railroad, do you not, Mr. Ridge?"

"I hope so. I am counting on the Pontchartrain Railroad to hold my position until I can return to New Orleans."

Lavinia stared at Mr. Trask's jowly face. This insufferable man! Two hundred fifty dollars was enough to live on for possibly a year or two if they were frugal. "So, you've covered everything, then?"

Mr. Trask carefully stacked the papers and pulled out a bag of gold pieces for each of them. "Here is your fitting out cash—two hundred and fifty dollars apiece. I'll look over the shop's bank accounts once all bills have been paid. There may be more funds to disperse at that time. Quite generous of Mr. Onslow, I must say. And if you wish the house to be appraised, I can handle that for you as well."

"Yes, that would be useful." William gave a nod. Lavinia noticed that a muscle pulsed in his jaw.

She then stood with some difficulty. She picked up the coin purse, took Daniel's arm, and took her leave of Mr. Trask and Mr. Mason as if in a dream. William picked up Sarah's bag of gold pieces.

"I'm sorry, Miss Lavinia. Miss Sarah. I did not know." Mr. Mason turned his top hat around and around in his hands.

Inside the carriage on the way home, Sarah and Lavinia could not stop talking.

"Mr. Mason! How could Father leave our family business to Mr. Mason?"

"I help to manage the shop. I help with the bonnet designs and the bookkeeping. I am intimately involved with every aspect of the business. Who will do these things?" Lavinia disconsolately leaned her cheek against the carriage window.

"I would like to look into challenging Mr. Onslow's will," William said. "This is most unusual."

Of course, William would say that. The thought of challenging the will seemed wrong to Lavinia, though. She didn't understand why Father had made this choice, but the odious Mr. Trask was right that it was his choice to make. She agreed with William—perhaps for the first time—that this was most unusual, but Lavinia did not trust his motives.

"Challenging the will sounds very time-consuming and unpleasant," Daniel said in a matter-of-fact tone.

"I agree, Daniel. My respect for my father makes me shy away from such a thing. I am still so shocked I don't know what to do, to be honest." With her embroidered handkerchief, she wiped sweat from under the brim of her bonnet.

"Perhaps he wrote a later will," William continued. "Sarah, we'll start searching your father's room when we arrive home. Meanwhile, Daniel and I need to discuss who will live in the house. It's fine for both of you to live there now but once there are families it will be a different matter."

"William, aren't you rushing things?" she asked. Was William truly suggesting that he should be permitted to dictate who should live in her childhood home? Both now and for years into the future?

"William, dear, there's no need to worry about that now," Sarah protested quietly, likely sensing the dangerous tone in Lavinia's voice.

"I foresee going with Lavinia to New Orleans, the place of my employment," Daniel said.

Did he, indeed? Maybe he'd like to discuss it with William. Lavinia clasped her gloved hands in her lap, willing herself to speak patiently. This discussion was quickly spiraling away from reason, and she needed to try to bring it back to something more sensible. "William, you and Sarah are not married. Until that time, Sarah makes the decisions about the house. Right, Sarah?" Lavinia squeezed Sarah's hand.

"We're engaged and of course I advise her. And we will be married very soon."

Sarah looked at Lavinia and squeezed Lavinia's hand back. The brim of Sarah's bonnet blocked William's view of her face, and Lavinia saw agreement there, but Sarah remained silent. Sarah might agree with Lavinia, but it was growing clearer that she was unlikely to be willing to cross William.

Lavinia spent the rest of the trip home in silence.

CHAPTER FIFTEEN

July 1838
Savannah

L AVINIA WENT TO her room when she returned from Mr. Trask's office, threw down the bag of coins, and sat down on the edge of her bed. She still breathed hard from emotional exertion and plain anger. She was furious with Mr. Trask and incensed by William's high-handed assumptions, but mostly she was hurt by losing the millinery shop.

Daniel came and gave her a quick kiss, telling her he was going out to talk with the railroad men again, but she barely noticed.

Through the open door she could hear William instructing Sarah to look under mattresses, in closets, in drawers and cubbyholes, as they searched for another will. She cringed as she heard Sarah and William in Father's room, opening and closing dresser drawers and closet doors. It seemed wrong that they should be going through his possessions in such a way.

She had never genuinely liked William, but only since the shipwreck had she become more willing to state it so plainly, even if it was just to herself. She had always thought him to be belittling of Sarah. Sarah had not held out for a marriage of passion, though she clearly enjoyed William's romantic attentions. Theirs was one of those practical arrangements condoned by Father. Lavinia wondered if Sarah truly loved him now. Or was it still more a marriage of convenience for her, a merging of two families who lived close to each other in Savannah who had similar resources?

William's behavior, however maddening, didn't surprise her, now that she was being this honest with herself. Of course William insisted on accompanying them to the lawyer's office to learn the contents of the will. Of course he would find an appraisal of the house useful. Of course he would question the will. She was not taken in by his tepid shows of concern in the least.

And Mr. Trask. Oh, what a horrid man.

But the most upsetting thing of all was the fact that Father had left the business to Mr. Mason. He had never reconsidered his earlier decision, even though she'd helped him for four years now? Surely, he had meant to, hadn't he? Mr. Mason was a perfectly nice man, but how could Father even consider leaving the shop to a person who wasn't related? William seemed determined to contest Father's will, but Lavinia knew that Daniel was right: contesting the will would be time-consuming and very unpleasant. She wasn't sure she had the energy for a legal battle.

Clementine paused for a moment at the door of her bedroom, interrupting her distressing reverie. "Mr. Daniel just left with the draft horse to go talk to the railroad men again."

"Yes, he told me, thank you, Clementine." She couldn't imagine what he had to talk with them about if, as he said, there was no chance of a job for him in Savannah. Maybe it just seemed familiar.

She took a deep breath and stood up. She would never be able to rest with so much anger brewing inside her. She went downstairs and found Clementine removing the black crepe from the windows and mirrors.

"I'll help you."

Clementine reached to pull black covering from one of the

dining room windows. "Nonsense, Miss Lavinia, that is not your task to do. What would your father think?"

Lavinia pulled the crepe from the other window. "I must do something. I can't just sit about, useless." She folded the crepe hastily and pulled the black shroud from the dining room sideboard mirror. It caught on the edge and ripped.

"Miss Lavinia, stop it, you're making a mess of things!" Clementine gave her one of her fond but exasperated looks. "I know you're at loose ends, but please go on now and let me be."

Wordlessly, she put down the black crepe, not wanting to upset Clementine but uncertain what to do next. Then she spied her hat and gloves still on the table where she'd dropped them after returning home, and she knew what she wanted to do. She put on her bonnet and gloves again and ran through the back courtyard to the carriage house, where Peter was grooming Daisy. Peter looked at her expectantly, and Daisy did, too, with her large, trusting brown eyes.

"Peter, I'd like to take the carriage out again. Daisy isn't too tired, is she?"

"I believe she could make a short trip, Miss Lavinia." He spoke slowly and eyed her with concern. "Where you figure on going?"

"I don't know. Nowhere in particular," she hedged. "I just want to go out for a ride. Maybe out Oglethorpe Avenue to the railroad tracks that they're building in the direction of Macon. I can drive myself."

"Well, I can hardly let you drive yourself, Miss Lavinia. You know your father wouldn't like that."

Here both Clementine and Peter were reminding her of what her father would want, as if what he wanted was all that was of importance!

"I used to ride my pony all over town! Of course he wouldn't mind."

Peter gazed at her. He had been with the family for her entire life, just like Clementine, and had always been a calm and thoughtful man. She had to admit he had talked her out of some foolish actions in the past. And today, it seemed, he would not be swayed. "I'll drive you. Give me a minute to get her harness on."

She twisted her gloves and took a deep breath. At last, she nodded. "I'll help you."

"You go wait in the courtyard, Miss Lavinia. I'll have the carriage ready shortly."

Lavinia paced the courtyard. She had a sudden desire to go out to the country and gallop on her little pony, Balderdash, for miles and miles. Let her hair stream out behind her. Let the road unfold under her. Be free of all that had happened, all that weighed her down, all the memories of the last month, the last week, the last day.

"The carriage is ready, Miss Lavinia." Peter came into the courtyard, and she followed him to the carriage house and climbed into the carriage behind him.

"If you don't mind my saying so, the railroad tracks are not a good place for women."

"I need to speak with my husband."

"Very well." Daisy set off in her determined way, twitching her ears to the sounds of their voices.

"So," Peter said after a moment. "Mr. Ridge is quite the railroad man."

"Yes, he helped start the railroad in New Orleans. He was on his way to Baltimore to meet the delivery of a new English locomotive, all of the funds with him, when our ship sank."

"That is a certain shame, Miss Lavinia, it surely is. Thank the Lord your lives were spared. And I say, you two fell in love mighty quick."

Lavinia smiled. Clementine was always happy to give her opinions—often valid, it had to be said—about her or Sarah's decisions or business, but Peter had always been more willing just to talk.

"Yes, we did. And maybe it was partially because he saved my life."

"Oh, did he now?"

"Oh, yes." She gave Peter all the details of the shipwreck and rescue he must surely be yearning for. "And so here we are, man and wife, no more than a few weeks later."

"Well, sometimes it does work that way. I fell in love with Zora the first time I laid eyes on her. We married no more than a month later. So, I don't at all doubt the truth of your love."

"Thank you, Peter." She could feel her tears starting up again. Peter and Lavinia were stepping over the line of confidence for an employer and an employee, but she didn't care.

Peter kept his eyes focused between Daisy's ears as he drove the carriage, but she could feel his sympathy and Peter didn't say more. She thought about the choices, or lack thereof, that Peter had had in his life. His look of understanding when she described the shipwreck made her wonder if he'd possibly known times when his own life was at stake. She grew silent, contemplating their similarities as well as their differences.

They drove past Colonial Park Cemetery, which brought tears to Lavinia's eyes as it reminded Lavinia of Mama and all the times she'd visited her grave, as well as the many who died on the *Pulaski*. It was there that Father's name would be placed on the family marker. And there was the infamous field where the hot-headed gentlemen of Savannah tended to have duels, which usually ended with one of them in Colonial Park, unless they missed each other, which occasionally happened. Then Peter turned right on Oglethorpe, and headed to the outskirts of town, to Louisville Road, where the clapboard train repair facility stood, and the railroad crew toiled, laying new track.

Daniel—in Father's old shirtsleeves and summer trousers—stood among the men overseeing the construction of the rails. With another man, he was looking at the surveyor's plans, and walking up the track bed, deep in discussion. She watched the sure way he carried himself—confident, completely engaged, quick-thinking—the same man she'd seen in action when he'd saved her life that dreadful night.

Peter and Lavinia sat in the carriage for a few minutes as she watched him. She had no idea how he had insinuated himself into a completely new situation like this with a group of unknown men. If only the railroad in Savannah could pay regular wages. Maybe if they were careful with her fitting out money they could hold out until the railroad was in a better financial position. She would discuss it with Daniel later.

The crew of about thirty men—all slaves or prisoners—laid the gravel and wooden ties and then the rails over the ties. After that they used pry bars to straighten the rails. They sang as they worked, the rhythm of their song helping them to work in unison, with the repetitive thump that the pry bars made as they pushed against the metal of the rails. It was back-breaking work. She could not fathom how these men could do this all day in the hot summer Savannah sun.

Peter watched, too, without speaking. They sat in silence, watching the men work, listening to their rhythmic chant. She fanned herself but felt a sense of discomfort, watching them work in the insufferable heat, though the rhythm of their singing and their movements were synchronized and powerful. How could they go on in this heat? She put down her fan, embarrassed to have the comfort of it.

"I heard that some of the planters around Savannah leased their slaves to the railroad." Peter said quietly. He pulled out his whittling knife and began working on another of his little wooden animal figures.

"I see." She smoothed the gloves in her lap in a nervous gesture. The idea that human beings would be leased out like a horse or piece of equipment made her very uncomfortable. It was not in keeping with Methodist teachings, yet somehow in Savannah the Methodists came to a silent acquiescence of the practice of slavery, and, though Father had been against it back in 1825 when the Marquis de Lafayette had visited, even he had become more complacent and less and less outspoken, too.

Daniel stood to the side with the white men, talking and

gesticulating while the slaves worked. He hadn't recognized the carriage or seen Lavinia.

"I believe we should go home now, Peter."

"You don't want to speak with Mr. Ridge?"

"I'll wait until he comes home. I'm sorry to have asked you to bring me out so late this afternoon."

Peter and Lavinia fell silent on the way home. She watched the people on the street as Daisy clopped by. As the late afternoon sun deepened the shadows on the streets, the women with their baskets, and the other household help with their aprons and kerchiefs headed for their own homes.

She remembered reading the paper one day in Smithville that two servants were in the lifeboats from the *Pulaski,* and that they both drowned while attempting to swim to shore because they didn't know how to swim.

With a suddenness that startled her, the incredible grace and pure luck of her own survival washed over her. She remembered that moment with Mrs. Gosher, the panic that had overwhelmed her, and the certainty when she'd realized that she needed to find purpose for her life. It was that same certainty come again, but it was transforming into something purposeful. With that grace and luck she felt a responsibility to do something useful with this life of hers that had been so miraculously saved.

Was it to be Daniel's companion and helpmate? To help her sister? To go to New Orleans? Her thoughts continued to preoccupy her when they arrived back at Oglethorpe Square.

"Thank you, again, Peter. I am sorry to have asked you to make that unnecessary trip. Can I help with Daisy?"

"No, I'll take care of her."

She went inside, still feeling ineffectual, and greeted Clementine distractedly, still thinking about what her revelation meant.

"Mr. Ridge received a letter." Clementine held out the folded letter as she entered the front hall, at the foot of the steps.

A return address from the Pontchartrain Railroad. Her chest tightened. The railroad management had written to Daniel.

CHAPTER SIXTEEN

July 1838
Savannah

DANIEL ARRIVED HOME to Oglethorpe Square so dusty and dirty that Lavinia insisted on toweling him off from the washbasin before they went into supper.

"You received a letter from the Pontchartrain Railroad today." She finished wiping the film of dust from his neck, and then soaked and wrung the towel over the basin. She wanted to keep the letter from him, but their marriage was new and fresh, and she suspected that secrets like that could poison it.

He turned to her quickly. "I did? Where is it?"

"Here." She took it from the pocket around her waist and gave it to him.

"I wrote them from Smithville. They must have sent it on." He tore open the letter and scanned it quickly.

Then, with a thoughtful look, he handed it to her.

Dear Mr. Ridge,

With amazement, we read your letter stating that you had survived the wreck of the Pulaski. This is truly a miracle of God. As you were not included on the lists of passengers in the lifeboats, we feared the worst.

Sadly, this meant we secured a replacement for you only just last week. Even so, I am certain we can find another role for you with the Pontchartrain Railroad. We are making good progress, and your skills and knowledge are of value here. Our current and growing needs are such that if you are able to present yourself at our offices by the end of this month, we should be able to discuss your prospects in more specific terms.

Though we were disappointed to learn that you were not able to salvage the gold pieces that were intended for the purchase of the steam engine, that is of no consequence compared to the salvage of your life. In any case, you wrote of marine insurance that you purchased before the voyage which should make good the loss of the gold pieces, so please do not trouble your mind further on that score.

Sincerely Yours,
DuPont LaPierre
Vice-President, Pontchartrain Railroad

"I must say, they hired a replacement for me without delay."

"I suppose they believed that you were dead. Though they do seem to have wasted no time, I agree." Maybe this would dissuade him from going to New Orleans.

"But still, they say I could have a future with the company if I can get to their offices by the end of the month, which is within a fortnight. We should go to New Orleans right away. I learned today about a ship leaving for New Orleans tomorrow."

"Tomorrow?" Her hand flew to her heart.

"Yes, tomorrow. I have only a fortnight to present myself. The voyage will be six days at the very least."

"You did get the marine insurance that they refer to in their letter?"

He looked insulted. "Of course, I did, Lavinia! Do you truly think I would lie about such a thing? Is that the kind of man you think I am?"

"I don't, not at all. Please don't get angry." An uncomfortable silence rose between them. "Shall we go down to supper, as soon as we finish washing up?" She tossed the water from the basin out the window and half-refilled it from the ceramic pitcher. "Maybe we can decide about New Orleans later."

"There can be no deciding later," Daniel rolled down his sleeves and buttoned them. "My employer has expectations, and a ship that will get me there in time leaves tomorrow morning. I hope you're willing to board the boat tomorrow, with me there to watch over you. But either way, I have to go."

"Daniel! Tomorrow? It's so soon! Do I have no say in this?"

Daniel turned to her sharply. "You'd prefer to stay here? Even though there is no longer a millinery shop for you to manage?"

The reminder about the shop stung. "It's not just the shop, Daniel. Don't forget, you and I do also own half of this house. And probate on my father's will is not yet complete." She drew a deep breath. "Maybe I should stay here at the house to secure my inheritance. William and Sarah want to challenge the will, and no one knows yet what will come of that. Perhaps you should go down to New Orleans alone and then send for me when you've re-established yourself again with the railroad."

"I understand that this has been your home for your entire life, Lavinia. I understand how much the shop and your sister mean to you. But we are married now. We are man and wife." He laid his hand on her arm. "We belong together. Again, I ask you, if there's no millinery shop to manage, could you not come with me?"

"Daniel, what do you mean? Why, my sister's wedding is in a few weeks. There's the disposition of my father's property, not to mention proper mourning for him. Someone has to be here to represent my interests. Do those things mean nothing to you?" Anger heated her cheeks, and she pulled away from his touch. She was shocked that Daniel was either unable or unwilling to see how important her sister and her home were to her and how difficult it would be to leave—and with only a few hours' notice!

But he couldn't see it. Or wouldn't. Disbelief still showed on his face. "And what about my need to rebuild all that I have lost?"

AFTER SUPPER, DANIEL and Lavinia usually joined Sarah and William out on the upstairs porch, but Lavinia couldn't stand listening another minute to William talking yet again about the meeting at the lawyer's office, or his instructions to Sarah to further ransack the house searching for a more recent will. He told Lavinia that when the time came, she should prepare to make a statement to the probate court about her work in the shop with her father and how much he depended on her. She would not need to appear in court, but William would represent her and read any statement aloud.

She was also eager to repair things with Daniel. She'd spent the entire meal going over and over their earlier argument in her head. Clementine's chicken, gravy, and rice, which usually appealed to her, had not tonight. She had a dry feeling at the back of her mouth.

"We could go crabbing, as we talked about when we were on the raft. It's almost high tide, and we could go to the Davis' dock," she suggested to Daniel after Sarah and William had gone outside. "They went north for the summer, but I know they won't mind. It's only a few blocks away."

"All right." Daniel, too, seemed relieved to have some time on their own after their quarrel.

She found a few chicken necks that Clementine was saving for soup (she would apologize tomorrow), and she and Daniel took a basket, a damp towel, a ring net, and string. They smeared themselves with vinegar to discourage the mosquitoes and headed for the Davis' dock on the river.

"I have something to confess to you," she told Daniel, after they had been walking in the direction of the water for a few blocks and the pink and yellow of the sunset spread across the sky. "Peter drove me out to the railroad site today, and I saw you working with the railroad men."

"You did? I didn't see you. It's a very rough place, Lavinia. That isn't safe for a lady."

"I had no idea slaves laid the track." Father had taken such quiet pride in not owning slaves. As they walked, they passed two chimney sweeps, boys no more than eight years old, trudging to the Yamacraw section of Savannah, carrying their brushes.

"Who did you imagine did the work, then?"

She felt uncomfortable. "I heard it was Irishmen, but I don't know that I had ever thought much about it. It just . . . surprised me, I suppose. The working conditions seem horrible."

"Yes, they are. It is infinitely less expensive to build the tracks here in the south than in the north because of the slave labor, which could give the south an economic advantage. And I share your objections, yet there is nothing that I can do about it."

"Well, you could certainly decide not be a part of it."

He made an impatient sound. "I don't want to sound dismissive, but you're speaking out of naivete, Lavinia."

"Don't call me naïve, Daniel! You sound like my father." In her last argument with Father, on the *Pulaski*, he had called her naïve. How much sorrow and pain did she have to see and experience before she would no longer be considered naïve by the men in her life?

"You are naïve."

"I am not!" Her voice sounded too loud, and she tried to speak more quietly so that those passing in the road wouldn't hear. "I helped Father with the shop, and I know more about life and business than many young women. I understand the south's reliance on slavery better than most. That doesn't mean I agree with it. Father didn't, either. Would you call him naïve if he were standing here?"

Daniel didn't answer.

Discussing the topic further would lead to further disagreement, and they had arrived at the Davis' dock. Without speaking much, they took their shoes off, tied the chicken necks onto the strings, sat on the gray dock, their bare feet dangling in the water, and dropped the strings so they hit bottom. Lavinia immediately remembered when they had dropped the line from the raft, with her earring, and she suspected Daniel was thinking the same thing.

"Well," said Daniel. "Certainly, we are not the desperate souls we were the last time we went fishing, are we?"

"Yet now we're using chicken necks and before we used a pearl and pink topaz earring."

They both smiled at the irony, a bit more at ease now. The sun slid lower and a cooler breeze from the water brushed their skin. They only half-watched their strings.

"Why did you go to the railroad site, Lavinia?" Daniel turned to her, with renewed interest.

"I went because I wanted to talk to you in private about what happened at the meeting with Mr. Trask. Losing the shop broke my heart. Yet you left and went out to the tracks. But then I didn't think it proper to interrupt you, so I had Peter drive me home."

Daniel remained silent for a moment, as if considering his answer. "I didn't realize how much the shop meant to you, and I'm sorry you weren't able to speak with me about it. But probably it was a good idea to have Peter drive you home."

Lavinia could see he was trying to make peace with her, and she was touched. "So there is really no chance that you might find a position here? New Orleans is to be our future?"

"The men here are eager to get my advice, since we've been running the cotton on a daily schedule down there for a few years now. But no, as I told you, the Georgia railroad's stock has plunged during the recession, and that's all they can pay me in. It's too risky. I must go back to New Orleans. I lost everything, Lavinia." He put one warm hand over hers. "And I would like to be on tomorrow's ship and bring my new wife with me."

"What if I were to stay here? Just for a while. For all the reasons I mentioned earlier—helping Sarah, and the disposition of Father's property?

Daniel let his hand drop from hers, yet its pressure still seemed to rest there. "Are we to separate, after all we endured out on the water? After we survived certain death? After those soul-searching days we spent together?"

She turned to him in the dusk and saw him looking at her beseechingly. The days they'd spent together had indeed been the most revealing of her life, teaching her about herself, about what she truly valued. She and Daniel had a love she had never thought she'd find. And she did feel that she'd been saved for a purpose, they both had, and possibly that purpose they might accomplish together.

"Can you wait a few weeks? Remember, Father left me two hundred fifty dollars. We can certainly live on that."

"The railroad said by the end of the month. The longer I wait, the less possibility there is that a position will be available for me. My pride doesn't allow me to continue to depend on your income, Lavinia. And the journey itself will take time." He hesitated. "But I will need to borrow money from you for the voyage. I'll reimburse you once we get to New Orleans and I've established myself again with the railroad."

At that instant, Lavinia's string went taut. "A crab!"

"Pull him in slowly," Daniel warned, jumping to his feet.

"I know, Daniel, I've done this before." She started to add that she didn't need his assistance but restrained herself. She didn't want to upset their delicate truce.

She pulled the string to her slowly, slowly, so that the crab didn't even know it was moving. When the crab was beside the dock, Daniel scooped it up with the ring net, then dropped it with its shiny blue shell into the basket and covered it with the wet cloth. They sat on the dock and caught a few more before dark, listening to the blue crabs they'd caught stirring in the basket, and the seabirds calling as they prepared for sleep.

They went home and steamed and picked the crabs, licking the juices from their fingers. It was just the two of them, as William had gone home and Sarah had gone to bed. Afterward they washed up in the basin, and as soon as they climbed in the bed, Daniel reached for her and his lips sought hers. She moved closer, inhaling the sharp but clean residual scent of vinegar.

━━━━━◦⟡◦━━━━━

CHAPTER SEVENTEEN

July 1838
Savannah

I N THE DEEP of the night, after Daniel had fallen asleep, Lavinia climbed from under the cotton matelassé bedspread and went downstairs to the sitting room and lay on the sofa. An hour crept by, and she pulled her knees up inside her nightgown and let her thoughts drift back over the time she had known Daniel. Only a few weeks ago she'd indeed been that naïve girl, traveling with her father. Now she was a shipwreck survivor and a wife. She felt forever changed. She could never truly go back.

She watched the lamplighter come by and douse the gas streetlamp as the morning light seeped from the horizon. A few servants walked by on their way to their labors. How quickly this night had passed! She shivered with pleasure, thinking of the time she and Daniel had shared last night. Yet, while she lay there watching the city wake up, she resolved that she would not go to New Orleans, that she would stay in Savannah instead. She wouldn't leave Sarah alone. Sarah needed her.

"What are you doing down here?"

Daniel, in his nightclothes, stood in the doorway in the gray morning light.

"Oh, just thinking."

He crossed the room, put his hand on the top of her head and stroked her hair. "Do you truly not want to come with me to New Orleans? It's a wonderful city. There's no other city like it."

"I think I will stay here while you go to New Orleans." She paused, wondering how to say what was on her mind, wondering how Daniel would react. "I just wonder sometimes if we made a hasty decision. We barely know each other. How can we make a life together?" When she sat up, he sat next to her, and she saw again his tousled dark blonde hair, his near-sighted eyes, his set jaw.

He took her hand. "Do you want to be separated from me?"

"Of course not. I want nothing but to be with you," she admitted.

"Lavinia, I feel that we couldn't have come to know each other any better over many years than what we learned over those harrowing days together on the water. And I cannot feel that there is any woman in this world who I would rather have as my wife. But to make a life together we must have faith and trust each other. I've made up my mind that I'll be on the ship leaving for New Orleans today. If you don't want to accompany me, I won't force you. But I hope you will come. Think about it. I leave this morning." He squeezed her shoulder, stood, and strode from the room.

She sat quietly, with tears running down her cheeks, as the sun rose and light slowly suffused the room and the church bells began ringing to announce the six o'clock hour. The shadows of the swaying Spanish moss played on the walls and floor.

"Miss Lavinia, what are you doing down here?" Clementine came in from the back of the house, as she arrived at work, her straight, full frame casting a shadow from the hallway in the morning light.

"Oh, I couldn't sleep." She looked away, hoping that Clementine wouldn't see her tears.

"It's beyond my understanding how a body could lie awake at night." Clementine came into the parlor and plumped the pillows beside her. "Why, some days I'm so tired I fall asleep on my own two feet." Clementine never stopped moving—always cooking, washing, or cleaning.

Now Clementine eyed her suspiciously, and Lavinia suspected that she had seen the tears. "Why don't you go on upstairs and try to rest your eyes before breakfast, Miss Lavinia." Clementine sometimes sounded brusque, but Lavinia knew she cared deeply for her and probably understood much more about Lavinia's conflicts with Daniel than she would speak about. After all, she was in their home most of the day and saw everything that wasn't behind closed doors.

Lavinia wouldn't have minded receiving some of Clementine's plainspoken advice now. She wanted to tell Clementine about Daniel leaving, but after a moment Clementine went into the warming kitchen and she lost her chance. Instead, she went upstairs and found Daniel in her room packing some of her father's clothes into a carpetbag. Now that all this was real, Lavinia redoubled her efforts to dissuade Daniel.

"Won't you change your mind? How long is the voyage?" She put on her dressing gown.

"We'll be six days at sea. Around the tip of the territory of Florida."

"Why don't you wait a few weeks and let me get things settled. I'm sure another ship will be going soon."

"Things are settled, Lavinia. I've checked, and this is the last ship that will get me there on time. I will be on it. I fear I must take twenty-five dollars of your fitting out money for my fare and food and other expenses before I arrive home." He indicated several gold coins he'd already removed from the purse, lying next to the carpetbag.

She nodded, her emotions swinging between fear of his departure and anger at his presumption. He could at least have asked before simply taking her money. What about the faith and trust he'd spoken of earlier? Did he think she would try to withhold it if he asked for the coins? Maybe it was only she who was supposed to trust him.

He closed the clasps on the carpet bag and made his own last appeal. "You could ask your sister to buy your half of the house from us. We could still go together."

"You know Sarah can't use her fitting out money to pay us for the house. She must use it for living expenses. And her trousseau. I could never ask it of her, and it's all too fast."

"Very well." He put his hand on her shoulder and kissed her forehead. "Will you see me off?"

"Of course. And you should let Clementine make you some breakfast."

They stayed silent at breakfast. She drank a cup of tea while Daniel ate the scrambled eggs, cheese grits, and sausage that Clementine prepared. Lavinia usually loved Clementine's breakfasts but couldn't find her appetite this morning.

Finally, Lavinia said to Clementine, when she eyed the carpetbag by the door, "Daniel is leaving for New Orleans today."

Clementine smoothly refilled Daniel's coffee. "And you're not going?"

"No."

Clementine nodded, still holding the coffee pot. "I see." Did she have an opinion about Daniel going and Lavinia staying? Lavinia didn't know. She had thought of Clementine as a motherly caretaking figure—a stern, but loving one—for her entire life, yet she wasn't sure that she could read her expression today. And Clementine would certainly never express her opinion now.

"Thank you for breakfast, Clementine, and for all you've done for me while I've been here." Daniel lined his utensils across his plate.

"You're welcome. I pray for safe travels." Clementine went back out the door and they heard her footsteps down the stairs from the warming kitchen to the back garden and heading for the main kitchen.

Daniel stood and put his napkin on the table. "I'll walk to the docks. There's no need to trouble Peter to get the carriage ready." He turned and looked into her eyes. "Good-bye, Lavinia."

She followed him to the door, her heart pounding. "Will you write and let me know how things progress?"

"Of course I will. And I will be ever hopeful that you will come and join me at the first opportunity."

"I don't know when I'll be able to come to you, Daniel." Her chin collapsed.

He put down his carpet bag and pulled her close in a tight embrace, then kissed her so hard she thought his lips might bruise hers.

Then he pulled away, lifted the satchel, and strode down the steps and up the street. Lavinia watched his progress silently, without tears. As he neared the corner, she heard Sarah's bare feet on the stairs behind her before her sister joined her at the door.

"What's happening, Lavinia? Where is Daniel going?" Sarah still wore her nightgown with her hair down in a smooth dark braid.

"He's going back to New Orleans." Lavinia heard the flat tone of her own voice.

"And the two of you are in agreement on this? How can you let him go? You're husband and wife!" Daniel turned the corner without breaking his stride.

"He had a letter yesterday from the railroad—he had to get back quickly to reclaim his position. But I'm not ready to leave, and you need me here to help with things. There are still a great many decisions to be made." She swiped a tear from her cheek. A terrible hollowness lined her stomach.

"Come on inside, Miss Lavinia, Miss Sarah." Clementine stood with her hands on her hips. "Don't be out here on the front porch in your nightclothes."

Sarah and Lavinia went inside to the dining room. Lavinia continued to cry as Clementine served them tea and toast and jam. Lavinia knew her tears were borne of anger and frustration.

She wished Daniel had not gone, and the fact that it was her own decision to stay did not ease the ache his absence had already left behind.

"Many married couples must separate at times," she told Sarah, wiping her eyes.

"I know, but I still can't believe he is gone. It's as though he was barely here." Sarah took a sip of the tea and spread jam on her toast.

"I agree. It seems we just arrived home. He had to go—I see that—but I couldn't bring myself to go with him, Sarah. I can't leave yet. This is my home. And how could I miss your wedding? You still need me here to help you."

"You are such a dear sister, but it pains me to think that you are separate from your husband because of me. A wife should be with her husband." Sarah gave her an earnest look. "William can help me. You know how much he wants to be involved in decisions."

That was an understatement, in Lavinia's mind, but she kept that to herself. Instead, she said, "For so many years it has been you and me and Father. We need time to grieve Father's passing. We need the time together."

Sarah's eyes filled now, too, and she nodded. "Thank you for staying with me, Lavinia." She laid her hand over Lavinia's.

She nodded and fell silent, thinking about the straight set of Daniel's back as he made his way up the street with his satchel.

CHAPTER EIGHTEEN

August 1838
Savannah

T HE FIRST THREE days after Daniel's departure were filled with discussions between Sarah and Lavinia. They talked of their father, of Daniel, and of William. They agreed that Father must have expected his daughters' husbands to care for them financially, and thus not felt the need to leave the millinery shop to them. But they speculated on Father's reasons for leaving them enough money to live on for only about a year or two. Having the business bequeathed away from the family was unusual and still troubled them, and Lavinia wondered why, since she had been helping him in the store for four years, he had not thought about changing his will. Why had he left the shop to an assistant instead of his daughters?

Neighbors and friends came on condolence visits, and Lavinia was touched to receive a letter from her old friend Harriet, who had seen the article about Lavinia and Daniel in the paper. Harriet expressed amazement at Lavinia's survival of the *Pulaski's* sinking and condolences about her father. Sarah and Lavinia in their turn also paid visits to express their sympathy and comfort others who had lost loved ones in the wreck of the *Pulaski*.

One morning Lavinia came into the warming kitchen from

the garden with a handful of blooming yellow jessamine vines she'd cut and searched in a cabinet for a large vase to put them in. Clementine, who was washing vegetables in the dry sink, said "I would like to tell you a story, Lavinia. My mama was separated from my father because they worked for two different plantations. They were allowed to see each other only once a week for a few hours when they attended church on Sunday. I know there are times when people must be separated from their loved ones. But if a woman can be with her husband of her own free will, I feel that's where she belongs." Clementine then pulled open a cabinet, handed Lavinia a vase, and went on with her work.

"Thank you, Clementine." Lavinia arranged the flowers in respectful silence. She had continued to wonder about Clementine's opinions on this matter and was humbled that she'd shared something so personal about her own parents.

William usually came to visit after dinner for a few hours, and they sat on the upstairs porch during the steamy evenings. Several weeks passed in this fashion, with Lavinia making concerted efforts not to get into quarrels with him, trying valiantly to focus on her stitching. His favorite topic of conversation was Father's will. He had wasted no time contacting a lawyer he knew to help contest the will, and a hearing would soon be scheduled.

"I will need you to write your testimony, Lavinia," he said abruptly one evening on the porch a few weeks after Daniel had left. Lavinia had rather hoped he'd forgotten about this. "You must be willing to state that your father had encouraged you to help in the millinery shop and that he had led you to believe that you and Sarah would inherit it."

Lavinia sat up straighter, feeling trapped. "He encouraged me to help, and yes, I did assume that we would inherit the shop. But Father never really promised it to us in so many words. I honestly just assumed. But still, I have mixed feelings about contesting the will."

"You would not need to testify before a judge, only provide

your testimony in writing. I will take care of everything else. And contesting the will is obviously in your best interest." William gestured dismissively. "The best thing to do is for you to draft a statement and I will review it."

"I will need some time to think about it."

"Not to put too fine a point on it, but sooner will be better than later."

When Lavinia continued with her stitching without responding, an awkward silence stretched on.

Then Sarah spoke. "Lavinia, William and I have decided we'll marry at the end of September, as soon as the heavy mourning period for Father is safely behind us. By then we will have limited our social obligations for three months, which I believe is what Father would have desired."

Lavinia, still thinking about whether to write the statement for William, glanced from William to her sister. "Father would want you to marry," Lavinia agreed. Indeed, they did need to marry quickly so that Sarah would have a source of income.

"And, with Father gone, and also since William's older brother and his wife and five children are living in their house with his parents on Chippewa Square, William thinks it would make sense for him to move in here with me after the wedding."

Not "with us?" Lavinia's throat went dry. Not that she was surprised; he'd been more concerned than anyone about the house that day in Mr. Trask's office. She decided to be non-committal in her response. "I see," was all she said.

A few moments later, when Sarah excused herself to get a shawl, Lavinia took a chance to question William on his resources.

"Just to pretend that I am Father for a moment, since he's no longer here, I am sure Father would have asked you if your income is sufficient to maintain the house." She forced a tone of lightness in her voice and remained intent on her needlework, as if this were a congenial conversation.

He gave her an annoyed look. "I had a close relationship with your father. He knew my income. We discussed this when Sarah and I became engaged."

"Of course. You must forgive my protective feeling for my sister, that's all. Especially since we no longer have the millinery shop."

"You don't need to be protective. I'll be taking care of her now."

She pressed him to answer. "Your income is indeed sufficient, then?"

He glared at her and looked away. "If you must know, yes, it is. Or it will be once my clerkship is complete. But I feel no obligation to answer questions like this, Lavinia."

She drew a deep breath and sewed another stitch, wishing she could poke the needle into the back of his hand the way Daniel had during the stagecoach robbery. At that moment, Sarah returned to the porch with her shawl. She had brought one for Lavinia, too.

"What did I miss?" she asked playfully.

"Oh, nothing," Lavinia said. She put down her stitching. It was too dark to continue, anyway. "I think I'll go inside." She avoided looking at William as she gathered her things and went in. With every conversation she disliked him more, yet this man was soon to be her brother-in-law, her family.

During the days she helped Sarah with her trousseau. They sewed six lace-trimmed nightdresses and drawers, as well as six lace-trimmed camisoles and six chemises. If Father had still been alive, they might have ordered ball gowns from Paris, but as it was, the two of them, with the assistance of Mrs. Thomas from the millinery shop, sewed a black silk traveling dress, two walking dresses in pique, and Swiss muslin evening robes. Mrs. Thomas brought some bonnets from the shop, and they chose one for each outfit. It may not be grand, but Sarah's trousseau would be presentable and still within their means.

As she stitched, listening to Sarah's conversation, she thought of her own wedding in Mrs. Gosher's wedding dress and bonnet and her own bridal night in the little rental house in Smithville. She hadn't even considered a trousseau. Nor had mourning traditions been a concern, since they hadn't at the time known with certainty whether Father was alive or dead. She hadn't been thinking about practical matters at all. Looking back, it seemed like a dream. She thought of Daniel on that night and could feel herself blush with the memory of their bodies touching each other.

And she had missed Daniel almost at once. Strange as it was for her childhood bed to also be her marriage bed, it now felt cold and empty without him. In those most lonely moments, she wondered if she'd made a mistake and should have gone with him instead.

She'd been so lethargic in the weeks since Daniel left, and a few mornings felt nauseated as well. Two mornings in a row she told Clementine she didn't want breakfast, even when she had made cheese grits. On the third morning, she actually had to run to her bedroom window and vomit into the yard. She feared she may have contracted malaria, which was rampant in Savannah in the summer, though no one knew what caused it. Sarah came into her bedroom when she heard Lavinia retching.

"What's ailing you, Lavinia?"

She turned from the window slowly. "I don't rightly know. Just a little under the weather, that's all. I just hope it's not malaria. I'd hate to call for the doctor for no reason." Father hadn't trusted doctors much since Mama died. He complained that all they did was bleed people, both with their leeches and their fees.

"Let's see how you feel as the day goes on."

She did feel tired, and her breasts felt swollen and sore. Had she strained herself while gardening, or getting into the carriage? She couldn't remember anything of that sort. She simply felt nauseated, slow-limbed and dreamy, as though she were swimming through warm water.

Clementine suddenly appeared in the doorway of the bedroom, in her white apron, with her normal ramrod posture. "Lavinia, when did you last have your monthly courses?"

Lavinia gasped and put her hand over her mouth. She thought back to the times she and Daniel had been together in bed and heat rose to her face. She couldn't remember having her monthlies since the shipwreck.

"Does your chest feel tender?"

She crossed her hands over her breasts as if to hide them, staring at Sarah and Clementine. She nodded.

The little she knew about this aspect of a woman's life she had learned from Clementine. Clementine had always made both Sarah and Lavinia remain indoors in the sitting room, and not go out in public, for the duration of their courses. They had both accepted her rules and the comforting dishes and teas she always made for them during those times, but they had both found these limitations extremely tiresome.

"That's it, isn't it? You'll be blessed with a child." Clementine smiled broadly.

"A child is a blessing, of course." In a daze of disbelief, she put on her cotton dressing gown. She didn't smile at Sarah, and Sarah didn't either. None of them mentioned the fact that Mama had died in childbirth, but Clementine had been there, so she surely thought of it, just as Lavinia and Sarah did. Many women successfully bore eight or nine children, but not Mama.

Father had told her that Clementine, who midwifed their mother, could not stop her bleeding during Sarah's birth, and Peter had fetched the doctor. The doctor delivered Sarah, but their mother died of infection a week later. Sarah nearly died, too, but managed to survive with the help of a wet nurse Clementine found, a brave woman living a few blocks away who had lost her own baby.

Lavinia ran her hands over her sore breasts, and down over her stomach, which wasn't at all enlarged, in fact felt flatter than before since her appetite had been poor of late. "How am I to know for sure?"

"There are signs. In early weeks the women feel poorly and have a touch of stomach upset," Clementine told her.

She nodded. She did feel that. Her mouth had tasted chalky, and she'd felt on the brink of throwing up for nearly a week.

"You'll be having you a spring baby!" Clementine smiled. "Mr. Daniel will be overjoyed!"

Would he be? She lay her palm over her stomach, thinking what it would feel like if he did the same. She did think that he would be pleased. He enjoyed children. And motherhood was meant to be such a blessing. Was it only because of Mama's death that she couldn't seem to feel joy herself?

"You're looking a bit peaked. Come downstairs and I'll fix you some ginger tea. That eases the morning sickness."

"All right." She followed Clementine downstairs and lowered herself into one of the dining room chairs. Sarah sat beside her and lay her hand over Lavinia's.

"Don't worry, Lavinia. Clementine will take care of you. Of us."

She nodded. She might not feel joy, exactly, but she did feel different. A tiny life grew inside her. Sarah and Lavinia had been taught, at church and by their tutors, that motherhood was a woman's highest calling, the most elevated role in life that a woman could play. She had never been able to reconcile this with what had happened to her mother, however. She didn't remember the horror of her own mother's passing, as she had been only three, but Clementine did. Clementine had officiated at hundreds of births.

"Well, if I had any desire to join Daniel in New Orleans, I would need to put that aside now." Women with child were not encouraged to travel.

"Maybe he will come back and join you." Sarah rubbed Lavinia's hand.

She had not yet had a letter from Daniel, which had begun to worry her. A letter would have had more than enough time to reach her by now, but she supposed he must be very busy with his sister and at the railroad, making up for lost time. She checked the mail Clementine brought into the front hall daily.

"I don't think I'll write him about this just yet. Who knows what may happen. And I don't know what might happen with his circumstances or his position."

Sarah looked at her closely, then nodded.

"I'll wait a month or two." She felt her heart squeeze with regret as she said it, wishing she could write Daniel immediately, wishing she'd had a letter from him, wishing anything were more certain.

"Whatever you think, Livvy."

"And Sarah, please don't tell William." She gave Sarah a significant look. "Please, let's keep it a secret only between us." She wasn't sure why this felt so important, but it did.

At that moment Clementine returned to the dining room with a cup of tea.

"Ginger tea with lemon and honey." She placed the cup on the lace tablecloth in front of Lavinia. "To ease the stomach. And, as joyful as this may be, maybe you should wait for the baby to quicken before making any announcements or writing to Mr. Daniel. It is a sad truth that not all babies make it into this world."

Relief spread over Lavinia as she understood that she and Clementine agreed on this. "Thank you, Clementine."

"You're welcome, Miss Lavinia. Now drink the ginger tea." Clementine left the dining room and headed back out through the garden to the main kitchen.

Lavinia picked up the flowered teacup and sipped the pale liquid. Like a balm, the spicy flavor did almost immediately ease her nausea.

CHAPTER NINETEEN

September 1838
Savannah

SARAH AND WILLIAM had decided on a morning wedding ceremony in Oglethorpe Square, with friends and neighbors attending, and a breakfast afterward in their garden. Lavinia spoke with Peter about getting their gardens ready. Clementine and Lavinia helped Sarah plan a menu of fruit cake with white frosting, sweetmeats, oysters, and tea.

In Lavinia's present condition, none of the wedding food sounded appetizing, especially the oysters, but they had become the rage the last few years, and they were in season.

Mrs. Thomas had been of such wonderful assistance with Sarah's trousseau that they decided to hire her again as a seamstress to make Sarah's dress for the ceremony and reception. The dress was pale lavender, made of chiffon and satin, with a V-shaped neckline, mutton chop sleeves, a wide embroidered satin sash, and a full skirt. Sarah could wear the dress again, perhaps dyed darker, for special occasions later.

Sarah and Lavinia discussed it one evening on the upstairs porch after dinner, before William arrived. "I know that the Scattergood sisters both wore white—and it's very fashionable— but it's impractical, don't you think, Livvy?"

"Yes, especially since we've just lost Father. We need to watch our expenses and try to be a bit less showy. People will already be wondering if you and William are rushing into the marriage after Father's death, even though you've been engaged for a while and the heavy mourning period is over."

"Do you care what people think, Livvy? After all, you and Daniel married a little more than a week after Father's death."

"I know. So soon after the shipwreck, all thoughts about what might be socially acceptable flew out of my mind. I was in a daze after all that had happened. Propriety and customs seemed silly after we'd come so close to death. But now that I'm back in Savannah I suppose the customs seem more real. Do you mind what people think, sister?"

William appeared at the doorway in the dusk. They hadn't heard his horse approaching.

"I care what people think. Lavinia, you know people are going to be asking where your husband is."

"I will tell them where he is." She turned to William with her chin set as he took his seat in one of the rockers. Why did they argue about nearly everything?

"I suppose the question most will have is why you are not there as well."

"She will say she stayed to help with her sister's wedding, William." Lavinia smiled at Sarah with gratitude. Sarah had also kept her promise and had not told William about her condition, otherwise she suspected William would have had much more to say.

"That reminds me, Sarah," William added, taking Sarah's hand. "I'd like to have a champagne wedding toast at our wedding. As Presbyterians, the folks in my family observe no rules against alcohol."

"I have no objection, do you, Livvy?"

Lavinia remembered the bottle of wine that had kept her and Daniel alive on the raft, and she smiled to herself. "No, I have no objection."

They continued quite pleasantly in their planning for several minutes before William inevitably turned the conversation to his most recent efforts to contest Father's will. He had hired another lawyer, who was perusing the will for veracity, and had also sent Sarah to search the stables and their father's office at Onslow's Millinery for any updated wills.

He then turned to Lavinia expectantly. "Lavinia, is your statement for the probate court ready for me to review?"

"I haven't written it yet." Lavinia wished he would admit defeat and never speak of Father's will again. Yet Lavinia had to admit she occasionally harbored a secret hope that William might find a new will in which Mr. Onslow treated his daughters more fairly.

"Please take the time to get it to me soon," William said.

Now, as William and Sarah moved on to other topics, sharing their activities of the day, Lavinia listened to the night creatures humming and let her mind wander, imagining what Daniel might be doing at that moment. Had he reestablished himself at the railroad? Had he told his sisters about her? Had he written to her? She couldn't stop herself from wondering if he had been in contact with the young woman he'd cared for before, the one his sister disapproved of. Sometimes at night she reached over to the empty side of the bed for him and imagined herself running her fingers through his dark blond curls again as she did in Smithville.

Lavinia pulled herself back to the present, as Sarah began trying to tease details about their bridal tour out of William. He had planned one that was a month long in a secret location known only to him. Lavinia wondered what would it be like to be in the house alone with Sarah and William after they returned from their trip.

THE NEXT DAY, Sarah stood on a foot stool in the parlor as Mrs.

Thomas put the finishing touches on her wedding dress.

"You look beautiful," Lavinia told Sarah. Sarah did indeed look lovely. The lavender complemented her ivory complexion and shiny dark hair, and the cut of the bodice accentuated the graceful curve of her neck and shoulders.

"Thank you, Livvy."

"How are things at the millinery shop, Mrs. Thomas?" She dearly wished she could be part of it.

"Oh, Mr. Mason is doing a masterful job at running it. You would be proud of him."

"That is wonderful." She was of course happy that the shop was doing well, but a part of her wished Mrs. Thomas had complained about Mr. Mason's poor management so she could swoop in and save the situation.

"You should come in to see the window displays. They are magnificent. And after the initial drop-off of business after the shipwreck business is picking up again nicely."

"Why, that is so good to hear." Lavinia bit her tongue. "I'm so happy that Mr. Mason is making a success of things. Have you sold many of the bonnets with the pink ruche lining that we talked about before I left?"

"Oh, yes, they are quite popular, Miss Lavinia. They'll put color in any girl's cheeks."

Lavinia felt satisfaction that her ideas were still being implemented. She'd seen some other new styles in the papers lately, showing a wider brim, like the headwear that had been worn at Queen Victoria's coronation, and wished she could run to the shop, as in the old days, to try out a pattern.

Mrs. Thomas removed the last pin from her mouth and spoke. "And Lavinia, what will you wear to your sister's wedding? Shall I make something for you to wear as well?"

"Oh, there's no need for me to have anything new. I have plenty of dresses."

"But you must have lost nearly all of your wardrobe in the shipwreck, didn't you, dear?"

"I did lose all of my finest frocks, to be honest, but I still have a few pretty ones to choose from." She hated to admit to Mrs. Thomas that they needed to be careful with their money.

"Can I help you alter any of your dresses, then, dear?"

Lavinia drew in her breath. She hadn't gained any weight yet, as she ate very little these days due to nausea, but she was filled with a sudden fear that Mrs. Thomas could somehow tell she was with child. She struggled to keep her countenance as she still didn't want any but Sarah and Clementine to know.

"You don't seem to have regained the weight you lost during your ordeal, and I imagine most of your dresses still hang on you," Mrs. Thomas went on. "We could take one of them in to fit you better."

Lavinia let out her breath with relief. "Oh, that's very kind of you, Mrs. Thomas. I will look through my wardrobe tonight and see if I need anything altered. I will let you know."

"Mrs. Thomas, perhaps you could alter one of mine for her." Sarah turned so that she could unbutton her dress. "The light-yellow silk gown that I wore to the Oyster Festival last year would look beautiful with your hair, Lavinia."

"I am closer to your size now." It did seem quite a practical idea. "You wouldn't mind, Sarah?"

"Of course not!"

After Mrs. Thomas left, and Sarah changed back into her day dress, Lavinia confided to Sarah, "I thought Mrs. Thomas had guessed. I was holding my breath."

"I was as well." Sarah gave her a pointed look. "Though you will indeed need to reveal your condition at some point."

"I heard that Belinda Pinckney was six months along before anyone knew."

"That was the tiniest baby I ever saw, too."

"And poor child, it only lived a few weeks." So many babies did not survive; almost everyone expected to lose a child at some time or another.

That afternoon Sarah and Lavinia moved to the dining room

and began working on the invitations, discussing those to be invited. They agreed on a small affair, just twenty-five friends and family. Yet, it seemed lavish to Lavinia when she compared it to her own nuptials, with only the Goshers there to witness.

"Do you think we should invite your old beau, Matthew Grogan, Lavinia?" Sarah giggled.

Lavinia laughed. "Matthew Grogan! He was *not* my beau, Sarah! He came to call once only."

"And you herded him out of the house. You practically told him he was an old goat." Sarah began laughing too. "I can still remember you telling me about that hat tip of his as he hurried down the steps. I believe he was smitten with you!"

Soon they were both lost in laughter, their sides aching and tears running from their eyes, and Lavinia remembered the way things used to be, before they lost Father. The two of them could sit and laugh over something silly for an entire afternoon, when just one look at the other would provoke more peals of giggles. She felt so happy and grateful to have recaptured it now, though she did regret they had recaptured it at Mr. Grogan's expense.

That night, though, in bed in the dark, her mind traveled over many paths. She ran her palm over the sheet on the other side of the bed, wondering if perhaps tomorrow she would at last receive a letter from Daniel. What was he doing, so far away from her? She pondered the fact that her sister would soon marry a man Lavinia didn't like and how that might affect their tender relationship. She wondered what would their father think about all that had happened. And then she floated into a somewhat agitated and shallow sleep, waking several times during the night.

CHAPTER TWENTY

September 1838
Savannah

A FEW DAYS after Lavinia and Sarah laughed about inviting Matthew Grogan to the wedding, Lavinia went down into the front hall in her dressing gown in search of her ginger tea. Clementine was in the back garden, picking herbs, and had left the tea on the dining room table under a cozy. Next to the tea lay a letter with the New Orleans postmark. It was wrinkled and creased as though it had crossed rivers and mountains on its way to her. She picked it up and ran her thumb gently over her name in Daniel's bold handwriting. She had never had much chance to see or study it. "Lavinia" looked spiky rather than flowing, with an ink blotch in the lower loop of the "L." Her heart thudded in her chest.

Relieved to have the chance to read the letter at leisure on her own, she took the tea and put the letter in her pocket and hurried back upstairs to her bedroom. She crawled under the matelassé quilt, curled away from the door, and pulled the letter out to look at it. She didn't tear into it, as she thought she might. Instead, she opened it slowly, removing the wax with great care. Then she read the letter through twice, savoring every word.

Dearest Lavinia,

I am home in New Orleans now with my sisters. The voyage was uneventful, though I must admit to some frightening moments and memories when I first boarded. I endeavored to spend every possible moment above decks as I am confident that strolling on deck saved us that night on the Pulaski. I disembarked with great relief at the end of the voyage and rejoiced to find my feet on solid ground.

I have met with the principals at the Pontchartrain Railroad, and I hope you will be pleased to learn that I have secured my old position again. The fellow that they hired to replace me said he could not bear to take the position of a man believed to be dead if he was still alive, and he stepped aside. I must say, this was very honorable of him, and I am much obliged.

However, there is one slight dilemma which I trust will be resolved soon. The maritime insurance I obtained before embarking on the Pulaski does not seem to be on record with the company, and I cannot find the receipt. Possibly it was lost in the shipwreck, though I was certain I had left it at the office. I will continue to search for it, but I may be required to resort to court proceedings. My superiors have not yet signaled their support, but I anticipate that they will.

Daniel spent the next few paragraphs telling Lavinia about the welcome his sisters had given him and how much food they seemed determined to make him eat. He seemed happy to be with them again. He wrote about renewing friendships with friends and regaled her with the sights of New Orleans, which he could not wait for her to see. The letter finished with affection and longing.

I think of you, my dear, every day, and regret that we parted with harsh feelings and words. I think of your lovely auburn hair, the softness of your charming, freckled skin, your integrity and bravery, and I regret that we ever parted. I continue to hope every day that you will join me here. Please say you will come and be by my side.

I have told my sisters much about you, and they send their regards. Of course, Sally is especially eager to meet you, and I'm sure you will become great friends. Please write to me and tell me of the passing of your days. No detail is too small to engage my interest.

With all my love,
Daniel

She folded the letter and placed it in the drawer of her night table. She sipped the cooled ginger tea, which still helped to settle her stomach. So, Daniel had indeed secured a position, his old position at that. And his words of endearment softened her heart. His sisters must be glad to have him home to care for them again. She wondered how they had fared in his absence, and she imagined their shared life. What did their home look like? Where might Daniel be sleeping? Her alert went up however—possibly it would be difficult for him ever to leave again due to his responsibilities to them. And who were the friends with whom he was renewing relationships?

And, though he didn't seem terribly concerned about it in the letter, she worried about the maritime insurance. Could his company expect him to pay back the gold pieces that were lost in the wreck? What would that mean for the two of them? How angry Daniel had become when he thought she doubted him about the maritime insurance. Usually he was so patient. Perhaps it meant that he was worried, too.

She wondered of course whether his sisters would like her and also if she would like them. It would be wonderful to become great friends with Sally. In her present exhausted condition, however, she could not imagine attempting the trip. She could barely prevent herself from writing him this moment about the baby. But she had promised herself—and Clementine—that she would not, at least until the baby quickened.

So she made herself get up and put on her nicest day dress

and bonnet. Evidence of all Daniel's activity made her feel that she too needed to accomplish something. Even though she felt tired all the time, she was determined to keep a normal schedule. She wasn't going to be like some of the Savannah women she knew who took laudanum and spent their days sleeping when they became pregnant. Soon she wouldn't be able to go out as much, due to her condition, so she might as well do it now.

She would go to the millinery shop and inquire with Mr. Mason and Mrs. Thomas about how things were going there. Who could say what might happen? Possibly this was a way of moving forward to discover a new and higher design for her life. Perhaps the memories of purposeful time spent at the millinery shop could also help her create new goals. Maybe, if she couldn't own Onslow's Millinery, she could find another way to do the things she was good at. At any rate, she couldn't seem to stay away. And she didn't care if she didn't have an escort. She would go alone.

Peter had the carriage ready within the hour.

"I'm going to the shop; do you want to come?" She stopped in the sunlit dining room, where Sarah had the invitations spread on the dark wood table.

"I think I had better continue addressing these invitations. Peter will need to deliver them this week."

"Very well. I know you don't need my help—my calligraphy is not nearly as fine as yours. And do you need Peter today?"

"No, not until tomorrow. Do you have an escort? Would you like me to send a note to William?"

"No, that's all right. I'll go alone." Certainly, she'd prefer to go alone rather than have William as an escort.

"Alone?" Sarah gave her a puzzled look.

"Yes, alone."

"Is that proper without Father there?"

"I'm not sure I care about whether it's proper."

"The shipwreck changed you, Livvy." Sarah turned back to her work as Lavinia heard the wheels of their carriage on the street outside.

A crisp day in late September meant the flies did not torment Daisy, so she clopped along with the surprising energy of a filly. Lavinia had not been out in a few days and enjoyed the sparkling sunshine on her face and the bright colors of the leaves on the red cedars and white oaks. When she arrived at the shop on Ellis Square, she immediately examined the window display with a critical eye. It featured two fall ladies' bonnets, but as she climbed down from the carriage, telling Peter she wouldn't be more than half an hour, she thought of several ways in which she could improve it. Another bonnet could be added—she liked an arrangement of three ladies' bonnets better than two—and her fingers itched to move the bonnets into a more artful placement.

The bell tinkled as she entered the store and glimpsed Mr. Mason, in his black waistcoat, behind the counter. He seemed to hold himself with more pride than before. She felt odd to encounter him now, knowing that he had inherited what he surely knew should be Lavinia's shop. He had seemed so apologetic that day; she wondered if he ever felt guilty.

"Good morning, Mr. Mason." She gave him a hesitant smile, not sure how she would interact with him.

"Miss Lavinia! A delight to see you!" He came out from behind the counter and swept toward her to kiss her hand. "How sweet of you to visit us!"

"Oh, I couldn't stay away, Mr. Mason. As you know, the shop used to occupy a great deal of my time."

He blinked, then rattled on, moving his hands nervously. "You would be so proud of how well things are going. We're still selling a few black bonnets, of course, for mourning after the *Pulaski,* but also new styles for fall with silk leaves and feathers. And the brims are wider, like the ones the ladies wore at Queen Victoria's coronation. Let me show you!" He hurried to a mannequin and carefully lifted a bonnet. "Isn't this a lovely shade of burgundy? And aren't these little orange-tinted leaves a nice touch?"

She did admire the bonnet and was impressed that Mr. Mason had noticed the new style of wider brims. "Did Mrs. Thomas make this one? It is indeed a lovely design, and just right for autumn.

"Why don't you put it in the window?" That would get the grouping of three Lavinia preferred.

"I didn't want it to fade in the sun." Mr. Mason shrugged apologetically. "That's why I located it centrally here, so it could be seen through the glass door." He considered. "But of course, that is a wonderful idea. Why don't you put it out there, Miss Lavinia? We have missed your artful touch here." He handed her the bonnet and mannequin.

She had to admit he acted more gracious than she felt. She stepped up onto the low platform in the front window with the new fall bonnet in hand and began adjusting the arrangement of the others. She turned them all this way and that until she had a nice triangular arrangement with more depth. She went back outside to examine her work, standing with her hands on her hips on the cobblestone street. Much improved!

Peter sat in the carriage, waiting for her, whittling a horse while Daisy munched on a sprig of grass she'd found growing beside the walk.

"Peter, I promise I will be only a few more minutes."

"I'm in no hurry, Miss Lavinia." He had waited for her so many times before, he knew what "a few more minutes" meant.

She went back inside and spoke to Mr. Mason. "All finished. I do think you will like the result. And I can't come for a visit without saying hello to Mrs. Thomas and Abby!"

"Of course not." Mr. Mason smiled and glanced at the back hallway.

She went past him and on into the milliner's room, where Mrs. Thomas and Abby were both at work on fall bonnets, both of which had the pink ruche inside the wider brims.

"Miss Lavinia!" Abby dropped her work onto the worktable and stood to give her a hug. "It's so good to see you! We've missed you, you know!"

A wave of pleasure swept over her as she hugged Abby and then Mrs. Thomas. She was used to seeing these two women nearly every day and had missed them, too.

Abby whispered, "I didn't know if you'd come back here again, Miss Lavinia. We couldn't believe that the millinery shop, well . . . isn't yours."

"It was difficult for me to believe, too, Abby." She gave a dry laugh, and then waved off the thought. "But I am glad things are going well for you all here."

"Mama told me that your husband Daniel returned to New Orleans. When will you be going to join him?"

She could feel her face heat up as she searched for a reply. The words from Daniel's letter, begging her to come, came back to her.

"Now, don't press Miss Lavinia about her plans, Abby. I'm sure she has much to think about." Mrs. Thomas saved her from having to answer.

"And Mama tells me Miss Sarah is getting married soon!"

"Oh, yes, in just a couple weeks." Lavinia was glad to change the subject. "She's working on the invitations now. The two of you and Mr. Mason are of course on the list."

Abby beamed, and Mrs. Thomas looked extremely pleased. "Oh, that means we'll need something pretty to wear, Mama!"

Mrs. Thomas drew a bit of the lavender material of Sarah's bridal dress from her pocket. "I confess I took this swatch when Sarah wasn't looking, and Abby and I would like to make her a matching bonnet as a surprise wedding gift."

"Oh, Mrs. Thomas, what a wonderful surprise! Sarah will be delighted. Thank you so much. And is Mr. Mason agreeable?"

"Of course Mr. Mason is agreeable," came Mr. Mason's voice behind her.

"Well, thank you, Mr. Mason, Mrs. Thomas, Abby. I will endeavor not to spoil the surprise!"

"Yes—don't tell her. We'll bring it over next week."

She stayed and talked with the women for a few more minutes, then became acutely aware of Peter waiting. "I should run on and not keep you from your work."

"Before you leave, I do have a matter that I would like to discuss with you." Mr. Mason stopped her as they came into the hallway beside her father's old office.

She looked at him, curious as to what he might have to say to her. "Yes, Mr. Mason?"

He pushed open the door to her father's office and she glimpsed the pedestal desk with the inkwell and the pen, the oil miniatures and Father's forever-waiting top hat. "I haven't wanted to move your father's things without your permission or your presence. I know they must be precious to you. Would you like to take his belongings with you now or send Peter for them later?"

The view of Father's office hit her like a blow. With all the turmoil of Daniel leaving, finding herself with child, and preparing for Sarah's wedding, she had forgotten that her father's things were still here in the shop's office, where they had been for so many years. A fresh wave of guilt washed over her for her forgetfulness. And naturally Mr. Mason would want to surround himself with his own things. Yet her heart ached. These last weeks she'd felt terribly emotional—Clementine said it was on account of the baby—and apt to cry at the slightest provocation and that is precisely what she did now. She held her hand over her mouth and tears leaked out of the corners of her eyes and her nose started to run.

Mr. Mason offered soothing words and produced his handkerchief, which she refused.

"Let me go fetch Peter." Lavinia didn't mean to use the brusque tone that came out in her voice.

Straightening her shoulders and wiping her face, she went out to get Peter, and between the three of them, they carried everything out to the carriage except the desk. The carriage had not room for it, and Peter would need to come back with the wagon. She immediately pictured Father's desk in her bedroom, in front of the window, a little piece of him now ever-present with her. Then she climbed back into the carriage, wiping away the last tears, and looking into the window she had so lovingly arranged and wondering if that was the last time she'd ever be there.

THE FOLLOWING DAY Peter and the neighbor's gardener returned to the millinery shop, loaded Father's desk into the wagon, and brought it to the house. There wasn't room in the sitting room without moving furniture around a great deal, and there certainly wasn't room in the dining room because of the breakfront.

"Do you mind if Father's work desk goes in my room?" Lavinia found Sarah still in the dining room, finishing the invitations. She pictured herself sitting at the desk writing a letter to Daniel or Harriet. Or possibly designing a bonnet for what had become the imaginary shop that she hoped one day she might own.

"Not at all, Livvy—you're the one who helped him at the shop."

Lavinia had Peter and his cohort carry it upstairs and put it in front of her bedroom window, and Lavinia sat at the desk for a long time, running her palm over the smooth dark wood, looking out at the trees, almost feeling her father's presence. But later, in the sitting room after dinner when Sarah mentioned the desk being brought home, William declared that he would find the desk useful for correspondence and paying bills once he and Sarah were married.

"Oh, William, I'm sorry, I didn't think about that," Sarah's face looked inscrutable in the candlelight. Lavinia felt badly for her sister, as she supposed she must feel torn between the wishes of her sister and her fiancé.

"I would advocate placing the desk here in the sitting room." William straightened his collar. "Then it could be accessed by all in the household. In Lavinia's room, it can only be used by her."

"You're quite right, William, we'll move it tomorrow." Sarah gave him an accommodating smile.

Lavinia remained silent for a few moments. Perhaps Sarah wasn't so torn. Was Lavinia being selfish to want the desk in her room? Possibly she was. Still, it was *her* father's desk, and William wasn't even a member of the family yet, and here suddenly his preference dictated every decision, large and small.

"And Lavinia, of course I would welcome you using the desk to write the statement we need for the probate court to contest the will," William added, with an air of impatience. "I need to review it before Sarah and I leave on our bridal tour."

"Yes, I have not yet had a chance to do that." Lavinia focused on her needlework. A wreath of flowers surrounded Sarah and William's names and their upcoming wedding date. She planned to either make it into a pillow or have it framed.

"You do realize that if we do not contest the will that you and Daniel will not inherit the millinery shop," William said. "And neither will Sarah and I."

"Of course I do." Lavinia had stitched white roses, for purity, jasmine for faithfulness, and a lily of the valley, for sensitiveness, all representing Sarah. For William, she had not been able to resist adding narcissus, for pride, and nettle, for defiance, among other more complimentary flowers. She didn't think William would decode her needlework and held a hope that Sarah would be too busy in her wedding whirl to notice.

CHAPTER TWENTY-ONE

September 1838
Savannah

T HE DAY OF Sarah's September wedding arrived, hot and
sunny. The bougainvillea, jessamine, and magnolias still
bloomed in their back garden, and the sun sparkled through the
trees. Clementine arrived an hour earlier than usual and put on
her Sunday apron in time to meet the oyster and ice delivery. She
had spent the previous afternoon frosting the fruitcake with thick
white icing, and Sarah and Lavinia had helped her with the
sweetmeats.

"Lavinia and Sarah, I'll thank you not to eat more sweets than
you make!" Clementine had smacked Lavinia's hand.

"Clementine! We're just trying the batter." Lavinia had
yanked her hand away, laughing, and glancing at Sarah.

Clementine was the only person in the house who seemed
truly calm. Sarah looked nerve-wracked, and Lavinia herself was
not much better.

How to sort out her complicated feelings about Sarah marrying William? Lavinia had married for love—though it was in a
whirl of emotion and grief after the shipwreck. But in Lavinia's
mind, Sarah's matrimony seemed to be more an economic
decision. Before Sarah's engagement, Lavinia had considered

what kind of work Sarah might do if she didn't marry. She had unsuccessfully tried to imagine her sister as a governess or teacher—Sarah did not have the strength of will to discipline a group of children. She loved enjoying new bonnet styles but didn't have an interest in actually designing or making the bonnets. Marriage did indeed seem to be Sarah's best option. Further, Sarah seemed fond of William, but Lavinia couldn't tell if it was love. It was clear that Sarah was eager to please him. Just as when discussing Father's desk or the decision to contest the will, she was quick to take his part. And they often inclined their heads together, their hands touching, as William instructed Sarah on some topic or another.

Yet Lavinia could not get past her personal distaste for the man. He seemed to have an autocratic nature that let him to behave as though Sarah were his own property. Also, William was deeply class conscious—an attitude that the shipwreck had brutally demonstrated to Lavinia as being false and shallow. He was dismissive and barked at Clementine and Peter and other tradespeople who came to the house when he thought the sisters weren't looking. She wondered how long that forbearance would last before he stopped caring who noticed. She didn't want to think too closely about what the years ahead might hold for Sarah after she married William.

Lying in her bed in her nightdress and listening to Clementine giving directions down below to the men delivering the ice and oysters, Lavinia began thinking about the institution of marriage, especially since she and Daniel were now separate. Without Daniel present, she functioned day to day as an unmarried woman, without the support or protection of a husband, but the little ceremony in Smithville changed her irrevocably in the eyes of the law. Women could inherit property as unmarried women but not as married women. She wondered if that difference in status would have made a difference in how she felt about contesting her father's will. It was true, though, that marriage brought romance and companionship, and safety, of course.

She didn't think, however, that Sarah would experience much companionship with William. When they sat on the porch in the evenings, mostly William pontificated while Sarah and Lavinia listened. And marriage did most often bring children. She ran her palm over her stomach, which had thickened slightly, enough for her to notice, though Sarah declared that it wasn't noticeable to others. But the care and tending of the children fell entirely to women. And that was in addition to the care and tending of the husbands.

She climbed out of bed and poured water into her washbasin. She had quite a lot to do today. It was certainly not a day to entertain thoughts such as these. She washed her face, trying to scrub them away.

"Livvy!" Sarah's voice sounded anxious. "You promised you'd style my hair!"

"Yes, yes, I will be right there!"

She hurried into Sarah's room and found her in her corset and chemise, sitting at her dressing table, nervously yanking the brush through her hair. "Hurry, Livvy, we need to be dressed and in the square in less than an hour."

She hugged her sister. "You look beautiful, sweetheart." She took the brush, and began separating her sister's dark hair into smooth, shiny sections. She braided and pinned, and they talked while looking in the dressing table mirror.

"Clementine will have everything ready when we walk back from the square. Do you have your case ready for your bridal tour?"

"Yes, William said to pack for cooler weather, so I have packed stockings and shawls. I still don't have the slightest idea where we might be going. Does Peter have the carriage ready?"

"I am sure he will."

Sarah caught Lavinia's eye in the mirror. "I wish Father were here."

Lavinia nodded. "He is here in spirit, Sarah, we must believe that."

"He would be so happy about my marriage to William. And you think I am doing the right thing, marrying William, do you not, Livvy?"

Lavinia pulled one of the plaits taut and wrapped it around the bun at the nape of Sarah's neck. She didn't answer right away.

"Lavinia?" Sarah turned and looked at her in alarm.

She focused on her own fingers as she pulled a braid tight. "Of course, you are doing the right thing, Sarah."

"You hesitated before your answer. I saw that. Why would you hesitate?"

"Sarah, I did not hesitate. I was braiding your hair."

"Was it because you don't think I should marry William? Whyever wouldn't you? And why wouldn't you say what you feel before my wedding day?" Sarah stood up quickly, scattering hairpins, and took the brush from Lavinia, her eyes flashing.

"Sarah, please. I didn't say anything. And you shouldn't upset yourself. The important thing is whether you love William. Does he bring you happiness, the way Daniel has brought it to me?"

Sarah's cheeks looked flushed, and her eyes began to brim with angry tears. "I would think that you would already know the answer to that! All the nights we have spent on the porch talking. All the times we have shared. Do I not seem as though I love him?"

"Yes, of course, you do." Lavinia gathered some scattered hairpins and did not try to meet Sarah's eyes, because they knew each other too well. Neither of them could fool the other with an untruth. And her fear wasn't that Sarah didn't love William. It was the reverse.

"And you let Daniel return to New Orleans—do you truly love *him*?"

Lavinia felt a mixture of guilt and avoidance—this was not how Sarah's wedding morning should go.

"Let's not talk about Daniel and me. Our situations are not the same. I've watched you, sister, and I believe that you do love William. I very much want you to be happy with him. So, tell me, are you?"

"Lavinia, why have you kept this from me?"

"Sarah, please." She picked up the brush and gently pushed Sarah back down into the dressing table chair. "Sit back down. I am almost finished. I've kept nothing from you. Of course you should marry William. You love him." What else could she say?

"All right." Sarah drew a deep breath and gave Lavinia one more searching look in the glass. "You believe it's the right thing." It was somehow both a challenge and a question.

"If you love him, it's the right thing. All finished. Now let's get your dress on."

Soon she closed the dozens of covered buttons up Sarah's back, her fingers racing.

"Beautiful, beautiful." Lavinia made sure her voice had a calming tone, as she clasped the amethyst necklace Father had given Sarah for her eighteenth birthday around her neck. "Father would be so pleased that you're wearing this. The prettiest bride in Savannah all year." She looked at Sarah in the mirror.

"Oh, Livvy." Sarah placed her cheek next to hers, her anger and alarm finally driven out by nerves. "What would I do without you?"

The guilt fell over her like a veil once more as she looked at her sister's hopeful face in the mirror, and then kissed her cheek. Oh, how she prayed that all would be well.

At that moment a soft knock came on the bedroom door, and Mrs. Thomas poked her head in. "May we interrupt for just a minute?"

Lavinia straightened, giving Sarah a last gentle pat on the shoulder. "Oh, certainly. Please come in, Mrs. Thomas, Abby."

The mother and daughter came shyly through the bedroom door, each holding an exquisite bonnet. Mrs. Thomas held one in lavender, for Sarah, with silk flowers and one perfectly placed white feather. Abby held one in pale yellow, matching Lavinia's dress.

"Our gifts to the two of you," said Mrs. Thomas.

"Oh, they are gorgeous!" Sarah stood, clasping her hands to her chest, tears of joy shining in her eyes. Lavinia felt tears coming too, that these sweet women had so diligently crafted these beautiful bonnets for her and Sarah.

"May I?" Mrs. Thomas asked, holding the bonnet up to help tie it over Sarah's shining, newly-braided hair.

"Oh, yes, I would be honored!" Deftly, with some happy tears of her own, Mrs. Thomas arranged Sarah's bonnet, affixed the hat pins, and she and Abby bustled out of the room.

A few minutes later, Lavinia had quickly pinned up her own hair and donned her newly altered pale-yellow dress and bonnet. Then she and Sarah skimmed down the stairs, grabbed their gloves, and hurried down the front steps, where William waited to make the short walk with them to the square.

How Lavinia wished Father were here with them.

REVEREND COLLINS AND his wife waited at the east edge of the square with their assembled neighbors, all of whom greeted the Onslows warmly and admired the bride. Reverend Collins, in his dark robes, waited for the Savannah church bells to finish tolling ten o'clock before clearing his throat and intoning, "We are gathered here today to join William and Sarah in holy matrimony."

During the ceremony, the Spanish moss draped from the trees stirred in a light breeze hinting of autumn coming from the water a few blocks away, and the last of the ivory blossoms glistened among the shiny green leaves of the magnolia tree in the center of the square. Lavinia was Sarah's bridesmaid, and William's older brother was his best man. One of Father's friends, Mr. Alexander, walked Sarah down a grassy opening between the standing guests. As Reverend Collins read the vows, Lavinia searched William's face for affection toward Sarah. She saw pride, maybe that always present sense of possession, and appreciation for Sarah's beauty. But she couldn't convince herself that she saw affection. Again, guilt coursed through her, and she had to restrain herself from speaking up when the minister asked if anyone knew of any reason why this union should not take place. But Sarah had said she loved him. And Lavinia chose to believe that she did.

As Sarah and William repeated their vows, Lavinia's own vows came back to her. At the time she had been frightened and nervous, leery of Judge Johnson, grateful to the Goshers, but most of all desperate beyond words for Daniel to take her in his arms. How could she have come to know Daniel well enough in those few short days together to truly love him in a deep and mature way? The question was, would true deep feelings of love develop as time went by? Or would the two of them drift apart?

Before she knew it, William and Sarah kissed and turned to the gathered guests, hand-in-hand. It was done. She couldn't help but feel a surge of sadness.

The reception in the garden passed as if in a dream. Clementine had hired her niece, Matilda to help serve, and she gave her directions with sharp commands. The poor girl seemed a bit cowed by Clementine. Lavinia smiled when she saw it—she could sympathize.

Their Savannah neighbors and friends, all in their finest clothing, ate the fruitcake and the sweetmeats, and congratulated William and Sarah. Lavinia watched William as he wrapped his arm around Sarah's waist.

"So good to have a happy event a few short months after the sad occasion of your father's death." Reverend Collins' tone was kind enough, but she wondered if he believed she and Sarah had not observed a long enough mourning period. He'd always been very attentive to issues of propriety.

"Yes, it is." She gave him a smile, and before she could say anything else Mrs. Pinckney, a widow from the next block and one of Father's most loyal customers at the millinery shop, accosted her.

"Where is that handsome husband of yours?"

She knew she would need to answer these questions. "He's returned to reclaim his position at the railroad in New Orleans."

"And will you join him soon?" Mrs. Pinckney sipped her tea.

"Oh, planning for Sarah's wedding has consumed all our days. I haven't had a thought to spare for travel!" she laughed, deflecting Mrs. Pinckney's attention back toward her sister. "Wasn't it a lovely day for a wedding?" Mrs. Pinckney allowed Lavinia to steer the conversation out of dangerous waters and she soon moved on. Lavinia then made her way across the grass to greet Mrs. Thomas, Abby, and Mr. Mason, where they stood beside the magnolia tree, in their finest attire and enjoying the celebratory occasion.

"Sarah looks so lovely in the wedding bonnet you made for her," Lavinia said to the milliners. She touched the brim of her own. "And I am delighted with mine. Thank you again for the very special gifts. And we are so pleased that you're all here."

"We would not have missed it," Mrs. Thomas assured her.

"It's an honor to be here," said Mr. Mason. "I wish your father could have been present. He would have been very proud and pleased."

"Yes, I think he would have," Lavinia agreed.

At that moment, William clinked his spoon against the crystal of his champagne glass to gain the group's attention. "Thank you for joining our wedding celebration and for your generous gifts. It is now time for us to take our leave, as our steamer sails at high tide for the glorious bridal tour I have planned to Niagara Falls with Sarah, now my wife."

Niagara Falls! Abby squealed and the other guests gasped and applauded. The most popular bridal tour destination of the last few years. Of course William would plan such a trip. Sarah smiled in delight, caught Lavinia's eye, and then William kissed her. Lavinia's misgivings began to dissolve. Perhaps, indeed, everything would be all right with William.

Everything unspooled from there in a whirl. The guests took their leave, Lavinia helped Sarah out of her wedding dress and into her traveling dress, and then, just as Sarah had said farewell to Lavinia several months ago before she boarded the *Pulaski* with Father, now Lavinia stood in the front hall saying goodbye to Sarah.

"Safe travels." She hugged her tightly. Sarah and William planned to take the steamer up north to the Hudson River and through the Erie Canal to the falls. The voyage north would take nearly a week, and they would be gone for over a month.

As they drove away Lavinia pushed away the recurring visions of the *Pulaski's* explosion, and of the dead man who had floated up to the raft. The chances of another disaster occurring had to be very small, she told herself, suspecting she would probably have misgivings about people traveling by water for the rest of her life.

THAT NIGHT SHE stayed alone in the house for the first time in her life. Clementine and Peter had gone home. She wandered around with a flickering candle, looking in Sarah's and Father's empty, quiet rooms. At last, she sat down in her own room at Father's desk, which no one had had time to move to the sitting room as William had asked. Not that Lavinia had been searching for a time to have it done. She dipped her pen in the inkwell and began a letter to Daniel.

Dear Daniel,

Sarah and William were married today. The ceremony in Oglethorpe Square and the reception in our garden were lovely. Then William and Sarah left for their month-long bridal tour at Niagara Falls. They will travel on a steamer! How I wish you could have been here.

Your letter was one of the happiest sights I have had these last few weeks. I am sorry that with the preparations for the wedding that I haven't had time to write you back until now. In truth, I was waiting to write so I could tell you about it. I was gladder still that you have regained your position with the Pontchartrain Railroad. How gallant of the new employee to relinquish his position to you! The situation with the maritime insurance is very vexing, and I hope that you have resolved it.

I, too, would love to meet your sisters. I have felt such closeness to my own sister as of late as we have prepared for her nuptials. No one can remember our life as children together except us, and that is a bond that in my mind can never be severed.

I am deeply touched and tempted by your entreaties to join you there in New Orleans. I do miss you and think of the short but intense time we shared together every day. Please understand my fear of travel.

She wrote several more paragraphs, describing the wedding in detail and the ways in which she had been passing her days, all the while wondering what his thoughts and expressions would be when he read them. Should she sign it with love? After some consideration, she signed it, "Your wife, Lavinia." She touched her waist, thinking about the small life growing there, and imagined Daniel's hand there too.

CHAPTER TWENTY-TWO

October 1838
Savannah

DAYS AND THEN weeks passed without Sarah. The leaves dropped from many trees in Savannah except the magnolias and live oaks, which remained glossy green with their gray capes of Spanish moss. The sun set earlier, and the evenings grew just a bit cooler. Lavinia carried Daniel's letters in the pockets of her dresses, and they grew soft and dog-eared from constant rereading and handling. Sarah had promised to write but so far Lavinia had only two short notes from her, both filled with descriptions of the wonders they were seeing on their travels on the Hudson River, but also complaining of the cold and her inadequate clothing. She must be very much enjoying William's company. Lavinia tried to be accepting of her sister's lack of further communication. After all, it was her bridal tour.

She received a letter from Harriet in Augusta. Harriet and Lavinia had been debutantes together four years ago, drawn to each other by their fondness for books, but Harriet, unlike Lavinia, had found a husband during her coming out season. Harriet was a thinker and a reader and had now taken up painting. In her letter, Harriet told Lavinia about her life in Augusta, considerably more rural and lonely. She had one child, was pregnant with another, and begged Lavinia to come for a visit. Lavinia valued Harriet's friendship, and replied quickly, but did not know when she might visit.

She saw more drawings of the headwear at Queen Victoria's coronation in a fashion journal, and could not resist driving to the millinery shop again to show Mr. Mason and the milliners. She insisted Peter need not come—all the time she spent alone was making her feel more independent than before, and once Daisy was harnessed, she could easily drive Daisy herself. When she arrived, though, she immediately felt that something was amiss. The bonnets in the window looked different in a way she couldn't quite describe. Upon entering the shop, she also sensed something had changed in Mr. Mason's attitude.

"Hello, Miss Lavinia. Delightful to see you." However, he didn't appear quite as delighted as usual, though, and he seemed to be standing purposely between her and the curtain covering the entrance to the back hallway.

"And how is business?"

"We have been busy." His tone sounded vague.

She examined one of the styles on display, a bonnet with a red ribbon and a red silk rose. "Did Abby make this one?"

He paused. "I'm not sure." He saw the fashion journal she carried. "Ah, you have more drawings from the Queen's coronation. Thank you for bringing this in. Let me take a look to see what ideas we can use."

"Of course." She handed him the journal. "I'll just go back and say hello to Mrs. Thomas and Abby."

"I don't think—" he began, but she went ahead past him into the back hall. There in the hallway, propped against the wall, stood a freshly painted sign in black and red that read, "Mason's Millinery." It hit Lavinia like a shock.

"Mr. Mason, are you changing the name of the shop?" She turned to face him.

"Well, yes, Miss Lavinia, I am. It seemed only right."

Her father's business, their family business—gone forever in the stroke of a paintbrush! Tears came to her eyes. "But all the years of goodwill we built with our family name will be lost, Mr. Mason."

"But the shop now belongs to me. I would like to build up that same goodwill with my name as well." He stood even straighter than usual, but he used a tone that sounded unsure. She noticed now that his dress was even finer than before. He now wore a silk cravat and a pocket watch, and there was pomade on his shiny brown hair.

"I just don't understand why it isn't mine!" she burst out.

"Please don't talk that way, Miss Lavinia."

Tears blinded her eyes. She swept down the hall and pulled back the curtain to the workroom. Two complete strangers looked up from their work.

"Yes, ma'am, may I help you?"

"Who are you? Where are Mrs. Thomas and Abby?" Her breath came in ragged bursts.

"They're sisters of my friends from the Bethesda Home," Mr. Mason said quietly behind her.

He gestured her ahead of him and she followed him back out into the hallway outside her father's office. "Do you mean the Bethesda Home for Boys, the one for orphans?"

"Yes. That is where I lived before your father took me in at the shop."

Lavinia knew Mr. Mason never spoke of any family, and she had assumed he lived on his own, but she had not realized that Mr. Mason had been an orphan. She chided herself for not being curious enough to find out such a thing. But her sorrow for him did not outweigh her concern for Mrs. Thomas and Abby. "You dismissed Mrs. Thomas and Abby? What are they to do for wages?"

"They're good milliners. I trust they'll find work. I gave them both excellent letters of recommendation."

"They had both worked here for years! I am heartbroken that you would dismiss them!"

"My friends' sisters need wages, too. Please understand, Miss Lavinia. Times are hard. It wasn't an easy decision."

She walked quickly toward the door. When she left the shop, she closed the door softly, wiping her tears so that people on the street would not see them, then stood in the street for long moments looking at the display window, wondering if she would ever be back.

Her heart went out to Mrs. Thomas and Abby. How could Mr. Mason have done such a thing to them? She must contact them right away and see that they were all right. She pushed poor Daisy almost to a gallop on her way home in her anger, and that night she cried herself to sleep. Father's legacy was gone.

AFTER THE BLOW of learning about the changes to the shop, Lavinia sent out inquiries and found that Mrs. Thomas and Abby had found work at a dressmaker's shop. This work most likely paid them lower wages, but at least they had a livelihood.

While taking care of household duties, Lavinia used some of the fitting out money Father had left her to pay Clementine and Peter. She hoped that now that William had married Sarah he would keep them on and share the expense with her when they returned from their bridal tour. With Sarah gone, Lavinia spent more time with Clementine, altering some dresses to accommodate her pregnancy, and at last couldn't keep herself from mentioning Mrs. Thomas and Abby to her late one afternoon when they sat together in the warming kitchen, trying to finish their stitching before the sunlight faded.

"Clementine, I felt so badly for Mrs. Thomas and Abby when I learned that they had to seek other employment. And I had not known until that day that Mr. Mason had been at the Bethesda Home for Boys. I was quite shocked, though I realize I probably should have wondered more about his situation over the years. I shouldn't speak ill of my father—you know how I loved him—but I admit that I am devastated Father didn't keep the shop in the family. I do not want to go so far as to contest the will, as William is determined to do, but I do at times wonder if Father ever made a later will."

Clementine remained silent, tightening both her stitches and her lips. Lavinia watched her a moment. Some in Savannah might have found this conversation improper for mistress and servant, yet Lavinia and Sarah had always been informal with Clementine since she had raised them from children, and she with them. If William were in the house and overheard this conversation, he might object to Lavinia being too familiar with the servants, but today there was no one in the house but Clementine and Lavinia, and who would be the wiser about what they discussed?

Lavinia took another stitch as the silence stretched, now feeling awkward that she had talked about such a thing to Clementine. She changed the subject. "I've always wondered, yet never asked, how did you end up as a free woman? There are not as many here in Savannah as there used to be . . . because of the changing atmosphere, I suppose."

"That's true, Miss Lavinia. I know some who have left to go north in these times. My mama bought her own freedom while she was expecting me, and I was born free."

"How did she do that?"

"She asked her master for a price, and he said if she could pay him four hundred dollars, she would be free. So she hired herself out to do sewing and was able to keep some of the money back, hidden in a gunny sack. It took her seven years to save the money, and by then I was on the way. But when she gave it to him, he was as good as his word and gave her the freedom papers. So, I was born a free girl. She told me every day of my life to look at myself in the mirror and to say out loud, 'I am Clementine Brown, and I am free.'"

"Your mother sounds like a strong woman." Lavinia tried to imagine, in her own expectant state, trying to buy freedom.

"Yes, she was, bless her soul."

"How did you get your training as a midwife?"

"My mama's sister-friend trained as a granny midwife, and from the time I was about twelve my mama told her to take me along so I could learn. She told me I needed to be useful so I could find my way in the world."

This hit Lavinia hard. Clementine, as a free Black woman, must have had a very difficult life, but she had also been taught the necessity of being useful from a young age. Sarah and Lavinia, on the other hand, white and merchant class, were taught to be decorative. They had not even been formally educated past the age of twelve, as Father had deemed it unnecessary. Lavinia had been lucky she had been able to pick up figures quickly when Father showed her at the shop. She returned to the idea that had recurred periodically since the shipwreck—that the grace of her survival with Daniel meant something and that she might try to find a higher purpose for her life. This was a thought that seemed to churn in the back of her mind.

"Do you feel that a person has a destiny, Clementine? That we might have been put on this earth to do something in particular?"

"I reckon I just feel like we do all the work we can while we're able." Clementine gave a rueful laugh. "And then we go to be with the Lord."

Lavinia smiled, too, but considered what Clementine had said. "I think for a long while I felt that the shop was my destiny. I felt that by and by I was meant to take over Father's role there. It is hard to accept that he didn't leave the shop to his own family. But since the shop is not to be mine, perhaps I have another destiny."

"Not all is as it seems," Clementine said after a wait, not meeting Lavinia's eye.

Lavinia looked up. "What do you mean?"

Clementine sat up straighter and spoke softly. "Perhaps your father did indeed keep the shop in the family."

Blood rushed to Lavinia's cheeks. "What do you mean? Mr. Mason is not in our family."

"I am sorry to say this, Miss Lavinia, but indeed, he is. He is your half-brother."

Lavinia's mouth fell open and she dropped her needle. "What?"

Clementine nodded, still refusing to meet her eye. "You know I have been midwifing for many years. Mr. Onslow did call me in one night—it was a few years before he met your mother—and I did deliver the boy of a young woman who used to work in your father's shop. Your father was in the next room in a terrible state of worry. That poor girl died that night, and your father paid for her funeral as well as the boy's keep at Bethesda Home for Boys. Peter used to take the money every month. He brought the boy to work in the shop when he turned fifteen."

Lavinia dropped the dress on the arm of her chair and got to her feet. "That can't be true. I am sure Father was just helping a poor woman in need. That was the kind of man he was."

"Your father was a good man," Clementine nodded in agreement. "But lonely." Clementine made a knot at the end of a seam and clipped the thread with her teeth. She stood and smoothed her apron. "Time to get dinner."

Lavinia could not feel her limbs. "Excuse me, Clementine, I believe I need to lie down." Nearly blinded by tears, she forced herself to walk calmly from the room and up the stairs. She'd never believe what Clementine had said about Mr. Mason. Never.

THAT NIGHT, WHILE eating her dinner alone and reading *Hobomok, A Tale of Early Times* written simply by "An American," which Harriet had sent with her last letter and described as "scandalous," she could hear Peter and Clementine laughing and joking in the warming kitchen as they ate together. No more would they have joined Lavinia here in the dining room than she would have joined them in the warming kitchen, but for the first time, as the only white person in the house, she became more acutely aware of their separation.

How could Father have done what Clementine said he did? And, if it were true, to think that Clementine and Peter had known for all these years, while Lavinia and Sarah were innocent of it. She thought of the way she had imagined Mr. Mason imitating Father's mannerisms. She realized with shock now: He could have *inherited* Father's mannerisms. What if he *was* his son? And if Father had a son, he would certainly leave his business to him rather than a daughter.

She tried to brush these thoughts aside. She would just be silent about this for a time. And she would never breathe a word of it to Sarah. And certainly not to William.

Reading *Hobomok*, which explored many of the same themes as *The Last of the Mohicans*, Lavinia found herself yearning to discuss the ideas in the book with Daniel. She remembered the letters about the equality of women and abolition by Miss Sarah Grimké that she'd hidden under her mattress before she'd left on the *Pulaski*. Later that evening, she pulled one out and reread it. Miss Grimké wrote that white women should commiserate with slaves since laws forced them into bondage to their husbands, and that men should not have so much control over their wives. So many of the ideas that had seemed so shocking before made more sense to Lavinia now. And she knew instinctively that she should keep the letter hidden from William. She put it back with the others and shoved them all more deeply under her mattress.

As THE DAYS passed and her pregnancy progressed, Lavinia craved sleep. Just thinking about Mr. Mason made her feel an exhaustion she could not put into words. One morning, a few weeks after

Sarah had left, when Clementine brought the ginger tea to the dining room, she touched her hand to her stomach.

"Clementine, I believe my nausea has improved. I may not need the ginger tea much longer. How long now before I should feel the baby quicken?"

"Maybe halfway through, at four to five months along."

That could still be several weeks from now, according to Lavinia's calculations. "And what will the quickening feel like?"

"It will be a feathery feeling, like a butterfly."

Lavinia held very still, trying to discern a fluttery movement, but felt nothing.

"Should I change my mind and write Daniel about the baby?" She wanted to share it with him.

"No need. It is a hard truth, but my eyes have seen things that would tell you to wait. Safe to wait."

Lavinia knew that not every baby lived. And not every mother. Lavinia knew that, too. A spark of fear rippled through her, remembering what happened to Mama. She would do as Clementine said. Yet, she had a new feeling, too—a fierce protectiveness for this life growing inside her, and a desire that this babe should live in spite of the odds.

SHE RECEIVED ANOTHER letter from Daniel a few days later. Because the letters took so long to arrive, receiving a letter felt like moving back in time and re-examining the past.

Dearest Lavinia,

I wish I could have been there for Sarah and William's wedding. Let us hope that William will care for your sister well, and they will have a good life together. Their exciting bridal trip to Niagara Falls naturally made me think that you and I had no bridal tour after our marriage, and I want to assure you that I would like to remedy that one day.

There are some interesting new ideas churning in regard to the railroad. While the major purpose of our railway is transporting cotton from the plantations to the docks, there has been some talk about us transporting people similar to a stagecoach, and I have seen some interesting railroad coach designs, interestingly enough, from Charleston. There is even talk that one day a special car for dining could be included. Right now it costs thirty-seven cents to ride from New Orleans to Pontchartrain. There have been some false starts and unfortunate circumstances, but it is my hope and belief that in the end we will also succeed in establishing a passenger train from New Orleans to Nashville. Ideas for financing are still being worked out, but I for one am intensely optimistic about the future of the railroad. It's true, though, that construction is not progressing well at the moment because of the swamps and bayous and the difficulty procuring red cypress for the cross ties. Furthermore, the mosquitos are atrocious.

However, for my position I am receiving nearly $100/month, which is an exceptionally good wage. I'm quite pleased with it, and I hope you are too. In fact, I have decided to invest in a subscription of stock in the New Orleans to Nashville. The city of New Orleans itself has invested, which gives me confidence.

The other good news is that I did find the copy of the maritime insurance policy that I purchased in the pocket of a jacket I had left at the railroad. So, the railroad will not need to accept the loss of the cost of the British locomotive. This is a considerable relief.

My cousins in Charleston are expecting another child, a baby sister or brother for the little thespian I told you about when we were on the water. It will be fun to have another child there to play with the next time I visit. Children bring such bright spirit and laughter to life. Perhaps one day we will be blessed with children.

I think of you every single day, Lavinia. I hope that now that Sarah is wed, you are one step closer to being back in my arms, and I remain hopeful that you will join me here in New

Orleans soon. I believe you would love this city, as I do, and you would be fond of my sisters. Please continue to consider this.

Your loving husband, Daniel

Lavinia folded and unfolded, read and reread the letter.

The fact that Daniel was interested in children of course came as a relief, and she was eager to respond. Should she tell him about the baby now? Could this be her opening? She thought about the wee baby she carried and a fierce, abiding love for it continued to consume her. She wondered if it was a boy or a girl, and wondered what Daniel might hope for, though whether the babe was healthy and vigorous was the most important thing. But so far, she had not yet felt a flutter of life. She sat down at Father's desk to respond that very afternoon.

Dear Daniel,

I submit that we did in fact take a bridal tour, though on a crowded stagecoach and in dilapidated inns rather than on a luxurious steamship like Sarah and William. And that trip nearly exhausted us both. Remember the week of recuperation we required when we arrived here in Savannah? And I will argue that we experienced an adventure too. But I would not refuse a bridal tour at some future date if you insist upon one!

I am glad the city of New Orleans is investing in the railroad, and it sounds as though you are using your salary wisely. I believe you're right that the railroad is a good investment.

I am pleased to learn that you foresee children in our future. I want you to know that whether boy or girl, I will feel a ferocious love for any child that we might be blessed with and hope you will feel the same when the time comes.

I, too, would like to meet your sisters one day. And please offer my best wishes for a peaceful laying-in and healthy baby to your cousin's wife.

Life here goes on, more quietly without Sarah. Since William is gone, I have been spared his demands for me to write a document supporting his challenge to the will. Like Odysseus' wife, I have kept delaying. Clementine and Peter seem to be more at ease with William gone, as well. Clementine particularly seems on edge whenever he is around. I have very mixed feelings about my sister's marriage, though of course I want it to be a success.

Being at home so much, especially since now I'm without Sarah, is strange. I used to spend so much time at the shop before and I dearly miss it. I have been thinking more about it, and I do believe that I would like to have a shop of my own one day. What do you think of the idea?

I have been plagued as of late with ideas about being useful, about doing something to show my gratitude for having our lives spared after the shipwreck. Have you had any similar feelings or inclinations? I feel that you and I have been kept on this earth for a reason and would like to know your thoughts on this topic.

Your wife,
Lavinia

She had been deliberately vague about children but hoped that she could write him the news that she was expecting in their next exchange. She wished she could tell Daniel what Clementine had told her about Mr. Mason, as she longed to know what he would think, but she much preferred to speak with Daniel about that in person.

She went downstairs to place her sealed envelope on the hall table the next morning just as someone knocked at the front door. Clementine was in the warming kitchen, so she opened it herself and was startled to recognize a familiar face—the ambitious and nattily-dressed reporter, Mr. Morgan, who had come to the Goshers' home in Smithville several months ago and raised Daniel's ire.

"Miss Onslow or Mrs. Ridge?" He removed his top hat. "Sorry to disturb you, ma'am." His boots had been recently shined, his waistcoat was of the newest fashion, and his mustache still well-groomed. But for the leather notebook and pencil he carried, he could have been a gentleman come to call.

She dropped her jaw and took a step back. "How on earth did you find me?"

"I checked the passenger manifest from the *Pulaski* and found that you were from Savannah. It was not a matter of much asking to connect you with Onslow's Milliners. The workers there were quite obliging with directions to your home. I have come in the hope of an interview with you and Mr. Ridge. Is Mr. Ridge here?"

His tenacity took her aback, and she was disinclined to give him information about Daniel's whereabouts. "Mr. Ridge is out at the moment."

"Our readers have continued to be fascinated with your story, and my editor sent me to find out how you and Mr. Ridge have fared. Are you indeed married? How is your life now? What has happened since you survived the wreck of the *Pulaski*?"

Daniel would be furious. And look at the cheek of this man— to follow them all the way to Savannah and now to be standing here on her front porch asking impertinent questions! Yet, she remembered that she encouraged his questions in Smithville because she thought he might in turn be able to learn something about what happened to Father. Perhaps he had thought he would be welcomed here.

The reporter must have sensed reticence in her face because he rushed on. "I appreciated your kindness to me when I first interviewed you. Yours was such a heartrending story."

Clementine would be aghast if she let the reporter in. Yet, she admitted she was grateful for the article he had written as it was how Harriet had learned she was still alive. Perhaps a short interview wouldn't hurt anything.

"Come in." She opened the door and gestured him inside hurriedly while looking up and down the street, not certain how her neighbors would accept a reporter in their midst. She shut the door and he followed her into the sitting room, where she sat in the center of the loveseat, quickly arranging her skirts.

"Please have a seat." She indicated the upholstered Queen

Anne chair. "What would you like to know?"

"Miss Onslow, many thanks for your cooperation. I am in your debt."

At that moment Clementine appeared, standing erect in the doorway in her apron, looking out of sorts. "Miss Lavinia? Do you need my help?"

"Yes, Clementine, thank you, this is Mr. Morgan from—

"*The Delaware Gazette.*"

"I would like some ginger tea and Mr. Morgan here would like . . . ?" She pretended not to notice Clementine's disapproval.

"Oh, any tea will do," Mr. Morgan said. "And please do not go to any trouble on my account. Many thanks, ma'am."

"Yes, ma'am." Clementine gave her a sideways look and left the room in a noisy fashion. Allowing a reporter into the house was, to her, scandalous.

Mr. Morgan looked after her and waited to speak until she was gone. "Thank you again for allowing me to come and interview you, Miss Onslow."

"Mrs. Ridge."

He tried to smooth his beard and hair without much success. "My apologies. So, do tell me, yes, you are now married to Mr. Ridge?"

She sat up straighter. "You know I am married, Mr. Morgan. I saw you standing outside the window of the Gosher's home that afternoon of our wedding, eavesdropping and taking notes. You saw our wedding yourself."

He reddened. "But I must confirm. You did say your marriage vows on that day but not on any other day?"

She nodded. "Of course I did." What was he getting at?

"I feel that I should tell you that Mr. Johnson, who married you, was not a justice of the peace. I tracked him down and found that he was an itinerant who posed as a justice of the peace and Mr. Ridge paid him a fee to marry you. He took the money and spent it on drink."

She felt faint. "Excuse me?"

"I fear you are not legally married, Miss Onslow."

CHAPTER TWENTY-THREE

October 1838
Savannah

B LOOD RUSHED FROM her head, and she had to steady herself on the loveseat.

"Miss Onslow, are you all right? Can I get you a glass of water?" The reporter's voice sounded very far away. He called into the front hall. "We need some help!"

A moment later he sat beside her, gingerly supporting her arm so that she didn't slide to the floor.

Clementine, just entering the room, let the tea tray clatter onto the tea cart and crossed the room in two strides. "Miss Lavinia! Excuse me, sir, I will assist her."

Mr. Morgan jumped to his feet and stood watching with his hat in his hands as Clementine framed Lavinia's face with her warm palms and patted her cheeks gently.

"Miss Lavinia? Do you need to lie down?"

"Yes," she breathed, and Clementine helped her to lie on the loveseat, plumping a pillow beneath her head.

"Sir, as you can see, my mistress is indisposed." Clementine's voice sounded curt, then she seemed to lose her composure. "What on God's green earth did you say to her?"

"Yes, I will take my leave, with the greatest apologies for

upsetting the lady. I surely had no intention of such a thing happening—"

"Wait." She raised herself to her elbow, before he left the room. "Tell me—did Daniel know? That Johnson was not a justice of the peace?"

Mr. Morgan twisted his hat. "I cannot say, Miss Onslow." Just the fact that he called her "Miss Onslow" rather than "Mrs. Ridge" gave her a pain near her heart. He produced a card from his hotel, which he laid on the front hall table. "Should you want to get in touch with me, Miss Onslow, please feel free. I'll be in Savannah for a few days and would still like to write another article about your story. Again, my most humble apologies." He shut the door quietly behind him as he took his leave.

"Land sakes, Miss Lavinia," Clementine seemed uncharacteristically upset. "Why in the world did you let that reporter into this house?"

"I don't know." She struggled not to cry.

"What did he say to you?"

"He says I am not married! He said he tracked down the man who married us, and apparently he was not a justice of the peace as he told us. He was an itinerant drunk who took money from Daniel and posed as one. I was in a daze, and I did not think to ask for a marriage certificate. And I don't think Daniel did either. Here I am with child, and I am not married!"

"Oh, my Lord!" Clementine helped her to sit up and wrapped her arm around her. "This is a terrible thing, Miss Lavinia."

She was ashamed that both she and Daniel had allowed that man to dupe them. Could Mr. Morgan be mistaken? But she remembered Mr. Johnson's seedy look and the whiff of whiskey on his breath and knew he wasn't. Had Daniel known? She could hardly credit it. Such a deception didn't seem to be anything that could be true of him, after their harrowing days on the water, days in which she had never felt so close to anyone in her life. Unbidden, a little voice in her head reminded her of how long he'd kept the secrets of his reversal of fortune and the railroad money that had been lost. In fact, he was capable of deception.

"Mark my words." Clementine sounded disgusted. "That reporter is going to go out and publish an article in the paper about you."

"I know." She felt bile rise in her throat.

Clementine helped Lavinia up to her room. Lavinia then crawled into bed and pulled the blanket over her head. Clementine assured her she would turn away any visitors and say that Lavinia was ill. In fact, she did feel ill—in a way the ginger tea couldn't help.

Her mind swirled, and she twisted around under the sheets, in regret and disbelief. How she wished Sarah were here so that they could discuss the situation. Just talking with Sarah could help calm her, help her keep a grip on reality. And Father. If only she could get Father's advice. But that was something that she would never get again.

What was the truth about Daniel?

HER THOUGHTS RACED restlessly for hours. She tried to read, she tried to make the list for the market, to plan the week's menus, and to trim the roses in the garden, but couldn't concentrate on anything and finally went back to bed and let her worries wash over her. She had questioned the wisdom of marrying Daniel only to find out now that she wasn't married at all. It seemed a perverse sort of irony. If it weren't for the baby, the four days on the water and the time together in Smithville could have been a nightmare or a dream.

That night, when Clementine, who had stayed late out of concern, brought some chicken soup, she suddenly remembered the letter she had left in the front hall.

"Did the letter to Daniel go out?"

"Yes, Peter took our mail to the depot. It is gone."

Gone! She would write another letter tonight and send it first thing in the morning. After the soup warmed her, she felt more energetic. She pulled herself from the bed and went to Father's desk, lit a candle, and wrote Daniel another letter. In it, she described the visit from the reporter and all that he had said.

She closed with:

Daniel, you must be truthful with me. Did you know that we weren't married? I can't go on without knowing.

Folding the letter, she crawled back into the bed and lay there thinking, wondering what the best course of action should be.

And as she lay there that night, she felt it. A faint, feathery flutter in her lower belly. Like a tiny butterfly turning flips. It was unmistakable. The sweet movement of a babe. The flutter felt so tender, so vulnerable and trusting, tears rolled from her eyes and wet her pillow. She crawled back out of bed, relit the candle, and added a line to her letter to Daniel.

I have something I must tell you in person. Can you come to Savannah?

TWO DAYS LATER, she sat in the dining room finishing her breakfast when Clementine interrupted by wordlessly bringing in the *Delaware Gazette*. Lavinia had asked Peter to find it and every local paper since Mr. Morgan had visited. And now, at last, Lavinia's worst fears were confirmed.

"Oh, no, Clementine, here on the second page is an article by Mr. Morgan about Daniel and me!"

Clementine's reading was rudimentary. "Read it to me," she said, leaning against the doorway.

So she did.

Savannah Debutante Tricked into Marriage

Miss Lavinia Onslow, a past Savannah debutante, survived the wreck of the Pulaski while floating on two settees lashed together by Mr. Daniel Ridge. Miss Onslow and Mr. Ridge floated for four days before they were rescued off the coast of North Carolina and taken by boat to the port at Smithville. When they were rescued, Mr. Ridge announced their engagement after the four-day ordeal. While in Smithville, they were married by a man named Johnson who claimed to be a justice of the peace. On questioning, however, Johnson revealed that he was not in fact a justice of the peace, making the marriage invalid.

Johnson explained: "I was happy to marry the two as they appeared very much in love, but it weren't an official ceremony, being that I am not a genuine justice of the peace." When asked why he posed as a justice of the peace, he admitted that he met the groom in a tavern and asked for a fee which the groom paid.

Mr. Ridge and Miss Onslow soon after traveled together by stage to the bride's home in Savannah, where they have been living openly as man and wife in the bride's family home.

When visited at her home in Savannah, Miss Onslow was taken ill by the scandalous news that Mr. Johnson was not a true justice of the peace, and asked for a cup of ginger tea, which, according to a knowledgeable source, is often used by women who are with child to settle the stomach. Mr. Ridge was not at home.

Lavinia could hardly finish reading the article. She stood and threw the paper to the floor. "That despicable Mr. Morgan!" From the headline to the final line, it was a total betrayal. And to add the line about the ginger tea—it was downright cruel! What in the world had she ever done to him to deserve this?

"Miss Lavinia, this is dreadful. You must not leave the house."

"What do you mean, Clementine? You think I should become a prisoner in my own house?" Yet she had a feeling of despair, a feeling of doom.

"Miss Lavinia, now that article's about, there'll soon be gossip about whether you are in the family way and unmarried." Clementine's voice sounded patient, as if she were speaking to a child. "You ought to stay in the house or travel somewhere until the babe is born and then maybe offer it for secret adoption."

"Secret adoption!" She took a breath, briefly placed her hand on her belly, where she had only recently felt the quickening. A tiny human being. Her child and Daniel's. "How could I possibly do such a thing?"

"What about your father's brother at the plantation outside Savannah?"

She shook her head. "We've never been close to their family. He and Father were estranged."

"Or maybe you could travel to Europe. One of the Maclean girls did that last year and people said she had a baby there and gave it for adoption."

"I can't think of getting back on an ocean-going boat, Clementine. And where would I find the money for an ocean voyage all the way to Europe?"

"We've got to do something, Miss Lavinia." Clementine gave her a look of desperate determination.

"Just give me time to think. As terrible as this article is, my situation now is no different than yesterday—only now it's just that everyone in Savannah knows about it. So, whatever I would do now would be to avoid gossip, that's all."

"Gossip and shunning too, Miss Lavinia. People are cruel."

"There has to be a solution." She took the stairs to her room and shut the door and leaned on it. She felt weak in the knees. She should have left with Daniel. Could she realistically remain in the house for five more months until the birth of the baby? That simply wouldn't be possible. Clementine was right. She had to go somewhere. But where?

She sat at her dressing table, taking down her hair, as her mind flitted over various solutions. She brushed her hair with long strokes, trying to calm down, telling herself that Savannah society had never meant much to her anyway. Sarah had enjoyed being a debutante when her time came, but Lavinia had found the social jockeying and the falseness of the interactions to be tedious—though she had enjoyed designing her own bonnets as well as Harriet's and a few of her other friends'—and she had done it only to please Father. But she loved this graceful city.

Thinking about the debutante balls and Harriet made her wonder suddenly if she could possibly go to Augusta and visit her, maybe even stay with her for a few months. She and Harriet could share their confinements before the births. She quickly got out writing paper and a pen and began drafting a letter.

As she wrote, her mind continued to whirl. She had trusted Daniel with her life and more when they were floating on the ocean, and she had so deeply admired his courage. Why, he had saved her twice—once from the shipwreck and again from the shark. And during the stagecoach robbery he had again shown himself to be resourceful and quick-thinking. His lack of interest in contesting Father's will had further persuaded Lavinia of his integrity. Did she still trust and admire him? What was the courageous thing for her to do now? She told herself that Daniel would not give a fig about gossip, but did that also mean he would not mind creating scandal? What did Daniel know about Johnson?

Lavinia had stayed in Savannah ostensibly to help with Sarah's wedding. That wedding was over, and Sarah and William were due back from their trip to Niagara Falls any day now. She wondered how things would unfold once they returned.

She stared at herself in the dressing table mirror. If she had thought William was her foe before, that status could be even more deeply set in stone now. Had Sarah kept her word not to tell William about Lavinia's child?

CHAPTER TWENTY-FOUR

October 1838
Savannah

"THEY'RE HOME!" CLEMENTINE rushed into the sitting room, drying a dish with a towel. "Someone just came from the docks with the message for Peter to go fetch them and their luggage!"

Lavinia stood, put down her needlework, and put her hand to her chest as if to still her fluttering heart.

They would be here within the hour. She hadn't dared to put any of her news in a letter to her sister, so it would all be spilled out today as soon as they heard about the bridal tour. She felt eager to discuss the situation with Sarah, whose ear she craved, but William would doubtless consider himself to be head of household now.

She skimmed up the stairs and quickly put on one of her altered day dresses and pinned up her hair. In the week since she'd read the article in the paper, she'd been lounging dispiritedly around the house in her dressing gown with her hair down until late in the mornings. As much as she'd meant to fight for the right to go out in her own city, she hadn't. And she hadn't heard a word from any of her acquaintances, except for one request to call from Helena Carter, probably to extract information for gossip. She wrote a note, declining. There hadn't yet been time to hear back from Harriet in Augusta, who she knew would be sympathetic in every way.

Her body seemed so changed that it was hard to imagine that others could not tell—her seemingly bursting breasts, her expanding abdomen—but Clementine assured Lavinia that only she was so intimately familiar with her own body and that to others the changes were subtle or not even noticeable.

When Sarah and William drove up in the carriage with Peter, Clementine and Lavinia were both on the front porch waiting. Sarah's eyes glowed with contentment, her cheeks had high color, and she and William laughed at something together as he helped her disembark.

"Welcome home, welcome home!" Lavinia waved her arms. Her sister looked happy and in love.

"Thank the Lord you've come back safe!" Clementine waved as well.

Sarah climbed the front porch steps and threw her arms around Lavinia, then Clementine. "Such a wonderful trip, but good to be home!"

"Peter, bring the luggage up on the porch, and then take the carriage around back," William commanded. Peter complied without a response, but Lavinia felt embarrassed by William's peremptory tone.

"Welcome back, sir." Clementine addressed William politely.

"Clementine," said William, with a nod, then, looking Lavinia up and down, "You're looking healthy, Lavinia."

Lavinia did not respond other than to say, "Welcome back," making sure she didn't say "home," as Clementine opened the door for William. Had Sarah told him about the pregnancy? It seemed an unusual greeting otherwise. She prayed inwardly that she was mistaken. It seemed wrong that William should know before Daniel did, and she was apprehensive about William's reaction.

Sarah quickly raised her arms above her head in the uncomfortable silence. "I brought gifts, I brought gifts!"

While Peter carried the luggage upstairs, Clementine went to prepare dinner. The rest of them moved to the parlor, and Sarah pulled her gifts from her carpetbag. In addition to a handwoven shawl and some illustrated notes for Lavinia, Sarah had brought Clementine a rock with the image of the falls painted on it.

"How beautiful and breathtaking! Tell me about standing near the falls. Could you feel the spray?" Lavinia wrapped the shawl around her shoulders. It was exquisitely made.

"Absolutely, yes, the spray billows out for yards and yards. And the sound of it—the constant ear-splitting roar! You'd never believe it, Livvy."

"There have been dozens of foolish souls who have attempted to go over the falls. Their fates were not kind." William was rather obsessed with this aspect of Niagara, and he went on about a daredevil named Sam Patch who had jumped into the falls. Then that led to a whispered discussion of the fact that people sometimes went to Niagara Falls to take their own lives.

"Men in financial straits and unwed mothers, I've heard." William's voice held a self-satisfied contempt. Silence filled the room. Lavinia had a hard time focusing through a sudden bout of lightheadedness. She needed to talk with Sarah alone.

William went on to describe a time that someone had sent a group of animals, similar to Noah's Ark, over the falls. The animals had included a buffalo, two bears, two raccoons, a dog, and a goose, all of which had perished except the bears and the goose. Horrified, Lavinia tried to change the subject by asking about their accommodations on the ship.

"Oh, it was wonderful, Livvy—quite luxurious. And we sat at the Captain's table more than once, which pleased William."

Lavinia remembered that Father had liked that, too. They were both men who were concerned with appearances, but she suspected William's reasons were different than her father's had been. Lavinia hadn't seen that until just now. William and Sarah had also met another newly married couple on the voyage who were planning a trip to Savannah and had promised to visit. Lavinia sighed inwardly. The account of the trip seemed never ending, and Lavinia was desperate to speak with Sarah. At long last, William left to speak to Peter about preparing the carriage so he could visit his parents, and Sarah stood, saying that she could use a rest.

Lavinia followed her to the top of the stairs and touched her sister's wrist. "Did you tell William?"

Sarah looked at the floor, unable to meet Lavinia's gaze. "I kept my promise, Livvy. But he . . . guessed."

Oh, she'd feared that. "I have something to show you." She pulled Sarah into her room and retrieved the inflammatory newspaper article written by Mr. Morgan.

Sarah's eyes skimmed over the headline and opening paragraph and she looked up at Lavinia with her mouth open. "Is this true, Livvy? You're not married?"

"I am afraid it may be true." Lavinia sat on her bed. "But there is so much I don't know. Most important, I need to know if Daniel knew. If he knowingly went through with a false wedding ceremony."

Sarah sat next to her, put her hand on her knee. "He seemed so in love with you. I just can't believe it. You must write to him, Livvy!"

"I did, I did. I wrote him that I had news that I wanted to share in person and asked him to return to Savannah so we can sort things out. I am waiting for his reply."

Sarah nodded. "Good. He must come right away."

"I will wait a reasonable amount of time to hear from him, but what if I don't, Sarah? I don't know what I shall do. Please, do not say anything to William, yet."

"But people who have read the paper will speak to him of it, Livvy. There will be no keeping it a secret. And you can't keep asking me to keep secrets from my husband. I haven't asked you to keep secrets from Daniel." Sarah squeezed Lavinia's hand and tilted her head as if Lavinia should surely understand this.

She'd suspected that marriage could change their sisterly relationship, but not how quickly it had actually happened.

LAVINIA HOPED THAT William would forget about moving Father's desk out of her room She had enjoyed writing letters and noting events of the day in her diary as she looked out her back window at their garden. But he had not forgotten, and the following morning before he headed to work at the law firm, William and Peter moved it down to the parlor in front of the window overlooking the neighbors' fence and side yard and placed his own inkwell and pens on the upper right-hand corner. Trembling with anger, Lavinia went up to her room and collected her own pens and inkwell. She promptly laid claim to the less convenient upper left-hand corner of the desk, sat down, and began another letter to Harriet. Again, she mentioned a possible visit.

As William passed by on his way to the law firm, Lavinia remained in her father's desk chair, composing the letter. She did not look up or greet him, even though she heard him stop in the front hall and could feel his eyes on her back.

She determined not to mention a word about her condition to him. If it were to be spoken about, she would force him to mention it first.

The silent tension between them only increased. That evening after dinner, Lavinia claimed the desk once again to write a note to Mrs. Thomas and Abby, to see how they were getting along, knowing full well that she was needling William. When William came into the room, she ignored his coughs and pointed rustling of papers. Though her back was to him, she could feel him fuming in the doorway of the parlor for a long moment, and then he stalked off, his heels sounding sharply on the hardwood.

At dinner the second night after their return home, William

waited for Clementine to leave the room after serving the plates and then addressed Lavinia.

"I have something of some import to discuss with you, Lavinia."

Lavinia's fork stopped in mid-air. Was he finally going to address her pregnancy? "What is it?"

William cleared his throat and carefully folded his napkin beside his plate. "As you know, I am in the process of contesting your father's will, and I have received some reports that Mr. Mason lives a depraved lifestyle and is guilty of obscene practices. I believe he can be arrested and even be sent to an asylum for such activities. I'll need you to provide some examples of this depraved behavior in your statement for my complaint."

Lavinia caught her breath in surprise. Whatever she had been expecting, this wasn't it. "Depraved behavior? I don't understand what you're saying, William."

"Surely you do, Lavinia. I believe him to be a sodomite, and since you have known him and worked with him, a statement from you could help nullify the will."

Lavinia nearly dropped her fork. "A sodomite? Mr. Mason? I can't imagine that's true. It broke my heart, too, to lose the shop, but I won't be party to such underhanded efforts to ruin a person's reputation. Mr. Mason is a perfectly decent man." *Who could be my half-brother*, she might have added, but didn't. "At any rate," she continued, "we have not found another will to replace the one that exists."

"You know he will never marry. He is depraved, and if given long enough, I can prove it." William leaned forward and pointed his fork at her.

"William, please," said Sarah, turning pale. "I thought I persuaded you not to pursue any of that any longer."

William shrugged and swigged his port. "And another thing: one of the lawyers at my firm brought an interesting article to my attention today. About you and your husband, Lavinia."

Lavinia caught her breath. She put down her fork and gave

William a level stare.

"You are not married after all," he said.

She continued to stare at him, offering no response.

"And you are expecting a child."

She involuntarily rested her palm on her belly, as if to protect the sweet baby growing there from this arrogant man.

"We cannot have a scandal at this house, with Sarah and me just beginning our married life. You cannot stay here if you are unmarried and expecting a child."

"William, Lavinia has been through a horrific experience." Sarah's voice cracked in protest. "She did not know the marriage might not be legal. She has written to Daniel already about the situation, and if Daniel comes back quickly, they can marry properly and solve the problem."

"So you knew all about this and didn't tell your own husband, Sarah?"

"I . . . have only known for a day or so." Sarah nervously pushed a stray strand of hair out of her eyes.

"You and I will discuss that later." He gave her a sharp look. "At any rate, it was illegal. Or close enough to be considered invalid." William carefully wiped his mouth with his napkin. "Lavinia, you need to find alternative lodgings, preferably not in Savannah."

"William! She is my sister. She has lived her entire life in this house. She does *not* need to find alternative lodgings."

"Thank you, Sarah." Lavinia felt heat rise to her face and her hands trembled. "I own half of the house." She felt breathless. "I will stay here as long as I like."

"You will be condemned by society." William gave her a prudish, judgmental look. "You already are, in fact. Just like Mr. Mason, I might add, who you refuse to condemn." He paused to consider her shrewdly. "In fact, I have decided that I no longer need you to write testimony about the will, after all, as your testimony as a tainted woman would be completely discounted. I insist you find alternative lodging immediately. There is no question of taking a voyage to Paris for the year or anything that some of these other fallen women do. There is not money for that, thanks to Mr. Mason inheriting your father's fortune."

"William! You cannot do this to her!" Sarah's voice went high with emotion.

"She's written to Daniel. You must give her at least the time it takes to receive a reply from him."

"I am the head of this household, and I will decide what needs to be done." William drew a deep breath, speared a beef tip, and chewed it.

Sarah, crying, threw down her napkin and fled the dining room. Lavinia could feel her heart beating all out of rhythm. Though she could barely eat, the baby needed sustenance. And she would not give in. She remained at the table and forced down her meal, one bite at a time, glaring at him. Clementine came through the door, saw tense faces and posture, and went directly back to the warming kitchen without speaking or picking up any plates.

William at last left the room to follow Sarah. Lavinia stayed at the table finishing her meal, chewing carefully, alone.

CHAPTER TWENTY-FIVE

October 1838
Savannah

THAT NIGHT SHE lay on the bed in her room and cried and listened to the raised voices coming from her sister's bedroom. Sarah was verging on hysterics, and it pained Lavinia to hear her so and to think that it was her situation that caused this. Eventually Sarah came into Lavinia's room as Lavinia had known she would. Her eyes were swollen and red and she seemed barely able to speak.

"I cannot persuade him of anything, sister. His mind is made up."

Sarah crawled onto the bed with Lavinia and put her arm around her waist. They lay there together quietly, sniffling and wiping away tears. Lavinia's throat felt raw, and her entire body ached. Of all the people in the world that she loved, no one meant more to her than Sarah.

And even though Lavinia had always tried her best not to speak against William, she did now. "How could you marry such a man?"

Sarah sat up sharply. "Livvy! How dare you say that about William? We have known him and his family since we were children, and he is a good man. I love him. I knew on my wedding day that you weren't being honest with me!

"Sarah, consider—he wants to have Mr. Mason put in an asylum and he is trying to throw me out of the house. Are those the actions of a good man?"

"I knew you didn't support our union. Well, the shoe is on the other foot now. I say to *you*, how could you marry a stranger you hardly know?"

"Sarah, I felt I did know him after those days on the sea!"

"Well, clearly you didn't. He betrayed you!"

"I don't know that yet! And I thought you believed him to be honorable. What has changed your mind?"

"My conversation with William—just now. He told me that he has heard people talking about you. I know you no longer care what anyone thinks of you, but I suppose it's too much to ask that you care that your scandal affects my place in society, too!"

"Please, dear sister, let's not fight!" Lavinia grabbed Sarah's hands between her own. She could just imagine what William had said to Sarah. William was filling Sarah's head with foolishness and lies. She had overheard snatches of their discussions.

Sarah drew a deep breath. "I admit that I know very little about Daniel and what kind of man he is. He did save your life."

"More than once."

Sarah stood up, smoothing her nightdress, wiping her face. "William wants you to leave in the morning, but I have at least bargained a few days for you to make arrangements. I want to help you more, Lavinia, but he is my husband, and I must obey him."

Lavinia looked at her sister's tense face and wanted only to somehow smooth all concern away. "I worry about you with him, Sarah."

"You needn't do so."

"Yet, I do. And you both seem to forget that the house he wants me to vacate is half mine."

"I'll make him give you your half, and I will sign anything that you like. He insists you not go out in public, however, between now and when you leave. I just don't know where you might go, do you? What about Father's brother at the plantation outside Savannah?"

"Clementine already mentioned him. But Father was estranged from them, you know that. I can't imagine them being willing to take me in."

Lavinia thought again of her half-formed plan to visit Harriet in Augusta. She knew Harriet would welcome her. Possibly she could leave tomorrow and need not even wait for Harriet's reply. She would need to take the carriage with Peter driving. She remembered Harriet's husband, and he was a kind, agreeable man. She was certain she'd find understanding in their home and a peaceful place to have the baby.

But what then?

She suddenly realized it was just Daniel she wanted. Not Harriet or peaceful Augusta. Not even Sarah and her beloved Savannah. Not anymore. As much as her feelings about Daniel confused her, as many questions as remained, Daniel still felt like home. She had to gamble on passion. It would be a frightening journey, but only one place held a realistic future for her. She pulled Daniel's latest letter from her dressing gown pocket and examined the return address in New Orleans.

She held the letter out for Sarah to see. "Here's where I'll go."

She had intended never to set foot on a ship again, and in her present condition an ocean voyage would be dreadful. The very idea filled her with terror. But there was no better way to travel to New Orleans. Going by stagecoach would take longer and, as Lavinia and Daniel had discovered on their recent journey, was no safer. The knowledge that she would rather get on a boat, uproot her life, and start over in a new city rather than stay here or even go to a kind friend, made her feel a little braver already.

Sarah's tears started again, and they hugged each other so tightly Lavinia could feel the bones in her sister's back. When Sarah left the room, there was something very final about it.

The next morning, after William had left for the law office,

Lavinia asked Peter to go to the dock and reserve her a berth on the next steamship bound for New Orleans, under the nondescript name of Laura Clark, just in case Mr. Morgan should still be tracking her, and meanwhile she "borrowed" one of Sarah's traveling trunks—since her own had been lost on the *Pulaski*—and began packing her things. As she folded and tucked her essentials in the trunk—nightclothes, a few altered day dresses, one bonnet, one pair of gloves, and a few chemises—she recalled in contrast the time she'd spent packing a dozen elegant gowns for the *Pulaski*. For the *Pulaski* voyage Lavinia had planned to be gone for a few months and had spent days preparing and packing. Now she might be leaving forever, yet she carried so much less. This irony didn't escape her. Possibly Daniel's sisters could loan her a dress or two if they were near her size. She guessed it would be even warmer in New Orleans than here, so packed only one shawl, the one Sarah had brought her from Niagara Falls.

She went through Mama's jewelry and found a plain silver ring that fit her left ring finger. Daniel had never presented her with a ring other than the lace one from her petticoat, but she would be safer traveling as a clearly married woman. And she could use it to obtain food or supplies if she grew desperate. Once she had the carved wooden jewelry box open, each piece she saw looked like safety, security, provisions. In the end, she took as much jewelry as she could possibly sew into her pockets—a gold bracelet, a double set of pearls, a pair of ruby earrings, her mother's cameo, and more. She left Sarah the amethyst earrings, because they were her birthstone, and the second set of pearls, but Lavinia took the rest. Sarah would understand or at least come to terms with it. She would get all the furnishings in the house, after all.

By the time Peter returned from the docks, Lavinia was almost ready and relieved to learn that the next boat left the following day, since she could now barely tolerate the idea of staying in the house with William for even a few more hours. She completed her packing and sewed the jewelry into her pockets that afternoon with Clementine's help.

Clementine spoke up after tightening the last stitch. "Miss Lavinia, this is a tragedy! I wanted you to be with your husband, but this should always be your home. I never wanted you to leave like this!"

Lavinia closed the traveling trunk. "I must, Clementine. I wish you could come with me."

"I had always thought I'd be the one to midwife your babies, Miss Lavinia." Clementine looked so downcast.

"I did, too. Until I met Daniel, I believed my life would always be in Savannah. If I sent a letter to Sarah, could you come to New Orleans to bring this baby into the world?"

Clementine shook her head. "If I go anywhere, Miss Lavinia, with times the way they are, it won't be south."

Lavinia thought her heart would break. So much of what Lavinia knew about the world had been taught to her by Clementine. But of course it would not be wise for Clementine to go south. She hugged Clementine as though they'd never meet again. And indeed, possibly they would not. She was doubly glad that William was gone and didn't see them as Lavinia cried on Clementine's shoulder. He would solidly disapprove.

She claimed Father's desk one last time and wrote Daniel a final, hurried letter.

Dear Daniel,

I am writing you to let you know about a change in my plans. As I wrote you before, Mr. Morgan has published an article about you and me possibly not being married. It seems you were right to distrust him in Smithville.

What you do not already know is that I am also expecting your child.

These two facts have made William, now my brother-in-law, feel that it is imperative for me to leave Savannah before I bring scandal to him and Sarah.

Therefore, I have booked a berth on the Utopia, under the false name of Laura Clark, which leaves Savannah tomorrow at high tide. The ship is expected to dock in New Orleans in six days. I hope that this letter will fly like a homing pigeon and find you quickly enough for you to be there to meet me.

Your wife,
Lavinia

She knew full well that the chances of the letter arriving ahead of her were poor. Yet, she had to write it. As she finished the letter and sealed it, she sat back and took a deep breath, catching the residual scent of her father's favorite pipe tobacco. She tugged on a small drawer that still held some of Father's smoking supplies. It was a day of lasts—the last time she'd sit and sew with Clementine, the last time she would write at this desk, the last time she would smell that scent.

She was awash in nostalgia as she jiggled the recalcitrant little drawer, and it finally slid grudgingly open with a resounding squeal. She pulled out the aromatic tobacco pouches, and brushes, laying each one gently on the desktop. As she reached for his small wooden pipe stand, her fingers brushed paper. As a little girl she sometimes used to leave drawings for Father in this drawer when Clementine used to take her and Sarah to visit him at the shop. But when she pulled it out along with the little stand, it wasn't a long-forgotten child's drawing, but a folded letter with "For Lavinia" written in her father's bold and confident handwriting.

Seeing her father's hand, her heart quickened. What was this? She would read it up in her room. She slid the letter into her skirt pocket, let her fingers caress the polished top of the desk, and went upstairs. Once inside, she shut the door and crawled under the covers. She withdrew Father's letter from her pocket and unfolded it.

Dearest Lavinia,

We stopped at the shop on our way to board the Pulaski so I could put this letter in my desk. If it becomes necessary to read it, I hope you might find it waiting for you in the drawer where you used to leave drawings for me as a little girl. My physician has let me know that my heart is not as strong as it could be. If you are reading this now, I must be gone, and you will have learned that I have left the shop to Charles Mason. He is my son, Lavinia. Though I loved your mother very much, years of loneliness before I met her resulted in a time of weakness on my part and I hope you will forgive me.

I cannot put into words how much it has meant to have your help in the shop, Lavinia. I know that Onslow's Millinery would be very successful in your hands. Your knowledge of style, your abilities with the books, and your passion for the work would make you an exceptional owner and manager.

However, though you and your sister may marry and be provided for, Charles has no such option, and I feel duty bound to leave him with a livelihood. The fact that you have a half-brother I am sure comes as a surprise to you. Though Charles does not know I am his father, I hope you will do your Christian duty to assist your brother in this endeavor. He has no family other than you and Sarah.

I feel confident that William and Sarah will wed happily, but Lavinia, I worry about you. I do hope that you will see your way clear to choosing an advantageous match. I know that you did not necessarily feel a connection to Mr. Grogan, the brickmaker, but a man like him would be good to you and care for you. For my sake, try to find such a man.

Your loving father,
Frederick Onslow

The letter was tear-stained by the time Lavinia finished it. She put it back into her pocket and turned her face to the corner. How could she have not believed what Clementine said— Clementine, who had cared for her all her life and always guided her rightly? She regretted her sharp words to Clementine that day and chided herself for not having more room in her heart for Charles Mason, an orphan and her half-brother.

If there was any part of her not ready to commit herself to Daniel and to this voyage to New Orleans, the letter put an end to it. She would not depend on inheritance. She would use what she had been given and what she could take with her and make her own way. She would choose Daniel.

But first, she would do what she could to protect Charles Mason, her brother, from William.

CHAPTER TWENTY-SIX

October 1838
Savannah

FIRST THING UPON waking, Lavinia often felt the small flutters of the baby. That morning she lay in bed and floated in the miracle of it for a few minutes, then drew a deep breath and rose with an assurance that she did not feel. She owed it to the tiny living thing growing inside her to survive. She buttoned herself into one of her day dresses, put up her hair, and slid the purse of gold pieces left from her fitting-out money and Father's letter into her dress pocket.

She took a moment to look out her bedroom window for the last time at the mid-morning stirrings on the cobblestone street, with carts and pedestrians passing on their way to their lives. She allowed herself to watch dreamily as one woman in a lovely straw bonnet passed, and how beautifully the balance of the bonnet accentuated the lady's swan-like neck.

Finally, she tied the latch on the trunk. Peter would come and fetch it to carry to the docks.

There still existed the matter of payment for the house. William had taken to lingering in the mornings before going to the law office, and Lavinia found him sitting at Father's desk. She stood in the doorway to the parlor and spoke to his back.

"William, I must request payment for half the value of the house, which the lawyer stated was the amount of four thousand dollars. If you are to buy out my part, I will need my two thousand."

He did not turn around when he spoke. "Give me your address in New Orleans and I will mail payment to Daniel when you arrive and have verified that you are indeed married."

What a scheme! If she didn't get the money now, she'd never get it. "I need the money now, William. If I am unmarried, then it is rightfully mine. If I am married, then you can write to Daniel and inform him that I am bringing it with me." She started to breathe heavily now and tried to control it.

"Daniel, if he is your husband, is the rightful owner of the property. Also, I must withdraw the funds from another account. Therefore, I cannot give you the money now." He turned and gave her a look as chilling as a stone.

At that moment she heard someone behind her. Sarah had come down the stairs in her nightdress and stood on the bottom stair with her arms crossed anxiously over her chest. Meanwhile, Peter had come down the hall and headed past her on the stairs on the way to fetch her trunk. Lavinia caught Sarah's eye, then quickly took several steps into the parlor, making fists of both hands in her frustration. "Give me the funds today, William, or, if you must, write me a check and I won't cash it until I arrive in New Orleans a week from now."

William hesitated. He glanced behind Lavinia at Sarah on the stairs.

As she waited, she thought she might lose control of her bladder, with the baby pressing on it. Her kneecaps trembled uncontrollably.

"I will send the funds to you once you arrive in New Orleans, care of your husband."

"You cannot do this, William. Half of this house is mine." She spoke in a level, firm tone. She was determined to stand up to him. For herself. For the baby. And for Daniel. She drew a deep breath and turned to look at Sarah. Tears stood in her eyes.

"My decision is final." William shoved past her and disappeared into the back of the house, his bootheels ringing on the floorboards.

Peter came downstairs with her trunk on his shoulder, and Clementine appeared from the warming kitchen, wiping her eyes with her apron.

"Good-bye, sister." Lavinia hugged Sarah and cried.

Peter was up front to drive the carriage. As she climbed on, she pulled down the thick black veil of her mourning bonnet even though anyone who might be about would recognize Peter and the Onslow family carriage and would guess who she was.

"Peter, before we go to the docks, I need to stop by the millinery shop."

"There is not much time, Miss Lavinia." Peter seemed nearly as anxious as she felt.

"I will be quick." She couldn't focus on the shaded streets she knew so well as they passed through, as she kept seeing Sarah's face. Though she and Peter had talked so often on drives like this one, today the two of them remained silent for most of the ride. Lavinia wanted to ask Peter about Mr. Mason and the money for the Bethesda Home for Boys but couldn't draw up the energy to ask the weighty questions.

Peter pulled up outside Mason's Millinery and Lavinia quickly alighted.

"I will be back in just a moment." The bell on the door tinkled as she entered. Mr. Mason was talking with Mrs. Pettigrew, a long-time customer, about a delicate blond lace cap with embroidery.

"We could add more embroidery if you like, Mrs. Pettigrew." Mr. Mason indicated places on the cap that might accommodate additional decoration. "Here. And here."

"Mr. Mason," Lavinia said, putting her hand on his arm. "May I steal you from Mrs. Pettigrew for just a minute or two?"

"Good morning, Miss Lavinia. Perhaps once I have helped her choose—" Mr. Mason crossed his arms over his chest.

"I am afraid it is most important. And Mrs. Pettigrew is so kind I am sure she doesn't mind waiting for just a moment, Mr. Mason." Lavinia nodded respectfully to the other woman. "May I speak to you in my father's office?"

Mrs. Pettigrew's plump face showed surprise, as did Mr. Mason's, but Lavinia left them standing in the middle of the sales floor and went back to father's old office, which now had a new, ornate desk with a quill pen adorned with a peacock feather. Mr. Mason entered a moment later and shut the door behind him.

"Miss Lavinia, what is this about? You yourself know that your father never kept a customer waiting."

"I have something very important to tell you, Mr. Mason, and then I must leave Savannah. I cannot say how I know to tell you this, but please be careful about your assignations." She whispered the last sentence.

"Assignations?" Mr. Mason gave her a look of shock.

"There are people who will attempt to arrest you and have you jailed for depravity if you are caught."

"I am sure I do not know what you mean." Mr. Mason gave her a look of disgust, but she saw fear in his eyes.

"Please, we are short on time, and I am not here to pass judgement upon you or cause you danger. I only want to warn you that you need to be very careful about your activities. Here is my new address in New Orleans. Please write me there and let me know how things go for you." She pressed a slip of paper with Daniel's address into his hand. "I hope you will continue to do well here."

Mr. Mason turned his face slightly away. "Why are you doing this, Miss Lavinia?"

She shook her head. The question was unanswerable. "I must go now. Please be careful."

She hurried out of the shop, giving the impatient and curious Mrs. Pettigrew a slight nod of her head, and climbed back into the carriage. "Let's go to the docks now, Peter."

"Gee!" Peter said to Daisy, and she trotted off in the direction of East Bay Street. At last, they approached the *Utopia* docked by the wharf, and Lavinia finally spoke to Peter as they drove along.

"Peter, Clementine tells me that you took money to Bethesda Home for Boys every month for many years for my father."

Peter turned briefly to look at Lavinia with surprise, but he recovered quickly and nodded. "That is true, Miss Lavinia. I did. I hope that's not why you're leaving."

"No, Peter. There are many reasons, but that's not one. The most important reason I'm leaving is because I love Mr. Ridge, and I hope he will still have me."

Peter nodded again, seeming pleased, then seemed to consider whether to speak, and, after a moment, did so "I should tell you, Miss Lavinia, that Zora and I are leaving Savannah tomorrow. We be going north, where it's safer for free people like us."

"Leaving?" Lavinia put her hand over her chest.

"Miss Sarah and Mr. Anderson don't know."

A whirlwind of emotions raced through her. All the years with Peter so efficiently saddling her pony Balderdash, driving Daisy, taking care of the Onslow back yard garden. He had been a fixture in their lives. What would Sarah do without Peter to depend on? Yet times were changing, and many people of color had left Savannah in the past few years for better lives in the north.

"I wish you and Zora Godspeed, Peter."

"Thank you."

They had arrived at the docks now, and Peter climbed down and called to some of the dock workers to come and take Lavinia's trunk. Once the workers had her trunk and were carrying it on board to storage, he helped her down. When her feet touched the cobblestone street, she looked up at the imposing sides of the vessel, the looming masts, and the sailors and slaves scurrying around preparing to set sail. Her heart seized and her mouth went dry. The bright image of the *Pulaski's* boiler exploding and the wheelhouse flying into the air flashed in her mind and she felt unsteady. She grabbed at the handrail of the gangplank, and drew two careful breaths, pulling herself together.

"Thank you, Peter, for all you have done for me."

"Safe travels, Miss Lavinia." Peter gave an almost imperceptible nod, tightening his lips.

She clutched the drawstring purse and jewelry in her skirt pocket for reassurance and, with Peter's assistance, stepped onto the gangplank. Lavinia began to shake uncontrollably.

"Can I help you to your berth, Miss Lavinia?" Peter's eyes focused on the shaking of her hand and filled with concern. "I'm sorry there were no first- or second-class staterooms."

"That's all right, Peter." Only Peter knew that, because the ticket had been purchased just the day before, only fourth-class berths had been available for Laura Clark's voyage. There would be no staterooms this time, as she and Father had had on the *Pulaski*.

"Have a safe trip, then. Regards to Mr. Ridge." She bid him good-bye—the heavy veil hid her tears—and climbed the rest of the way to the deck, avoiding looking at the water below. The first mate did not greet or direct her this time; fourth class passengers were expected to find their own way.

She drew deep breaths, endeavoring to remain calm and avoid looking at the smokestack and wheelhouse. She took one last look at Savannah's busy and beautiful waterfront, gleaming in the sun, then, as the church bells announced the eleven o'clock hour, she carefully climbed down the narrow stairs, past the rows of staterooms, down several more levels, and at last found her berth, the lowest of two horizontal wooden planks stacked atop each other in a stale-smelling cavernous room.

She immediately lay on the hard plank and closed her eyes. People streamed in, talking and arguing about who took which berth, and shoving belongings into corners. A fight broke out over a berth in the men's section, and the ship's crew halted it and threw one man off the boat. She tried to ignore it, but the shouting made her heart pound. Eventually the ship's horn blew a deep startling blast and the boat started to move beneath her.

She tried to keep her breathing even.

As the ship got underway, the cook came around and gave each fourth-class passenger their allotment of food for the six-day journey: six biscuits, sugar, a cup of molasses, a cup of rice, and a few ounces of tea. All fourth-class passengers shared a small kitchen near the entrance. Lavinia stacked her food in the corner of her berth, wondering if it might be stolen if she fell asleep. This was a far cry from the sumptuous meals the staff served Father and Lavinia as stateroom passengers on the *Pulaski*.

A mother with a little boy and a baby occupied the top berth above her. One of the children cried. As more people filled the space and the ship's movement intensified, the smells became more intense. The mother in the berth above struggled to change her baby's swaddling. Bile rose in Lavinia's throat, and she put her handkerchief over her mouth.

This would last for six days. She would find a way to endure it.

CHAPTER TWENTY-SEVEN

October 1838
At sea

AFTER A DAY or so, Lavinia felt able to converse with the woman in the berth above with the baby and the little boy. Her name was Callie, and she and the children were to meet her husband in New Orleans now that he had secured a position as a shipping clerk there. Callie had stringy hair and a plain country drawl. The little boy and the baby wore clean but worn clothes. Lavinia couldn't imagine the sort of life Callie must have, but she accepted what companionship she could find and was grateful for it. She did not tell Callie why she was traveling, and Callie was too harried with both children to ask. It was difficult for Callie to lift the children to the upper berth, so Lavinia offered to take the upper berth and gave them the lower one. Callie didn't seem very grateful, but she acquiesced to Lavinia's suggestion.

The movement of the ship felt more intense than on the *Pulaski*, but possibly that was because Lavinia was farther down in the belly of the ship, without much ventilation, or possibly it was because the water in October was rougher. Or because she was pregnant. At any rate, she was seasick.

Between the seasickness and the circumstances of her departure from her home, she felt beyond miserable.

Roaches and rats crawled on the floor of the fourth-class compartment, which actually made her upper berth preferable, and she quickly understood why Callie wasn't pleased with her offer to change. Even with her seasickness, Lavinia could see how overwhelmed Callie was with the two children, and she dragged herself to the crowded kitchen, helped Callie cook, and shared some of her food with her. After all, they were three and Lavinia was only one. And she felt too sick to eat much anyway. For the first two days they picked the bugs out of the rice before they cooked it. By the third day, they were both so exhausted and hungry they just cooked and ate it without bothering.

Callie had limited swaddling for her baby, Henry, which she had difficulty keeping clean and dry with the limited amount of water, and Lavinia helped occupy the older boy, Ephraim, while she changed the little one. The baby cried because of his raw, chafed bottom, but nothing could be done.

Lavinia lay in her berth, overwhelmed with nausea, listening to Callie tell Ephraim about meeting his father soon, and thinking of Daniel and her own baby. Would Daniel be there to meet her? Would her baby be a boy or a girl?

She got very little sleep, and time seemed to pass slowly. She kept her hand in her skirt pocket closed around her drawstring reticule, as she didn't know what she'd do if she were to lose those gold pieces now. With the jewelry, it was all she had. Again and again, she checked the other pocket for the weight of the sewn-in jewelry. These items were the only way she would be able to make a new start if things went poorly with Daniel. She and Callie took turns leaving their berths, for fear someone might take their belongings or their food. She reread Father's letter until she had it memorized.

The day before the *Utopia* was set to dock, Lavinia felt so nauseated that she asked Callie if she would watch her berth and little remaining food while she tried to settle her stomach with a walk above decks.

"Sure, you go right ahead. I hope it'll make you feel better."

She put on her shawl and her bonnet with the thick black veil—days wedged into the corner of her berth had flattened it, but it was tolerably presentable—and made her way up the narrow stairs, acutely aware that she had not been able to properly clean her face or hands or even comb her hair while on the ship. She must look a sight. But she assured herself that Laura Clark would never see anyone on this ship again, so it didn't much matter.

As she stepped onto the upper deck, the late afternoon sun beamed over the choppy water. The blustery roaring wind immediately blew back her veil and she had to close her eyes from the brightness after staying below in the semi-dark for several days. She staggered with the shock of it and grabbed onto the railing. As her eyes adjusted, she saw others on deck, grasping the railing, holding onto their hats.

Keeping one hand on the railing, she struggled to make her way around the ship. The fierce wind made her stagger. How easy it would be to slide under the railing and into those heaving waves. Yet the freshness of the air felt so bracing, and the sunlight so uplifting, that she remembered walking around the deck of the *Pulaski* and seeing Daniel. How handsome and studious he had been, sitting on that settee, with his spectacles, his cravat, and dark blonde curls. How long ago that had been. And how much had occurred since. As she allowed herself to be lost in memories, for the first time since she'd embarked on the *Utopia*, her constant unease at being on the water again began to subside.

"Miss Onslow! Miss Onslow!"

Was someone calling her? She tried to pull the veil down over her face, but to no avail. The wind gusted again and blew it back. She finally stopped and turned around.

A man with deep-set eyes and a well-trimmed beard stood a few feet behind her, dressed in a brocade waistcoat, and a fine top hat, the kind that she'd seen often in Savannah. The past few days had left her slightly disoriented, and she tried to focus on who this might be.

"Miss Onslow, I thought I recognized you! What a coincidence! It's Matthew Grogan. Matthew Grogan of Grogan's Brickmaking, I called on you once a few months ago, do you remember?"

Matthew Grogan! Matthew Grogan, the potential beau she had believed to be too old, too stooped, too bald, and had nearly run out of the house. She remembered with chagrin that she and Sarah had laughed about him that night and that they had joked about whether to invite him to Sarah's wedding.

"Matthew Grogan." In her shock and weakened state, she could manage nothing more than his name. He still had the same graying beard and thinning hair she recalled from the summer. But as she looked at him now, she saw that his eyes were kind.

"What a delight to see you on the *Utopia*. I hear your sister recently married William Anderson and they enjoyed an extended bridal tour at Niagara Falls. Wonderful!"

"Yes. A sweet wedding." She felt a stab of guilt over the way she and Sarah had joked about inviting Matthew Grogan. She attempted to smile at Mr. Grogan and then swayed.

"Are you feeling quite well, Miss Onslow? You seem—"

"I am a little unsteady on my feet, yes."

"The wind is considerable. Come inside and sit down. Can I offer you some tea?"

He took her arm firmly and guided her down the stairs to the dining room. It was not as elegant as the one on the *Pulaski*—it was, in fact, little better than a tavern—but he found a small table for them topped with a green oilcloth. She paused in her habitual reach to remove her bonnet, knowing that her hair looked like a rat's nest and anyone staying in a stateroom would have had an opportunity to comb their hair. She decided to leave it on.

As he left to find a waiter to bring tea, she quickly pulled a handkerchief from her pocket and tried to wipe off her face and hands as best she could. Her seasickness had eased while on deck and now she felt weak and dizzy with hunger.

In a moment Mr. Grogan returned. "Tea will be coming up in

just a few moments." He took the seat across from her. "That will warm you right up."

At that moment, the waiter brought a basket of warm yeasty-smelling rolls, and it was all she could do to prevent herself from snatching one and devouring it in one bite. The food in steerage was so sparse. She chose one from the basket with deliberation but couldn't resist taking a large bite.

"So, what takes you to New Orleans? And how unfortunate that you don't have an escort."

She couldn't answer around the roll, but that gave her a moment to contemplate her answer. Father would have been appalled at something so unladylike, but Mr. Grogan didn't seem to mind, and he continued talking while Lavinia ate.

"The brickmaking business has been taking me to New Orleans for many years. And recently there has been an increase in purchasing since there has been such a need for bricks for lanes and thoroughfares. There are shortages everywhere."

She nodded but still chewed, utterly preoccupied by the warm bread in her hands. Where was that tea?

"I was so sorry to hear about your father. He was a respected gentleman in the community and very kind to me."

"Thank you." Now her eyes welled up. She was having difficulties holding up her end of this conversation.

Mr. Grogan saw and tried to change the subject. "And what an amazing experience you had floating on the water before being rescued after the *Pulaski*. And I hear you have married the man who rescued you?" He pointed at the silver ring on her left hand.

She glanced down at it, nodding. So, he had read the articles about the accident, but possibly hadn't seen the recent one by Mr. Morgan. That was very lucky indeed.

"Yes, I am indeed married, and am meeting my husband, Daniel Ridge, in New Orleans, where he is employed by the railroad."

"A railroad man. It's a burgeoning business."

"Yes."

The waiter brought hot tea at last, and Lavinia eagerly washed down her roll with a sip of the strong, scalding liquid. Dare she wrap the other roll in a napkin to take to Callie and her children?

"May I also have a bowl of soup, please?" She caught the waiter before he turned away. Both the waiter and Mr. Grogan looked a bit surprised to see her order for herself, but, after the bursts of fresh air above deck, her appetite had returned, and Lavinia felt famished.

"Potato soup or oyster soup?" he asked.

"Yes," she said quickly, then recovered herself and favored the waiter with what she hoped was a genteel smile. "Potato soup would be delightful." He didn't seem convinced.

"I shall have some too," added Mr. Grogan, smoothing over the slightly awkward pause. "And please put the meal on my bill."

The waiter nodded and left.

"Oh, no, Mr. Grogan, you need not pay for my meal. I have money with me." She carefully patted her pocket to make sure the gold pieces were still there, then blushed to be speaking of money in this way. She seemed to have lost her sense of appropriate social discourse. She looked down at her hands in embarrassment and caught sight of her skirts. Her dark blue dress had wrinkled horribly from lying on her berth and sleeping in it for several days. How could Mr. Grogan not notice?

"I insist. And no more argument."

She looked at him earnestly, thinking to refuse, but then nodded. She may need her own money later. As a brickmaker, Mr. Grogan was certainly quite well-off at the moment.

"It must have been difficult for you to set foot back on a boat. After your dreadful experience," he said gently.

"Quite." Mr. Grogan did not seem nearly as old as he had when she met him initially. Lavinia had to admit, he was also kind and observant, which wasn't something she'd been sensitive enough to give him credit for in June.

The waiter brought the soup. The edges of her hunger had been dulled, and she was able to eat the soup with a margin of decorum.

"Well, I must congratulate you on your marriage." Mr. Grogan looked a bit wistful. "I must confess that I had hopes when we met. I flattered myself into believing that your father approved of my suit, but he assured me that you were a very independent young lady and would make the decision yourself. As you did." He smiled sadly.

Lavinia had finally had enough food to enable her to focus on Mr. Grogan's conversation. Here he bared his heart to her! She felt doubly ashamed of how cruel and childish she and Sarah had been. "Oh, Mr. Grogan, I was young."

He brightened. "The color has returned to your cheeks, Mrs. Ridge, whereby I deduce that you must be feeling better."

"Yes, I am, thank you so much for your kind attention. I am much better."

They passed a few more minutes talking about memories of Savannah—the terrible fire in 1833 that destroyed a full block of homes, and another time that a storm rolled in and lightning struck two men having tea in a waterfront home and they fell unconscious for several hours, singed from head to toe. One of the men had been holding a baby which had thankfully remained completely unharmed. They discussed two recent tragic duels that had started at the free-flowing barroom of the white four-story City Hotel on Bay Street. When she asked more about his business, Mr. Grogan referred rather modestly to the success of his brick-making business since people now demanded brick streets to avoid the muddy ponds that horses and carriages alike became mired in after every rain. Not to mention the ongoing construction in Savannah of Fort Pulaski, which crews were building completely of bricks. Lavinia wondered if the bricks were made by slaves, as the railroad beds had been, but she didn't ask.

Lavinia must have been looking weary, because Mr. Grogan

suddenly said, "If you've finished dining, please allow me to escort you to your room."

She froze and felt a panic beginning to rise. The conversation had been so pleasant—she couldn't bear to see the look of pity in his eyes if he discovered she was traveling in fourth class. "Oh, Mr. Grogan, you do not need to escort me. I may take another turn or two around the deck."

"Allow me to accompany you, then. An unaccompanied lady should have the protection of a friend."

"Please, do not trouble yourself. I made the acquaintance of a woman the other day while on deck," she quickly fibbed, "and she is in fourth class. Frankly, I would like to take her the rest of these rolls. I don't know if you're aware, but the food allotment in fourth class is horribly lacking in comparison to the sumptuous way we eat in staterooms." Boldly, she wrapped the napkin around the two remaining rolls—one for Callie, the other for Ephraim—and slid it into her pocket as she stood. She ignored the staring eyes of those at a nearby table.

"You have a kind heart, Mrs. Ridge. Well, if you are visiting fourth class, you will indeed need an escort." Grogan stood to pull out her chair. "I can't imagine you'd go there alone."

"I truly couldn't trouble you, Mr. Grogan." She rose from her chair and straightened her wrinkled skirt. "Fourth class is a difficult place to visit, much less to stay—." She stopped abruptly, realizing what she'd said.

Realization dawned on Mr. Grogan's face. "Are you . . ."—he cleared his throat—". . . *staying* in fourth class, Mrs. Ridge?"

The heat of shame flashed into her cheeks. She couldn't hold Mr. Grogan's eye. She looked at the floor as they exited the tavern and tried to prevent the wind from grabbing her bonnet as she entered the stairwell to the upper deck. But why should she be ashamed? These circumstances were none of her own doing. So, she straightened her shoulders, and looked Grogan in the eye. "Yes, Mr. Grogan. Yes, I am. I must conserve my resources, so I am staying in fourth class."

Mr. Grogan's mouth worked, and he appeared momentarily speechless.

"If you don't mind my asking, Mrs. Ridge, is all well . . . ?" His deep-set dark eyes studied her face with concern.

"Well, in truth, all is not completely well." On impulse, she decided to tell him the truth. Perhaps it was the compassion in his voice. "You see, there has been some confusion about whether I am truly married. And, as I am with child, my brother-in-law would prefer that I no longer live with him and Sarah in Savannah. So, I'm on my way to New Orleans, but my husband doesn't know. I . . . am not sure if my letter has reached him. So, that is my story. It's been lovely to see you. Thank you for the soup."

Suddenly unsettled by her own intemperate honesty, she gave him a polite nod and quickly headed for the stairwell leading to the fourth-class compartment, holding her head as high as she could manage. He had been kind and she didn't want to embarrass herself or him further. This way he would have the chance to make a graceful exit.

She didn't think he would try to follow her under the circumstances. But he did, and when he caught up with her, just as she reached the stairs, he pressed a printed card into her hand and held it there a moment.

"Mrs. Ridge, here is the address of my hotel in New Orleans. I do wish you well in meeting your husband. But . . . if perchance you have difficulties or need an escort in New Orleans . . . or should you perchance need anything at all—." He gave a small tilt forward of his head, not quite a bow, and gave her hand a gentle squeeze as if to imply much that hadn't been said. "Anything," he repeated, "please call on me there. It was a delight to see you. Please do take care."

And then he turned and headed back down the narrow hall and then up a flight of stairs toward the most spacious upper-level staterooms. She watched him go, thoughtful, then concentrated on carrying the rolls safely down the tight staircase to fourth class.

She did put the card into her pocket.

Callie was so overcome by the rolls she began to weep. "Ephraim look, here is a roll—still warm—that Mrs. Clark has brought us!" The little boy ate with alacrity, as Lavinia had an hour before. He grabbed for the second roll, but she pulled it away from him and pressed it into Callie's hand.

"I insist that you eat as well, Callie. You need your strength."

Callie wiped her tears and turned away, abashed by her display. But Lavinia felt pleased because Callie had the roll all to herself.

CHAPTER TWENTY-EIGHT

October 1838
New Orleans

T HE FOLLOWING DAY was docking day, and everyone climbed up on deck to watch as the ship approached the teeming New Orleans wharfs. The weather in New Orleans was still warm and sunny and the wind considerably diminished. The passengers crowded near the railing, gaping at the city of New Orleans spread before them—the flatboats, steamboats and schooners lined by the wharfs, the elegant homes with decorative iron balcony railings, the people waving and shouting.

Lavinia took Ephraim's hand as Callie carried the baby. Lavinia had never seen a city this size, and she suspected Callie hadn't either. She drew a deep breath, hoping little Ephraim wouldn't notice that her hand trembled. She could hardly believe that her letter would have arrived by now, but she let her eyes travel over the hordes of people, hoping to see Daniel anyway, and wondering how she'd find him if she didn't.

Once the ship docked, passengers rushed to the gangplank. Bodies pressed against her, and she felt her breath quickening.

"Thank you for everything." Callie gripped her hand then took hold of Ephraim's. "I won't never forget what you've done for us."

"Goodness. We helped each other. You go on. I'm going to stay up here for a bit longer to see if I can spot Daniel."

She tried to hug Callie and the children but then people swarmed by and they were torn apart and finally separated. Lavinia, by standing on tiptoe and leaning just so, was able to keep her eye on Callie's dark hair, though, until she saw that she and the children had disembarked, and she watched jealously as a wiry young man in shirtsleeves approached and hugged Callie and swung Ephraim over his head. Then the couple, with Callie carrying the baby and Ephraim riding on his father's shoulders, strolled away from the dock, hand in hand. Lavinia's heart squeezed.

The dizzying, frightening feeling of being alone in a new and bustling place overwhelmed her and she let the people carry her toward the gangplank, fearing to meet anyone's eye. Her heart pounded, and her head swam in the cloying heat. Lavinia stumbled and nearly fell as she stepped from the gangplank onto the muddy landing, her shoe sinking deep, catching her breath with a soft shriek.

She kept the black veil on her bonnet pushed back so she could breathe easier, but lord, the New Orleans air felt suffocating. She waited for her trunk to be unloaded, searching the sea of churning faces eagerly, hoping to see Daniel's face. Would he have changed?

She had never seen so many unusual-looking people, with a variety of skin tones, clothing, and accents. There were Indians with bare chests, men wearing top hats and others wearing turbans, women with extravagant feathers in their bonnets, and there stood a slave market right in the square not far from the wharf, where the hawkers shouted out prices in smooth southern voices for their human goods. A group of men played a spritely tune on their trumpets and trombones, their instrument cases open for coins. The smells of horse manure, urine, beer, and human sweat nauseated her.

She didn't see Daniel anywhere. Yet, truly, she reminded

herself, the letter would never have arrived in time. But still she searched for him.

The crowd thinned as more trunks were unloaded and lifted onto carriages. A man with dark blond wavy hair faced away from her and was talking with someone. Daniel! Oh, thank God, he had come! Relief and joy flooded through her body. She picked up her skirts and bounded through the thick muck in his direction. Then he turned, and she realized it was only a stranger, someone she'd never seen. Her chest tightened and tears came to her eyes. She turned back toward the gangplank in disappointment just as the crew brought her trunk down and dropped it unceremoniously onto the dock with a crash.

"How do I get my trunk to my destination?" she asked the sweating dark men who dropped it, but they climbed the plank for another trunk without a reply. Possibly they spoke a different language? She stood beside her trunk, trembling, hoping Daniel would appear, but knowing he wouldn't. Why hadn't she thought about transporting herself and her trunk across the city earlier?

Again, she scanned the now sparse crowd for Daniel without success. Her spirits sank. She couldn't seem to will her heart to slow down. Minutes crawled by, the crowds thinned, and eventually she was among the last few on the wharf. She became so panicky she hoped to see Mr. Grogan again, but then she remembered that stateroom passengers were always allowed off the boat first on a separate gangplank, so he would be long gone.

She sat on top of her trunk, feeling lightheaded, terrified, and numb with disappointment. The baby kicked. She felt she might swoon.

"Need a carriage, ma'am?" A driver with a green cap driving a dilapidated open two-wheel carriage drawn by a mule addressed her with a distinct drawl.

She hesitated, then stood, feeling dizzy. "Why, yes, I have an address." She reached into her pocket for Daniel's letter with shaking hands and read the now faded return address in the corner.

The driver nodded. "I know where that is. Not too far." He climbed down and with a groan hauled her trunk into the back of the carriage. She wasn't sure she could trust this man, but he had already claimed her trunk.

"Come on now, honey." His voice had a charming lilt. The mule turned her head and stared at Lavinia with welcoming but rheumy eyes. She reminded Lavinia of Daisy from home. Solely because of the understanding eyes of the mule, she allowed the driver to pull her up into the carriage with a calloused hand.

The mule started off with a toss of her head and ears, and they headed down Canal Street, soon passing a sprawling new hotel with soaring columns, occupying an entire block.

"That is the new St. Charles Hotel. Brand new, yessir, brand new."

Was that the same hotel where Mr. Grogan stayed? She reached into her pocket to peek at the card he'd given her. "St. Charles Hotel" was written below his name in a firm hand. Well, at the very least, if she were desperate, she could return here and ask for him. In her previous life she would not have hesitated to feel she belonged in a place like that, but in her current circumstances she could not imagine herself in what surely would be a grand lobby.

The carriage creaked down the muddy streets, and they passed other landmarks and new construction, which the driver occasionally shouted out to her in his thick accent. "This is the St. Charles Theater. And this is the St. Louis Cathedral." At last, they arrived in a quaint and quiet new neighborhood with houses. They were smaller than her own and built of clapboard, but not so different otherwise. Though it had to be said it was an eclectic mix of architectural styles, including quaint cottages and the Greek Revival style which was popular now, featuring rows of columns, upstairs porches, and front steps.

"Here we are. Whoa, Jennie." The mule came to such a sudden stop Lavinia nearly fell out of the carriage.

"Careful." He helped her down to the muddy street.

"What do I owe you?" She stared at the house—was this Daniel's house?—and nervously pulled one gold piece from her purse, careful to leave the purse in her pocket so the driver couldn't see that she had others.

"That'll do." He smiled, revealing a blank spot where a tooth should have been, as he pocketed the gold. She could see right away that she'd given him too much, but the coin was already warming in his pocket, and she had more important concerns pressing on her as she gazed up at this house they'd come to. She laid her hand over her chest to try to calm herself. It was a neat house painted a light green, with five columns, an upstairs porch like at home, with curved bay windows extending out onto the porch, whose railings were white wrought iron forming delicate patterns. As the driver lowered her trunk to the sidewalk, she looked in the tall, narrow front windows to see if anyone was there, but couldn't see anyone.

"Need me to put the trunk on the porch?"

"Yes, could you?"

He heaved the trunk up the short flight of stairs and onto the wooden floor of the side porch. She felt grateful that he didn't let it drop loudly. Maybe the gold piece was worth it.

The driver tipped his green cap. "Best of luck, young lady."

"Thank you."

And within a few seconds he climbed back on the carriage, slapping the reins on the mule's neck and calling, "Gee!" With another weary shake of her head, Jennie clopped down the street and out of Lavinia's sight.

Lavinia stood on the porch with her heart racing. If her most recent letter hadn't arrived, then Daniel would have no idea she was coming here. He might even have left and be on his way to Savannah if he'd heeded her previous letter. She still wore the bonnet with the black veil pushed back, and she tried to smooth it along with her hair and skirts. She hadn't washed up since she had boarded the *Utopia*. She was dirty, wrinkled, and must smell foul after so many days without washing up.

What would Daniel think? What would his sisters think?

The entrance to the house appeared to be on the side, where the trunk was, so she hesitantly walked past it along the side porch, and, after taking a deep breath, she knocked on the door. She wasn't expecting Daniel to answer. Even if he were in town, he would probably be out working at the railroad offices.

After a moment she heard footsteps, and someone pulled back the curtain on the window beside the door. A pair of green eyes very like Daniel's, even with spectacles similar to his, looked out. The eyes widened and the curtain dropped. She stood trembling on the porch, again smoothing her hands over her skirt, and at last she heard the lock sliding and the door creaked open.

A woman several years older than she was, but who looked very much like Daniel, with the same square jaw and wavy dark blonde hair, stood in the doorway. "Yes?"

"Hello, you must be Daniel's sister. You look so like him!" A breeze blew her veil back over her face and she pushed it back. "My name is Lavinia. I'm Daniel's wife."

The woman gaped at her. Had Daniel not told her he was married?

"I wrote to Daniel saying that I was coming, but perhaps my letter hasn't arrived. I just came in on the *Utopia*."

The woman glanced at her trunk, then back at Lavinia. Was she ever going to invite her in?

"Have you come to stay?"

"I . . . don't know. Is Daniel here?" Her mouth went dry. She had eaten very little since the soup with Mr. Grogan last evening, as her own food supplies had been nearly exhausted by that time. She had rather hoped for a warm greeting, possibly a bite to eat, and a sisterly hug, at least from Sally.

"He is at the railroad offices."

"But he will be home later? May I wait for him?"

At last, the woman stepped back and held the door open. "I'll have Claude get your trunk."

"Thank you." Her eyes adjusted as she stepped inside. Just off the narrow front hall, the neatly arranged parlor featured a small piano, furniture in worn green velvet with white antimacassars, and a bookcase stuffed full of books of all shapes and sizes.

"What a nice collection of books."

"You must know that Daniel loves to read. We all do."

"Yes. In fact, when I first saw Daniel, he was reading *The Last of the Mohicans*." She hesitated, remembering the moment and their later discussion as they floated on the sea. "Are you . . . Sally or Imogene?" She remembered Daniel telling her that Sally would be happy to meet her, but Imogene might not.

"Imogene. Sally is at the market."

Well, Daniel had been right. This certainly had not been a very warm welcome so far. Lavinia gave what she hoped to be her most engaging smile.

"It is a pleasure to meet you, Imogene. I've heard a lot about you from Daniel."

"Probably about his overbearing big sister."

"No, not at all!" Though it wasn't entirely truthful, the remark relaxed her a little.

"That was quite a story, Daniel saving your life after the wreck of the *Pulaski*."

"Yes, he did save my life. Your brother was so kind and brave, I could not help but fall in love with him. Those four days on the water with Daniel were among the most memorable of my life."

Lavinia hoped for a friendlier encounter after that, but Imogene just nodded without asking anything more. "Well, you must be hungry. I'll ask Seraphine to get you something to eat."

Lavinia was again growing lightheaded with hunger and was grateful at the mention of food. She thanked Imogene who then showed her to Daniel's room, at the top of the stairs and very small, to wash up in before eating. A narrow bed with a worn quilt in colors of red, blue, and green stood next to a wardrobe. It would be a tight fit for two.

Before washing, Lavinia took a moment to explore the small room. Inside the wardrobe were two suits and a few shirts and breeches that had belonged to Father. There were a few other suits and shirts that must have been Daniel's from before. Lavinia buried her face in one of the suits, breathing in the familiar scents, and thinking about all that had happened to lead her here.

As she pulled her face away, she saw, folded in the pocket, a woman's handkerchief embroidered with lace. Hesitantly, she pulled it open. In the center, in a flourish of embroidery, was the letter "B." Not Imogene's or Sally's, clearly.

Perhaps it could belong to the young woman Daniel had spoken of on the raft, the one he was involved with years ago. She wondered if he had seen her since he'd returned to New Orleans, if they were still friends. Lavinia could think of no other reason why he would still have her handkerchief.

Claude had not yet brought her trunk, so there was no chance of changing into a fresh dress. She took off her bonnet and washed her face and hands the best she could with the pitcher of water, basin, and lye soap that she found there.

She sat down on the bed, suddenly feeling very tired and scared and alone. What would Daniel say when he saw her?

LAVINIA IMMEDIATELY WARMED to Seraphine, their young Cajun cook, when she brought her chicken and dumplings prepared in a style similar to Clementine's. Seraphine was short and sprightly and appeared to be several years younger than Lavinia.

The small dining room featured an oak table and chairs much plainer than her dining room at home in Savannah. A sideboard displayed a few serving dishes that, in her previous life, she might have passed over as being not fine enough in contrast with the hand-painted English china she was used to.

Imogene didn't join Lavinia in the dining room—she sat in

the parlor reading a book—so she thanked Seraphine and ate by herself, hurt by Imogene's aloofness, but also relieved that no one watched the way she wolfed down the food, which tasted spicier than Clementine's and smelled wonderful. She returned the dishes to the warming kitchen when she finished, and thanked Seraphine again.

"You are most welcome." Seraphine gave her such a pretty smile that Lavinia was filled with hope that she might have an ally here.

With a full stomach for the first time in nearly a week, she suddenly felt exhaustion wash over her. From the doorway of the warming kitchen, a portion of the parlor was visible, and she peeked in where Imogene sat reading.

"Don't mind her," Seraphine said in a quiet voice, which renewed Lavinia's courage, and she crossed into the parlor, lifting her chin.

"I do appreciate your hospitality, Imogene. I would like to visit, but I'm feeling very tired now and think I should go upstairs and rest until Daniel comes home, if you don't mind."

"As you wish." Imogene looked up very briefly, then back down at the printed page.

She climbed the stairs slowly and tried to understand Imogene. In Savannah, hospitality was paramount, even when a person didn't feel very welcoming. She tried to put herself in Imogene's position, however. Here her only brother had, on a whim, married a girl from halfway across the country. How would Lavinia feel if Sarah had done something like that? She might be equally surprised and doubtful about the wisdom of the decision, but she hoped she'd at least be civil.

She laid down on the colorful old quilt and felt the baby begin to kick. It always was more active when she lay down and after eating. He? She? She laid her palm over her shifting stomach. Was that a foot? A shoulder? An elbow? She wondered if she would need to tell Daniel, or if he would guess. She briefly wondered about the handkerchief in Daniel's pocket but quickly told herself it was not good to dwell on such things and tried to push it from her mind.

She felt so tired, but for a while her thoughts still swirled around the *Utopia*, the mule-drawn carriage, this house with the robin's egg porch ceiling, and Imogene's face, so like Daniel's yet without the warmth. Then, even in the unfamiliar and uncertain surroundings, she fell asleep.

"LAVINIA!"

She woke with a start. Daniel leaned over her, his expression both joyous and concerned.

She raised herself up onto one elbow, her other hand protectively over the baby. He glanced down at her hand, recognition bloomed in his eyes, and he leaned over and kissed her.

She was relieved beyond measure to be in his arms again, to feel his lips against hers. Doubts and fears from the last months melted away.

Some, though, still lingered.

CHAPTER TWENTY-NINE

October 1838
New Orleans

"YOU CAME HERE—ALONE—IN fourth class!" Daniel's green eyes were wide behind his spectacles, and his voice cracked with disbelief.

"Yes." They had finished dinner together and were in the parlor with Imogene and Sally, who had warmly accepted her, giving her a sisterly hug, for which she was extremely grateful.

"You slept on one of those tiny berths for the entirety of your journey?" Sally had dark hair, unlike her brother and sister, and looked slightly round and jolly. She sat near the lamp so as better to work on her embroidery, while Imogene still had her book on her lap. The parlor had just begun to cool on this late-October evening, as the sun had set early. The lamps flickered in the dusky light. Lavinia had been sorry to see Seraphine leave, as she already felt a sense of closeness to her, but had noticed with pleasure that a dapper young man waited to walk her home.

"I did." Daniel and Lavinia sat together on the love seat, and he kept her hand in his in a protective way. She felt acutely aware of him sitting next to her and felt much the same as she had while on the settee with him on the water—safe.

"That's extraordinary, Lavinia! I'm horrified that you should endure such a passage—especially in your condition. Why did no one escort you? I thought you were determined never to get back on a boat!"

"That's true, and that's how I felt. But it's amazing what you can do if you know you must."

"Are you quite sure you haven't contracted lice?" Imogene narrowed her eyes.

"Imogene!" Sally threw a glance Lavinia's way. "You'll embarrass Lavinia."

Taken aback by the question, but remembering the circumstances in steerage, she admitted Imogene had good reason to ask. "I can bathe with lye soap tonight." Then the power of suggestion came upon her so greatly it was all she could do to prevent herself from scratching her head.

"You shouldn't sleep in the same bed if there is a chance Lavinia has lice," Imogene said to Daniel as though Lavinia wasn't in the room. Then she leveled a look at Lavinia. "There must be some reason why you left your home in Savannah so quickly. Were you pining for my brother, or is it related to you being with child?"

She had not wanted to tell Imogene about the baby so soon, but her condition was obvious by now, and once Daniel had recognized it, he had immediately gone to the top of the stairs and called down, "Imogene! Lavinia and I are to have a child!" Lavinia had not heard her response, but Daniel's exuberant reaction had given her a great deal of joy.

"Of course, I desperately desired to be with Daniel." She glanced at him, and they shared a private smile before she continued. "But yes, my brother-in-law, because of my pregnancy, preferred for me to find another place to stay."

"William? He asked you to leave the house?" Daniel asked.

"Yes."

"I can't imagine why he'd do something like that." Daniel's voice held a puzzled tone. "I know he is somewhat pompous, but I always thought he was a decent man."

"Things changed after they returned from their wedding journey. I explained everything in my last letter, but I seem to have arrived ahead of it." She didn't want Daniel's sisters to know exactly why she had to leave. It would be better to tell Daniel everything in private. "I am afraid I feel quite exhausted after all the traveling and excitement of the week. If you'll excuse me, I believe I'll take a bath and retire."

A LITTLE LATER, she and Daniel were upstairs in the bedroom while she prepared for her bath, and she asked, "Daniel, what was the last letter you received from me?"

"The one in which you described Sarah's wedding. Why, should I be expecting another?" he asked with a smile.

As she thought, he hadn't received her account of Mr. Morgan coming to the house. She took a breath. "Do you remember Mr. Morgan, the reporter?"

"Of course, I do—I thought he was a nosy boor."

"He appeared on my doorstep one day a few weeks ago and informed me that he had interviewed the man who married us—"

"Mr. Johnson." Daniel nodded.

"Yes, Mr. Johnson, and he—" she searched for the right words, and at last she plunged on, "—he told Mr. Morgan he wasn't actually a justice of the peace. He admitted he performed our marriage service just for a bit of money. Mr. Morgan thought he used it to buy drink." She couldn't look at Daniel. She looked at their entwined hands. "You didn't know this, did you, Daniel?" Even as she said it, she knew the answer. From the moment he'd seen her today, Daniel had enveloped her in love and care. She knew he had not purposely deceived her in this. She shifted to face him directly, searching his face. "No. I can see that you would never knowingly participate in a false marriage ceremony. But I must admit that when we were apart, I doubted."

Daniel's face showed surprise and disbelief. "I would never do such a thing. He was not a justice of the peace?"

"He said you met him in a tavern."

"I did. But he told me he was a justice of the peace who traveled from town to town and would marry us for a fee. I asked Dr. Gosher to lend me that fee and so he married us. I never suspected he was untruthful! Are you sure this reporter was telling the truth?"

"I am afraid he might have been. And we never received a marriage certificate, did we? Did Dr. Gosher never suspect anything either?"

"No! It was because he was itinerant, I suppose, and there seemed at the time to be no reason for him to lie. And I was so desperate—I had gone to the Methodist Church, and because I was Catholic the minister wouldn't marry us. I wanted nothing more than to marry you after those four days on the water. I believed Mr. Johnson to be a legal justice of the peace."

"Well, according to Mr. Morgan, he was not."

"Then we must solve this immediately. I'll get our priest to marry us at the first possible opportunity. Tomorrow! Then there will be no question."

Lavinia let her shoulder relax against Daniel's and her entire exhausted body had the consistency of a wet noodle. Then she had a realization.

"I'm not Catholic. Would your priest marry us?" She remembered her discussion about religion with Daniel when they were on the water. There had seemed to be only one god, the god of nature, when floating helplessly there. Would Lavinia convert, if necessary? She didn't even know how long such a thing took.

"No, you're right, he wouldn't." Daniel furrowed his brow, squeezing her hand. "Then we must locate a true justice of the peace who would be willing to do us this favor. I'll find someone this week."

She curled closer to him. "And we must try to keep all of this from your sisters if we can. I'll bathe with the lye soap, and tonight you could sleep downstairs if for no other reason than to avoid getting lice, as Imogene suggested. I hope that tomorrow you can find someone to marry us."

"I hate to give in to Imogene." Daniel leaned in to kiss her. "Truth be told, I'm head of this household."

"I know, but I feel as though if we are to live harmoniously in this house, we must make an effort to please your sisters." She leaned into his embrace.

That night, for the first time in her life, she heated water for her own bath, which Daniel had kindly carried in, making numerous trips from the well, since Seraphine and Claude had already gone home. Then she bathed in the copper tub by candlelight in the main kitchen out back. The lye soap felt painfully harsh on her skin, but Sally brought towels to dry her skin and hair. Then she changed into one of her nightgowns. On the way back upstairs, she passed Daniel lying on the sofa, covered by a blanket, still in his clothing, with his spectacles folded on the side table and his eyes closed.

Deep in the middle of the night she felt his arms slip around her. She turned to him and their lips met, and she remembered that salty kiss on the water months ago.

"This will be our secret," he whispered.

As they drew close together, warm skin against warm skin, Lavinia thought about the handkerchief in his shirt pocket. She'd ask about it tomorrow. She also remembered Clementine telling her that relations could be bad for the baby, but Daniel kissed her neck and shoulder, and she didn't stop him.

CHAPTER THIRTY

November 1838
New Orleans

DANIEL LEFT FOR work early the next day, so Lavinia had breakfast with the sisters. Seraphine's eggs and spicy sausage were delicious, the chicory coffee was strong, and Lavinia could feel her strength returning. Thus bolstered, she hoped to win both sisters over, especially Imogene.

"Imogene, I noticed that you are a reader. I am, as well. What manner of books do you prefer?"

"My Bible, of course, the catechism, and books about the natural world. I have no interest in novels, of course," Imogene said.

"Of course." Lavinia repeated, nodding, sipping her coffee, trying to think of something she had read that Imogene might like. "Did you perchance read Ralph Waldo Emerson's essay called 'Nature' that was published a year or two ago?" Harriet had sent it to Lavinia before her trip on the *Pulaski*, and Lavinia had found the idea that God was in all of nature to be compelling, even though it challenged many of the Methodist teachings of her youth.

"Certainly not," Imogene replied, straightening her spine. "But I have heard of its contents. That is dangerous—even worse than novels—and you should not be reading it, either."

Lavinia refolded her napkin, realizing her mistake, considering how to respond, but Sally fortunately spoke up.

"I'm planning to go to the bookshop today, Lavinia, in case you'd care to join me."

"I would like to very much." Lavinia gave Sally a grateful smile.

They set out together later that morning. Sally showed her some of the sweeping Mississippi River views and they stopped to watch the ferry arrive at Jackson Point. The bookshop was tucked back a few blocks from the river, and it was charming, with an enticing selection of stories, essays, and poetry. Sally had ordered a copy of Charles Dickens' new three-volume book, *Oliver Twist*, and she was pleased that it had arrived.

"You are welcome to read it when I've finished," she offered to Lavinia, who had been looking at some stories by Washington Irving but wondering if she could afford to buy a book.

"And of course you are welcome to anything in our home library, Lavinia. Imogene doesn't like novels, but I do!"

"Oh, that's very kind of you, thank you." Lavinia had begun to feel at ease with Sally already and enjoyed their walk back to the house.

Lavinia had hoped that Daniel would find a justice of the peace the next day, but that night when he came home from work, he said he'd had to visit the swamp where the railroad was being built. He hadn't had a chance to look but promised to do so the next day. Meanwhile, Imogene became colder and colder toward Lavinia. More than just her choices in reading material, Imogene seemed to find fault with everything Lavinia did. She even left the room once when Lavinia entered, and Lavinia wondered if it had been deliberate or if she had just imagined it. Often, if Lavinia spoke, only Sally would answer.

That night Daniel and Lavinia lay in bed whispering with each other.

"A man died today," Daniel said into the darkness, after

Lavinia had extinguished the candle and crawled under the faded wedding ring quilt that Daniel had told her his mother had pieced.

"How?" She could hardly form the word, thinking about the horrible ways in which men could die while building the railroad. Being felled by an axe. Exhaustion. Being shot by a foreman.

"Snakebite. On the foot."

She could not help herself, she wept for the poor soul and pictured a man with a foot swollen beyond recognition. She tried to hide her wet face from Daniel.

"Building a railroad is a dangerous enterprise."

She was quiet a moment. "It could have been you. What if it had been?"

He wrapped his arm around her and stroked her hair. "That's what Imogene has always said about the railroad. She thinks it's too dangerous."

They lay in silence for a while.

"What would you do, Daniel, if you discovered you had a brother you never knew about?"

He glanced down at her. "That's an odd question. Why, I'd make his acquaintance right away."

"What if you already knew him, but you hadn't known he was your brother?"

Daniel's eyes gleamed in the dark. "Well, then, I'd endeavor to establish a warm relationship. I'd be overjoyed to have a brother, to be honest."

"Mr. Mason, the new owner of father's millinery shop, is my half-brother. That's why Father left it to him."

"Is that so? Well, that is certainly a mystery solved, isn't it? How did you find out?"

"Clementine told me, and then I found a letter from Father in his old desk confirming it."

"That does explain a great deal." Daniel did not speak for a moment, then rubbed her shoulder. "Well. Let's think on this. Your father's shop may belong to another, but you know that you can have your own millinery shop one day if you work hard for it. You did mention in your last letter that this has been on your mind."

She didn't answer right away. "I'd like that. I've been thinking often about what might be my purpose in life since we were saved, and I wonder if that could be my purpose. Perhaps it is." She sat up, pulling the quilt around her. "Would you be willing to write a letter vouching for Mr. Mason's good character that might counteract anything that William might do? He is so dreadfully determined to find a way around Father's will and has already threatened slander against Mr. Mason. William knows nothing of the family connection. In truth, I fear what he would do with that information. I would write a letter of support myself, but it might not be acceptable coming from a woman."

"I would be happy to."

They lay in silence a few moments more. How would Sarah feel about Charles Mason being their brother? And how would Mr. Mason feel? Lavinia was amazed at how accepting Daniel seemed of this newly discovered member of her family and the complicated situation they were all in. She wondered about Daniel's own complicated situation.

"Imogene—why is she so unhappy?"

Daniel sighed. "Our mother had a wasting sickness from when we were young, and Imogene acted as my mother. She feels rather proprietary toward me still. I even courted a young lady a few years ago, when I had first started with the railroad, but Imogene felt she had a weak character and disapproved so vehemently that I broke it off with her." He paused, thoughtful. "Imogene also fell in love when she was young. She was always a serious-minded young woman but with a kind spirit and deep feeling—a bit like you, really. She became engaged to the young man, and we all thought well of him, but then in a humiliating scandal he married someone else. He jilted Imogene just weeks before their wedding. All the guests had to be written. I don't believe she's ever healed completely from it. Perhaps now she's decided that if she can't be happy, no one can."

"Do you believe she will ever unbend, if I try to win her over?"

"I think we both must try. She is protective of our family—herself and Sally and me—and it may take some doing for her to accept a new person."

The talk of love and courting brought the handkerchief again to Lavinia's mind. Now was the time to ask Daniel about it, to ask about the woman he had courted before. She turned to look at him, the question on her lips, but he groaned. "I have a horrible headache."

Another time, then. "Oh, I'm sorry. That man's death must have been horrible to see. Let me try to smooth it away." She massaged his temples for a few minutes. "Better?"

He shook his head. "Not much. But first things first. I will find us a justice of the peace tomorrow after work."

The next day Daniel went to work, and she had determined that pregnant or not, she would look for a house for them. She had gone out the door, realized she had forgotten her gloves, and turned back around, but just then a wagon pulled up outside the house and two men began carrying Daniel up the front walk on a plank.

"What on earth?" Her heart lurched, and Lavinia, Imogene, and Sally all rushed to his side.

"He collapsed at the work site. Just keeled right over." The men lifted him up onto the porch and into the front hall.

"It could be the yellow fever. Other men have come down with it as well."

Heart pounding, she put her palm on his forehead. "Hot as fire."

"I knew working on the railroad would be the death of him. I'll get Dr. McCallum." Imogene put on her bonnet and hurried out the door.

The two men carried Daniel upstairs to the bedroom and lay him on the bed. Lavinia put his spectacles on the nightstand and helped him into his nightclothes, and Sally rushed to the kitchen for cool water and a cloth to bathe his fevered face and neck.

"I'm so cold." Daniel's teeth chattered. "My head is splitting."

With Sally's help, Lavinia continually bathed his face and chest with water, frantic to keep Daniel's skin cool while they waited for the doctor. When Imogene finally led him in, Dr. McCallum, thin and pale with a small mustache, sat next to Daniel's bed, laid his hand on his forehead, and used a wooden stethoscope to listen to his heart.

"Have you got a headache?"

"Yes," Daniel groaned. "Quite terrible."

"Muscle aches?"

Daniel could barely nod. He turned his eyes away from the light coming in the window and Lavinia closed the curtain.

"Sensitivity of his eyes to light as well. I think it is the yellow fever. Many of the men who have been working on the railroad have succumbed to it. I am afraid we still don't know what causes it, but we think it may be vapors around the swamps. I understand that's where he's been?"

"Yes," whispered Lavinia.

"Oh, heavens." Sally's face went pale.

"Is there a cure?" Imogene asked.

Dr McCallum shook his head. "No. There is nothing we can do for it but wait and pray. If he survives the next four days, then he should live. But if his skin begins to turn yellow, the disease might have its way with him."

Lavinia gasped. "But can't we do anything to help him?"

Dr. McCallum shook his head again. "Just keep trying to keep him cool and keep the fever at bay. See if you can get him to eat and drink. I'll come back tomorrow to check on him."

The next day passed in a nightmarish haze. She didn't leave Daniel's side, as he tossed in the bed, moaning, burning with fever. She soaked his entire sheet in icy water and then draped it over him. She could feel the heat from his feverish skin rise up through the cotton within moments. That night she slept on the floor next to his bed. Sally brought him soup, but he had no appetite and vomited up anything he managed to get down. Imogene went back to get the doctor the following day at daybreak. By the time the doctor arrived, Daniel was worse. Dr. McCallum looked grave, and repeated that he could do nothing to cure him.

Thoughts tinged with regret tumbled chaotically through Lavinia's head as she sat by Daniel's bed. Regardless of whether the justice of the peace was real, Daniel was her love and her husband. What she would do without him, should he not survive this, she didn't know. Should he not survive, where would she go? She couldn't stay here, not with the way Imogene felt about her. And she couldn't go back to live in Savannah—even if she could make a legal case for staying in the house, being there with Sarah and William would be untenable. But right now, she couldn't let her mind go to those dark places. She pushed the thoughts away and concentrated only on Daniel. While he tossed in delirium, she talked to him; whether he understood her she couldn't tell, but she talked to him anyway, holding tight to his feverish hand.

"Daniel, I love you deeply. You are the bravest and most loyal and most loving man, and I count myself so blessed and I count every day with you as a gift. Please stay with me, with us, with me and your child, Daniel."

His eyes were closed, and he breathed heavily with the effects of the fever. If he could hear her, he didn't respond.

She wet the sheet again, and lay it over him, and afterward lay back down on the floor beside him, reached up and took his hand, and fell asleep.

THE THIRD DAY was even worse, a torturous series of hours with Daniel barely conscious, interrupted only by the dreadfully delayed delivery, at long last, of the letter Lavinia had written to him before boarding the *Utopia*. It was wrinkled and smeared with dirt, as if it had fallen off a stagecoach somewhere. The letter about Mr. Morgan seemed to have gone permanently astray.

Imogene handed it to Lavinia. "I suppose this is from you."

Lavinia put the letter in her trunk and resumed her ministrations to Daniel, who seemed near delirium.

ON THE MORNING of the fourth day, a slanted November sun peeked through the closed curtains in Daniel's bedroom. Lavinia pushed herself up onto her elbow, looking into Daniel's sleeping face. He looked less flushed, with no hint of jaundice. Cautiously, she lay her palm on his cheek. It felt cool, and his nightclothes felt damp with sweat from the breaking of his fever.

"Daniel?" she whispered.

His bloodshot eyes opened slowly. "Lavinia." He squeezed her hand.

She gasped, and jumped from the bed, pulling her robe on and running into the hall. "Call for Dr. McCallum—the fever's broken!"

An hour later, when Dr. McCallum arrived, Daniel was already sitting up in bed, drinking tea that Imogene had made for him and eating some rice pudding that Sally had prepared.

"He's survived the first fever."

"The first fever? What do you mean?" she stumbled over her words.

"I didn't want to alarm you before. Most people who survive the first fever will indeed live. But I must warn you that sometimes, within a few days, a second fever occurs, and that one is much more dangerous. If he gets the second fever, the likelihood of survival is low."

"Why didn't you tell us that before? How do I know whether

to believe you now?" Lavinia's irritation toward the doctor flared. Did they not take an oath to care for their patients? It was not caring to allow them all to only know half of what they needed, to give them hope only to throw them into turmoil again! She remembered her father's disdain for doctors after her mother's death and sympathized with it as she never had before.

"Lavinia, we must do our best to trust the doctor, tired and fearful as we are," Sally said, laying a patient hand on her arm.

An exhaustion followed unlike any she had experienced except on the water with Daniel after the *Pulaski*. She didn't know if she had the energy to continue to nurse Daniel through a second fever and wondered if her weakness now might make her susceptible to the yellow fever herself. Or even if exposure to the illness might affect the baby. But Dr. McCallum assured her that in his experience those nursing yellow fever patients did not catch it.

Over the next two days, the sisters and Lavinia floated like ghosts through the house, taking care of Daniel's every need, ever watchful for the return of the fever. The slightest change in Daniel's countenance caused all three of them to rush to his side.

"I feel fine." The color had returned to Daniel's face. "In a day or two I will have the strength to get up and go back to the railroad. Please stop fussing over me, Imogene, Sally. I shall allow Lavinia to continue to fuss, as she is my wife." He smiled, and took her hand, showing his humor, giving her hope that he was indeed on the mend.

Blessedly, the third day came and went, with no return of the fever. Dr. McCallum returned, examined Daniel, and declared him finally free of the disease. Sally, Imogene, and Lavinia all burst into tears of joy and relief together.

"However, you will need several weeks to regain your strength, Daniel. Wait at least a fortnight before returning to the railroad."

Lavinia helped Daniel downstairs so he could continue his recovery on the couch, and that day, he was even able to join them in the dining room for the midday meal. Lavinia, who had been waiting for Daniel to recover a bit more before asking him about the handkerchief in his shirt pocket, decided he was now well enough, and she determined that she would ask him that night when they retired to the bedroom.

That afternoon though, came a knock on the door. "Hello, miss," said an elderly bearded gentleman in a dark suit, stepping inside and removing his hat when Sally opened the door. "Is Mr. Ridge at home?"

Daniel was lying on the couch covered with a quilt, and his face suffused with excitement. "I have a gift for you, Lavinia. This is Edward Fiore, justice of the peace. I made arrangements with him before I became ill and sent him a note this morning confirming the time and place. I've seen his credentials. He'll give us a marriage certificate and marry us right now, here in our own parlor, without requiring that banns be read."

She gasped, clutching Daniel's arm. At last, they were to be married officially! "Oh, a pleasure to meet you, Mr. Fiore." She gave a slight bow to the gentleman.

"And you, miss." He reached into his jacket pocket for his Bible, his eyes straying briefly to her increasing abdomen.

"What is this?" Imogene sat up straight in her chair. "If you are already married, why would you need to be married again?"

"I will explain later, Imogene," Daniel said firmly.

From inside his jacket pocket, Mr. Fiore produced a completed marriage certificate. "And the two of you are not related to each other?" He looked from Daniel's face to Lavinia's.

"Heavens! No, sir." Daniel squeezed Lavinia's hand.

And so, for the second time, Daniel and Lavinia were married by a justice of the peace—a real one—this time with Daniel lying on the couch, Lavinia standing next to him, and Sally as a witness. In the middle of the vows, Imogene got up, threw her book down on the seat of her chair, stomped upstairs, and slammed her bedroom door. Mr. Fiore only raised his white eyebrows and continued with the vows.

When Mr. Fiore told Daniel he could kiss his bride, Daniel smiled at Lavinia. "We are truly and finally married this time."

"Truly."

And Daniel kissed her, his lips at once firm and soft.

The moment Mr. Fiore left, Imogene rushed downstairs. "What just happened? Why did the justice of the peace just marry you? I thought you *were* married!"

"We are now. It turned out that the first justice of the peace may not have been official, and so Lavinia and I wanted to be sure of it."

"So, you have been living in our house in sin?" Imogene's hand covered her heart.

"We acted in good faith at all times. And no one knew except us." Daniel glared at Imogene.

"We will never live down such scandal! No priest!"

"Imogene, I would thank you to be more supportive of our situation. None of this has been deliberate."

"Daniel, as usual, you give very little thought to the way your actions affect the women of our family. You have brought this woman into our home falsely. If this were ever to become known, our reputations would be ruined!"

"Imogene, there is no scandal unless you create one." Daniel squeezed Lavinia's hand even more tightly, and her face burned. She hated being talked about as though she wasn't present or didn't understand plain English.

"I think Lavinia should leave this house!" Imogene exclaimed.

Now Sally's calm voice contrasted with the other two angrier ones. "That is not reasonable, Imogene. Even if she wasn't officially Daniel's wife before, she certainly is now. And you seem to forget that it is Daniel's money supporting us and his roof over our heads. You and I live here only by his kindness." Sally pulled her stitches tight. "He is the one who inherited the house when Father died but has never said one word about asking us to leave, out of the goodness of his heart."

"Is that what it's come to, then? Daniel throwing us out into the street?"

"Of course he would never do that!" The very thought that Daniel would be cruel to his sisters compelled Lavinia to speech. Her days of doubting him were gone, and anyway he was no William.

"Oh, you think you know your so-called 'husband' so well? Better than his sisters who grew up with him?"

"Enough, Imogene!" Daniel stood. "Imogene, perhaps we can talk more about this tomorrow. I am sorry, but I'm very tired. Come, Lavinia, let's go upstairs. This discussion has ended."

"Your marriage has been a sham for all these weeks! What will people say?"

"Let's please be civil to one another." Sally gave Imogene a beseeching glance.

"Come upstairs with me, Lavinia," Daniel was looking weaker after the argument, so she followed him up the stairs with her hand supporting his back. Once they were in his room, he shut the door.

"I am sorry about Imogene. Possibly I should have talked to her about the situation beforehand. But part of me was afraid she would become very angry and possibly try to prevent Mr. Fiore from coming. At least we are truly married now."

"It's all right, Daniel." She put her palm on his cheek. "She can't take our joy away."

Lavinia glanced at the closet, and decided, since they were indeed now married, that perhaps there was no need to bring up the handkerchief at all.

CHAPTER THIRTY-ONE

Winter 1838-39
New Orleans

THOSE ENSUING DAYS, while they waited for Daniel to regain his strength, Lavinia especially missed Sarah. How she missed talking with her about everything, their discussions about people and ideas, their silly high-spirited laughter. She wondered how Sarah was getting along in keeping up the house, stable, and yard without Peter's help. Had William hired someone new? She worried her closeness with Sarah could be forever lost.

Christmas, now only a month away, would feel strange and lonely without her. She found a book of poems by Anne Bradstreet that she wanted to send Sarah as a Christmas gift, and composed a letter to her, describing Daniel's illness and recuperation. After a great deal of thought, she also wrote a short letter to Charles Mason.

Dear Mr. Mason,

I hope all is well at Mason's Millinery. I enclose a letter vouching for your good character from my husband, Daniel Ridge, based on my work with you over four years in Onslow's Millinery Shop. I hope this letter may be of help to you should it become necessary in any legal disputes.

Also, I have seen in fashion plates from Europe some fluffy turbans with pearl-lined headbands and fringe. Have you seen these? I would be interested in your thoughts. Do you think the ladies of Savannah would take to them?

I hope that you will write back and we can keep up a correspondence. I do know that you loved my father, as did I.

Yours truly,
Lavinia Ridge

She placed Daniel's letter vouching for his upstanding character with her personal note, but she didn't immediately post them. She had lost some faith in the postal system, since two of her important letters had not made their destination before she did, and when they did arrive were in sad condition, and one hadn't arrived at all. So, bundled up in a cloak and accompanied by Sally, she went to the St. Charles Hotel, with its enormous Corinthian columns and cupola, hoping to find Mr. Grogan still in residence there. A hotel page was sent to find him, and he kindly met her in the ornate lobby, wearing his usual brocaded waistcoat and top hat. She asked if he would be willing to take her letters to Sarah and Charles with him on his next trip back to Savannah.

"I'll be delighted to take these letters to your sister. I return to Savannah at the first of December. How are you finding your stay here in your husband's city?"

"Oh, it is quite lovely. And I must introduce my sister-in-law to you, Mr. Matthew Grogan. This is Miss Sally Ridge."

"How nice to make your acquaintance," Mr. Grogan said with a sincere smile.

"Likewise, Mr. Grogan." Sally, with color rising to her cheeks, offered her hand to be kissed.

"New Orleans is such an exciting city," Lavinia said. "And Mr. Grogan, I want to thank you again for your gallantry while I was on the *Utopia*. You have no idea what your kindness and the warm soup meant to me that day."

"Mrs. Ridge, my only wish is that I could have done more."

He gave her a fond smile. "I am so pleased to see you doing well."

This kind man might have become her husband had she agreed to court him, and if she had tried to please Father rather than follow her own desires. She would certainly have wanted for nothing, since his brick business had found such success. But though he truly did seem to care for her, she suspected there would have been no passion as she had with Daniel. Her heart felt at peace, and she hoped Mr. Grogan might yet find the sort of happiness she had, too.

"Good day, and thank you again, Mr. Grogan. I very much hope you have a merry Christmas."

"You, as well, Mrs. Ridge. And so lovely to meet you, Miss Ridge," Mr. Grogan added.

"I feel the same," Sally replied, with a polite inclination of her head.

As Lavinia and Sally walked home, she imagined how Sarah would react to having Mr. Grogan come to their front step in Savannah with a letter and gift from Lavinia in his hand. She wanted to talk to Sarah about the way she'd been treated by Imogene, never mind the fact that William's treatment had been even worse. She wished that she and Daniel might somehow leave his house, but moving to another house would be difficult in her present condition.

Lavinia felt she could spend money more freely these days and enjoyed the luxury of shopping trips and purchasing Christmas presents for her family. Daniel had recently received a generous increase in salary from the railroad management, as the maritime insurance that Daniel had acquired before the voyage on the Pulaski had finally paid for the loss and the railroad was more solvent again. Also, Mr. Trask, father's lawyer, had at long last sent Lavinia her portion of the shop's earnings before it was turned over to Mr. Mason.

Lavinia wanted to give Daniel a perfect Christmas gift, and in the following days spent time wandering about the city, often with Sally, searching for just the right thing. At last, she found him a pocket watch, and had the back engraved with both of their initials and the message *I was adrift in time until I found you.*

In the sweet little bookseller's shop Sally had shown her, she purchased books for both sisters. She immediately found a romantic adventure tale she thought Sally would like, but at first wasn't sure whether to buy a gift for Imogene or not, as she guessed Imogene would not get anything for her. In the end, she chose a book about nature for her that was beautifully illustrated. In a flash of inspiration, she also chose a copy of *The Last of the Mohicans* for Daniel, to replace the one he'd lost on the *Pulaski*.

A few doors down from the bookshop, Lavinia passed a millinery. She stopped to examine the window, with several stylish and feathered white winter bonnets for ladies, displayed with luxurious kid gloves.

Oh! She had completely forgotten to wear gloves today. Memories of past days spent designing the window for Onslow's Millinery swept over her. How was Charles Mason doing with the shop? She was satisfied with her life here with Daniel and was, in fact, glad that she hadn't fought him for Father's shop. After all, he was an orphan and she and Sarah were his only family. She did not go inside, but at that moment she renewed her pledge to somehow acquire her own millinery someday.

THE NIGHT BEFORE Christmas, Daniel took her in the carriage to see a special New Orleans tradition—the lighting of the bonfires along the levee of the Mississippi River. The tall, cone-shaped burning structures looked eerie and cheerful at once. One of the organizers offered them a spicy hot bowl of gumbo. The bonfires, Daniel explained, served as a guide for Father Noel.

On Christmas morning, the four of them enjoyed a pancake breakfast together, which Seraphine had made the day before, since she would spend Christmas Day with her own family, and enjoyed a leisurely cup of coffee around the table before opening gifts. Sally seemed delighted with the book Lavinia gave her, and in turn gave Lavinia a book on motherhood, as well as a pair of extra gloves, with a note saying, "In case you lose your other ones," which warmed Lavinia's heart. Imogene was in a more amiable mood than usual, and, though she complained that the print in the book Lavinia gave her was too small, she spent quite some time contemplating the illustrations. Lavinia thought that she liked it, possibly in spite of herself. When Daniel opened his watch, he put it on immediately, and took Lavinia's chin in his hand and kissed her right in front of his sisters. And when he opened the book, tears came to his eyes.

"Now I can finally finish it!" he declared.

For her present, he gave her the engagement ring that he had promised so many months ago, a beautiful diamond surrounded by small pink topaz stones, to match the necklace from Father, and to stand in the stead of the topaz earring she'd lost on the raft.

"How ever did you shop for this, as sick as you were?" She felt overwhelmed.

"I sent a note to the jeweler." He smiled.

Daniel and Lavinia took a leisurely stroll down Canal Street that Christmas day, just the two of them. Daniel had continued to improve and went into the railroad offices most days, but he still needed to be cautious of his health. As they walked, her arm in his, she reflected on her gratitude for Daniel's life. Daniel wore a top hat that reminded her of Father. What would Father think about how her life had unfolded were he alive?

As they strolled, another couple approached arm in arm, and Daniel seemed slightly nervous at the sight of them. Lavinia, both concerned and curious, examined the two people approaching. One was a middle-aged gray-haired man, handsomely dressed in a top hat, brocade waistcoat and long frock coat, with tailored pantaloons, and the other was a young woman, about Lavinia's age, lovely, with blond hair pulled into a sleek chignon, wearing one of the most stylish white winter cloaks Lavinia had ever seen. Her expression was sweet but sad, and, from the angle of her cloak, she appeared, like Lavinia, to be expecting a child. As they neared, the woman also seemed to become uneasy, glancing more than once at Daniel.

"Mr. Ridge," the woman said as they neared, stopping and inclining her head with a little sigh. "Merry Christmas."

Daniel seemed to gather his wits. "Merry Christmas to you, Belinda. Allow me to introduce my wife, Lavinia Ridge."

"A pleasure to meet you." Lavinia smiled cautiously, watching the two of them closely. Belinda—the B on the handkerchief.

"And this is my husband, Zachary Jones."

"A pleasure." Daniel shook hands with the gentleman. "It has been a few years, has it not, Belinda? Or I should say Mrs. Jones."

"Indeed, two Christmases ago was the last we saw each other." It might just be the chilly breeze, but Lavinia thought she might see a shimmering of tears in Belinda Jones' eyes.

"Did you meet through the Charity Hospital?" asked Mr. Jones, clearly oblivious to the emotions passing between his wife and Daniel.

Belinda glanced at Daniel, then nodded. "Yes, the Charity Hospital." Lavinia didn't think that was how they had met at all.

"Very good. Well, a merry Christmas to you both!" Mr. Jones bowed briefly and led his wife forward.

Lavinia and Daniel also continued walking along together for a short while, passing through a grove of ancient sycamores that were slowly losing their broad leaves in winter, with the gray bark peeling from the large trunks, revealing the white bark beneath. Carolers passed, singing "Hark the Herald Angels Sing," which Lavinia recognized from her Methodist upbringing, and was comforted by thinking that there were Methodists, if only a few, here in New Orleans.

"There is an embroidered handkerchief with a 'B' on it in a shirt pocket in your closet." Lavinia snuggled her hand closer on Daniel's elbow, where she could feel the pumping of his blood.

"Yes." Daniel blinked then nodded. "That is Belinda's."

They walked on in a charged silence.

"She is quite beautiful. And she still cares for you." Lavinia realized she held her breath.

Suddenly, Daniel stopped and faced her, taking her gloved hands in his. "I did care for her, Lavinia. And I wish the best for her. Yet nothing can compare to what I feel for you. You are my compass, my life's companion. Those days we spent together between the sky and the sea forever sealed my enduring love for you. Lavinia, never doubt me."

With joy, Lavinia took his face in her hands and touched her lips to his, lightly at first, then more deeply. He had indeed vanquished every one of her doubts.

As the weeks passed, Daniel grew stronger and Lavinia grew larger with child. She started to have difficulty climbing the narrow stairs to their bedroom and felt uncomfortable in almost any position while trying to sleep. Many of the Cajun recipes that Seraphine prepared tasted good but then caused pain later. Lavinia spent her time knitting and crocheting a few blankets and wraps for the baby.

"Oh, will this baby never arrive!" She expressed her frustration one morning after breakfast, when only she and Seraphine were in the dining room, to which Seraphine replied cheerfully, "That baby is less trouble now than it will ever be, Miss Lavinia. You can be sure of that." Seraphine was especially happy these days, as she had become engaged on Christmas Day to her young man.

February in New Orleans meant the Mardi Gras ball, and Daniel and his sisters, along with apparently everyone else in the city, all were wrapped up in who was invited, who hosted, and all the details. No one from the Ridge family expected an invitation, but the committee announced that for the first time this year, 1839, there would be a Mardi Gras parade in addition to the ball. Daniel decided that it would be too indecorous for Lavinia and his sisters to attend the parade, but he would go. When he returned, he told them that revelers teemed in the streets, and an enormous rooster that appeared to be six feet tall, riding in a carriage, and crowing loudly, was the most entertaining feature of the parade. Lavinia wished she could have gone, but she would have been far too worn out by such an event anyway; still, it would have been exciting to be amongst all those people and especially to see all the fashionable headwear.

A few weeks later, at the end of March, she woke feeling strange but didn't mention it to Daniel—she often felt strange these days. He kissed her goodbye and left for the railroad offices, promising not to be too late. That morning she sat for an hour in the parlor with Imogene and Sally, feeling queasy and somewhat disconnected from her own body, as Imogene addressed statements to Sally, but not to Lavinia. She read her book, a treatise on the blessings of motherhood that Sally had given her for Christmas, trying not to focus on Imogene's childish behavior, and suddenly a release of warm fluid rushed between her legs.

"Oh!" She leaped to her feet, gathering her skirts.

"What is the matter with you?" Imogene demanded.

Already feeling on edge and sensitive, Lavinia burst into tears. If only she were at home in Savannah, with Sarah and Clementine by her side. Her mother had died giving birth to Sarah. The worry that Lavinia had held at bay all these months was suddenly upon her in full force. Was this her last day? She could not leave Daniel with a motherless baby. She was determined to see her baby's face, to care for the baby and raise it to adulthood if it was at all in her power. She simply would not let these be her last hours.

"Lavinia, let me help you upstairs." At least Sally was kind. "Imogene, fetch the midwife."

THE DAY PASSED in a blur of pain. Lavinia felt aware of screaming in a way that she could hardly believe herself capable and a release of her inhibitions and any other care. In brief flashes, moments came back to her from that day on the water when she and Daniel saw the boats go by and screamed and screamed with hopelessness and despair when the ships disappeared. And then when Lavinia was sure she had no more strength for anything, the skilled midwife, a mother of three who lived nearby, said, "One last push." And miraculously she summoned the fortitude and bore down, nearly losing consciousness with the effort.

And then it was done.

"Here is your little girl. She's beautiful. She's perfect."

The midwife handed a warm and damp bundle into her arms already with dark blonde curls like Daniel's and a tiny red face. After that the midwife allowed Daniel into the bedroom, and together they named her Lily, after Lavinia's mother.

DURING THE FIRST week of Lily's life, Lavinia waited to weaken and die, but she did not. She grew slowly stronger and took sheer delight in every moment holding her baby, examining her tiny fingers and toes while she nursed, touching her tender little head, gazing into her eyes. While her feelings for Daniel were powerful, she had never felt a love so peaceful and encompassing as her love for Lily. Just Lily's smell made her dizzy with love. Daniel acted smitten, too, coming straight to the bedroom from work to admire Lily in the upper drawer of their dresser, which served as her crib.

Lavinia remembered feeling awkward with other children, but she had become more at ease, as with Henry and Ephraim on the *Utopia*. She'd had some anxiety with Lily at first, as she was so very tiny and helpless, but eventually, using the mothering book that Sally had given her and her own common sense, she learned to nurse her, bathe her, and dress her. Sally and Seraphine also helped Lavinia with the extra washing Lily created and by rocking the baby so that Lavinia could sleep, which she greatly appreciated.

And Imogene seemed to have changed overnight; one would have thought Lily was *her* baby. Imogene adored her.

"Do you think the baby needs another blanket? Might she be hungry? Look, I believe Lily smiled at me." Imogene knitted one set of booties after another.

But this didn't change Lavinia's mind about finding a place for herself and Daniel and the baby. When Lily turned three weeks old, Lavinia brought up the subject with Daniel as they sat together in the dining room having breakfast. Imogene and Sally had gone to the market, and Lily, after her morning feeding, had fallen asleep.

"Spring is here. What would you say if we left this house? We could use what's left of my fitting out money and proceeds from the shop, as well as what you've saved from your salary, to buy one of our own, and your sisters could continue on here."

"I agree, Lavinia, that we should leave this house." Daniel took a careful sip of chicory coffee. "I have been watching, and even though Imogene has changed since Lily was born, I see how difficult this is for you. And there are too many of us in this house; you and I need our own. Do you remember Mr. Bishop, the man with the top hat on our ill-fated stagecoach ride?"

"Yes, he gave you his card, did he not?"

"He did. It turns out, he decided, after our conversation on the stagecoach, to become involved with the new railroad in Charleston. He wrote this week saying they needed some quick-thinking men like me in Charleston and asked if I would like to come aboard. I've been talking with some of my colleagues and many believe that the new future of railroads in the south is Charleston. What would you say to moving there?" He gave her a look of significance, his eyebrows raised behind his spectacles.

"Oh, Daniel, that could be the perfect spot for us!" Charleston! She entwined her hand with his, thinking of the possibilities. And Charleston was so much closer to Savannah. Could she and her sister reconcile if she were nearer? She'd received a short note after Christmas from Mr. Grogan saying he'd delivered her letters and gift and that everyone appeared well. She had even had a tentative letter from Mr. Mason thanking her for her good wishes and asking about the millinery fashions of New Orleans. But she had heard nothing from Sarah.

And so, at the end of April, Lily, only weeks on this earth, Daniel, still thin from his bout with yellow fever, and Lavinia, still weak from childbirth, set out for the docks for their steamship voyage to Charleston. Lavinia had tracked down the driver who had brought her from the docks a few months ago, and on the appointed day he arrived, with Jennie plodding along and twitching her ears.

"Hello, Jennie," Lavinia said, removing her gloves to scratch under Jennie's forelock, filled with emotion with the memory of when she had arrived. The driver and Daniel loaded two trunks with their clothes, books, and supplies for Lily—including several blankets hand-knitted by Imogene—into the wagon. After Lavinia climbed in as well, she realized that while petting Jennie, she'd neglected her gloves again and dropped them into the street. Daniel, with a fond smile, retrieved them, gallantly handing them back to her.

Daniel's sisters stood on the stoop, Sally wiping her eyes, Imogene with her arms crossed over her stomach and tears rolling unbidden down her cheeks. Daniel had promised to send money each month and to continue to pay the taxes on the house. They would be safe and taken care of.

As the driver slapped the reins for Jennie and they pulled away from the house, Lavinia looked at Daniel's profile—his strong jaw, his dark blonde curls, his green eyes behind his spectacles. She felt again a sense of wonder that the two of them had found each other adrift in the middle of the ocean and forged such a love over those four harrowing days. In spite of whatever troubles their journey might bring them, they were embarking now, and for the rest of their lives, together.

EPILOGUE

Five years later
June 14, 1843
Charleston

Dearest Sarah,

Thank you for your letter. I cannot tell you how much it meant to me, after sending so many that went unanswered. Being estranged from you for these past five years, along with the shipwreck and Father's death, have been the most painful experiences of my life. When I sent you that letter and Christmas gift by way of Matthew Grogan and you did not answer I was devastated. What a welcome sight your letter was yesterday!

I have just put Lily and little Danny to bed and finally have a few quiet moments to write you back. The weather has been extremely warm here, and people are complaining of the heat. Daniel is busy at the railroad—he has been working on the line to Cincinnati. He says Charleston and the south can recapture their importance if the railroad can provide a route to the west. He works long hours, which worries me, as he does not have the stamina he did before he was ill with the yellow fever. He tires so much more easily. The fact he is away a great deal makes me thankful that I have the millinery shop to keep me occupied and to bring in extra money. I want to send both children—yes, Lily, too!—to college so this money will be useful for tuition when the time comes. I've hired a young woman as a tutor for Lily who also helps me with Danny when I need to go to the shop.

My shop, Lavinia's Hatpin, has been very busy as of late. The new styles have been introduced from England and the girls and I are working our fingers to the bone to keep up with them. The women of Charleston are more adventurous in their bonnet desires than even in Savannah! Even though Daniel owns the shop, he gives me a free hand with how it's managed and calls it "the project of Lavinia's heart." I have begun hiring unwed mothers to teach them the millinery business so that they will have a way to support themselves in the future. I suppose that time when I was considered an unwed mother myself gave me a kinship with them and a further purpose to my life. We have taken several such desperate girls into our home for a time to help them get settled in safe situations. Some people criticized us at first, but today, Mrs. Crenshaw, one of the most prestigious women in the city, came in and ordered two new fall bonnets, giving us her tacit approval. We were overjoyed. Her seal of approval can do wonders.

The children have been blessedly healthy, except for a bout with whooping cough last winter. Danny is teething, and has had some fevers, but they haven't been severe. It was wise of you to have the twins vaccinated against smallpox. We vaccinated our children as well.

We've enjoyed living close to Daniel's cousin and his family here in Charleston. Our connection has made it easier for us to get to know people here. His daughter likes to mother Lily and Danny, and she has begun to give them small parts in her plays, which delights them to no end.

I will admit that I did know that Peter and his wife Zora

had left Savannah—he told me before I left that they were planning on leaving. He was part of our lives for so long, it's hard to imagine our childhood home without him. I'm terribly sorry he hasn't been there to help you with the garden and the horses. I pray that he stays safe and has found a better life. I fear for him. I have heard horrible stories about people being captured and forced into slavery, but he surely is safer in Chicago.

I was sad to hear that Clementine left your house, too, yet I am pleased that her midwife services are so needed and admired throughout Savannah, and that she is training her niece, Matilda, to follow in her footsteps. You must miss her so. Though she could be stern with us, I think she was as good to us as any mother could have been. Do you agree? And I was overjoyed to learn she midwifed your twins and comes to visit now and again. What a happy miracle they were born healthy! When I gave birth to Lily and little Danny how I wished she could have been there with me. I so feared having children, after what happened to Mama.

I can't remember if I mentioned it before, but we have no servants here; though Charleston is a major slave trading city, we live in a section among Methodists who do not keep slaves or even servants. How are you adjusting to having two of William's family's slaves? Does it sit well with you? It would not with me. Yet, I must admit, with two children, no servants, and a millinery shop to run, I sometimes feel exhausted, especially as Daniel travels so much. He has mentioned moving out west, to follow the railroad. Though I have always lived in the south and would hate to leave, the railroad in the west is not dependent upon slave labor, which puts my heart more at ease. It is something Daniel and I have often discussed. We will see.

Daniel and I went to New Orleans last month. His sister Sally married Matthew Grogan! Can you believe it? He treasures her good humor, which quite pleased Daniel. And how wonderful that the two of them have found each other. His other sister, Imogene, who had become a hopelessly doting aunt to our children, passed away last year from a stomach ailment, and for a while, Sally lived in the house alone. Since Sally will be moving to Savannah to live with Mr. Grogan next month after their bridal tour of Europe, Daniel has sold the house. I hope you will get to know her once she settles in Savannah. I think you will like her. And Mr. Grogan, despite our thoughts about him in the past, is a kind and generous man.

It felt strange to stay in that house again, where Lily was born and where I felt so like a fish out of water. New Orleans is as bustling and exuberant a city as ever, and I felt freer to experience it this time.

Something happened the other day that you might find amusing. Daniel and I opened the paper and saw an article from none other than that reporter Mr. Morgan, who followed us from Smithville to Savannah and wrote that article that caused all the trouble for me. Somehow Morgan has ended up in Charleston, of all things. I proposed to Daniel that we contact Mr. Morgan and ask if he would like to do one last story about us. After some hesitation, Daniel agreed, and Mr. Morgan seemed to leap at the opportunity and came to our home. We were perfect hosts, serving him tea and cakes and introducing our children. We gave him tours of both Daniel's railroad offices and my millinery shop. His profile of us as a Charleston success story was very complimentary, almost abashed, and I am enclosing a copy of it here. I have come to the opinion that Mr. Morgan is not a bad man, just perhaps sometimes too avid in his pursuit of a good story and selling more papers.

It grieves me to hear that things are not going well between you and William. Marriage can be a challenge, especially when the two people do not always see eye to eye. I think back to your wedding and our argument that day. How I wish I could be there to talk about this with you, and I hope one day soon we can talk about it all in person. It breaks my heart to think that you are not happy. Meanwhile, remember that William never paid me or Daniel for my half of the house, which means that we still own half. Please remind your husband of that if you think it will help you.

And how I wish the cousins could meet! I've told Daniel

that I would like to bring the children to Savannah to meet you all. It is nearly incredible to think that it has been five long years since I've seen my beloved sister! What would you say to a late summer visit? Would William agree? Our shop is usually closed during the month of August, and the children are old enough now to make traveling easier. We will stop in Augusta to visit my good friend Harriet, and then could come to Savannah to see you. We will continue from there to Milan to buy the straw for next season's bonnets. Yes, if you can believe it, Daniel and I are both getting back on an ocean-going vessel. If you by any chance would like to join us with your children, we would welcome you with open arms. That might also give you and William time to reflect on your differences and decide how to move forward.

I don't suppose you've been to Mason's Millinery since William tried to contest Father's will. I confess I was overjoyed that he did not succeed. I will say that I did ask Daniel to write a letter in support of Mr. Mason's good character, and I hope it helped him. I would like to visit, and to see Mr. Mason when I come. He and I have been corresponding. Perhaps you could come too, and we could all talk. I found a last letter from Father before I left Savannah and I think you both might like to read it.

Daniel and I are doing well. Ever since he had the yellow fever, I have been grateful for each day we have together. To think that we fell in love floating on two settees in the middle of the Atlantic Ocean, exactly five years ago today. What an adventure it has been, and still is. Life and love are most amazing things.

Your loving sister,
Lavinia

ABOUT THE AUTHOR

Between the Sky and the Sea is Lisa Williams Kline's first novel for adults. Her stories and essays have appeared in *Literary Mama, Skirt, Sasee, Carolina Woman, moonShine review, The Press 53 Awards Anthology, Sand Hills Literary Magazine,* and *Idol Talk,* among others. She is the author of ten novels and a novella for young readers, a short story collection for adults called *Take Me* (Main Street Rag), and an essay collection called *The Ruby Mirror.* She lives in Davidson with her veterinarian husband, a cat who can open doors, and a sweet chihuahua who hardly ever barks. They treasure frequent visits with their grown daughters and their husbands.

IG: @lisawilliamskline
FB: lisa.kline.566

www.ingramcontent.com/pod-product-compliance
Lightning Source LLC
Chambersburg PA
CBHW071210210726
48293CB00002B/370